# A-B-C

# A - B - C

*BOOK TWO*

*of*

*The Madness of Power*

## STEVEN J. CONNERS

Steven J. Conners | Reno, NV

# CONTENTS

## A

## B

# C

# Preface

Through the years as I read of humankind's wars and plagues, despots and good people, social and religious conflicts—even though I found this history spellbinding, it always seemed like chaos. It has a great plot and one hell of a cast, but my exploration of the past and comparison with the present caused me to conclude—as most others have—that history does repeat itself.

Apparently, it's always been the same old game, with nearly identical circumstances replicating themselves over and over. Maybe the idea was only to admit new players as the game went on. From the use of sticks, stones, bows, arrows, knives, swords, guns, cannons, tanks, aircraft and bombs, all kinds of weapons have been used by humankind to intimidate and kill fellow humans. Our ingenuity in the killing process seems boundless. Humankind appears to enjoy conquest, and actually hungers for it. Yet the conquests are usually short-lived. They are always met with rebellion and, eventually, life goes on until the arrival of the next conqueror.

I've earned my living mostly on the road, traveling throughout the U.S. and Canada. I've met and spoken with hundreds, if not thousands, of my fellow citizens. At one point, I took notes on what I heard. I became fascinated by human behavior and by people's reactions to danger or possible threats. I spent time—lots of time—in libraries and on the Internet.

The results of my research were rather intriguing. I suppose it was no surprise to learn that most people had no new ideas as to how to solve society's problems. Instead, my astonishing, if not alarming, discovery was that there was a common, shared opinion. The fact that it was so common was what made it most revelatory. Most people had confidence that their government would always fix the problems in their lives.

And so, I envisioned a cautionary tale, and intended to produce a screenplay based on my research and conjecture.

But it was such a big project. There was so much detail and minutiae; so much I didn't want to leave out. When my daughter, Jane, then an executive with Orion Pictures, told me my story would be better served in novel form, I had to agree. She was right. In this form, I could capture the depth of the large and small, almost sublime machinations of a New World Order.

Fascinatingly, after I'd completed my first draft, elements of my story were taking on a quality of verisimilitude. In January 1994, while traveling cross-country via Amtrak, I met a man who introduced himself as a psychologist. His comments caused me to have doubts about my little story. This man read my entire rough manuscript. He said it was good, but very dangerous. He felt that such a fiction—one this rational and straightforward—might possibly become a primer for an anarchist or opportunist. He felt it was too factual and repeatedly asked me how I knew these things. I told him my story elements were merely based on facts as they were at the time (1993) and that I had quite simply and logically proposed how the future might unfold. He became quite serious and I became frightened.

He cautioned me to not to publish my book. In fact, he said I should destroy it. I never saw that man again, but I'll always wonder if he was with the CIA or FBI, or just a nut.

After hearing these negative comments and objections, I did become a little apprehensive. I certainly didn't want problems with the government. Maybe I had discovered too much. Maybe my scenario of the future was too close to the truth.

Now, as we venture into a fresh century and a new millennium under the umbrella of the possibility of a real-life "New World Order," and as we live with the energy crisis, global warming, crime, poverty, terrorism, the consequences of 9/11, the Patriot Act, Homeland Security, The NSA, Operation Iraqi Freedom, The Immigration Act, The Real ID Act, The Mental Health Act, etc., my story seems all the more prognostic.

Is it life imitating art? Or vice versa?

Whatever the circumstances may be, I feel the need to present this tale as originally conceived, over a decade ago.

What if one solitary man decided he could rule the world and, for the first time in history, he succeeded? And what if this man didn't use weapons for control and everyone ended up happy?

In this day of caution and conflicts, with all of our laws and checks and balances, could one person gain total control of the people? And, based on the history of humankind's evil toward itself, how would the people allow it to happen?

I quote now the last guy who tried to rule the world, Adolph Hitler: "How fortunate for governments, that people are so stupid."

I want you to know that the story you are about to read is, of course, fiction; it hasn't happened—yet! But, by recognizing the issues that we are still facing today, this might be a valid scenario of what the future could hold for us. I want to be very clear: my intention is not to frighten you. This book is intended to be an entertainment. However, much of what you'll read here really is happening now. These ideas are truth, not fiction.

Humankind's moral principles and ethics are forever in conflict and disarray. This *hydra* that has been with mankind forever may now finally have an opportunity to be corrected.

If our government and the governments of the world continue in the direction they are heading, then the entire set of circumstances, as I have proposed, will actually happen.

Personally, I think it's too late to do anything to stop it!

And, if I'm right, then we can only hope and pray that we will get a compassionate, benevolent and honorable dictator.

Steven J. Conners
Reno, Nevada
2006

## PREFACE TO THE SECOND EDITION

The state of our nation nearly ten years after publication of the first edition is just as I imagined it might be when I started writing this book in 1993. I find that many aspects of my cautionary tale are no longer fiction. Humankind continues to ignore and oppose wisdom and rationality.

Today, we may have a latent dictator in our current president. I hope he reads this book. Billy, though lethal, seemed to be a really nice guy, too. Believe me...

Steven J. Conners
Vista, California
2017

DEFINITION—HYDRA:


A multifarious evil not to be overcome by a single effort.


–MERRIAM-WEBSTER.COM

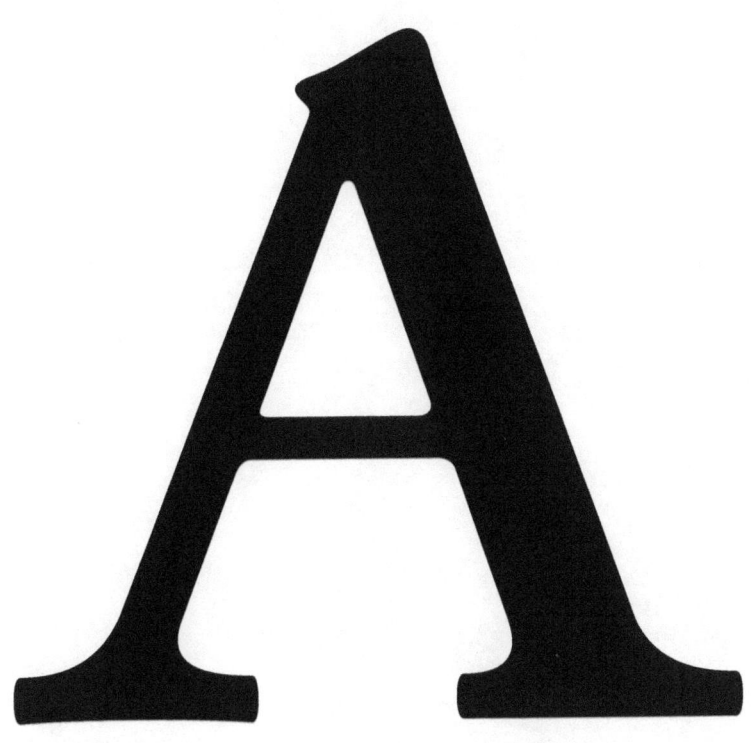

# 1

## *THE DESERT*

The desolate desert sky was a beautiful deep shade of blue with just a few wispy clouds. It was hot, but the strong breeze made it tolerable. A group of uniformed men looked high above the horizon into the brilliant vastness. There was no sound. It was very still.

Far in the distance a small speck, just a black spot in the blue sky, moved rapidly toward them. They stood motionless, transfixed. The object came at them at an ever-increasing speed. Impact! With a blinding flash the missile hit the ground and exploded with a tremendous, jarring roar. All sorts of military equipment and human parts catapulted up violently, all flying high through the hot desert air, a slow-motion ballet of bodies and pieces of bodies combined with the fragments of olive-drab hardware. They all rose together and then fell in fractured syncopation, lightly, seemingly gently, to earth.

Billy thought: "Oh my God, it's happening to me again."

Screams do not echo in the desert. They are heard quite individually—one at a time. The silence in between screams becomes almost as eerie as the screams themselves.

Not at all like the jungle, Billy remembered. In the jungle, one voice could seem to come from everywhere. These, now, were his last thoughts, as he was hurled through the air. Spinning. Floating. Then the inevitable crunch, as he hit the ground. Then, deep blackness.

The hospital wardroom was small and fiercely hot. The smells were not of an ordinary hospital. The mixture of old and new death combined with hospital clean made for an unusual, slightly repugnant odor. The ward was part of an old World War II British field hospital, constructed of rough stucco walls and exposed wooden beams. Numerous cracks spidered along the cream-colored plaster walls, intermittently interrupted by divots from hundreds of bullet holes in countless places. Layers of dust covered every surface in the ward, including the very white bed linens. Rows of wounded men and a few women lined the wardroom. As one might expect in war, there were many severely wounded.

Billy lay in the hospital bed, his head bandaged, leg in a cast, arm hung in a sling. There was blood on the pillowcase. Burn ointment seeped through the gauze encasing one of his hands.

Several men gathered near his bed, speaking quietly among themselves. Billy, still unconscious, was obviously a very important man. The men stood at his bedside, waiting.

At last, one of them spoke aloud to the others. It was Henry Gillespie, a tall, thin man in his late fifties. He was quite upset. "I am so very lucky. It could have been me, you know. I was standing next him. Boom! I was thrown to the side, but Billy got it square on. Oh God, why him? He has so much left to do. So many people are counting on him."

Irving Penitz spoke, "Henry, what you really mean to say is, 'Why did we all have to see the war up close?'"

Gillespie interrupted: "Billy always has to know what's going on—says he wants the people to see him in the thick of things, says they'll admire his courage, says it gives them faith in him and the movement. I happen to think he's right."

The well-known Senator from Montana, the honorable Avery Harrison, ignored Gillespie's sympathetic comment. The fact that he, too, was a lawyer, like the respected Irving R. Penitz, allowed Avery to have a certain cynical pragmatism that he felt only attorneys were permitted to have.

Avery bent over and looked closely at the wounded man lying in the old hospital bed. He shook his head and spoke almost mockingly in that old-time orator way he used so often. "Well, gentlemen. Here's to our dear William F. Johnstone, the next, or should I say, the ex-Third Party presidential nominee. Too bad. Too bad."

Col. Robert Collings, retired from the Marine Corps, was Billy's personal *aide-de-camp*. Collings addressed the doctor, who was reading the chart, in his usual brusque, military manner. "What are his chances of getting out alive? How bad is it? Can he be moved? And how soon?"

The doctor, a young Australian replied, "Broken femur, dislocated hip and shoulder—all of which have been reset—a few small first and second-degree burns on the body, and more severe burns on the right hand and wrist. Lacerations of the face, neck and upper back, concussion via multiple skull fractures—pressure has been relieved—previous fractures of the skull—kind of a mess in there—a lot of brain pressure and I don't like his prolonged unconsciousness."

The doctor addressed the entire group. "Unfortunately, considering his condition at this time, I wouldn't chance moving him."

Gillespie, still noticeably shaken, groaned "And only two weeks before the campaign would have started."

The doctor continued. "It could go either way, you see, and I don't think that..."

"They'll never elect an injured man," interrupted Penitz.

They all nodded in quiet agreement.

Billy opened his eyes and struggled to sit up on one elbow. "Not dead! Not even dyin'. Broke' leg and a little concussion. It's happened to me before—could happen to anyone. We're still in the game. Now listen up, you clowns: you get to my chief of propaganda and tell him not to spare one detail of this situation. I want pictures, video, stories, the works. Goddammit. I'm a vet! A full-blown, blown-up hero. Billy F. Johnstone ain't gonna die in no desert! Don't worry, boys, 'cause everything's gonna be all right, and that's a promise. Now git your worried asses out of here and go make it happen. I'm flyin' back to Hurricane House tonight. I'll be well enough to do a press conference there in the morning. And that's a fact! Now git!"

The men exited quickly.

Billy could hold on no longer. The pain in his head was horrible. His black-brown eyes stared toward the ceiling as the room swirled and darkened. The dark infinity peaked with blips of light, blending into a surreal montage of shapes, colors and sounds. Billy, unconscious again, fell into a very deep dream.

The dream swirled and Billy saw himself as a little boy of ten, sitting in a small rural church.

In his dream, Billy clutched his mother's hand. He squeezed it so hard that she whimpered in pain. Billy was very frightened.

The pastor was a huge man, tall, fat, and red in the face as he screamed the words of his sermon to his frightened flock. "The end is not just nearby, my friends; the end has come! You were supposed to help Jesus, supposed to convert all the sinners, make 'em good for the Lord."

He looked straight at young Billy. "The Lord sayeth, 'He who conquers evil in my name, to him I will give power over the nations of the world and he shall rule the people with a rod of iron.' But, those who see sin and don't try to correct it, those that abide Satan and his ways, those that don't help to cleanse the world, they will die and spend eternity in hell. Oh, yeah. Got to do your job. Got to help the Lord, that's what you're s'posed to do. But oh, you wicked, you terrible, you sons and daughters of the devil, you haven't done your job. He knows of your works. You're not the helpers of the Lord. You know it! And you're gonna die for it. You're gonna burn in hell! You'll never get to heaven!"

The pastor wiped his face and calmed a bit. "The little ones," he looked at Billy again, "they have some time, yet. Not much time, but they could grow up to help Jesus. They can fix the world like the Lord wants it to be, like He demands it to be. Oh yeah, the young people still have a chance."

The pastor seemed to grow larger as his passion grew. "But the rest of you are in deep, deep trouble, 'cause Jesus will be back and he's not gonna be the 'I love y'all' kinda guy he was the last time...Oh, no. Oh no!"

The pastor, flushed and sweating, yelled even louder. "He's a-comin' back and he's a-gonna be a killer and he's a-gonna kill you all 'cause you didn't do what you were s'posed to do. He's gonna raise the dead from their graves—the good ones, that is—and take 'em all up to heaven and give them ever-lastin' life.

A fiendish smile broke across the preacher's face. "And then. Then he's gonna come back and set about to destroy you sinners. Repent now, while you can. Make your ways the ways of the Lord, for He is coming to judge us all. Oh, my brethren, it will be Hell on Earth and pain and suffering to those who didn't do right, to those who didn't help our Jesus. The four horsemen—the terrible battles—the pestilence—the sickness—the death—the absolute horror. It'll be fire this time. Fire...fire...FIRE!"

Billy's dream cut movie-like to a jungle battle scene with a close-up of a mortar firing, then dollied back to reveal soldiers lying prone in the mud.

The camera of his mind zoomed into Billy's eye, then turned around to see the battle from Billy's point of view. The enemy charged toward him.

In his fear and panic Billy once again heard the old pastor screaming, "...fire and death and hell on earth. He'll kill those who haven't done right. He'll destroy the sinners, for they're the enemy of the Lord. Destroy the enemy and Jesus will save you, destroy the sinners and He will let you rule the world."

A North Vietnamese soldier broke through the foliage and came right at Billy and his platoon. The soldier was almost in his face as Billy lifted his automatic weapon and fired. He kept on firing at the man until his clip was empty. The Vietnamese soldier's head and one arm hung limp, severed by the intense firepower of Billy's weapon.

Billy shouted and ranted biblical verse at the dead soldier until he heard another voice screaming from behind him: "Incoming! Incoming! Incoming!"

The shell screamed to earth. Explosion.

Billy again saw himself and others thrown high into the air.

Billy landed hard on the jungle floor among his dying comrades.

For a moment, there was total silence. Everything was still.

As the smoke and falling debris subsided, the wounded began screaming and writhing on the ground like so many large bloody worms.

Billy couldn't move, but he could see. To his right, Captain Collings was up on one elbow and Major Fenwick was flat on his back groaning in pain. A few of the others were recovering from the blast and were beginning to move about.

Soundlessly, the enemy rushed again, firing and stabbing bayonets at the wounded and the already dead.

Billy wanted to move, but he couldn't. He felt the hot pain of his wound and then a different kind pain—a ragged bayonet thrust into his side.

Again, silence.

Billy could still see. He thought maybe he was dead.

Billy saw the North Vietnamese checking the dead American soldiers, taking items and papers from their lifeless bodies and jabbering in their very foreign talk. He heard one of them shout and Billy turned his eyes to the right.

Captain Collings struggled to get on his feet.

The enemy soldiers forced Collings to pick up the wounded Major Fenwick and carry him away.

Billy could see it all happening but he couldn't move to stop it.

The enemy quickly disappeared into the thick underbrush.

Once again it was silent.

Then the animal sounds of the jungle began. Billy lay among the dead for a very long time.

Finally, he succumbed to the awful pain in his body and fell into the warmth of that welcome, black unconsciousness.

Billy's desert hospital dream continued to mix his present circumstances with memories, creating a whirlpool of reverie and confusion. In this darkness time expanded, contracted and bounced from trauma to bliss.

The dream exploded into bright sunlight. A graduation exercise was in progress on the beautiful, palm-surrounded grounds of a university.

Billy saw himself coming up the steps to the platform to receive his diploma. He moved to the other side of the stage, accepted his diploma, and continued down the steps to the small group of people waiting for him.

A beautiful dark-haired girl, Suzzanne Berlois, beamed approval and admiration toward Billy. As he descended the steps, she threw her arms around him and kissed him passionately. She was the love of his life.

Billy declared out loud that she would become his wife.

Billy's mother was there, too, crying with joy and hugging him. Billy told her that becoming a soldier, his high marks in school and earning his degree had all been for her.

Billy felt all warm and wonderful. His mother was, is, his first love.

On this special graduation day, his oldest and dearest friends, Charles Gertz and David Barnston, were there, too, shaking his hand and patting him on the back. Billy was proud, triumphant. He felt magnificent!

Billy wanted to stay in this part of the wonderful dream forever.

Suddenly the dream cut to black and then to Billy and Suzzanne being married in a church.

The pastor spoke to them in a serious, commanding tone. "...and as long as you both revere the Lord and do what the Lord expects and commands of you, you will receive His blessings from heaven. If you do not obey God and the laws he has set out for mankind—if you sin, or abide sinners—you will perish into eternal Hell."

Billy's knees buckled. He collapsed, fainting at the altar.

Suzzanne knelt beside him, clutching his child-like face contorting in anguish and fear. Wide-eyed with terror he screamed: "No, God, no. Please don't hurt me! No. No. No..."

Billy's dream cut quickly to another scene of himself holding a salesman's large sample bag.

An unseen prospect barked at Billy: "You're not listening to me, kid. I'm not interested in buying anything from you!," and brusquely shoved him out of an office door.

Similar rejections swirled in a montage of many offices. In each of these fantasy situations Billy feverishly pitched, trying to sell something to someone.

Finally, the whirlwind stopped.

At last, in a brightly lit office, a prospective buyer nodded, yes, and shook hands with Billy.

As Billy let go of the buyer's hand, and was pulled back into darkness, as the dream continued. He felt himself falling, then floating.

The light returned as the fluorescent brightness inside an ultra-lavish office building, then he moved down a hall and into the interior of a large meeting room.

Billy, slightly older now, told a group of people: "Business is war. If you want something you have to make it happen. Plan a good assault, kick their asses, and kill the bad guys first before they figure out who you are. You'll impress the good guys and they'll all do what you want. They'll know they'd better listen to you or they'll be gone, too."

Billy paced back and forth. "Do it right and they'll love you. Yeah, they'll actually love you, 'cause you will have become their hero." He smiled in his grand fashion. "And the devil knows, they always need a hero."

Billy stopped pacing. "Now get out there and sell my damned medical products and don't give me any excuses about competition or hard luck or difficulties. Just do it! Do it, or get away from me, 'cause God don't love a loser and neither do I. This meeting's over."

Even with the pain of his wounds, Billy smiled in unconscious reverie.

His dream cross-faded to a sunny outdoor scene. Blue sky above. A soft breeze. A beautiful day.

Billy stood on a platform decorated with red, white, and blue bunting, making a speech to a large group of people. "Ya see folks, the world's in a mess and this country's in an even bigger mess. I can't fix it all by myself, but, be assured, it can be fixed! You, the people, must fix it and I'm gonna help you do it. The very first thing we got to do is get elected. And we're gonna win."

The crowd signaled its approval with a mighty cheer. "Now, our opposition doesn't think it can be done. But we are gonna do it, you and I. We're gonna win this election! Then we'll lead the mighty people of the U.S. with all of their God-given rights in a full crusade to free and enlighten the people of the world."

His audience whistled and shouted: "Bil-ly! Bil-ly! Bil-ly!"

He continued, "See, it's as easy as *A-B-C*. A: We're gonna take our country back from this big government stranglehold. And B: you're gonna put me in office so I can do the job they always said they would do...and I promise you, I will do it! And C: we're gonna kick those old bureaucrats so far out of the game that they'll all have to go back home and get real jobs, 'cause their fat, soft, political careers are gonna be over. And now, don't y'all worry, 'cause everything's gonna be all right...all right...all...right..."

The crowd cheered and cheered as the dream went out of focus, the sounds of the crowd mixing with Billy's words and the wildly surreal band playing weird rally music.

Suddenly, the dream was over. The flashes of light and garbled sounds faded into a deep and wonderful sleep.

# 2

## *AS EASY AS A-B-C*

By the next morning, Billy's wishes had been obeyed. Overnight, he had been safely transported back to his home, back to the place he called Hurricane House.

A piercing clap of thunder rocked the foundations of the large Southern mansion as the wind picked up and whistled through the palm trees surrounding the fenced, very private patio area. The Gulf of Mexico lay beautifully quiet in the background, framing the huge home set back in a Louisiana bayou. Located on or near the spot where rumors say that Lafayette, the pirate, had his famous hideout during the War of 1812, the huge old mansion was certainly as mysterious as it was beautiful. A dream of Billy's since childhood, this house was his first big personal purchase.

Rob Collings informed Billy that more than fifty reporters had gathered to hear about Billy's exploits in the desert war. They wanted to confirm or dispel the rumors that Billy was permanently injured or even, as some said, dying from his wounds.

Some of the news-hawks were already seated; others were checking their equipment out on the patio filled with snakes of wiring, lights, lots of videocams, still cameras and microphones. This was an important interview. Anxiously, they all awaited Billy's arrival.

Billy made his entrance seated in an ornate wheelchair—one arm in a sling, right leg in a cast—dressed in a simple eastern-style robe with a cowl top, partially covering his heavily bandaged head. Suzzanne wheeled him to the huge cluster of microphones waiting for him on the low podium. The reporters' noisy chatter quieted, and they listened with rapt attention.

A reporter called out, "Hey, Billy. You okay?"

Billy responded immediately. "Of course, I'm all right. Got blowed up in 'Nam worse than this and still had the stuff to survive and build my biomedical business to be the biggest in the world, didn't I? Got shot by those damned terrorists two years ago and healed up real fine, didn't I? Hell, this is just a broken leg and a bump on the head. It only happened the day before yesterday and here I am today, feeling real great, ready to get on the job and go to work for all of you. You're my bosses and I'll show up for work and that's a promise!"

Another reporter asked: "Tell us about that war over there, will you, Billy?"

"Well, we're doing the right thing, that's for sure. God don't like some of those A-rabs, and we don't like 'em either, so we're s'posed to fight 'em—the bad ones—until they see it like the Lord wants 'em to see it. It's in the Bible. These wars, I guess, they just can't be avoided. The brave men and women of our armed forces over there in that desert are doing a great job. They're kickin' ass and takin' names. My God, you'd have to see 'em fight. They really are great Americans!"

Then from another reporter: "Billy, if you're elected, what's the first thing you'll do as President of the United States?"

"Well, that's a 'when,' not an 'if,' my friend. Listen, I'm gonna have a meeting with all those ol' boys in the House and the Senate and set 'em straight on what the deal really is, that's the first thing."

The questions came fast. "Can you tell us your plans, Billy? Specifically, what can the American people look forward to if you win?"

Billy hesitated, and then answered in that now familiar style. "Sure, I can tell you. But I'm not gonna. Gotta keep it a secret, you know. It was once said, 'never let your right hand know what your left hand is doing.' The day I tell those ol' boys on the Hill they'll know, you'll know and the whole danged country and the world will know. But nobody is gonna know 'til then. But, don't worry, folks, 'cause everything's gonna be all right, and that's a promise! Fellows and ladies, this meeting is over. I got work to do!"

The reporters broke up into groups and began to talk with Billy's aides. The drinks flowed and the very hungry press corps eagerly consumed the elaborate buffet.

As the reporters filed reports, David Barnston, Billy's chief publicist and campaign manager, listened closely to their conversations. It seemed that the normally cynical media had arrived at a consensus. Not only did they believe what Billy had told them, but they agreed that Billy would almost certainly be the next President of the United States. Billy was the man for the job. They all loved this guy. They trusted him. Billy wasn't a politician in their eyes. He was one of them.

Rob Collings, now the head of corporate and campaign security, wanted his man out of the commotion. He quickly wheeled the beaming candidate off to the library sunroom.

Safely inside, Billy ordered the door closed. He turned to Collings and said, "Rob, I want you to get Gertz, Barnston, Harrison, and Wilhelm out of there and in here now."

When everyone had gathered in the sunroom, Billy motioned for Wilhelm, his oldest son, to push the wheelchair over to the bar. "Well, Willy, the fat is in the fire. I guess we'll have to go all the way now!" Billy rapped on the bar with his cane. "Gentlemen, what'll you have? Fix us all a drink, will you, son?"

Billy wheeled around and addressed Collings. "I hope that glorious *Semper Fi* still runs hot in your veins, old boy. Plan A—Becoming President of the United States—has been put in full, formal, and forward motion!"

With an eye on his father, Wilhelm served the drinks and sat down next to Barnston, Collings and Gertz.

Billy sipped his scotch, then wheeled his chair over to the table. "Well, let's make an assessment. The incumbent administration is following through with the plan that was put in place way back in the early 60s, right after JFK was shot: the slow, steady, bureaucratic government control of the masses—hook 'em, tag 'em, dazzle 'em with misinformation and you've got control. More and more media pressure, using primarily the Madison Avenue version of the old Pavlovian principle: 'If they can hear and see the message, we can make 'em do anything.'"

He stopped just long enough to take another sip. "They'll respond to any message—they'll buy anything. Those ol' boys have caused the people to forget cash and savings and convinced them to use credit for everything. And they've got 'em so hooked on buying, that the American public have become completely dependent on living paycheck-to-paycheck. It's become an odd form of modern slavery.

"With this foolish and extreme use of credit the typical American is forced to fill out an average of 8.73 credit applications each year, and now with the new National Mental Health examination in the wings the government hopes to finish the systematic identification and cataloging of every person in the U.S., Canada, Mexico, and Central America. They'll be able to tell exactly what you had for breakfast yesterday! And, with the North American Trade Agreement in place, and the Immigration Department letting anyone into the country just so they can be tagged and identified, the information bloodhounds are headed even further north and south of our borders at an alarming rate.

"Outbreaks of TB and other communicable diseases have been political footballs between the government and the media for years and have only confused and caused further paranoia in the people. I mean look at that AIDS virus! Imagine impressing the public with propaganda strong enough to make them afraid to have natural sex! When the media speaks out on AIDS they covertly persuade the public to doubt their own natural feelings, producing a fear so potent that people literally have to abstain from sex or masturbate, or become voyeurs, or even worse. It's emotional madness. But it does prove that the 'control machinery' works!"

Charles grabbed a napkin from the center of the table, flipped it, scrawled some indecipherable combination of numbers and letters, smiled, then shoved the napkin in his pocket. He grabbed his drink and took a long satisfying gulp, while turning his attention back to Billy, who'd barely taken a breath.

"It's very fortunate for this incumbent president that crime has continued to be another big psychological issue. They keep giving shorter prison sentences and earlier releases to the very limited number of real criminals. They turn them back on the street and then talk up the rise in criminal activity. Hell, they've even used CIA killers to commit random murders just to enhance the picture of rampant and unsolvable violent crime. With the 'justice' system we have now, they can pin the charges on anyone—preferably a foreigner or a person of color—then make a big public trial, and after months of press coverage, the judge will render a minor sentence for a major crime and then we'll get another trial to watch the next week. You know, they tell me that watching the real and put-up crime coverage on television has a greater daytime audience than the old soap operas."

Billy took a pull on his scotch and held the glass up for Wilhelm to fill. "They've wired the schools with TV to deliver the 'news of the day' propaganda as a 'current events' class instead of civics and government. They feed the kids on CNN, MSNBC, FOX and the

World-Wide Web sites and constantly revise the textbooks each year. They've rewritten history taking aim at the future—our children.

"The schools in this country look like prisons. They have internal police more vicious than Hitler's Gestapo. They have instituted juvenile detention camps and quasi-drug rehabilitation programs for the urban youth criminals that are so controlling that the young of this country are firmly convinced that they have no future.

"The 'drug problem' is, of course, a totally manufactured issue, used as a cover to make payoffs at various levels and convince the people that a steady increase in police for every city, as well as along our borders, is vitally necessary. They have quadrupled the number of prisons in the state and federal systems and by using an absurd schedule called 'mandatory minimum sentences' they have turned the federal courts into nazi-style prosecutor's courts, making the judges all but impotent.

"The passage of new federal drug and anti-terrorism laws now permit totally illegal search and seizure—confiscation of private possessions, real estate and bank accounts. They can arrest anyone they think is a terrorist and hold them without a lawyer or trial. There goes another piece of our great Constitution. In fact, these latest laws have made our Constitution look like a piece of Swiss cheese. The majority of crimes that are committed today are not physically hurting anyone. Most of the criminals could really be dealt with in other, more effective ways than using the police, courts and prisons.

"And their stupid war on drugs has locked up hundreds of thousands of young people simply because the government believes these kids are potential resistance leaders. They worry that their 'control shit' is gonna set off an armed rebellion and..."

Collings surveyed the wall of CCTV screens. He knew this was going to be a long one. The glass of his noticeably untouched drink was sweating. Carefully, he wiped it clean. He never drank on duty. But, he knew better than to refuse a drink from Billy.

Billy hadn't taken a breath. "...so they can't storm the White House.

"Now they want 'new laws' to 'prevent crime.' And they'll get the public support and it'll end up in the eventual removal of all firearms from every American citizen. 'Let's lock up all the guns, and the public will obey us unconditionally.' They are definitely afraid of rebellion.

"But it's the media and the police that are their weapons of control. Very sinister. Illegal! Immoral!"

Barnston silently thought that Billy sounded a lot like Huey Long on a good day. Billy was on a roll. Barnston listened intently for pieces he could use in the campaign.

"You oppress the people and they will rebel. Always have, always will. Of course, we can't go on the street and tell the public what's being done to them. First, they wouldn't believe it and, second, the opposition would literally kill us, dead. If we announced to the public any of what I've been telling you, the press would label us as radicals. 'Never blow the whistle on another guy's game,' so I've been told. It could be dangerously fatal if you do!

"But don't worry, boys, when we get into office I'll show you how we can use this slow and stupid government oppression and turn it into something very, very beneficial. For now, though, we have to inspire the people of our country and continue to focus on the hot issues of the day: terrorism, unemployment, poverty, crime, drugs, health, education, and the general economy. We have to convince them that the new Third Party will be the 'cross bearers' for the people of the North American continent."

Wilhelm shifted in his chair. None of this was new for him.

"We'll continue to keep our opposition off balance. The old guard uses very slow methods, you know, and most of them don't work. In the end, they'll have no choice but to oppress the people and that, historically, doesn't work for very long. The people always resist the oppressor. The dictator becomes the vanquished and then the pendulum swings back the other way. Mankind has been doing this same silly dance throughout its existence. What is really needed is a way to not just control the people, but make 'em happy. 'Cause if they're happy they won't want to kill you!"

Billy took another long pull on his scotch and lit an expensive Cuban cigar. "Rest assured, gentlemen, I have done my homework. I do have a solution to these age-old problems. But that's for another time."

Billy smacked the table to make sure they were all paying attention. "Now, both camps have a lot of tough old-school birds—we'll have to fight 'em without any traditional political campaign strategies. The incumbent party has had two terms and has convinced a certain segment of the population that their strong government policy will work. It hasn't, and it won't. They still want the poor to remain poor and the disenfranchised to be even further from the real decision-making. If the Republicans get back to the gravy trough and eat any more of this country, we will surely have a revolution.

"Now, between the two parties, they have plenty of corporate backing. And they both have some organized labor and organized minorities and special interest groups. 'Organized' is the operative word here. Somebody got them organized years ago and now they're just phone numbers that the campaigners call. I think we should look at what's left over. I think we should use a good old-fashioned 'let's make it happen' grassroots campaign and utilize all this great new media technology to wrap them up as our supporters."

Barnston pulled out a notepad and started writing feverishly.

"We'll go directly to the thousands of bypassed organizations: the students, the non-union working people, the poor, the old. We'll use all the groups that the other two parties ignore and think are too small or not effective and bring them in as major Third Party supporters. I think you'll find that they will add up to a mighty, loyal, cooperative and winning force. We can go to these people and tell them how poorly they have been treated in the past and just how badly the politicians in the previous and existing administrations have cheated them. We need to lay off the stronger government and constitutional stuff and stress the concept of 'more for every man and woman;' you know, that old 'chicken in every pot' and 'every man a king' platform. It's worked before and it'll work again. We'll give them all a voice and show 'em that the problems that afflict them can be solved by action and solidarity, not politics. When we bring in these new groups, the unions and the minority groups will fall into place. We'll convince them that we alone are the answer; the only true way to salvation.

"Now, that's the plan, boys, and that's how I want to sell it, and here's the bottom line: This next election is the whole ballgame. The Democrats have allowed the Republicans to stay in office for two terms. They want the presidency back and they intend to keep it for a very long time. Get the big picture, boys? The fiber optic highway will soon be completed, probably, just in time for the first nationwide vote-from-your-home election, and those interactive cable boxes will sell like hotcakes on a cold morning. The president who wins next will take the people of the United States all the way and right into the history books and the big, bright new future. And boys, I want to be that President!"

Billy wheeled his chair in a circle and then stopped abruptly, facing them all once again. "If you men give me 'til the end of this week, I'll be ready to go on tour. Now, my good Doctor Gertz, how long can I keep this cast on my leg—and be legit, I mean? I want to use this wheelchair for a while, then crutches, then get the cast off and use a cane. Then I want to run and jump for the cameras, show 'em I'm completely well and fit for the job of President of the United States. Get it?"

Dr. Charles Gertz was not a practicing physician, but he knew his medicine. Billy always had him cross-check anything medical. He was Billy's business partner and a trusted old friend. Charles examined

Billy's leg and then looked closely at the medical reports and X-rays. "Billy, I would say that you could definitely be walking on your own in less than four weeks. I would follow the scheme you just outlined. Wheelchair for about two weeks, then to crutches, cast removed, cane as a prop until you don't want to use it anymore. Yes, it's a good medical plan, and you do heal very quickly, Billy."

"Thank you, Charles. Now Mr. David Barnston, you start me out on this tour at rallies with the older folks, 'cause they'll sympathize with my current injuries and my status as a war veteran. Then, when I get this cast off, David you get me straight into the colleges so I can start that big youth demographic jumping and moving for us. I want to see an idea for a route by tomorrow morning. I really feel good, and I'm rarin' to go."

Barnston remembered that since they were children, through grade school and high school, Billy always got what he wanted or he wanted to know why, and you'd better have the right answers.

Billy brought the meeting to an end. "If you will, gentlemen, I need to talk to Rob, alone, so I bid you all a good night and thank you as always for your friendship and loyalty. May we win this political war and have peace for America during our administration. And don't worry, 'cause everything's gonna be all right. And, that's a promise! Goodnight, fellows."

Wilhelm stood up with Charles, looking back at his father. He never was sure how much he was involved; never sure whether to stay or go. Billy gave him a nod and Wilhelm and Charles departed as ordered, leaving Billy and Collings alone.

Now, Collings was off the clock. He mixed himself a fresh drink.

Billy watched him and silently mused, "Colonel Robert J. Collings, USMC, retired—my man."

Though Billy had known David Barnston his entire life, it was Collings that grew to be his closest friend; a man with whom he had shared his plans for the future, his ideas, his philosophy of life itself. The two had participated in many high passions during that long friendship; events that included large doses of love, hate, and greed. They had both killed many men in their lifetimes. War. Duty. Otherwise. Tonight, though, all of that seemed to be far away in the past. The best was yet to come.

Collings was a career Marine when Billy saved his life. When Major Fenwick's reconnaissance platoon was attacked, the enemy captured Collings and Fenwick and put them through some terrible torture. Billy was left for dead. After Billy recovered from his battle wounds, he went against orders and formed a rescue team to liberate Collings, Fenwick, and five others held as POWs. For this almost superhuman feat, Billy won the Congressional Medal of Honor, the Distinguished Service Cross, the Purple Heart and the lifelong love of Collings and Fenwick. After he was released from the POW camp, Collings quit the Marines and swore a new oath of allegiance to another great American cause: William F. Johnstone.

Billy broke his own sweet reverie. "Rob, do you think I'm nuts?"

"No more than any great man has ever been, Billy. You can't help yourself. Don't worry. In the end, you'll find that it will all have been worth it. In life, you do whatever you have to do. You told me that, remember? The ends always justify the means."

They spoke little more about the political campaign. It was relaxed conversation now between two very close friends. Talk about their good old days and remembering long into the quiet night.

# 3

## *THE SELLING BEGINS*

The very next weekend, on a clear, cool Sunday afternoon, David Barnston organized a rally at the National Congress of Retired People convention in St. Louis—just as Billy had ordered. Some eight thousand people were on hand, all over the age of sixty, with a solid representation from every state. This was the first big rally for Billy and a real test to see what kind of response this normally conservative demographic would give to his new Third Party.

Billy was not the only one on the rostrum that afternoon, and was not the principle speaker. The program noted that he was a presidential candidate for the new Third Party.

Barnston knew this was a great opportunity to "catch the pulse" of the old guard and he and his staff had several table locations giving out brochures, buttons, hats, and T-shirts. David never missed a chance to make any event into a strong "Billy for President" rally. He was good at what he did, and getting even better as this campaign rolled along.

Barnston was worried that Billy was allotted only five minutes to speak. Somehow Billy thought that he didn't even need that much time to "sell 'em." Billy was introduced and he wheeled his chair toward the microphones. Barnston held his breath.

"Good afternoon, ladies and gentlemen. I hope you don't mind a youngster talking with you today. I'm only fifty-four—just a little kid."

The audience laughed and Barnston began to feel confident that his man might be able to connect with these people after all.

"For the record, I did join your association a few years ago, and I've listened with very great interest to what is going on in your organization. As you may know, I am running for president on a third party ticket. Now I know that probably makes most of you feel like I'm a crackpot or a nut. Until a few years ago I was—and always had been—a card-carrying Republican."

The people shifted in their seats, harboring a quiet skepticism.

"About that time, I began to look at the shape this nation was in. I didn't like what I saw. And I liked even less what I came to find out after a little investigation. For all the years you and I have lived and all the wars we've fought for this country—I was in Vietnam, and I know we've got World War II, Korean, and Vietnam men and women out there today. Throughout all those wars and the social changes that came from those wars, we have all been lied to by our government."

A loud murmur bubbled up from the audience. "Oh, I know that sounds like a radical statement, but listen up. Here's the real truth: Our taxes are higher now. Our health care does cost more and gives us less, and inflation is now growing. The infrastructure that we fought hard to build is falling apart and you senior citizens—those with the wisdom and experience that have come from living—you've become third-class citizens in your own country. You are not listened to; they don't want to hear from you. They would like to just shove you off and let you be forgotten."

This was a different kind of quiet. The audience was paying attention.

"But they tolerate us because, you and I have real dollars, the genuine wealth of this country. We have made real investments. We have honestly paid our way. We have a true understanding of life and the necessary wisdom to aid our country. But this government, especially the boys who are in power now, they ignore us. How dare they ignore the people who built and own this country?"

The applause rippled throughout the audience.

"Well, when I become President, I won't let that happen, folks. And I'm counting on you people, the group that really should be the most important and powerful group in this country, to help me make a change for the immediate benefit and future of all senior men and women. We must make our government give back to us what we have put in, and we must do it today, before it's too late."

The cheers and applause rumbled up like a roar.

Billy shouted over them. "Listen, you get behind me in this coming election, and I'll do the job for you. With your help, I know we can win this election. So, don't worry, 'cause everything's gonna be all right, and that's a promise!"

The people jumped to their feet in support.

Barnston was more amazed at Billy than ever before. Billy, in less than three minutes, had tailored his message to what had always been considered a tough, loyal Republican crowd and made them stamp and cheer like a bunch of liberals. Billy had some real magic. David's creative mind was on fire with the many campaign possibilities for this charismatic figure.

That evening, following the rally in St. Louis, they took the WFJ corporate jet back to New Orleans and then flew in the company helicopter to Hurricane House in Grand Isle.

On Monday morning, Billy went to his offices at the factory in Larose, Louisiana. He got there at 8:55 a.m. and went immediately to the boardroom.

By 9 a.m., Billy was steaming. Collings had promised that all of the officers of WFJ Polybiotech would be at this meeting on time.

Even though he was in a wheelchair, he managed to wheel about pacing the floor.

9:02 a.m. No one was in the boardroom. This was not like any of them. They all knew that Billy hated to be kept waiting. Another long minute passed as Billy simmered and wheeled up and down the length of the boardroom table.

The door opened and Collings entered, followed by the entire management of WFJ Polybiotech Corporation. "As you ordered, sir. They're all here. I even captured Charles for this one."

"Yes, but I said exactly at 9:00. It's four minutes after…"

Without looking at his watch, Collings went to the phone in front of Billy, dialed a number and put it on the speaker. "The time now is exactly 9 a.m."

"Correct your watch, sir." Collings took his seat at the table.

Billy smiled at Collings and sucked in a deep cleansing breath, then exhaled. Fully. Calmly.

"That's why we're a great team here. We watch out for each other. And we admit when we're wrong. Thank you, Mr. Collings, for that correction."

Focused, Billy continued, "And good morning to all of you. Now, if I may have an update on sales of new products and then products under development…Sam Karsting?"

"Good morning, everybody. Our sales last month on the new Hemo-Tester, the AIDS home-blood testing units, were just short of phenomenal. That was a great suggestion to use a television infomercial. Right on target. They tell me we'll launch a third shift in our Missouri facility just to keep up with the demand."

"Thanks, Sam, and well done, boys, well done. It's nice to hear that our butter and egg business is still going strong. You're doing a great job with the sales, Sammy.

"Look at the sheet, boys. A little item that costs us under a dollar to manufacture and a couple more to market, we wholesale at $18 each. The retailer prices it at between \$32 and \$39, and in the first week out we've moved over three million units in the U.S. market alone. All from a little innovation and some smart marketing.

"Now Charles, what's the next moneymaker going to be? What's new from your sci-fi department?"

"All okay and looking good, Billy. I can't talk too much to the group here and now. Not in any detail, anyway, about our newest discovery—legal stuff and all. But I can say that this next little number will put us on the top of the heap in the hospital/general healthcare market. I think we've got another 'they can't live without it' product, if you'll excuse the pun. But seriously, in the very near future, because of the development of this product, humans will live longer and enjoy better health. Sorry I can't tell you more right now."

"Sounds like another winner for WFJ Polybiotech—if we ever find out what it really is! But I have faith in your genius, Charles. I'm sure you'll tell us when it's ready."

Charles retreated willingly from the center of attention and moved back to his chair.

Billy wheeled himself to the head of the table. "Now to finish up today, I am sad to say, you are all going to lose a valuable player from your team. I am forced to remove from your ranks one of the best computer men in the world. He will never again work for WFJ Polybiotech or any of its affiliated companies. He is finished here. Felix Hansen, I'm talking about you. You're all done, my good fellow. Finished. Kaput. Out!"

The group was stunned.

Felix was in shock. He turned bright red and then the color drained away, leaving his face a deathly white. He stumbled to his feet and turned to Billy. Charles jumped from his chair and came to his aid. Felix was about to pass out.

Billy brought his wheelchair about and quickly went over to him. "Felix! Felix hold on, buddy. Wait, I'm just kidding. You're not working for Polybiotech anymore, but you're still working for me...on my campaign! I need you. Oh god, that was a bad joke. Look at him... Charles, help him. Somebody get some water or..."

Collings had a small glass of brandy and a tumbler of water already at hand. Felix gulped it down the liquor and chased it with the water.

"You mean I'm not fired, Billy?" he stammered.

Billy threw his arms around Felix. "No way! No way! You are my main computer guy. I can't live without you." Billy released Felix from his bear hug. "Sorry for the scare, pal."

Billy returned to the head of the table. "Gentlemen, as of this day Felix will be working with Barnston, Collings and me as we put together the most awesome presidential campaign the world has ever seen."

After a little more talk, the meeting with his managers came to a close, and Billy guided his wheelchair back to his own office.

Billy was pleased. After years of service and many serious conversations with Felix Hansen, Billy had decided that Felix should be brought into the "Inner Circle." This man would be a welcome addition. Felix was skilled, loyal, and shared the IC's vision. Soon the others in the IC would confirm him and then he, too, would swear his allegiance to Billy and the new Third Party.

Billy loved meeting with the guys. It was play to him, not work. They all inspired each other. Billy was the boss, but he was also their hero and leader.

Billy smiled. He lifted himself out of the wheelchair, sank into his big soft leather office chair and swiveled to his left to look out the window.

The view from this office window was bleak, barren and quite depressing. The scene featured several bubbling waste ponds that held highly toxic byproducts. Billy, an environmentalist at heart, had the entire area around the dirty ponds ringed with concrete retaining walls set deep into the earth to prevent the dangerous wastewater from leaking into the aquifer. Within this polluted area, the grass would not grow and all of the trees had died, leaving a brown, parched, surreal view that truly was dismal and ugly. Sometimes Billy sat for hours looking at this desolation, pretending to be depressed when he thought he needed to be.

By nature, Billy was an optimist. By turning just 90 degrees in his chair and looking out the window on his right, the land was bright and verdant. Billy thought that this view was possibly as beautiful a scene as nature could provide: green grass, rolling hills, trees and a sparkling clear stream. Billy often switched from side to side as he was thinking.

This office was one of his favorite places. It represented the start of his success and the vast fortune it had brought. It made him proud and happy. It all happened here. This was the house that Billy built. Charles' genius for finding and designing new products and Billy's great ability to get them to market made for a long-lasting happy partnership.

Billy loved to dream and get lost in memories. Reverie came easy to him, especially when he was in this room. He remembered meeting with Charles Gertz in the student union at Great Southern Tech. He remembered the eagerness and vitality that they both enjoyed in those days. They were full of faith in themselves and their ideas. They had even greater confidence in the absolute goodness of life and all that the future would hold. So far, Billy thought, it had been a very good life. And he believed it was going to get even better. Real soon.

As Charles often said: "Life is a lot of fun, if you ignore the fact that you'll never get out alive!"

Charles was the same age as Billy. They met in high school and went on together to college. Billy dropped out after his freshman year to join the Marines and fight in Vietnam.

That first year they roomed together at Great Southern Technical University, and Charles almost drove Billy mad with his inventions and ideas. Charles was a genius, without a doubt. Billy decided then and there to back the weird ideas of Charles Gertz. They formed WFJ Polybiotech Corporation that year. Billy owned seventy percent of the stock and Charles held the other thirty.

While Billy was in 'Nam, he sent half of his monthly pay to Charles and the rest to his mother. When Billy came home from the war, he enrolled again at GST. Charles was still there working on his doctorate in biochemistry and through those years, too, Billy continued to financially support Charles and his projects.

Billy remembered how shattered he had been when he came home from 'Nam and discovered that his father had died just the week before. Then, to lose his mother, the other most important person in his life, shortly after he graduated from college was totally devastating. Billy remembered the torture of living with his mother's slow death from cancer and the vast empty feeling that came from being helpless in her time of need.

After his mother's death, Billy was truly alone. No brothers or sisters or aunts or uncles or cousins. His mother's death was the end of their family. He was alone. But not for long. The world became bright again when he married Suzzanne Berlois. The sun came back into his life and he knew that with this woman's love he would once again have that wonderful feeling of family. He loved her deeply and recalled just how great it felt to be loved by Suzzanne.

They were married, and Billy stayed on at GST and began to work as a salesman to support himself and Suzzanne—and Charles, too. Billy worked day and night making sales calls, in between writing his dissertation to complete his doctorate in political science. It was hard work It was during those exciting and happy times that his first son, Wilhelm, was born. Billy was determined that he would make a great future for his son. Happiness had returned to Billy with the birth of this child and the security of Suzzanne's love. He enjoyed caring for them, and he knew that the terrible desolation he had experienced in his life would never return. Over the passing years, it never did.

Today, as he sat in his office at WFJ Polybiotech, he was far from alone. Rob Collins, Charles Gertz, David Barnston, Alfred Fenwick, George Osher, Henry Gillespie, Irving Penitz and Avery Harrison—that wonderful assembly of friends—had evolved into a solid core of allies. They were the secret Inner Circle that he had formed years ago, and he knew they were with him for the rest of his life.

Charles was the first to swear the oath. Then Billy invited David Barnston and Rob Collings. Charles brought in his mentor, Professor George Osher, and Rob brought Major—now General—Alfred Fenwick. Billy brought law professor, later to become Senator, Avery Harrison, and the distinguished lawyers, Irving Penitz and Henry Gillespie. And now Billy had invited in the ninth and final member of the Inner Circle, the computer genius Felix Hansen. Each in turn had sworn allegiance to the Inner Circle. Collectively they had become the board of directors of WFJ Polybiotech. They had personally supported Billy's ideas and comforted and protected him for many years. Billy accepted the idea that he really was something special and, with their encouragement, Billy had decided that he was going to be the "real guy" Kurt had expected him to be.

"A man zhat von't just talk about it; a man zhat vill do somesing about it!"

The old German's words echoed in his memory, inspiring Billy's every waking hour.

# 4

## *THE WHIRLWIND TOUR*

Billy and his political advisers needed something sensational and different to help focus the public's attention on his campaign for the presidency. Paraphrasing Lincoln, Billy wanted "to be seen and communicate with all of the people, all of the time."

David Barnston suggested a nationwide tour using a train. This gigantic traveling campaign headquarters would embark on a one-year, 150-city tour to sell Billy and the new Third Party.

It all sounded great to Billy. He loved trains.

The train concept received a lot of attention, even from the first press releases. Big picture stories followed in all the print media reporting on the construction of the train, followed by even bigger stories as the train was finished and the tour schedule announced.

Barnston was right. The campaign train quickly became an icon reminding people of America's ingenuity and strength. It was a press agent's dream come true. The campaign had all the excitement, color and style of an old MGM movie and enough class and energy to stimulate the imagination of the American voter.

Billy purchased thirty-five old train cars and two brand new German diesel-electric engines. The rail cars were totally overhauled and refurbished, Billy-style: Good work, fine design, delivered ahead of schedule, and under budget. Billy's custom-built train, decorated smartly in red, white, blue and silver, with all the bells and whistles, emerged completed and ready to roll, in less than six months!

Billy stated to the media, "If we can do this kind of work in the private sector, why can't our nationalized rail system make a go of it? Well, I'll tell you. When the people are in charge of the trains again, we'll make it the best railroad system in the world!"

Today, Billy met the press, who were assembled in one of the refurbished Pullman cars, and took them on a car-by-car tour of his train. "Look at this marvel of American enterprise and hard work. We took these old cars, American-made over sixty years ago, tops in their day, and now we've modernized them to be functional way into the 21st century. All the electronics you'd ever want, excellent climate control, comfortable day or night, with cell phones, computers, satellite Internet, faxes, individual TVs, stereo sound—and the cost was small, folks. You know, there are hundreds of these great old train cars sittin' around in yards all over this country just waitin' to be returned to duty. Keep that in mind. Repair and refurbish what we've got, then build new!"

They moved into a dining car. "Good solid railroad china and silver in here and the food is cooked to order. No frozen stuff on board. Now let's move to the club car." The group of cameras moved on. Everyone was genuinely impressed with the decor and smart redesign of the old cars.

"Now, folks, here is the sin car. Whiskey, beer, wine and if you'll look in the back there, a complete section for any fool who still wants to smoke. I'm against cigarette smoking myself. I'm not against anything any of you might want to do, as long as it doesn't hurt anybody else. There's plenty of air cleaners in this car, as well as in each of the compartments in the sleepers, so nobody should ever be offended by second-hand smoke. After a glass of fine cognac, I like a good cigar myself, once in a while. And now, if you'll exit down the stairs here, I'll go on to the back porch of this rig for that big announcement I promised you."

The reporters and camera people dutifully descended the stairs to the outside and went around to the back of the last car.

The platform area had been slightly enlarged and PA speakers and special lighting had been installed. It certainly looked like every newsreel presidential train picture you ever saw. The media got their cameras and equipment assembled and waited for Billy to enter the "back porch," as he had put it. Somehow, everything this guy did looked and felt good. He knew human nature and was a master showman.

The press didn't notice, but several hundred people had assembled in back of them. As Billy made his entrance, the cheers from the crowd added just the right sweetening to make a great picture for even a bad cameraman. Billy stood still as the crowd yelled: "Billy! Billy! Billy! Billy!"

Then he held his hands up for them to quiet.

The yelling stopped and the people waited in hushed silence.

"Well, what do think of your train?"

The audience shouted again and Billy continued. "It's really great, isn't it?" It cost me 241 million dollars. I say, 'your train,' 'cause I'm just gonna use it for a short time to go across this great country and talk with all your brothers and sisters. And after they've heard what I have to say, you're all gonna send me to work in Washington and I won't need this train anymore. So, I'm gonna donate it to our national railroad system and then you can all take a ride!"

The crowd erupted with their approval. Billy wasn't kidding them. The media kits were being distributed and each one further explained how Billy would actually give the train—all thirty-five cars and two engines—to the national railroad, whether he won the election or not. This was the beginning of one of the greatest political campaigns ever waged in American history.

The first car, the one right behind the engines, was Billy's. The living quarters for himself and Suzzanne were lavish. This car also housed Billy's private office, a meeting room, and reception area. The entire car was heavily armored and protected, not only against bullets but even light missiles.

Rob Collings occupied the second car and was on-call to Billy day and night. He could also keep an eye on anything that happened throughout the train. Inside this car were Collings' top security men and the latest surveillance equipment. His living room was like a large hotel suite with a sitting-dining room, a bedroom and Collings' private office. Collings' car was noticeably even more plush than Barnston's. This was Billy's idea of a conspicuous "caste system."

David C. Barnston occupied the third car. His car had living quarters and a layout similar to Collings' and was quite well appointed. Collings' watched Barnston, and Barnston's car was right in front of the news-making machinery. Billy believed in a pecking order that kept tabs on itself.

The next five cars, the "Campaign Cars," were under Barnston's total direction. These cars had everything needed for the publicity and promotion staff. The first car was for strategy and planning and had offices for a compliment of eight full-time publicists. The next car housed two still photographers, four digital video cameramen, a production studio with full editing facilities, as well as Billy's personal voice-over announcer and a complete audio studio and two recording engineers. The adjoining car had a huge offset printing press, two pressmen, laser color copiers, two graphic artists, and four layout people. Then came an entire car devoted to the Internet. Here, the brightest and most capable computer minds created the website and chat rooms to engage young voters. These experts knew how to get into every nook and cranny of digital communications. The last car was the boiler room with a telemarketing staff of thirty people and sixty computerized auto-dialing machines.

There were three dining cars and three club cars for the staff; an elegant restaurant car and a sophisticated exclusive nightclub car for the management.

The next car, the video press car also functioned as a movie theatre. It had a large two-sided HDTV screen in the middle that allowed two presentations to occur at the same time and was used daily for briefings and nightly as a cinema.

Two reception cars opened for the campaign supporters in each city. One car carried a museum of "Billy history" featuring interactive A/V displays.

Two sleeping cars housed the national press corps stringers traveling with the campaign and the general staff occupied another six sleeping cars.

Next was a gym, spa and hair salon car, then a car for housekeeping, laundry and dry-cleaning, and then one that housed mechanical shop and general supplies, followed by a car carrying a custom bus.

The Presidential Car was last, with its luxury appointments and the "back porch" for Billy's many speeches.

The train was virtually a world unto itself. Contained in those thirty-five cars was manpower and material enough to manipulate the political thinking of the entire country. And that was exactly what was happening.

Barnston's train idea was great, but when Billy got his hands on it, it became inspired genius. Billy loved the acronym "KISS" (Keep It Simple, Stupid). He had his own little twist on this phrase and always followed with: "Make it look difficult. Keep it simple and don't be stupid." The endeavor did appear to be a huge and costly undertaking, but it was uncomplicated to Billy.

The truth behind the truth was that this fabulous train hadn't cost

Billy one red cent. Oh, he fronted the money, but the cars were all retrofit and the interior furnishings were provided by the companies that wanted the future railroad business, and the two new gas-fired steam-electric engines came from that nice German company that wanted to sell a lot more of them to the American railroad system.

The cost of running these steam-electric engines was less than one-third of the cost of standard diesel engines currently in use. In addition, the natural gas closed-steam boilers created more than twice the power of diesel engines. The big oil company lobbies had successfully engineered passage of laws to prohibit the importation of such locomotives until they had been proven under complicated test conditions. Billy fixed that by paying the testing lab fees and getting all necessary temporary permits and insurances to conduct the tests. The German company, of course, was a substantial contributor to Billy's campaign fund. The company that owned the train, WFJ Railroads, Inc., would reap millions more as a tax deduction when it donated the train to the people. If this was the last gasp of capitalism, as Billy thought it was, it should be a big one. When all was said and done, Billy's plans for the new economy would make this little endeavor look like small potatoes.

The campaign tour began with a bang. The "Billy's Train" story was released to each town well in advance of each stop via radio, TV and newspapers. The media everywhere sopped it up. Barnston and his staff filled in the blanks of the advance release forms and dispatched them by the thousands:

> *A thirty-five car, red, white and blue train loaded with its own high-tech equipment and the Third Party candidate, William F. 'Billy' Johnstone on board, has been launched to tour the nation. This traveling political headquarters has a museum, theatres, nightclubs and restaurants, its own laundry and dry-cleaning facilities, a photo lab, a printing company and many more amenities. It is, in fact, a traveling city. This mobile marvel carries*

*an on-board staff of 211 people and is coming to [city]
on [dates]. It will be parked on a siding at [location]
for [number of days] while the Third Party presidential
candidate, William F. "Billy" Johnstone appears at the
[local venue] college campus for a rally with the students.
Billy, as his friends call him, will also do some radio, TV
and newspaper interviews while he's in town and promises
to tour many of the local [city] businesses and factories.
Candidate Johnstone will hold a massive public rally at
the local [city] arena on [dates/times] and many name
entertainers, local dignitaries and guests will be on hand.
Watch the [newspaper], radio and television for more
news. For more information call 800-555-1234.*

The local news media in each city quickly churned the public
into hot action at absolutely no cost whatsoever to the Third Party's
campaign fund. All day long, in every city, group after group came out
to Billy's train. They each got buttons, hats, signs and brochures from
the able campaign staff that charmed and wooed them into becoming
loyal supporters of Billy and his New Third Party.

In each city, the Boiler Room car was connected to local telephone
cables so that the army of telemarketers could continue, "burning up
the lines," getting commitments of support from the local populace.

Barnston developed another great gimmick using bookstores in
major malls. Billy's book signings served a double purpose. It put Billy
in the intellectual but casual atmosphere of a bookstore and provided
the local media with good "art" background. Because it was a high
traffic area, thousands of people were sure to drop in. Sales of Billy's
book, *Americans Want a Change*, were fantastic.

If a bookstore in a particular city had enough customer traffic, or
the bookstore agreed to sponsor a big ad campaign, then Barnston
arranged a book-signing appearance for Billy. These appearances were
not only a great photo-op for the traveling press corps and the local
media, they allowed Billy an occasion to talk, one-on-one, with the

people. Barnston liked to say it gave Billy the opportunity "to be Mark Twain or Will Rogers, or Mr. Rogers or Roy Rogers or Ginger Rogers, or whomever Billy thought it was best for him to be that day."

At each train stop Barnston set up mass rallies to include every kind of local club or organization that might be helpful in that city. In bad weather, these rallies were held at the biggest arena in the city and in good weather in outdoor stadiums. Farmers' groups, labor groups, fraternal clubs, social clubs, the big and the small got involved. Barnston's idea was to give everybody a chance to hear Billy's message in person. To ensure that Billy had good coverage, Barnston also bought half-hour segments on each of the local TV and radio stations. These live simulcasts assured that the opening of the campaign headquarters in that city would have a tremendous kickoff and the most extensive exposure possible.

The same coordinated advertising design occurred in each city. A "stereotype" campaign beginning with a four-page, full-color insert in the newspaper the Sunday before the train arrived. Then the radio and television stations were serviced with the interesting video programs that closed with the "where and when" details of Billy's visit. These ads were sponsored by local retail merchants—loyal party members— and had a tremendous impact.

In addition, campaign brochures went out in the member-mailings of every club and organization throughout the city. Hundreds of posters, billboards and bus cards were plastered everywhere. Barnston had done his homework on how to publicize and excite a city: it was strictly circus-style. Although what he was doing was not new, not even Ringling Brothers could advertise in a town and reach that many people. It was a powerful and effective advance program, and it was developing strong local Third Party organizations in every city Billy and his train visited.

The disenchanted and disappointed ex-Republicans and ex-Democrats in each city were very experienced political supporters.

As they joined up they soon became a great and fresh strength for the new Third Party machine. With unsullied faith and devoted zeal, they attached themselves to Billy's hybrid-platform as though they had written and organized it themselves. Billy and Barnston cleverly designed each of the planks of their platform to resemble the issues of the other parties. This allowed these disillusioned supporters to feel right at home with the principles of the new Third Party.

Billy's enthusiasm and innate ability to deliver speeches with content the people wanted to hear was remarkable. His growing army of supporters eagerly committed to the rebuilding of America. They felt that they had a place in this campaign and that they could help make a difference. It was real magic to see Billy at work with the people. He was the strong, benevolent leader they had long been waiting for. They loved him and trusted him. He was not a politician in their eyes; he was one of the people. The fact that he had become a billionaire only sparked the "American Dream" perception that lived in each of them.

"If I can do it, you can do it!" Billy encouraged over and over.

The timing for this campaign was perfect. Life was strained for most people, and they wanted things to get better. Some had known prosperity and wanted it again. Some had never known anything but poverty and hard times throughout their entire lives. All of them had confidence in Billy and the promises that were being made by the new Third Party. For the first time in a long time, new hope and faith exploded throughout the country as the people prayed that they would finally have a chance at a good and fair life. City after city got on the Billy bandwagon.

It was a bright and sunny day in Detroit, Michigan. Billy, on board his luxurious "Land Yacht," was on the way to a local rally. The "Yacht," a custom-built red white and blue bus, was carried on the train to move Billy and his entourage from the train site to the various personal appearances in each city. As usual, a few of the local leaders from some of the supporting clubs, unions and organizations were on board with him. The bus was set up with tables and seats along walls. Billy had a clever little seat with wheels that allowed him to travel up and down the aisles, stop, sit a while and talk with every person. Billy liked people, and they liked him. He wanted to hear what they had to say and always carried a little note pad to mark down those things and those people he found interesting.

On this day, Billy was on board with the bosses from every union in the Detroit area, representing a big part of the labor unions that traditionally voted Democrat. These guys were along for the ride, the fun, and the free booze. No one yet had moved these organized labor leaders from their loyalty to the Democratic party. This was the kind of challenge Billy loved a chance to spar with the best. It thrilled him more than anything.

Dan Hartley was on board. Billy knew that he would have to get Hartley, the biggest of the labor bosses, on his side—a seemingly impossible task. Without Hartley, there was no union support. Billy remembered what he had learned as a kid: always pick the biggest guy in the mob to whip and the rest of them will follow you. So, he'd start with Dan Hartley, the long-time head of the Auto Laborers.

"Big Dan Hartley! How've ya been, my friend?" Billy put his hand in the bear claw of this very large man.

"Billy-boy, this is a better shindig than those Republicans throw when they're out after our vote. You got real style, Billy and we'd vote for you, if you were gonna win!"

The whole bus erupted in laughter.

"Well, I like an honest man, Dan. Now let me tell you something. The Democrats have had their shot, and they didn't help your unions or this country. And I'll be damned to hell if I'll let the Republicans back in, win or lose. But, Danny-boy, the Third Party is gonna win this one. I won't give you any condescending talk like the Republicans do. When we win this election, and we look back and find out that you and your unions didn't support us, well, I'm gonna take it personal. Not maybe. Definitely. Then I'll finish that union busting job the Republicans have been dancing with all these years. Yeah, I think we could put you completely out of business, in say...three months. You guys will all be working for minimum wage. You should watch who you insult, Danny-boy. Now you drink our very expensive whiskey and eat all the food you can stuff in your fat gut, and if you want to really talk with me, I'll be in my private room in the back of the bus."

The angry murmurs from the rest of the union leaders made Billy confidently smile to each of them as he moved down the aisle. "Well, when you kick a hornet's nest, sometimes you can get stung," he thought.

Billy reached his compartment, closed the door, sat down and began to quietly sip on his scotch. He waited patiently for a sign from Hartley.

The wait was short. Within a few minutes, there was a knock on the door. Billy slid it open. It was one of Dan Hartley's men. "Yes? Oh, how are you, Fred?"

"Fine, sir. Big Dan wanted me to tell you that he would like to see you tonight on board your train...about 10:30, if that's alright?"

Billy nodded yes and the errand boy departed. The game was on.

It was a good rally that night. Forty-eight thousand people, they told Billy. A very satisfying day.

Billy had returned to the train and was just finishing a late dinner with Collings and Barnston. There was little talk, a sign that Billy had something on this mind. Out of courtesy the other men did not speak.

Finally, Billy broke the silence. "I want to see the entire IC in my car at 10 o'clock, sharp." He got up from the table and left the dining car.

Collings issued a coded memo via the "Locator" to inform each of the IC, Billy's "Inner Circle," that the boss wanted to see all of them in his car in fifteen minutes. Something very urgent must have happened to bring them all to a meeting at this late hour. Even though everyone was working late on other projects, they dropped what they were doing and headed toward the front of the train to attend this emergency meeting.

This was the first time that the Inner Circle had been together since the train began its journey. Barnston and Collings had been meeting on an as-needed basis with Billy several times every day. Avery Harrison, Billy's vice-presidential running mate, and General Alfred Fenwick started Billy's days with early breakfast meetings. Felix Hansen was constantly busy with the installation and maintenance of the computer systems, and Dr. Charles Gertz and Professor George Osher, although members of the Inner Circle, were usually busy in the laboratories of WFJ Polybiotech and conferred with Billy occasionally via cellular phone and email.

They were all assembled in the office of Billy's private car, which connected to Billy's living accommodations. The car also provided the living quarters for Charlene Grainger, Billy's personal secretary. The office was set up to easily hold fifteen people, plus Billy, who was always seated at the head of the long T-shaped conference table. The chairs were big and covered with soft leather. There were no windows and the heavy steel rail car walls had been disguised by expensive walnut paneling. The indirect lighting from the ceiling coves, deep thick carpeting, a small bar area, and a large picture of Billy over the mantle of the propane-fired fireplace, made one feel quite comfortable.

Everyone was seated and talking with one another when Billy made his entrance. They all stood up immediately. Billy took his place at the head of the table and after he sat down, the members of the Inner Circle sat down.

"Gentlemen, in exactly twenty-five minutes I will be meeting with Dan Hartley of the Auto Laborers Union. Some of you may have heard that I had words with Mr. Hartley this afternoon. It's true. I told the son-of-a-bitch to throw in with us, or I would bust all of his unions down to minimum wage earners, where they belong. He was pissed, but I left the door open, and I think he'll come in."

Senator Avery Harrison interrupted. "Billy, I don't like this kind of compromise. We are all in agreement that the unions have gone too far. They alone may be the reason that so much industry has moved out of this country. The existing union labor force basically lacks good production values. They're poor workers. You'd be lying to him if you told him we would play ball with him."

"Avery, you've hit the nail on the head. That's what I intend to do. Lie to him. I have no compunction in telling that man a lie. He and his kind have made a profession out of lying. No, my friend, I wasn't asking for advice on this issue. I know exactly what I intend to do. My reason for this quick meeting is to make all of you aware that this opportunity to corral the unions is at hand."

Billy stood up and began pacing.

"Further good news is that the public is truly on our side. I believe they will give us a landslide vote in November. But there is also a downside position. What if the public vote is great, but we don't have reliable majority in that damned electoral vote? You know what happens, the way it's set up, we lose. We could win the battle and lose the war. I am charging each of you with securing full commitment from the electors. Without that assurance, we could still be in the manipulative hands of the established political machinery. Review history, gentlemen. Find out how we can be doubly sure, legal or not. But, don't let me worry you boys, 'cause everything's gonna be all right. We're gonna win, and that's a promise. Good night, my friends. This meeting is over."

His loyalists departed, leaving Billy to arm-wrestle with the union boss. Within minutes, his I-Com buzzed, and Charlene told him that Dan Hartley was in the reception area. Billy gave security the OK to bring Hartley to his office and glanced at the wall clock. It was 10:30. Hartley was on time. Billy resolved that Big Dan had just thirty minutes to make a deal, or else.

Dan Hartley swaggered into the office. Billy got up to shake his hand. The hand was huge. The man was big: six-foot-four or -five and probably 250 to 275 pounds. This guy was an old-school ruffian who had made good, but there was a lot of soft fat on top of that old muscled body. It could be a nasty and interesting fight, but it wasn't going to last very long.

"Dan, thank you for taking your time to see me. I know it's late, but I think we can accomplish a lot tonight, so let's get started."

"Just hold on a minute, Billy. I don't want you to think I'm here to take a dive, like you suggested I do this afternoon. No way. I'm in here with your recorders and security cameras running to tell you that you don't have a deal with Dan Hartley or the unions of North America. So that's the way we'll open the conversation. Now, what is it you wanted to talk about, Billy?"

"Well, I hope you've got all that off your chest, Danny-boy. And by the way, when did you start speaking for all the unions? You really got them all in your pocket like they say?"

"Yeah, Billy, all of them. Every goddamned worker with a union card of any kind will jump when Dan Hartley sends down the word. And you can go to the bank on that, Johnstone!"

"Well, that's just what I want to do, Hartley. I want to bank on it. Why don't you join us? We're gonna win and all the rank and file and both of those obsolete political machines combined can't stop us!"

"You know where my loyalty is and has been, Billy. If you had some track record, I might consider it, but a first-timer? No way. No way!"

"Look Dan, I don't have time to play your amateur game of chess. Let me make this clear. I'm the new broom. The old boys haven't got the guts to tell you, but you talk with the newer crowd, and you'll get the news. This election belongs to the American people, and I've got the people. Now let's look at the facts. The union leaders are going to oppose me. Great, go ahead. But the union people are going to vote for me, and then I'm going to turn that huge rank and file on you anti-Billy guys and watch them eat you alive. This country doesn't need a union and hasn't for fifty years. Imagine what might happen if I make unions obsolete. You've got a few minutes before I throw you off the train, Danny-boy, so how 'bout a drink?"

Dan Hartley stood up and towered above Billy's five-foot-ten-inch frame.

"I ought to take you apart, you little…"

"Danny, Danny. You're in my office, on my train, with my guys outside waitin' to kick your ass if you keep talking like this. So sit down, boy!"

Billy went to the liquor cabinet and poured each of them a good half glass of scotch. Hartley sat down and became extremely quiet. Billy handed him a folded piece of paper along with the glass of whiskey. Inside the typed note said:

> *Dan—You're right about the recorders and video cameras. So far, you haven't sold the 'boys' out and you're not going to, because now you're going to pretend to force a deal on me. Have a drink, and then propose to me that you might turn the union vote to me if I would agree to some real pro-union planks in my platform, and you will want to write the conditions. I'll agree. You'll agree. We'll shake hands and it'll be over. Just follow my lead. —Billy.*

Big Dan Hartley turned sideways in his chair and met Billy's eyes. He knew that he was trapped. The next move he would make would be his best, or his last. He turned back to Billy's note and took a sip of his whiskey.

"Well Dan, it's late. Let's quit fencing and make a deal. Are you going to do it my way? What do you think, ol' Buddy?"

"I think this, Mr. Politician. I think you're a goddamned smart-ass. You've offered me nothing for my people, but you want me to knuckle under. Here's what I have to say to you: I just might turn the union vote your way Billy, if you would put some solid union planks in your platform. And I mean solid. The deal would have to be in writing. Real drafted planks in your policy for my unions, and I want to do the writing. Can you live with a deal like that, Billy?"

Billy remained quiet. To be convincing, he waited to answer.

"Okay, Dan, you win. I know what the Republicans have offered you, and it's very weak. Ultimately you know that the Republicans want to kill the unions. And the Democrats? Well, they just want your vote. They'll lie to get it and they'll make no changes for your people. I'm the new guy, Dan. You will find that I am a man of my word. I will back your union principles if you will deliver the union vote. And yes. You get to write the deal, Dan!"

Big Dan was happy. They clinked glasses and shook hands. Hartley had followed Billy's script to the word. He had convinced Dan Harley. Billy was, in fact, a very good liar!

Collings made his way back to his own rail car. The pep meeting with the Inner Circle was over, but Rob Collings himself, had run out of pep. He was really tired. Using a handheld computer, he sent a memo to the Locator notifying his chief of on-board security: "Collings Off Duty—DND [Do Not Disturb]"

Rob settled into his compartment. A little relaxation, he thought, and then a good night's sleep. He fixed a drink and opened a file folder. After a few moments reading, Rob looked out of the window and watched the countryside clip by. The bright moon and cloudless night sky gave the illusion of a surrealistic world seen through a light blue filter. The whiskey was working on him. He relaxed and went over the security plans for tomorrow's rally.

Rob Collings had a very tight security system for Billy and the campaign staff. All personnel had holographic photo-ID badges with a computer chip laminated in the card. The chip would activate a computer file that contained all the pertinent data on that individual. Use of this card was required to pass into any area that was involved in the campaign operation. On board the train, infrared and laser units installed in each car were connected to a central computer. By calling up a person's number and simply requesting "Find and Track," one could follow that person's activity as he or she moved about the train.

Every time a person came on board, an invisible spray dusted that person and by using the microwave and infrared scanners in each car, the computer could match ID's with 'NO ID' and tell if anyone was on board without a pass. Each time the train left the station, the computer made a tally of all personnel on board and Collings would know who was missing and where they were. When a person left the train, tracking continued via a satellite global positioning system using a similar locator program. Rob worked with Felix Hansen to design the program using most cutting-edge security techniques. It was almost error-free.

Collings helmed all security and protection details for the most elaborate political campaign ever staged in American history. He was responsible for the very life of this new candidate. And he was the right-hand man of the future president. Sometimes it was hard for him to realize the real import of it all. Imagine him, Robert Collings, having gone so far, having become so important.

That glass of smooth *Maker's Mark®* hit him just right. He tossed the file onto the stack on his desk and tilted his chair back.

This was a good life. But Rob sometimes wondered if it would not have been better to have died in that damned Vietcong prison. Ridiculous. What a stupid thought. Besides, Billy wouldn't have let that happen, anyway. Rob knew that. Even then Billy had plans for them both.

The good warm whiskey and his fatigue allowed the memories to rush in upon him. He began to talk out loud.

"Oh, my God. For as bad as those years were, it was a great time to remember. That little SOB Billy sprung Fenwick and me out of our cells, then, right under "Charlie's" nose, he got us out of the camp. How he did that, I'll never know. The three of us killed the guards in that blockhouse and freed the other prisoners and Billy led us and that small group of hungry, nasty smelling grunts on an all-camp raid that made Rambo look like a church social. Shee-it! It was fantastic! When it was over all the Cong were dead...all of them, real dead. And us white hats, jus' like in the movies, not a scratch on any of us. Never lost a man! Then we burned the place to the ground, blew up ever'thing, and Billy rigged the enemies' radio set and just like he was hailing a taxi in New York City, he called I-Corps for a pick up! What a dude. It was like Billy knew exactly what to do and how and when to do it. After that little outing, we all got purple hearts, and were on TV. Billy Johnstone, all-American hero and my good fren...giddin' real drunk now...talking to myseff...real tired."

For that bit of true bravery, Collings had committed himself to Billy and would forever be the devoted guardian of the lives of Billy and his family. This long association would be the closest thing to a real friendship that either of the men would ever know.

# 5

## *REMEMBERING KURT*

The train leaned sharply to the left. Billy was startled out of a very sound sleep. Usually, the gentle rocking motion of the train made a wonderful place to sleep. But this sudden lurch of the car surprised him.

Billy was wide-awake now, visibly shaken. He looked over at Suzzanne. She was lovely, even when she was sleeping. Billy hated to wake her—it was three in the morning. But, he needed to talk.

"Suzzanne. Suzzanne, honey. Wake up, honey. Wake up."

Suzanne sat up quickly with a worried look on her face. "What is it, Billy? What's wrong? What time is it?"

"It's okay, honey. Nothing's really wrong, I...I just had another dream. I need to talk about it."

"Ugh." Suzanne dropped back onto her pillow.

"Please get up. You can sleep in today. You don't have anything to do until three in the afternoon. Come on, babe, get up. I'll call for some coffee. Or would you like some hot chocolate and some cookies, ma cherie?"

Struggling to sit back up, Suzzanne looked at him. She was mildy annoyed, her eyes barely open. "You're a clever little boy, I'll give you that. You know the buttons. All right. Hot chocolate and cookies'll do."

Billy jumped up into his robe, slid into his slippers and reached for the phone. He called back to the dining car for pots of coffee, hot chocolate, and a tray of cookies.

One of the dining cars was always open. Many worked through the night on this busy campaign train.

Billy, still unnerved, sat down at the dining table.

Suzanne hauled herself up, sat on the edge of the bed and pulled on her robe and slippers.

"Suz, it's happening every night now. I go to sleep and have the same dream. Exactly. The same. Just like the dreams I had years ago. But they're happening every night."

Suzzanne was awake now, standing near him at the table. "How long has been happening?" She gently squeezed his shoulder as she sat beside him.

"I don't know. The last couple of weeks. I'm making this speech and there are thousands of people there...it's a big auditorium, I think. Anyhow, they're all cheering and suddenly I get light-headed and fall down. Someone picks me up. The crowd is hushed and..."

The entry buzzer interrupted.

Billy looked up to the CCTV monitor and saw old Franklin, his personal porter. Billy got up and let him in.

"Hey, Franklin. Did they wake you up to bring me this?"

"No, sir, Mr. Billy. I was up and if I'm up nobody can bring you food or anything. That's my job, sir. And here I am." Franklin brought the tray inside and placed the carafes of hot chocolate and coffee on the table and looked up at Billy. "Everything all right, sir?"

Billy reached up and put his hand on Franklin's shoulder, guiding him back to the door. "I'm okay, folks." Billy took a deep breath.

"Fine, fine. Well, Suzzanne and I thank you. We won't be needing anything more tonight, so you go to bed, Franklin. We've got another big day tomorrow, old friend."

"Good night to you, Mr. President." The old man quietly left the room.

"Mr. President...He's called me that since the start. Guess I've got his vote, for sure."

Billy sat down again.

Suzanne watched him carefully. "The dream? You fainted and somebody..."

"Oh, yeah. Well I get up and I'm standing now and I'm looking at the crowd. They're as quiet as death. Not a sound. I say the same damned thing every time. I say: 'I'm okay, folks. God doesn't want to take me now. He wants me to stay here and help his people.' And they just go wild and start cheering. I hush them up and just as I'm about to speak I get this piercing hot feeling behind me. I turn and see the most blinding light ever—but it doesn't seem to hurt my eyes. And then..."

"Drink a little coffee, honey." Suzzanne carefully handed him a cup. He was revving up. She saw it. "It's made the way you like it. Just sip a bit of coffee, and you'll feel better."

Billy took a sip and barely missed a beat. "And then, believe me, God talks to them. God speaks!" Billy was quite agitated now. Saying it out loud, talking about the dream made it more real and that upset him.

Suzzanne grabbed his hands and tried to look in his eyes, but he struggled away, stood up and turned his back to her.

She wanted him to get it out. All of it. "Billy. Go on."

"Suzzanne, God says the same thing night after night. The same thing!"

"God." She kept her voice neutral.

"He says: 'Listen my people, this man before you'—meaning

me!—'will guide you. Hear him for he speaks my commands. Obey him in every way, for I have inspired this man for the good of you all. He is here to repair the damage you have done to my world. Let no man harm him for he is my anointed...'"

"Anointed." Suzzanne's face was as neutral as her voice. She knew this was no time to react. Just take it in, she thought. Just take it in.

Billy was breathless. It was difficult to tell whether he was elated or afraid. "Those words—verbatim—every time. Then I wake up. It's the same every night. Exactly the same."

Calmly, Suzzanne took another sip of hot chocolate. It's his eyes, she thought. His eyes seemed so..."Billy, you are taking the rhetoric of this campaign much too seriously. You've developed a sense of responsibility that's too large. I think you need to ease up a bit. You're mixing reality with emotional dreams, honey."

She looked deep into his eyes, straightening up in her chair.

This was what he needed. Her calm, practical, centered strength.

"You're such a very good man. And I know you think you're the savior of humanity. But, you're not. You're just Billy Johnstone, a mortal man, who is trying to do a very big job."

"But Suzzanne, it's so real. And why is it always the same?"

"I know it seems real. But if you continue to think that it's real, you could lose your grip on reality. You might develop a messiah complex, Billy. I'm afraid you'll have a breakdown and then you'll never complete these wonderful plans you have."

Billy relaxed and pulled himself together. "I know you're right. It seems so real...Well, you are right. It's not real. Just a dream. I need to stop trying to make sense of it. It is just a dream."

For a long time neither of them spoke. They ate cookies and sipped their warm drinks. But Billy could not stop thinking: What if God could speak to us? Speak to us all at the same time? Wouldn't that be a great thing? It would glue the whole world together once and for all.

"Jeez, that's total madness.," he thought. "It was just a dream. She's right. I'm pushing too hard. It's just a dream. Not real."

He looked at his beautiful wife. "Let's go to bed, Suz. I'm feelin' pretty darned tired, now. I'm sorry I bothered you with all that craziness. I sure do love you, woman."

They turned off the lights and went to bed and made wonderful love to each other. It had been a long time since they remembered to make each other happy. With just a tiny sliver of night remaining, they fell into a sound sleep, as the train sped forward into the breaking dawn.

That morning the train pulled into Wilton, Alabama, home of Billy's alma mater, G.S.T.—Great Southern Technological University. Billy agreed to do Barnston's rally at the big regional mall, but he wanted it scheduled for noon. There would be no night rally in Wilton. Instead of the usual public rally, Billy asked Barnston to set up a student-only assembly in Huntington Hall at G.S.T. and to invite some of the students from surrounding colleges to attend as well.

The day was a busy one. Shopping malls were odd places to stage rallies, but it was a well-known community location that everyone could easily find. The rally went very well, but the effects of the day-after-day public appearances and speeches had left Billy drained. Later, as Billy sat, exhausted, at yet another late afternoon luncheon, his head nodded. The G.S.T. student rally was scheduled for seven. Barnston knew he had to get his guy out and into the limo for a quick rest.

As the limo silently drove toward G.S.T. University, Billy fell asleep.

The car came to a stop and the driver announced that they had arrived at their destination. Before the nap in the car Billy had been tired, but his vitality returned to him very quickly. The excitement of coming back to his *alma mater* had him aglow. Billy wanted to walk for a while and remember and savor the memories of this great place of learning that he loved so much.

The drop point, as Billy had ordered, was about two blocks from the main entrance to the campus. Collings' special security men followed Billy as he walked down the street and through the main gates of G.S.T University. He walked down the flagstone pathway toward Huntington Hall. Tonight, Billy wanted to be alone. No entourage. No press. As he walked, he planned his format for the student rally. First, he would give a speech about the new Third Party. Then, he would participate in an open forum with the students. It would be simple and effective—Billy style.

He was going home. Tonight, being alone felt particularly good. Even though he liked to think he was all alone, Billy knew that Collings' bodyguards were tailing him. They were off in the shadows. He was sure Rob had told them to lay back so as not to be seen. Still, Billy knew they were out there. These security guys even went to the bathroom with him. No, he was never alone, really. But tonight, he pretended that he was.

As he walked on the campus of Great Southern Tech, the memories were coming fast. Memories of the good times during those free, exciting days in school. And now the future of the world was in the hands of these new kids, just like it once was for him. He vowed to make it a better future for them. Get rid of all the chaos and make it a kinder, gentler world.

It seemed as if he might have heard that one somewhere before.

Billy stopped walking and stood very still. There was the old Rock of GST. He climbed up on the huge granite boulder just as he had done so many times years ago. As he looked out over at the central library building, the time-rush was overwhelming. He remembered all the good fun with Charles and Kurt and Hilga during his college days. Tonight, the long walks and good talks they had together were alive again in his mind.

He recalled that day, long ago, when he first met old Kurt. It was during his senior year at GST, after coming home from 'Nam. He was majoring in political science and business administration, but the course that day was in cultural anthropology. The material was tough and confusing.

The professor went on and on. Finally, the class ended. As the rest of the students began to leave, Billy remained in his seat. His mind had caught fire after some the statements made by the usually boring Professor Holland. The professor commented that the Malthusian Theory had been debated without proof, agreement or conclusion that either side was right, for over 150 years.

Billy vividly remembered what he had been thinking that day, all those many years ago. It was Billy's custom, when deep in thought, to talk to himself out loud. "Was Malthus right? Professor Holland thinks so. Following the Malthusian theory, then, our population is increasing, and the production of the necessary sustenance will not be able to keep up with that increase. Well, not everywhere in the world. The US could hold its own. But then maybe Malthus was right. I don't know. Maybe we've all become brainwashed with propaganda and can't see the truth. Still, it seems to me that there are just too many people in general. People are starving in most third-world countries; that's been going on generation after generation. And they do nothing to help themselves. The help that the world offers to them, they don't even use. You know, this seems to be the same problem that has existed throughout history."

Billy remembered that he then stood up and began to pace as he spoke. "The village, the city, the state, the nations of the world have always found it difficult to support an increase in population. So, even with good, well-meaning help some of the population always starved. Is it true? Is it a fact, or was the real problem that all of the available goods were not being fairly distributed to everyone? Yeah, it was probably simple human greed. The many always seem to work to benefit the few. But why, then, did these elitists always penalize the lower classes? Why did they impose such harsh taxes and severe punishments on the masses? And why, then, did the people revere the kings and emperors, even though those very rulers were cruel and dictatorial? Why, why, why?"

Everyone had gone. Billy was alone in the lecture hall. His words echoed back at him. "Why, why, why?"

A loud, authoritative voice with a thick German accent answered. "Because, zhe people vere dependent upon zheir rulers und zhe rulers vere dependent on zhe people. Vhen zhe people found out how important zhey vere, how powerful zhey could be, zhey vould alvays rebel, kill zhe king und put anozher king in his place. Zhat new king vould, of course, qvickly begin to act just like his predecessor und zhe resentment from zhe people vould begin vonce again."

Billy turned to the voice, homing in on the clipped, precise, thick German accent.

"All revolutions, you see, start mit zhe poor und are alvays aimed at zhe rich, whom zhey hate for being rich. Und vonce zhe poor are installed as zhe rulers, und are zhen zhe new rich, zhey become zhe sing zhey hate und had rebelled against in zhe first place. Zhese new rulers are qvickly dispatched by zhe poor, in exactly zhe same vay as zhe previous rulers. Zhey vere killed. Und zhe cycle zhen continued, *ad infinitum*."

The voice in the darkness from somewhere underneath the front rows, continued. "Zhe poor, zhe ignorant, zhe weak, zhe infirm are alvays Zhe dissidents, und because zhey have alvays been zhere—zhey never go avay—zhey are alvays zhe real problem. Only a few men in hiztory have had zhe vision to deal mit zhis problem in zhe correct und efficient vay."

Billy looked around to see who was talking. He saw only an old custodian sweeping the floors near the top rows. There was no one else in the hall. He called out to the man. "Is that you talking?"

"Yah. I vas just speaking my mind, if you please."

Billy got up and went down a few steps to the first row of seats. He sat down and motioned to the man.

"Come down here, will you? You speak as though you may know something about this subject."

The janitor was tall and slender and had a bush of snowy white hair, but he moved with an agility not often seen in an older man. He laughed, a little. "Yah, yah, I know very much about it. I know vhy it hasn't vorked sroughout hiztory und vhat it takes to make it vork. But you tell me, young herr. Do you really vant to do somesing, or is dis just curiosity. Vould you change it all if you could? Now, mein herr. You tell me!"

Billy leaned forward. "I think about these things all the time. Why our government process doesn't really work. Why the world in general doesn't work well. It's all a mess. So confusing. Yet there must be a way to fix it, to fix it once and for all; to eliminate these recurring problems that have plagued mankind since the dawn of civilization. I've got plenty of questions and very few answers!"

The old man propped his push broom against the wall and took a seat near Billy. "I vill repeat. Are you just curious, or are you a man who vill do somesing about it?"

Do something about it?! Billy's thoughts suddenly jolted back to the present. Today, Billy was trying to do something about it. He had learned so much from Kurt in those early years. Kurt's teachings fashioned Billy's thinking and set him on the course he was on at this very moment.

Billy, Kurt and Hilga had become inseparable during Billy's postgraduate years, and no matter how much he badgered Kurt for the answers, all he got from his mentor was more questions. It was during this exciting time in Billy's life that he began to discover a hint of what his true destiny might be. Kurt seemed to know that Billy was going to make it big in the world and the old man felt proud to play a part in the grooming of this bright new star.

Kurt had opened Billy's mind and had taught him more in that first night than Billy ever thought was possible. Billy emptied Kurt of the knowledge that had taken Kurt a lifetime to acquire. Billy was insatiable. The task might have been refreshing to the old man, but Billy was sure that it must have been exhausting for him, too.

And sweet, dear, beautiful, Hilga. Hilga was Kurt's young house-keeper, cook, assistant, librarian and researcher. She had graduated from GST with a master's in history. Blonde, blue-eyed, buxom with perfect skin and features, Billy always called her "mein sexy Aryan." Sometimes he wondered if that phrase was more accurate than the joke he meant it to be.

Even though Billy was happily married to Suzzanne at the time, he still had that wandering nature about him. He loved women. His sense of loyalty, however, was best described in the old lyric: 'When I'm not with the one I love, I love the one I'm with!' It had always been that way with him, and he felt no shame. An affair with Hilga was not to be avoided. They were soul mates. And, Hilga was definitely in love with Billy.

When Suzzanne did accompany Billy to Kurt's house it was as though nothing had happened with Hilga. Hilga knew her place in Billy's life, and she was more than satisfied to play second fiddle to Suzzanne. Billy and Hilga loved each other in a spiritual way. They were the best of friends.

The memories flooded back again to the day that Billy was awarded his doctorate in political science. Kurt, Hilga and Suzzanne were there and after the ceremonies, they all went to *Ollie's*, the local campus hangout, to celebrate. As usual, the pizza and that "one glass of beer" went on for hours. Billy was full of pride for his own accomplishment, but was always awed in Kurt's presence. Even on that special evening Billy would not stop questioning Kurt.

Kurt finally held his hand in the air and said. "Enough, young Vilhelm, enough. You vill stop mit your qvestions. You are a Doctor now. You have zhe answers to zhe qvestions, und zhis certificate proves it!"

"Okay. Okay. But, please, oh great and powerful Genie, grant me just one more wish, if you will?"

"All right. Vun. But just vun. Und zhis vill be zhe last qvestion. Agreed?"

"Agreed. Now for, yea, these many years, we have danced around the great mysteries of life. I always ask the questions and you, in your great wisdom, send the answers back to me in the form of more questions. A fine technique for an empty head! You forced me to find out more and so that is what I have done. But now, the last question is a repeat question—but I want this answer from you, not me. So here goes: If Malthus is correct, and I think he is, and if Darwin is correct, and I think he is, and if Marx is correct, and I think he is, then, pray tell, oh keeper of the truth: tell me concisely, succinctly, pragmatically and exactly what is it, then, that we are to do with these conclusions?"

"Zhe same qvestion. Und you really vant me to answer it, don't you? Vell, I vill make an arrangement mit you. I vill write zhe answer to your qvestion on good paper und place it tomorrow in an envelope. You must continue to pursue zhis problem, even if it takes years. Pursue it until you feel you have zhe true answer. Zhen you vill come back here to me mit your answer—also written on good paper und sealed in an envelope—und zhen, ve vill exchange zhe envelopes. Ve vill open zhem und read zhem both. If you do zhis as I have suggested, you vill find zhat, qvite remarkably, both of zhe statements vill be zhe same. And zhat, my young friend, is zhe end of zhe qvestioning...at least for a few years!"

Billy and Suzzanne laughed and Kurt and Hilga laughed, too. They all drank beer and sang and talked and had one of the best evenings they had ever known. There were no more questions, just fun and friendship.

Oh, what a night it had been. It seemed like it was just a few days ago, but in fact, it had been almost twenty years since that great night. Billy had seen Kurt and Hilga quite regularly over those years but usually just for a few hours at a time. Kurt would always find a way to ask for the envelope. And Billy seemed always to have forgotten to bring the envelope. But tonight, Billy did have it with him and would present it, as ordered, in person to Kurt. He was excited with the anticipation of seeing his old friends once again.

# 6

## *THE COLLEGE TOUR*

Billy came out of his wonderful daydream and, like a little boy, jumped down from the rock. He continued his walk and finally reached Huntington Hall. Quite a large group of students had turned out. Billy was thrilled at the big response and looked forward to the evening that was before him. He began to walk with the crowd into the entrance of the auditorium. No one seemed to recognize him. He sort of liked that, too.

Billy went down the aisle and took a seat near the front. He listened to the students as they discussed their problems, the school, the news of the day, and so forth. Two boys to the left of him were talking about how, even with a college degree, the job market was glutted and that maybe they should have learned a usable skill as a backup to their college education.

In front of Billy, a boy and girl were discussing the merits of politics. The girl whispered loudly to the young man. "I don't know why we're wasting our time tonight, Michael. We both agree that the political system doesn't work and hasn't worked for a long time. This man is a politician, so why is he going to be any different?"

The boy motioned for her to speak more softly. "Listen, I think this guy might be all right. What I've read about him sounds good. This Johnstone knows that the Democrats and Republicans have grown to be practically the same and that both parties are unproductive. Both parties cater to the big corporations and private interests. And neither party serves the people. That's why he started this Third Party. I think you'll change your mind after you hear him speak!"

A young man approached the microphone on the platform. "We are waiting for our guest, William F. Johnstone, to arrive. We understand he is on campus and that he should be here soon. To open the program, we have another guest, Dr. Sally Hawthorne, a visiting professor of political science, who will outline the agenda for tonight's program. Dr. Hawthorne?"

Dr. Hawthorne, a confident young woman, stepped to the podium. "Thank you and good evening, ladies and gentlemen. Tonight, we'll hear from Mr. William F. Johnstone, an alumnus of GST and the exciting presidential candidate from the newly formed Third Party. Mr. Johnstone is a brilliant..."

From the audience: "Dr. Hawthorne, please call me Billy. Billy Johnstone. I'm down here with the crowd. Sorry, I know that I should've been backstage, but I've been enjoying myself out here listening to some very exciting ideas and conversations."

Billy left his seat and quickly walked up the steps to the stage. When he reached the podium, he couldn't help staring at Sally Hawthorne. To him, this gorgeous young redhead had the most perfectly shaped body he had ever seen. Her face was unusually beautiful and her gray-green eyes seemed to sparkle and twinkle mischievously in the stage lights. "Sorry I'm late, teacher. I do apologize. Please continue, Dr. Hawthorne."

Typical, Sally thought. What she hated most was being judged by her looks. "Thank you. I will put aside my personal comments. I know we're all anxious to hear what Mr. Johnstone has to say. We're honored to have you as our guest, Mr. Johnstone."

"Billy, if you please."

"All right, then. Billy Johnstone represents a new political movement simply called 'The Third Party.' Mr...", Sally launched a barbed glance at Billy. "...excuse me...Billy, is the presidential nominee for this exciting new Third Party, and tonight he'll explain—in some detail, I hope—the purpose of having a third party and what his party stands for, after which, he has graciously agreed to answer all questions that you may have, in an open forum. Ladies and Gentlemen, William, ah...Billy Johnstone."

There was a smattering of polite applause from the audience.

Billy began. "Well, thank you, Dr. Hawthorne. See, I've been Billy all my life. No sense in getting formal now, when all I want to do is talk with some friends. Most of you don't know me, unless you read *The Wall Street Journal* or *Forbes*. I'm not a politician. I'm a businessman and I've been pretty successful and pretty lucky, I guess. I went to college here at GST and graduated without a clue as to what I wanted or could do to make a living. Didn't even think, in those days, what it was I could do for my country or my fellow man. Just wanted to make my mark, realize the American dream, become wealthy, maybe even do something important someday. I assume that's why most of you are here in these hallowed halls of learning—to better yourselves."

The audience quietly squirmed.

"Well, let me play a little game with you. What if you worked hard for four or eight or twelve years and when you got all that education and were ready to apply all that good learnin', the world had changed so much that you couldn't fit in anywhere? Unemployment got higher. The job requirements got higher. Inflation got higher. Crime was everywhere, and this great nation of yours had to become a police state in order to stay together.

"Not a pretty picture, is it? Okay, now I'm gonna sound like a politician. The reason that scenario could happen is because our country is in the hands of a government and not under the control of the people. By the way, all of those problems are happening right now and the only answer ol' Big Brother has is more laws and more police and more prisons. The other two parties have been passing the baton so long that there's not much difference between them, just different names. But it's still the same old game.

"See, those old bureaucrats say: screw the people; let's take care of us. Us, to them, means private interests: banks, Wall Street, big corporations. Those fat cats have turned our senators and congressmen, our President, and all of the officials we have trusted to protect our rights into fat cats, too. Our taxes pay our elected officials' salaries but, in fact, they're really getting the big bucks by working for the giant corporations and private interests. Doesn't seem fair, does it? Well, it's a fact. Our guardians of the Constitution have sold us out. And they did it a long time ago. Our government has the media under their control now and feeds us pap by the hundred pounds. When it looks like we might have had enough and maybe we might rebel, they just twist the media/propaganda machine a turn or two and out comes some more promises and lies. You see, because we're all good people at heart and we want to believe in our so-called representatives, we listen. And hope. And we depend on their promises. But for some reason, they lie to us. And you can't have faith in a liar. That's why we need a Third Party."

Billy took a long drink a drink of water from the glass on the lectern and changed the pace of his delivery.

"If you know anything about brainwashing, then you know that if you lie and confuse people and keep them bewildered, after a while, because they have been told they don't know right from wrong, they're afraid to think, afraid to respond to anything. They can't react. They become apathetic. So as not to go totally insane, these confused people may break this apathy by doing extraordinarily bizarre things. They might tattoo themselves, or pierce their skin, or start talking to themselves or completely change personalities or run away from their jobs or homes or steal from each other, or start fighting, or even killing each other. These are the people, the so-called nuts and criminals, who have been squeezed until they went over the edge. But a Big Brother government has an answer for these folks, too. Mental hospitals, prisons, detainment camps, and coming soon, the return of capital punishment for all kinds of new crimes. And that's why we need a Third Party."

Groans and murmurs came from the audience, but Billy continued.

"Well, those crazy and criminal people have become extremists, haven't they? Ordinarily, most people listen to reason and obey the laws of the land. Why? One word: authority! When your big boss employer or your big boss government says don't do such and such, most people will stop, look and listen. That's because we've been conditioned all our lives to obey authority.

"See, from the day you were born, you and the rest of the population of the United States of America have been conditioned to trust the current administration—Democrat or Republican—even though, in general, each administration represents continuing confusion. Now, let me tell you. The good-old-American-dope always does what he's told, even though he suspects that he's been lied to over and over and that he's being lied to again. Our government, right or wrong. That's how we were raised.

"Well, we've reached the time in history when our government has become wrong, not right. And let me tell you why I say that. As American citizens, we still have the great potential to make this country the most powerful, influential and productive nation in all the world's history. We the people, not we the government, can do it. You see, these guys in Washington are supposed to do exactly as we tell them. Our representatives are supposed to work for us and, if they don't follow our orders, our Constitution and all the advice given to us by the likes of Jefferson and his buddies tells us that we can fire them—remove them from office—by force, if necessary.

"Now, it's a fact that these Washington fat cats just haven't been taking care of our business. They've allowed our educational system to go to hell and are responsible for allowing nearly three generations of our people to fall into illiteracy, immorality, and family degeneration, thereby creating a very sick subculture in our country. And that, ladies and gentlemen is why we need a Third Party and why I will need your help to make it happen!"

There was no response from the audience. Billy immediately thought that maybe the truth had shocked them into silence. Undaunted, he smiled and rolled on.

"Oh, I know what I've been telling you sounds unreal. And, it certainly is negative. But, it's true. Want to know where it all began? How it happened? See, during World War II, for the first time in our history, Mom, a single parent, ran eighty-five percent of all households. After the war, when some of the Dads came home, the family had to get busy keeping up with the economy. Soon, Mom and Dad both had to work to make ends meet. Our schools became babysitters instead of teachers and, because of their schedules, both folks working, we now had zero-parent households and the term 'latchkey children' was coined. The family, as we had known it, had come apart. Without the family unit working hand in glove with the schools and the churches, a lot of little fellows and gals that could have been helped to grow up right just didn't get any help at all. Without the necessary parental guidance, they drifted off into serious and sometimes dangerous antisocial behavior and when drugs and crime grew rampant in all our cities, big and small, citizens began to fear each other and were even afraid to venture out of their houses because of the danger in their cities."

Billy paused. The silence was beginning to annoy him so he spoke louder.

"Today, constant fear is a way of life. I can tell you that I personally do not like walking around our streets feeling like I'm going to get killed. And neither do you. We must face it; our streets aren't safe anymore. In addition to the crime, we've got millions and millions of people on welfare, people that don't work, don't know how to work, and never will work. A million or more mentally and physically disabled who have become homeless and need help. An infrastructure that is falling apart, a national debt that can never be paid, pollution that is rapidly killing us, a food chain that is breaking down, infectious diseases on the rise, poor health care, people literally starving to death, and war and rumors of war. Sounds like a description of the middle ages or a few lines from *Revelations* in *The Bible*, doesn't it?

"Well I'm talking about today and I'm talking about the United States of America, the most powerful and bountiful country in the world. America the beautiful, the land of the free and the brave! How could this have happened to our great country and, better, why did it happen? Well, in business we call it poor management: no fiscal responsibility, bad fiduciary controls, leading the company into peril, embezzlement, fraud, false accounting, you name it. It's all just plain corruption! Any board of directors would remove a person that handled a business like they're handling our country. And furthermore, they'd put 'em straight in jail! And so, my friends, that's why we need the new Third Party."

The audience responded with solid applause. Some even shouted out little cheers. Billy felt the tide turning. Maybe they were interested in what he had to say. They seemed to want more.

Billy took another drink of water, looked at them intently and held his hands up for quiet. He dropped his voice and spoke firmly, but quietly.

"We the people, the owners of this great country, have allowed our government to perform these corrupt and criminal acts of mis-management over and over. Then, as though we forget and forgive their inequities, four years later, we elect a new bunch of liars and thieves to do it to us all over again. Are we nuts? Yes, I think we, the people, have become crazy, 'cause we keep on believing it'll work and that our elected officials won't lie and steal. But it never does work. And they never do tell us the truth. And that, ladies and gentlemen, will make anyone absolutely crazy!"

The audience responded with solid applause.

"So how do we fix this problem? Well, if the same old parties, those Democrats and Republicans, don't change, and we can't change them, then let's get a new party—one that is for all the American people who need and want a change. And then we'll do just like Jefferson said: we'll start our country all over again. My friends, that is exactly why we need a Third Party to represent us!"

Loud, sustained applause filled the auditorium. Billy's eyes adjusted to the bright stage lights. He could see the faces in his audience. They smiled and nodded to each other, and some had clenched fists raised high.

"This Third Party is your party. It will be made up of American people who want a new administration for our country. Listen, we've got good people with us. We've got the plan. And for the first time in a long time, you will be the bosses. And we—your elected representatives—will work for you to clean up and strengthen this great nation."

Billy had the hook in. They became quiet again.

"I just want to make it happen for you and my children and all the children of the future. Together we can do it. And people—listen—it really needs to be done and done now, before it's too late! That's all I have to say, except to tell you that, personally, I've got about twelve and half billion dollars—all that I've earned during my lifetime—and it belongs to me and my family. And I want you to know that I'm willing to throw it all into the pot to make this happen for you. If you'll tell me what you want, I'll go up to Washington as your good and true representative and—believe me, my friends—I will get the job done!"

There was silence. Billy's words echoed in the large auditorium. Then the place exploded into thunderous applause.

Billy basked in the enthusiastic response from this young audience. He waited and then motioned for them to sit.

"Well, thanks for the approval. You've heard what I had to say and now it's time for you folks do some talking. I'm serious, now. I want to hear from you. Start talking. We need to figure this out and time's a-wastin.' So, let's get to work. The gentleman down here with his hand up..."

A student near the front called out: "Tell us, specifically, why your Third Party is different from the other two parties."

"A good question. Well, our party has no previous political affiliation, so we can move on the important issues without owing anything to any special interest or power group. We can and will quickly eliminate crime and criminals, fix the economy, improve the health and educational systems, provide needed housing, reduce the size of government, balance the budget, put everyone to work and stop poverty and starvation in this country. And, get this, people. We can and will do all that before the end of our first year, because it can be done."

There was another thundering ovation from the audience. Over this roar an insistent voice was heard from the audience: "That's exactly what Hitler promised."

Billy didn't miss a beat. "Right. Well, he had the right plans. He just used the wrong methods on the wrong people."

The audience laughed. Billy had them. He was on a roll.

"See, old Adolph started out with some good ideas and probably good intentions to help the German people out of the economic and emotional depression that followed World War I. In the process, he got impressed—no, obsessed—with himself. Because the people had faith in him, he ultimately fell prey to the power that the people gave him. He really thought he was God. Hitler became an extremely selfish and cruel ruler and, as history has finally revealed, his interests for the good of humanity or the good of the fatherland got clouded and confused. Adolph got lost in his own self-centered ideas. He became a huge megalomaniac and lost his mind. He became insane. Ultimately, Hitler failed not only himself, but the German people as well.

"Our country is suffering nothing new. Throughout history, all over the world people have always had these same problems to deal with: unfair laws, inequitable enforcement of basic freedoms, and disproportionate distribution of goods and services. In the past, as now, it was caused by just plain bad government, bad rulers. This happens because the leaders are invested with unmerited power. Remember how power works: After you have all the money you can spend, after you've done all the things that money can do for you, you become bored and want to play God. Then you begin to push people around and create laws that control the way people live and behave and think. That happens only because the people allow it to happen. They don't speak up and demand a fair and just government."

From the audience: "Can that happen in the United States?"

"Well, it already has, I'm sorry to say. It's happening right now. But, because we have these fantastic checks and balances our founding fathers so intelligently put into our Constitution, we still have a chance, for a while, to prevent our government from becoming altogether tyrannical. Here we are in free speech and open assembly. We can still be in charge of our country and, if we act now, together, we can ensure and resolve once again, to never let a Hitler-type get the best of us...not ever!"

The crowd cheered and applauded again.

"Another question, Billy. Why do we have so much crime?"

"I'll try to answer that, but God himself, or herself, is the only one who really knows for sure, and he or she doesn't seem to be talking, but here goes. As I see it, crime is the human response to being born and living in fear and insecurity. When humans, rich or poor, are oppressed, starved for food or love, or they are mistreated, or their basic freedoms are taken away, they become insecure, frightened, confused, and finally apathetic. As they awaken from this apathy, they slowly embrace a warped reality. They have nothing, think then that they are nothing, and are perceived by others as nothing. With this out-of-focus perception that they now firmly believe, they can now do whatever they please without any regard for the consequences or society or its rules. They are out of the social loop and have nothing at all to lose. In this nothingness, with total abandon, they finally break out of their apathy and to maintain their sanity, they become neurotic. They believe they are something new and different. Their motivation could be to do good and great things, or sadly, they could become a lawless, unfeeling, psychotic criminal. The elite of the world create the criminals by depriving people of basic human rights, making them feel like non-humans. You know, we have an old saying here in the South: 'Justice is all about the big criminals hanging the little criminals.'"

The audience laughed, nervously and Billy laughed with them and then immediately became serious.

"Man's injustice toward man has been, historically, very cruel. It is probably better stated as, 'The rich man's justice for the poor man is not really justice, only punishment.' Say, I'm beginning to sound like one of those long-winded professors. But that philosophical stuff does stay with you. You, too, will learn all about how man has treated man and all that exciting history before you get out of these hallowed halls."

He slowed down and spoke quietly again.

"The problems today are very much the same as they have always been. In this beautiful world that God has given to us, there is plenty to go around for everyone. It just isn't being distributed very well. Now here's the problem: How are we going to make it better? Anyone got any ideas they'd like to share with us?"

Hands went up throughout the audience, and a voice shouted out: "How do you propose to redistribute the wealth?"

"Same man who asked about Hitler. Well, I can't see you very well out there, but I'll bet you're not enrolled as a student here."

The audience laughed knowingly.

The man spoke again. "No, I'm a professor here and quite honestly, what you're telling these kids frightens the hell out of me. I'm aware of Hitler and his reign of terror. The world, at present, is much better off than it was when he was making promises to the people like you are doing here tonight."

The audience didn't like this man. Some booed. The mood of the happy crowd was becoming darker.

Billy held his hands up requesting order. "Wait. Wait a minute. I guess that's an accusation. This is still America. I could ask you to give a little more evidence and not so much innuendo, or I could just ignore you. I don't think you know me, or what I'm trying to do. I think I just look like something frightening from your past and because you did nothing about it then, waited until it was too late, you think it has come back to haunt you. The evil that Hitler represented has always existed. It exists now. Evil can only win when you do nothing—when you pretend like it won't bother you and hope that it will go away. You have to fight evil or it will become strong. You have to fight, professor. Fight!"

The crowd was on its feet again, cheering: "Bil-ly! Bil-ly! Bil-ly!"

The professor was on his feet, too, and he slowly walked up the aisle and out of the auditorium.

Billy calmed them again. "That man had a right to speak out because he is an American citizen. He knows what I'm saying is correct. He's just not sure I'm the right one for the job. But what do you think?"

They responded again with thunderous applause.

The questions came fast. Billy ran forty minutes longer than scheduled. He had to beg to leave the platform. The students didn't want him to go.

Finally, he walked off the stage as they continued to chant: "Bil-ly! Bil-ly! Bil-ly!"

This night proved to Billy just how easy it was for him to convince the people. If the people want to believe something, they will. Billy remembered a quote from Adolph Hitler: "How fortunate for governments that the people are so stupid."

Backstage, the students mobbed Billy as though he was a rock star. He signed books and backpacks and whatever the kids put in front of him. One of his security men reminded Billy of the hour and just as he was about to walk out the side door, someone tapped him on the shoulder.

"Mr. Johnstone?"

Billy turned to see the beautiful, beaming face of Dr. Sally Hawthorne. "Yes, Dr. Hawthorne. Thank you, again for..."

"Sally, please. Billy, I'd like to work with your campaign!"

"Well, that's real nice, Sally, honey. I'll tell Mr. Barnston, the man who's running my campaign, that we got a real pretty volunteer who..."

Mocking his tone, Sally cut him off. "Okay, Billy-honey. I want to work directly for you. And for pay, not as a volunteer. I know what you're missing. With my help, you will be the next President of the United States. I don't need this job—I want this job. I want to do something that's going to make a difference. Throwing in with you and your team is it. I can pick up and go wherever you go, whenever you want me to go. Do your research. You'll find I'm the real deal. Let's meet before noon tomorrow. I'll see you in the morning then, Mr. President. Good night." Sally turned and walked away.

Billy was flabbergasted. He watched the backside wiggle of this beautiful girl as she walked away and thought: "Mr. President, eh? She just might be what the doctor ordered!"

He went out the side door of the auditorium and down the steep steps from the hall and was once again on the old walkways that curved through the dark campus. Nothing had changed.

He walked toward Kurt's house just as he had done so many times, over so many years ago, taking all the old short cuts. He reached for the door of the engineering building and, to his surprise, it opened just like it had in the old days. It was never locked. He entered the old building and took the stairs to the lower level, turned left and went down the long empty hall to the opposite side of the building, turned right and went out the exit door and down the ramp. He remembered that this little move saved about six minutes of walking. His heart was racing a bit now. He was full of expectation. Billy wanted to see Kurt and Hilga. It had been a long time.

As he rounded the corner, there it was: the big familiar house that had been his second home. Billy bounded up the steps and rang the doorbell. There were no lights on. He hesitated and rang again. From inside, a light came on. Then the porch light brightened and he heard the sounds of bolts being undone. The door slowly opened.

It was Hilga.

"Hilga. It's the pest, Billy!"

"Oh Billy, it is you. Oh, Billy, Billy come in, come in!"

Entering this house made Billy feel like a pilgrim entering Mecca. Babbling like a young student, he could barely contain himself. "Is Kurt in bed? I hate to wake him. I have so much to tell him. And, yes, tell him I've got it this time!

Hilga ushered him in and shut the door. She just stood there in the dimly lit room not knowing where to look.

"Hilga!" Billy said excitedly, grabbing her shoulders. "Come on! Get the old man up!"

Finally, she met his gaze, squarely. "Kurt is dead, Billy. He died last week, of old age, very quietly."

Billy's arms dropped limply to his sides and he stared at her for long moment.

"What? No...He...He can't be...No!" He fell into a chair and began to cry. Hilga comforted him.

After some time, Billy spoke.

"Talk to me Hilga. Tell me what happened. Was he sick? He always told me he was feeling fine. What happened?"

"He was no kid, Billy. He was 92-years-old. He died in his sleep. He didn't suffer. He just got old and passed on."

"Hilga. The times the three of us had. Oh, my God, that man taught me a lot."

Regaining some of his composure, he struggled to speak. "I'm gonna miss him more than anyone I have ever known."

Billy followed Hilga to the living room and sat down in a chair, his chair, as he had done so many times before.

"Talk with me a while, Hilga. How long have you been with Kurt?"

"I've known Kurt since the year he stopped teaching. I was one of his students. Except for you there has never been another man. You two were the men of my life. I knew Kurt very well. There were few secrets between us. This is the right time to ask you. Did you bring your envelope?"

"Yes, I have it right here. My god, you remembered? Did he tell you to ask me, Hilga? The last time Kurt and I spoke he mentioned our old 'arrangement,' as he liked to call it. He reminded me, as always, of how negligent I had been, and he that he had written his end of the deal the night he made the bargain with me twenty years ago. He was still waiting for me to come through. Six weeks ago, the last conversation I had with him, I hung up the phone and sat down at the typewriter and put it all down on good paper, as we originally agreed and I've carried it with me this month hoping to hand it to him in person, and now..."

She interrupted him. "And now, we will have a few steins of good German beer and some schnapps and talk some more of Kurt. Then we'll exchange the envelopes, just like he wanted you to do."

Hilga brought in the beverages and, as if by magic, produced a tray laden with cheeses, sausages, and pickles that Kurt would have approved of as a fitting snack. They drank and ate and talked for hours. Billy observed Hilga. She had grown older, but she was still a beautiful and sensuous woman. She had that genuine beauty, the kind that glows from inside; the kind that comes from being a true and good human being.

Billy was happy. He was home.

Calling the merriment to a halt, Hilga produced the envelope from Kurt and Billy produced his envelope.

Billy spoke first. "Hilga, this is not the right time. I can't think about philosophical stuff right now. Why did Kurt have to die before I became somebody? I wanted him to see me succeed, to use all that he had taught me."

She spoke reverently. "I know, I know. Kurt was the most brilliant man I have ever known and one of the great thinkers of this century. I have all his writings, Billy. He unquestionably cared for the human race and believed that we, as a civilization, should have done better by this time. It's so sad. Because of his affiliations with the Nazi party as a very young man, he did not want his work published while he lived. He had a fear of having his ideas misunderstood and probably a more real fear of jail or death. Fear. That's why he stopped teaching, you know."

"We never discussed his past, Hilga. I'm sure I asked him why he wasn't teaching, but he had a way of ignoring my incessant questions if he didn't want to answer them. Tell me what you know, Hilga."

"Well, it was in the 60s when he stopped teaching. Kurt came to this country in 1937, before the war in Europe started. He saw what Hitler was doing and quit the Nazi party flat and came to America.

Kurt told me that after he arrived here he quickly understood what the people of this country were all about and realized that he never was a Nazi. He felt he was an American who was unfortunately born in Germany. Kurt loved this country and the potential of its independent people. In those early years, he had many menial jobs until the war ended. Kurt wanted to return to teaching, so in 1947 he applied to several universities.

"He was offered a full professorship at GST in 1948 and taught here for many years. In the 60s, somehow, they found out about his Nazi affiliations. Rather than go through the terrors of an investigation, he simply resigned. He took the janitor's job and continued to teach and influence hundreds of students until his death. Kurt used his spare time for research and writing and he tutored someone every day of the week. He drank beer and held Socratic discourses with the students at night at Ollie's or here in this house. Quietly, Kurt became famous at GST and probably caused more kids to think than all the professors put together. Hundreds of his 'hard heads', as he used to call them, showed up for his funeral. It was wonderful."

Hilga moved closer to Billy. "I tried to contact you. I know your office took the messages, but I didn't hear from you. Oh, Billy, you and I were the only ones he had real conversations with. Kurt had very strict rules that he followed, stemming from those old fears of reprisal, I imagine. With the other students, he would merely ask questions. Make them talk to themselves. He never had discussions about anything controversial, except with you and me, Billy. I think we became his children, the children he never had. I truly loved him, in every way."

"Were you two, um...lovers?"

"Yes. When I was very young we made love. But, at least from my side, he was not my lover. I loved him as one loves someone who is great. Kurt was my teacher and my good friend, and I gave him physical love because he needed it. The only man I have ever been in love with is you."

Hilga got up from the couch. She took Billy by his hand and led him to her bedroom. That night they renewed the love that they had for one another. They both knew it was to be the last time.

Hilga had set the alarm to ring at 3 a.m. She got up and let Billy sleep a while longer as she prepared the coffee. Then she went upstairs and awakened him. She gave Billy one of Kurt's robes and told him to come down to breakfast.

Billy drank the hot coffee and shuffled through some of Kurt's papers until the overpowering smell of Hilga's cooking pulled his attention away. He looked up and walked over to the stove where Hilga was frying ham, eggs and potatoes. It suddenly dawned on him what must be done.

Billy grabbed Hilga's shoulders, spun her around and looked into her eyes. "Hilga you are the only one in the world that I can openly talk with about certain issues. Because of Kurt's teaching and inspiration, I've started on a great adventure, a quest, a high mission. I'm going to become the President of the United States and in doing so I will begin to correct some of society's age-old ills, the 'harmful sickness,' as Kurt used to say, 'a disease that has been with mankind throughout history.'"

Hilga loved Billy's strength and character. Since the day they'd met, Billy had always been enthusiastic, forceful, and very sincere.

"Billy. I'm going to ruin breakfast, here."

"Hilga, I will become president, but I'll need your help. I want you near me. I want you to become the head of my household staff in Louisiana. You'll be in charge of everything. It's a big job. Suzzanne is so very busy now helping me with the campaign. She'll be even busier as First Lady. I need you, Hilga. I need your brain, your love, your support, and your help."

"But Billy, this house, Kurt's papers and library..."

"You can easily sell this house. As for the library, I'll have it packed—under your direction, of course—and shipped to Hurricane House so that we can both have use of it. It'll be better protected there. Do we have a deal, my beautiful soul mate?"

"How can I say no? I know you won't take no for an answer."

"Hilga I can't lose you, too. Say yes."

"So...my answer is yes. It will probably tear my heart out to see you loving Suzzanne—it always did. But, I can handle it...Mr. President!"

# 7

## *SALLY*

Billy got back to the train about an hour before sunrise. He made his way to the Action Room located in Collings' car. He was scanning the daily schedule when the I-COM phone line rang. The Caller-ID displayed 'Collings.' Billy lifted the receiver greeting him with a a very tired, "Hello, Rob."

"Good morning, Billy. Glad you made it home before we pulled out. My boys had to stand out in the cold all night. Hope she was worth it. You and your broads. You're gonna have to be a bit more careful, Mr. President. Now listen up. I've got a crazy woman here who claims you hired her last night. You should tell me these things. You know I check everybody out first."

"Sally Hawthorne's her name. Got a hunch on this one, Rob. Get her vitals and begin a full check on her. Give me about twenty minutes to freshen up, then you bring that little girl over to my car, and we'll both give her a going over. Okay?"

"Ok, Billy, have it your way." Never gonna change, Collings thought.

After a quick shower, Billy walked from his living quarters to the private office section. Wilhelm was waiting for promised campaign updates.

Their conversation was interrupted by the entry buzzer—Collings, punctual as usual.

Wilhelm looked at the CCTV monitor. Collings and a beautiful girl waited in the hallway.

Billy motioned for Wilhelm to open the door.

Barely inside, Collings snapped at Wilhelm. "Willy, remember how your Uncle Rob told you to always ask who is at the door, make them identify themselves and move into camera so you can see if anybody is hiding in back of them? One of these days somebody'll just blow you away, Junior. Then you'll figure it out!"

Embarrassed, Wilhelm got the "high-sign" from Billy and excused himself.

Sally immediately moved over to the front of Billy's desk and stood smiling at him.

Billy looked up into her gray-green eyes. "Well, well. You are a man of your word, aren't you, Sally Hawthorne? Here you are, and it's still before noon. How'd you get on this train without a pass? Got that one figured out yet, Rob?"

"Yeah, she stowed away. Came in with some of the local visitors last night, I presume. Don't know how she got past the scanners, though. I've got my security people revising the programs and procedures right now. I assure you, it won't ever happen again, Billy."

"I'm not the least bit worried, Rob. You guys take better care of me than the security for the current President. Now, Ms. Sally Anne Hawthorne, talk to me. What's your real scheme, honey?"

"Not a scheme, Mr. President. I told you last night, sir. I want to make a difference, and I believe you're the way I'm going to do it. I've been following your campaign, and I believe in what you say and what you say want to do. I know I can help you make it happen. It's that simple, sir."

"All right, let's say it is that simple. Lord knows we can use all the good talent we can find. I do like your assertiveness. If you had gone through the normal hiring methods it might have taken weeks, maybe never. But, you're here now. Mr. Collings has a background search in motion, so let's see who you are and what you're about and then we'll talk some more. In the meantime, Mr. Collings will escort you to the dining car, where you will stay until he returns. Please enjoy some of the fine food and beverages we have on board. If you check out and Collings and I think you'll fit, you're in. Otherwise, you're off this train at the next whistle stop. Got it, Sally Anne?"

She gave him a little salute and a wink.

"Got it, Chief. I'm gonna like working for you and you're gonna like me, too."

Sally and Collings left Billy's office. Soon, Billy's I-Com rang again. It was Collings.

"Billy, I've got about thirty pages printed out on that little girl. I'll be right over. We should talk about this alone before we call her in."

When Collings came into Billy's office he plopped down in a chair and poured over the Sally Anne Hawthorne dossier.

Billy waited patiently.

Finally, Collings spoke. "I'll read, you listen. We've got to think this one out. She's 29 years old, born in Westport, Connecticut, daughter of Amos I. Hawthorne and Edith A. Sterling Hawthorne. Private schooling at Smith, entered Harvard Business school when she was 17, graduated with a law degree at 23, went abroad to Cambridge for two years, then some graduate work in Hong Kong for about a year and a half, and now the better part of two years here at Great Southern Tech as a visiting Professor of Media and Political Science. Add it up. She's a rich girl, a professional student, a part-time professor...she's a flake! Sound like that to you, Billy?"

"Yeah, could be. How about political affiliations?"

Collings continued. "Member of the DAR when she was sixteen. Then Young Republicans at 18, a Democrat at 24, and then, oh my god, the Socialist Party. Nah, Billy, this girl's a nutter."

"Well, Rob, if she's able to sort it out, she certainly comes with more than a standard liberal education. It looks bad, but maybe there's something more, Rob. There's something we're not seeing. Any troubles? The law, bad groups, you know."

"Her criminal record is clean. I mean clean. Not even traffic tickets. I couldn't even find that she's ever had a record expunged. No Billy, she's really clean."

"Marriage? Divorce? Children?"

Collings looked at the sheaf of papers again. "None."

"Ever linked with anyone that would raise an eyebrow? Mob?"

"Not a thing, Billy. She's squeaky clean. An exemplary life, except for the string of schools. This is a tough one to figure out, ol' pal."

"Put a call in to her father, Amos Hawthorne. He's a staunch Republican. I want to talk with him right now. Maybe she's been sent here to spy on us. Christ, how would we ever know? Get Amos on the line, will you? We met once at the New York Athletic Club. He'll remember that. We had quite a row, as I recall."

Collings processed the call and handed the phone to Billy.

"Amos Hawthorne, please...Amos? Billy Johnstone here...Great. And you? Swell. Now listen, I've got your daughter, Sally, here, and she wants to come to work for me on my presidential campaign. Can you tell me if that's a good or a bad idea—and why?"

He listened to the answer.

"Hmm. I see. All right. Well thank you Amos...And to you, too. May the best man win. Goodbye." Billy hung up and stared out the window for a moment.

He turned to Collings. "Amos says that she is a very strong-willed, single-minded girl who ought to have been a boy, the way she thinks.

He believes she could bring a lot to any party that she chose to tie in with. He's been trying to get her actively involved in the Republican cause for years. Says she has never campaigned for anyone, Republican or Democrat. Says I should be honored. I'm going to be her first. Wished me well, etcetera, etcetera. I hit the record button. It's all there for you to review. This whole deal makes it seem like I shouldn't do it."

"Should I have one of our men bring her back here?"

"Yeah, Rob. Let's get it over with. I've got other things to do."

Collings called the dining car and gave orders to have Sally brought to Billy's car. Within a few minutes, Collings heard the door buzz. He let Sally in and directed her to a seat across from Billy. Collings remained standing and moved to a panel that controlled a video camera. He wanted this interview recorded.

Billy spoke first.

"Well, Sally Anne, you're clean as a brand-new pistol. Tell me— why all the schools? Nothing to do but spend Daddy's money?"

"I have a curious mind. I can't seem to learn enough. I always want more. I followed my interests as they occurred. I realize that's a privilege few people can afford, both in time and money. And now that I've found you—a real challenging project, I suspect—for the first time in my life I really want to be a part of something big. I think you are destined for greatness, Mr. Johnstone and apparently most of this country does also. You are going to make changes, not just talk about them, and I want to be part of that when it happens."

Billy smiled at her and turned to Collings. "Well, let's put her in the boiler room for a few days, Rob. She sure can talk. Give her a limited access pass so she can move around the train and get an idea of what this tour is all about. Sally, you don't have a 'green light' with me yet, so don't waste any of your time on board. Talk with as many people on our staff as you can so you can come up to speed on what we're doing and why we're doing it. I want to see you again day after tomorrow. Then you can tell me specifically what position you want and why you should have it. If I agree, I'll hire you. End of interview."

Sally and Collings left. Billy wondered how much trouble this girl might become. He smiled and thought that getting into a little trouble with her, now and then, probably wouldn't be all that bad.

On Thursday, as ordered, Sally Hawthorne called Billy's office car for an appointment. It was early, and Billy's secretary told her she would be able to see Billy at 9:30, and only for fifteen minutes. That sounded good enough to Sally.

She was up and ready to go, so she decided to visit the main press car for a while. Her pass did not permit her to be in that car, but Sally had met one of the campaign reps over drinks the night before, and he said she could take a peek inside. Sally was clever and lucky, too. If she got that far, she would get in to see the entire operation. Sally rarely followed rules.

She traveled down the narrow hallway toward the end of the car and stopped at the solid steel door marked: "Class A Pass Only." She knocked on the door. No answer. Looking up she saw the CCTV camera and beamed a smile and cute wave, hoping that the press agent she met last night was near a monitor inside. The door opened.

"You're not going to let a girl stand out in the hallway, are you?"

The press agent, a tall, heavy-set man, opened the door and grinned. "Hello, beautiful. Glad you stopped by. Come on in."

She had made it!

Once inside, the first thing she noticed was the beehive of activity. It was electric. In the front room of the car the staffers were chattering away on headset cellular telephones. A computer screen in front of each of them displayed lists of names, addresses, and phone numbers. The callers were prepping the next town by talking with the major companies and organizations. It was much like the boiler room she had observed yesterday evening, but in the boiler room car over fifty people had been calling residences in the upcoming town to invite them to a rally. This car was another link in the campaign chain, Sally observed.

The overweight man who had let her in was speaking authoritatively about what the people were doing on the telephones. His mumbling trailed off as Sally walked out of that room and into the next. He quickly followed and began to tell her about the next area. Here were several cubbyhole style offices. Again, everyone was on the phones, and from what she could hear of their conversations, they were talking to the media in the next town. At the end of this section was a wall with a door in the middle and a brass plaque that named the occupant: "David C. Barnston."

"Who is Mr. Barnston?" Sally asked.

"Mr. David C. Barnston is the president's director of communications. He's the head storyteller. The best of the prevaricators. The greatest of the deceivers. The main liar. Our chief of all media."

Sally batted her eyes at her guide.

"Can I meet Mr. Barnston...uh, I forget your name, honey."

"Roger Cormsby, Sally. Ol' Roger-dodger. Well babe, I don't know. I've never really talked with him myself. I've seen him lots. Hell, let's try it."

Roger knocked on the door. The I-Com on the wall sounded.

"Speak!"

"Uh, ah, Roger Cormsby, here. Is Mr. Barnston available?"

"This is Barnston. I don't know your name. What do you do here, and what do you want of me?"

"I'm in the corporate-calling room, Mr. Barnston. I, uh..."

Sally interrupted Cormsby. "David, this is Dr. Hawthorne, from GST. Mr. Cormsby was nice enough to show me to your office. I'm the one who'd like to speak with you. I only have a moment before my meeting with Billy at 9:30."

The door opened. A very tall, very large, middle-aged man nearly filled the doorway. "Doctor...Sally Hawthorne?"

"Yes, Mr. Barnston. The very same Sally Anne Hawthorne in the briefing memo sent to you this morning."

Looking her over, up and down and back again, David said, "Do, come in, Sally. That'll be all, Cormsby, and thank you for assisting Dr. Hawthorne."

Barnston gave a slight bow and ushered Sally through the door, closing it in Cormsby's face. Barnston turned to Sally. "That memo— the one entitled *Yesterday's Recap and Opinion*—it did catch my attention. I tried to track down its origin, but..."

"That was my publication, Mr. Barnston. I just reduced all the information and gossip that I had discovered since coming on board yesterday afternoon, put it in newspaper-ese and whipped up a cheery morning read for the staff. At least, I hope it serves that purpose."

Barnston offered her a chair and seated himself behind his desk. "Well, yes it did. Interesting, succinct and humorous. I might want to continue publishing that little rag. Want to be its editor?"

Sally brightened. "Sure. It'll give me something to do over coffee each morning with you, the senior editor. You've got yourself a deal, boss, and you buy the coffee!"

"Deal, young lady, and I will have the final edit."

"Mr. Barnston—David—I don't mean to be rude, but I must excuse myself. I don't want to keep the President waiting."

Barnston laughed, extended his hand to Sally and showed her to the side door of his office. She quickly moved through the aisle of the press car. It was 9:35 a.m. and Sally was late for her appointment with Billy. She literally ran through the last two cars until she came to the door marked: "No Admittance Without Prior Clearance." She pushed the button and the receptionist answered the I-Com.

"Hello. May I help you, Miss Hawthorne?"

Breathlessly, she answered. "Yes, I have an appointment with Mr. Johnstone and I'm afraid I'm a little late..."

"Yes, eight minutes. I will admit you now. I am sorry, Miss Hawthorne, but you will only have seven minutes with Mr. Johnstone."

The scene was the same as yesterday. The door buzzed and opened. Sally went into the reception area. A woman came through a door and guided Sally down a narrow hallway to another door, where she punched in a numeric code placed the palm of her hand on a sensor and the door opened. They went further down a hallway to an armed guard station. Sally signed the board and was admitted to a small, four-chair waiting room.

Soon after, a man came in and directed Sally into the office. Billy was sitting behind his desk and Collings was standing. Sally came in, shook hands with both of them and seated herself opposite Billy's desk.

"Well, Sally, with you as the editor of *Yesterday's Recap and Opinion*, your little sheet will certainly be considered one of America's newest and most independent newspapers, eh?"

Sally smirked. "Wow. You guys sure have an effective communications system. News travels fast around here!"

"Very fast. Sometimes we even report it as it's happening," Collings added matter-of-factly.

Billy shot a glance at Collings. "You're pretty resourceful and creative, yourself, Sally. Since we are constantly in 'start-up' mode with our campaign, opportunities are usually where you make them. You've seen some of our operation, as you've indicated in your morning tab-sheet. Where do you think you can best help us?"

"I'd like to be assigned as your personal information/media liaison. I can help correlate your observations and funnel them to David for use as you and he see fit."

Billy sensed this could be both useful and fun. "Highest priority, eh? Well, Mr. Collings, have you found out anything about Sally that would prevent her suggestion from happening?"

Collings reluctantly shook his head no.

"Done, then. Sally Anne, I put you now in the very capable hands of my closest friends and associates and the two men most responsible for helping me frame this new Third Party, Rob Collings and David Barnston. You will answer directly to Barnston and myself, and will treat Collings' word in all matters as if it were mine. Is that clear?"

"Yes, sir. Thank you for this opportunity. I'm honored to be working with you. I'll do everything I can to help you and your cause." Sally stood and extended her hand to Billy and then to Collings.

"Thank you, Sally, and welcome to the team. Rob, this little spitfire is yours now. Show her what she needs to know. Sally, I will expect you to check in with David on an hourly basis. Rob, give her medium clearance and outfit her with a locator so I can find her when I need her. That's it, you two. This meeting's over!"

In the weeks to come, Billy spoke to thousands of college students all across the country. Because of the impressive results at Great Southern Tech, Barnston now included a student rally in every town. With Sally Hawthorne in charge of the final coordination of these school rallies, Billy always played to enthusiastic and packed houses. The response from this young segment of the population was thrilling. They were all intelligent, well informed, and most eager to hear about the new Third Party and anxious to join Billy and support his plan to revitalize the country. The young vote was swinging toward Billy.

One evening after a college rally at the University of Central Michigan, Billy, Collings and Sally managed to escape the well-wishers and supporters by going to the dressing room backstage, shedding the campaign business attire, and changing into hoodies, t-shirts, jeans and sneakers. They crawled out a window and walked right through the crowd in front of the hall. It was Sally's idea, of course. The three of them thoroughly enjoyed the little escapade. It was good to be free for a minute or two, away from that blinding public spotlight.

As they walked across the university campus, Billy turned to Collings. "Ok. I'm just an average citizen, right? No more 'Bil-ly! Bil-ly! Bil-ly!' Just a guy and a girl and the guy's best friend, right?"

Collings knew what was coming.

"And you want to get rid of 'the guy's best friend' so you can spend some quality time with the girl, right."

"Yeah. And the best friend will make sure the bloodhounds behind the trees go with him, too ... right?"

"All right, but you have to have this 'jail bait' and your old ass back on the train before 11:30. Agreed?"

"Agreed. Goodnight, mother!"

Collings knew Billy needed a little play time, and he liked the work Sally was doing for the campaign, but he wished that she, and Billy too, would realize that Billy was a married man and a very public figure.

Sally had made plans to capture Billy in each town they had been in, but this was the only time she had successfully created the oppor-tunity. First, they would go to the campus hangout to have something to eat and a few beers. Then, she might rape the great Billy F. Johnstone.

Right now, she was starving, and she wanted to just eat and talk. The sex would come later

*The Old Bore's Inn* looked like the perfect place. A grade up from the usual campus pizza places, this was more of a faculty hangout. The front bar area was packed with younger professors and TAs. In a separate dining room off the bar, a mixture of old and young sat at tables talking and enjoying themselves. Billy and Sally opted for a smaller, quiet dining area in the rear and walked to an empty table. The place was busy and that was good for blending in and not being noticed.

A young man came by the table and put down water, a dish of lemon wedges, napkins, silver and a one-page menu. "Somebody, maybe even me, will be with you in a minute for the food order, but I'll take your drink order if you want."

"Glenlivet and soda for the gentleman and Jack Daniels, neat, for me, with a beer back."

The waiter raised his eyebrows and left the table.

Billy smiled. "A boilermaker...You really are one of the guys!"

"Listen, I've been drinking shots and beers since my cousin Larry and I learned how to break into my old man's library bar. Loosens me up...just enough."

"Let's get this straight before it goes too far. I'm married, and I don't fool around, and if I wanted to fool around, I wouldn't fool around. That is, if I wanted to fool around. Got it?"

"Oh, I read you loud and clear." Sally slowly leaned across the table. She stopped too close to his lips, grabbed the bowl of lemon wedges, pulled herself back into her seat and rhythmically squeezed the lemons into her water with both hands while looking longingly into his eyes. "What you really mean is you don't get caught, right Billy-boy? Never mean what you say. You're a politician now, re-member?

Barnston had Billy performing something unique and different with the local people in each city. These contrived media opportunities were recorded and edited and sent out to the wire services and networks. The media enjoyed these unusual bits, and they used them. No one wanted to miss the continuing adventures of Billy. He had become the darling of the public, and the press as well.

The senior vote was in the bag. The students were behind him and, with the deal cut with Dan Hartley, he had the union vote locked up. Now they wanted to galvanize the remaining sections of the popular vote and decided to use the media as the messenger.

Barnston knew that by showing Billy in unusual situations and environments he would reinforce the standard sell that was being done on his candidate. The public got to see Billy in beer commercials. He didn't speak. He didn't drink. He just raised his mug, the camera zoomed in and Billy mouthed: "This one's for all of us."

Billy appeared in no less than one music video every month. He sat down for several MTV interviews. Oprah, Dr. Phil, Geraldo, Conan, Letterman, Leno, O'Reilly, Hannity and Regis. He scored with all of them and was booked for returns whenever he became available.

Billy gave the opening prayer for the nationally televised Easter sunrise services and was a part of the Yom Kippur services in New York City's David Ben Yedid Temple. He gave the graduating class speech at the ultra-right-wing Liberty College and addressed the Harvard graduates, as well.

As a pre-fight stunt for the heavily televised world heavyweight boxing championship from Las Vegas, Billy actually boxed a full round with the champ. Proceeds to charity; publicity to Billy.

Later that day Billy and Hulk Hogan mixed it up in an exhibition wrestling match and the next day he played in the Bob Hope Golf Classic and pitched an inning for the Los Angeles Dodgers. He drove the pace car at the Indy 500 and a semitrailer at the Teamsters national meeting. He became an honorary Sioux chief, plowed fields with the farmers in Kansas, helped assemble cars in Detroit, played round ball with the Celtics and kicked footballs at the summer training camps. He was everywhere, every day.

Billy's fame and political support were growing. He was no longer the underdog, the oddity. He was a real, bona fide contender for the highest office of the land. Billy and the new Third Party were steaming across the country. Every day he was getting favorable press in all the newspapers and magazines. The major talk shows wanted return engagements. The opinion polls put him ahead of the incumbent and the challenger. All that was necessary was to keep the movement alive with the people and to solidify that damned electoral vote. Everyone everywhere was confident that William F. Johnstone would be the next President of the United States.

# 8

## THE DEBATES

Now came the long-awaited presidential debates. Billy was about to play hardball in the world series of politics. The people of the United States would be in their homes watching his every move on television. Billy wanted this opportunity more than anything else.

In the limousine, on the way to the first debate Billy bolstered his nerve by speechifyin' a little with Barnston and Collings.

"These damned fools—these politicians—they'll finally be seen by the public as the incompetents that they really are. They can't win with me in a debate. They'll have to play by the rules that they, themselves, set up. They can't tell the people everything. They have to hedge their answers. Avoid. Shade. I've got 'em both 'cause I don't have to play by their rules. I'll just tell the truth. Cite the facts. Put 'em both on the spot. Whatever they answer, they'll lose."

Barnston chimed in to keep Billy's fire going strong. "The records of both parties will be very fresh in the minds of the people and this time they'll want real answers. Most people feel that they've been lied to by both parties. America is definitely looking for someone to restore their faith. And I think they're hungry to believe in someone new."

Billy concluded, "I think they'll believe me. You know, I've got a real advantage, boys. I've never lied to them before!"

The location for the debate, Ideola University, was an advantage to Billy. He had delivered one of his best speeches to this college audience just a few months ago. It was solidly Johnstone turf.

That evening, backstage in the large auditorium, a political advisor—a so-called "handler"—was prepping Billy on the issues as the makeup person put final touches on his face.

Suzzanne and Sally watched and listened.

Sally couldn't hold back her "two cents." "Billy, these guys are gonna get tough with you tonight. You make fools of them and their parties every chance you get. But tonight, they're out to get you."

Billy had tuned her out, but the handler picked up Sally's idea. "Yes, sir. The one thing you can count on is that they're going to make you declare exactly what it is you're going to do with your new party. You've stated the problems, they know the problems, and the world knows the problems. Now they want you to specifically declare the planks in your platform. When you do they'll take you apart, board for board, so watch it. Now, on the economy issue, I think you should go easy..."

Billy turned the swivel chair and looked sharply at the man. "You listen up, pilgrim. You're a bright young man and I respect you and I'll take all the facts you can discover for me. But about this 'advice' stuff—what you think I should say—well, don't try to tell grandma how to fry chicken! They might hurt me in the first couple of rounds, but that'll just show me what they've got. Then...well, you just watch, son. And learn. Get this, and remember it: I'm the winner and a winner just doesn't lose!"

It was almost show time. The floor director introduced the studio audience to Marvin Koel, the moderator for the debates. Marvin had an engaging personality and began to kibitz with the audience, reminiscent of the days when Ed McMahon warmed up the old Tonight Show audience for Johnny Carson.

The crowd was made up of young people and their mood was high. Koel had lots of experience with TV audiences. He knew how to get people laughing and responsive. The audience was in good spirits and but was clearly eager for this presidential debate to begin.

The floor director interrupted Koel's banter and announced that it was just five minutes until airtime. Koel skillfully adjusted his tone, and soon a more serious mood permeated the auditorium. The young audience listened raptly. "Okay, okay, we've had a little fun, but I ask all of you now to calm down a little and give these presidential candidates your attention and the respect they deserve."

Backstage, the candidates awaited their introductions. Suzzanne and Sally each kissed Billy lightly on the cheek. The women were then escorted to the green room to watch the debate.

Billy was guided to the wings and found himself standing next to the challenger, Larry Trompe, a former Democratic Vice President and the great "new hope" of the Democratic Party. Billy reached over and smacked his opponent good on his backside. The obviously tense candidate jumped forward shocked, indignant. He looked at Billy. Trope's anger quickly melted and he forced a smile.

Billy quipped: "Used to do that to our quarterback in high school just before we went on the field. He was a tight-ass just like you are, Larry. Relax, my friend. One of us is gonna impress the hell out of them and win them over; and two of you guys are not!"

It was showtime. The opening credits rolled as the camera panned the auditorium. The staff announcer introduced Marvin Koel. In an almost prizefight voice, Marvin shouted: "And now, introducing the worthy opponent from the Democratic party, the former Vice President, Mr. Larry Trompe, ladies and gentlemen. Mr. Trompe."

The level of applause was sound, but noticeably polite.

"And now the candidate from the new Third Party, Mr. William F. 'Billy' Johnstone."

The crowd chanted, "Bil-ly! Bil-ly! Bil-ly!" Billy briskly walked out with that now famous smile on his face, thinking, "At least he didn't call me the challenger."

"And finally, ladies and gentlemen, the candidate for the Republican Party, Mr. Harlan A. Bennedict."

The audience responded with loud, respectful applause and a few boos.

The candidates took their positions on the dais behind individual lecterns as Marvin Koel spoke in a more reserved tone. "Gentlemen, once again, I repeat the rules for our audience, both those here in the Ideola University auditorium, as well as those watching on television and listening on the radio. You will each have your opening remarks. I remind you that, as the moderator, I may, at my discretion, decide to have an open debate and each of you—in polite, courteous fashion— may respond spontaneously to the last point made. Those responses must be limited to not more than one minute. Here we go. Mr Trompe..."

The moderator started the clock.

After rambling on, Larry Trompe got the 30-second warning light and began to wrap. "And so, my fellow Americans, you are all very much aware of the remarkable job that has been done by the Democratic party, and I know you have been listening to me during this campaign and that you have heard the good news that we have for you as we go further into this century and this bright new millennium. Thank you."

The audience soundly applauded.

"Thank you, Mr. Trompe. And now, your opening statement, Mr. Bennedict."

The clock started again for the Republican challenger.

"Thank you, Marvin. I think the real issue here is just exactly what

Mr. Trompe has touched on. But I do want to focus on the job that has been done by our party over the last eight years. It has not been a bad job, not a bad job at all, and in fact we have served the people of America and have accomplished much. The American people have had a constant barrage of promises from the Democratic Party, and yet nothing has really been done. They have provided a great publicity and image campaign, but if you go beyond the sound bites and look closely, they have nothing to say...empty promises...no real change."

Marvin shuffled his stance a bit and looked directly at the camera. "Here are the facts: Our Republican administration has decreased unemployment, lowered taxes, lowered the crime in this country and all without an increase in big government. The economy continues to grow, and our foreign policy—well, you know our record since the 9/11 disaster, and we've become the most powerful nation in the world. On the other hand, I can tell you that without the constant opposition of the Democrats in Congress, we could be further down the road. They oppose everything. Rest assured, when I am elected this fall, I promise to tackle each unfulfilled issue with vigor and demand that answers, solutions, come forth. Our party has always been a party that has been for the people of this country and not for big government. I can tell you that I, as well as the people we have assembled to work with us, will not sit by and let this country go to ruin. We intend to continue the good work that has been done. Thank you."

Bennedict finished to better applause than Trompe, and he finished exactly within the allotted time.

Over the applause, the moderator said, "You have an amazing internal clock, sir. Exactly two minutes...to the second! Now, the Third Party candidate, Mr. William, uh—oh, I've done it now. Billy John-stone!"

The crowd laughed and that great grin spilled across Billy's face. "That's right, Marv. Just plain ol' Billy. Thank you, sir, and good evening to all of you out there and here in our audience. Now, I'm not a politician. Just a hard-working businessman who has been pretty lucky."

Billy spoke slowly, taking care to pause after each phrase. "I want to read to you how the *Oxford American Dictionary* defines the word politic, as 'Showing good judgment, prudent, the body politic.' And then, a politician is 'a person who is engaged in politics.' And of course, politics is, number one, 'the science and art of governing a country;' and number two, 'political affairs of life.' And three, 'wanting, maneuvering for power, to govern within a group.'"

Billy took off his reading glasses and paused. He looked out into the audience and let this sink in.

"These guys never read the primary definition, but the lowest definition, number three, suits them to a tee: 'Wanting, maneuvering for power, to govern within a group; as to govern, to rule a country, its people, its affairs of life.' Well, that's the game these two guys are professionally engaged in. Both of them. They're real pros. See, they'll do anything to get that power for themselves and their parties. Power over each and every one of you. And it's not 'to show good judgment,' or 'to be prudent,' or 'to help the people.' No. They stand before you now to simply gain the 'power' and to use that power for their own selfish special interests. Listen to what they've said tonight and how they said it. You'll hear the shocking truth that's mixed into their politics and hidden by their double-speak. People, we need a change."

The audience cheered and applauded enthusiastically.

"Thank you, Mr., uh, Billy. You went a little over. Please watch your time. Now to the interrogation of our candidates. These questions, by the way, came from citizens all across the nation and were picked by the candidates themselves. Now, the first issue, gentlemen: How will your administration reduce crime? Mr. Trompe."

"Thank you. After a long battle in Congress, the Democrats have just gotten approval for a second, and more effective crime bill. We do need more police and more gun control. This new crime bill will stress stronger efforts in the war against drug abuse and, in our assessment, will destroy the criminal base that has been plaguing our nation. Crime is rampant in every urban area of this country. The people can stand no more of the violence that occurs in their daily lives. Without intervention by our government and strong new laws to give the police and the courts more power, crime will continue to grow. I can tell you that we cannot allow this to happen, and when I am elected, I will not allow crime to increase during my administration."

Very little applause greeted the Democratic reply to the crime question.

"Thank you, Mr. Trompe. And how will another Republican administration stop crime? You may rebut anything Mr. Trompe has said, Mr. Bennedict."

"Thank you. First of all, let me say that I disagree with adding more tax burden to the people of this country by enacting still another crime bill, but it's done now and we'll have to live with it. You know, we have enough police to do the job, and enough courts. We do need to build more prisons and use longer terms for these habitual violators. The laws are there, the methods of curtailing crime exist, but the courts are hampered in making swift decisions and meting out longer sentences because there are not enough cells for these criminals. We need more prisons. We cannot release the criminals we have incarcerated just to replace them with more of the same. We need to build more prisons to lock up these violators for a long time, and we need to start building them now. This will result in less crime because there will be fewer criminals on the streets to commit those crimes. More prisons, now!"

There was no applause, just a low murmur and a few groans.

Marvin Koel was not impressed, either. "Um, well, thank you, Mr. Bennedict. And last—your response to the crime issue, Billy."

Billy shook his head in disbelief. "Boy, oh boy, oh boy. Ya see, that's what I mean, folks. Let's look at what these two good-old political birds are telling us. The first one, heart and soul of the Democratic party, suggests that we need a bigger police state and that we need to make more severe laws and penalties and have stronger courts. And recently he said to the press that we need to take the guns away from the registered gun owners. You know, the ones who are holding their own, defending themselves against the criminals because they can own guns. That's what the Democrats have said for years. Then the other guy, the Republican, who also wants to be president, says the real problem is that we're letting the criminals back into society too early. Too many of them, he says. He suggests that we build more prisons so we can have longer imprisonment. Doesn't that sound like a Republican response? Whew! Wonder if these guys know which side they're on? They certainly aren't for Americans being free!"

The audience roared with laughter. Billy smiled and went on.

"Both ideas are really dangerous. See, these guys haven't got any idea what to do, and they haven't got guts enough to tell us that what they have done in the past, and what they'd like to do in the future, hasn't worked, and probably won't ever work. They're clueless and they don't tell the whole story. Now listen. Our party has done a great study on this issue. We don't want to enslave all the people just to deal with a few bad ones. We know the truth. We have a plan, and it will work!"

Exuberant applause arose from the audience.

"All right, Billy, thank you. And now, the next issue for your consideration, gentlemen. Poverty and starvation rates in this country are extremely high. How will you address these problems and how soon will your proposed solutions have a noticeable effect? Mr. Bennedict will go first this time."

"Ah, thank you. Well, ah, as I see it, again the Democrats are still fostering the continuation of a welfare state and all the programs that support that failed idea. We do have millions of people in this country who are living at the lowest possible level of poverty and this appalling condition has existed for many, many years. Nearly three generations of American families have grown up with this welfare mentality. We need more jobs and a total reform of the welfare concept as it exists now in our country. We should continue to redistribute our surplus food products, those that are not earmarked for distribution to third world countries, and move that food back to our people through those 'relief' and 'fresh start' programs that are already in action now. When I'm elected, I promise you that our administration will take a big bite out of the poverty problem."

The audience responded with bored applause, scattered boos, and muttered comments.

Koel raised his hand for silence. "Thank you. Please, audience, if you will, no more of that, let's remain courteous. You will all get a chance to show your approval or disapproval by way of your comments during the open forum a little later. And now on the poverty issue, to you Billy."

"Well, that was one of the best politicians' double-talk I've heard, in a long, long time." Turning in Bennedict's direction Billy shouted. "Old buddy, you didn't even answer the question. Remember? 'What are you going to do about poverty and when will what you do have a noticeable effect?' Since you didn't give us an answer, I will. It's real easy. It's just fundamental thinking."

Billy spoke directly to Bennedict.

"Use logic, Mr. Republican. Just stop giving away the food we produce in this great country to make business deals in faraway countries for your fat-cat corporate friends. Stop burning the crops and destroying the livestock to keep the commodities markets unfairly prosperous. Put the great surpluses that we have back in our own food supply chain so this country, our people, can all eat well and be healthy every day. Spread out the food we produce evenly and lower the prices so everyone can afford all the goods, all of the time. Stop cheating the people of this country!"

The audience started to respond, but Billy signaled for them to wait. He pointed his finger at the Republican.

"You know how to do it, Harlan, and you need to see that it's done now. Not after you think about it, not after you form committees to investigate it, not after you pass that old poverty football back and forth with Congress. Do it now. Do it today Harlan, not after, or only if you're party is elected. Feed all our people today. Or as sure as you've ever read a history book, if you don't feed 'em, they'll get so hungry and angry that they'll storm your White House and those other overfed thieves in Washington 'til they get what they need. Oh, hell, I won't waste any more time on the obvious. It's just too simple. We need to feed our people, not talk about it!"

The audience cheered so loudly that the moderator had to ring his bell furiously to calm them down.

Larry Trompe may have been inspired by Billy's remarks. He removed his coat and rolled up his sleeves. For just a moment the audience believed that they were really going to hear some solid statements. As the camera came closer, it could be seen that he was sweating. Trompe hesitantly began to speak on the poverty issue. He had much less conviction than Bennedict and offered no new ideas or promises. He was ambiguous at every turn and his remarks were even less impressive than the Republican candidate's had been.

Billy, in just a few words, had all but destroyed the people's confidence in both parties. As Larry Trompe rambled on, his comments continued to prove that he was a part of the problem, and that he had no answers.

The next question put Billy up to bat first. The moderator asked: "Our next issue, gentlemen, is simply unemployment. How will you fix it? And again, when will you fix it? Billy?"

"You know, I've said these things over and over throughout my campaign all across this great country. See, it's easy if you don't play politics. If you just deal with the problems, problems are easy to fix.

Identify the problem. Get the right people on the job and fix the problem. Do it now, not later or when you get around to it. Listen folks, I couldn't run my company, deal with my competitors, my employees, my suppliers, my bankers or any of that on a 'well, let's have a meeting, let's put it under advisement, let's move it forward to next quarter.' Hell, my competition would eat me alive, my employees would quit and the whole damned business would fall apart.

"I make a decision. I act. I make it happen. I get off my ass and work to achieve what has to be done. Lack of effort and follow-through is why this country has failed in the past and is failing now. All of our workers aren't working, and they really want to, believe me, they do. These millions of unemployed are not producing anything for themselves or their country. No man wants to take charity or be on the dole. No man wants to be unemployed and the unemployed don't have to be retrained or re-schooled at a cost of billions of dollars to the taxpayer. That's stupid.

"Let me tell you, the reason people don't like or trust their elected representatives anymore is because the government is allowing our big businesses to give the good American jobs to any country in the world that will work for cheap wages. Cheap wages produce high corporate profits, don't they? The major shareholders are making a killing. Hey, our people are suffering and our country is going broke because of this kind of selfish thinking. Let me tell you: it's bad busi-ness to have this kind of discontent throughout our country. It's bad business to let the fine and able people of this country, the heart of America, get sick and depressed. You elect me and put me in there and all this nonsense—you know: no-sense—why, I'll make it stop. And real damn quick, too."

The cameras panned the auditorium as the audience rose to its feet and cheered: "Bil-ly! Bil-ly! Bil-ly! Bil-ly! Bil-ly!" The people doing the shouting were the old and the young of the country; the rich and the poor and the middle class and every ethnic background and socioeconomic level that was represented in the auditorium this night. They loved what this man represented: Power returned to the people. It was obvious that the audience believed him and wanted him to be their president.

For the first time since presidential debates began, the moderator could not regain control of the audience. They had become riotous, out of control. They kept up the chant: "Bil-ly! Bil-ly! Bil-ly! Bil-ly!" as if it were a Third Party convention. The entire audience seemed part of the Third Party campaign. "Billy for President" signs were everywhere. Viewers at home were treated to a wild scene, an unprecedented, unrestrained, unbelievable uproar. The TV cameras panned the arena floor, bringing the bedlam home to millions of viewers.

The candidates were unable to continue. Lawrence Trompe approached Harlan Bennedict's podium and the two of them spoke very intently. Billy stood down on the apron of the stage, waving to the audience like he was on the back porch of his train.

The ABN TV commentator did his wrap-up, struggling to speak above the noise of the crowd. "What a night for American politics. This is real, old-fashioned politics in the raw. Three political parties now, all about to fight it out for that coveted presidential seat. And before the debate had even finished, the new Third Party candidate lowered the boom on both the Republicans and Democrats with a full measure of truth. The audience here heard him well and has not stopped applauding and cheering and shouting 'Billy, Billy, Billy.' Just listen to that noise. Ladies and gentlemen, this presidential debate is so disorderly that...no, I don't believe it, the Republican and Democratic candidates, totally bewildered, have both left the stage. This debate is over, ladies and gentlemen. It's over."

The camera tightened on the commentator. "My analysis is this: The public has a great fear of the future and, as we have seen tonight, they are brimming with resentment for the past incompetence of our government. It is for the two traditional political parties to convince the people that there is a better future for America than they have given us in the past. The public is fed up with politics and politicians. They want results, not just meaningless answers and broken promises."

A cameraman with a handheld unit delivered a shot of Harlan Bennedict, and then back to the commentator. "Then we had the candidate from the Republican party. A known quantity. Occasionally articulate, though often not very precise, he came to us spewing that same old Republican rhetoric. I think I even heard some boos following one of his remarks. Maybe not. Well, at any rate, even though his song has been sung many times before, I think the people want to forget that particular tune."

Another camera switched to backstage showing Larry Trompe huddled with several advisers as the commentator continued. "And here's Larry Trompe, the Democratic candidate, who has been on a whirlwind selling spree all summer long. He is really fighting to get the Democrats in office. Tonight, we saw him in a pose that we haven't seen before. He took off his coat and rolled up his sleeves. Was it as hot as he said or was he trying to convince us of his resolve to work harder, if he is elected? To me he looked more like Willy Loman than a nominee for the job of commander-in-chief of the most powerful nation on earth."

Billy sat on the stage steps with a huge mob around him. He was laughing and chatting with the people. The TV cameras focused on him.

"And finally, the new contender, a man with no political background, no seasoned political machine to support him, but definitely the one who probably has the greatest chance of throwing the knock-out punch, the Third Party candidate, William F. 'Billy' Johnstone. Folks, this guy may be the man the public has been waiting for all these years. He sure won't play politics with these guys. He slashed and burned all evening on topics that the other two men would never touch. When he addressed them on the issues of unemployment, crime, poverty, the economy, he skillfully proved to us that these men either didn't have answers or just refused to tell us the real story. From my point of view, the people still don't know exactly what the Republicans or Democrats intend to do if elected. Billy, on the other hand, told us, in no uncertain terms, what he would do. It was a glorious performance by Johnstone. Billy took over the debate and made history here tonight. Hear the crowd? The people, seem to really want Billy."

The networks continued to show instant replays clips of the debate. It revealed the devastation of the Democrat and Republican as their talk before millions of Americans continued to fall apart.

The commentator continued. "At the close we saw the Republican candidate straining to keep up and the Democratic candidate almost standing mute, fumbling and stumbling, not able to, or afraid to, get into the fracas again. Sweat was rolling down both their faces. Billy had put them on the spot in front of the voters. Clearly, whatever the outcome of this year's election, Americans will note that we now have a very powerful and organized Third Party and that Billy Johnstone and this new Third Party may, in fact, represent the true sentiments of the people. As Billy said: 'No more promises and vague answers, no more politics. The people want action; and they want it now!' This time, Americans will only give this election to the man that represents the possibility of cleaning up the old ways and who will act immediately to benefit all the American people. Right now, it is this old scribe's opinion that the obvious winner of tonight's debate, and the only one who appears able to win this race for president, is the dark horse, William F. 'Billy' Johnstone. This is John Bawling, for the ABN network, saying good night!"

At the end of this important debate, it could easily be said that Billy had been brilliant. He debated with his opponents in his own unique style and the audiences cheered him. He clearly emerged victorious. The media analysis reported on his "sage and forthright manner" as "purely American" and "just the tonic necessary for this ailing country."

Billy was golden. There was little doubt that he felt invincible. His enthusiasm allowed him to become even a little overconfident.

# 9

## *HIS FINAL PROMISES*

With just three weeks remaining before the election David Barnston, in true theatrical tradition, had saved his best act for last. He created another big whistle-stop tour, but this time it was to be by airplane. He wanted a big, prominent, highly visible tour to the top 50 cities in America, including Anchorage and Honolulu. Three rallies in three different cities each day and the entire tour completed in just twenty days. The venues were to be big-league ballparks, with major media coverage and tens of thousands of people in attendance and millions more viewing these massive rallies on television. The arrival by Billy's private jet and the long motorcades from the airport to the ball-parks led the media to tag the whole spectacular the "Barnston & Billy Circus."

This circus had an impressive lineup of acts.

In each town, Barnston carefully choreographed the parade to begin with sixteen motorcycle cops, eight patrol cars, the mayor's limousine, the police chief's car, the fire chief's car, and Billy's big red, white and blue stretch limousine with the bulletproof bubble on top.

Then came ten white stretch convertibles carrying the greatest stars from the entertainment world, three fire trucks, the local university marching band, three garbage trucks, the best local high school bands marching in formation, a large group of VFW members, three post office trucks, an augmented Salvation army band, three farm tractors, marching members of the FFA, a road grader, a front-end loader, a dump truck, followed by the members of the trade unions carrying their union insignias and a simple banner that read: "Vote For Billy."

Then came twenty-one red, white and blue Lincoln, Cadillac and Chrysler convertibles containing all the prime local supporters of the new Third Party. At the end of this huge motorcade was a shiny new semi rig, with bright banners on the sides of the trailer and back doors that proclaimed: "Freedom For The People!—Follow Me And Meet Our Man Billy In Person!—Vote For Billy!—Elect Billy For President!"

The motorcade was the pied piper and the people followed it to the big rally at the local ballpark.

Everyone wanted to be involved with this new "pride of the people" named Billy Johnstone. The red carpet was rolled out from coast to coast and border to border. Every night portions of this extravaganza were the featured highlight on network news programs, providing millions of dollars of free exposure, building strong public support and lasting reinforcement. Barnston believed in the motto: "Say it. Say it again. Then, say it again!"

One week before election, the polls ranked Billy far ahead of the Democratic and Republican candidates combined, with an unprecedented 85% popularity rating.

Now Barnston would play his final card. The "B & B Circus" stirred up the greatest marketing blitz ever seen. After tying up the national media for the previous twenty days for free, the paid media campaign election week rivaled anything that AT&T, McDonald's, Coke, or Pepsi had ever done. Barnston made the largest advertising buy ever made for a single purpose. America had become Billy-crazy and the results were unbelievable. Barnston crafted a hoopla campaign that carefully drew people together to support of Billy and his new Third Party.

David Barnston was the true genius of Billy's crusade. In this last effort to win over the people, he blew the budget. His masterful print and broadcast campaign grafted together video clips and still photos acquired all year long from each stop during the train and plane tour, publishing and broadcasting to every city the local experience of Billy's campaign appearances, and closing with the people's local leaders' endorsements of Billy for President, repeating the same words of confirmation:

"I believed in him in the beginning and I'm going to vote for him on Tuesday. Billy is our only answer. Billy must become our President!"

The exact message was repeated everywhere. The world too, had been primed and was awaiting Billy's final pre-election message. It was to be Barnston's *coup de gras*.

Barnston even got corporate supporters to sponsor this program on every television network, cable TV service, and major radio station in North America. This would be the prime delivery system for Billy's final campaign speech. By not buying spots throughout the year, Barnston had made sure that this media bombardment would create a private broadcasting network of unprecedented impact. It was timed to occur during the last four days before the election. It meant a virtual blackout for the other contenders. They just couldn't compete with Barnston's strategy and buying power.

This time Billy would be heard simultaneously on all broadcast media, and his words interpreted for the many non-English speakers in in the United States. In an extraordinary and unprecedented move, his speech was to be aired on stations in Canada, Mexico, Central and South America with hundreds of pickups from media outlets world-wide. Billy was campaigning for world support. It was the first time anyone had designed and delivered a worldwide multilingual radio and TV simulcast.

To make it even more unique for the viewers and listeners, Barnston booked Radio City Music Hall as the point of origin for the program and provided the press with the story of how Billy had invited nearly 5000 of his friends and most loyal supporters to attend this last speech. Billy wanted his loyal followers to be seen with him. He told them he was going to win, and he was going to celebrate the win in advance.

After the broadcast, Billy's guests were to attend a fabulous party at Madison Square Garden. This pre-victory party would rival any private gala or ball ever held. It was rumored that the party itself would cost over $15,000,000. Each couple paid $10,000. Billy and Suzzanne paid $1,000,000 for their pair of tickets. Billy worked his people magic once again and got the hall and all the union help, the food, the wine—everything—at no cost to the Third Party.

This mammoth affair would be televised worldwide, and all the corporate sponsorship money, as well as all the cash taken in, would be used to buy food to feed the millions of hungry people in the United States. This food would be distributed in the name of the American people to food banks across the United States. It might have looked to old-time politicians like buying votes with meal tickets, but it was all very legal.

In every city in the country, Billy's grassroots campaign organizations staged little "Big Victory Parties," and raised money for food banks. At these local parties the main entertainment for the evening was the projection TV viewing of the event in Manhattan. It would be a fantastic and wonderful night—all complements of Billy!

Barnston knew this would solidify voters. To insure prompt and loyal viewership for this all-important pre-election speech, Barnston had persuaded some of the most famous celebrities and show business artists to precede Billy's historic global speech. The *crème de la crème* of the entertainment world would delight the people with forty minutes of great music and amusement before Billy arrived.

The stage was now properly set.

Vice Presidential running mate, Avery Harrison, was slated to introduce Billy. Even though he was well grounded in the history and science of politics, Harrison was a bit nervous. A veritable genius at political strategy and a veteran campaigner, he knew this was the last opportunity to galvanize the voters for the Johnstone/Harrison ticket.

Harrison had been Billy's professor of political science and his long association and loyalty to Billy gave him credibility. Harrison may have deluded himself into thinking he was a seasoned candidate. This synthetic confidence propped him up tonight and, as Billy liked to say, 'If you believe it, it is so!"

David Barnston provided a quick introduction to the vice-presidential candidate. As Harrison approached the podium the noisy crowd quieted down. "Ladies and gentlemen, citizens of the United States, and of the world, my fellow Americans. It is my pleasure to introduce to you the next President of the United States of America, William F. 'Billy' Johnstone!"

The crowd of 5,000 was on its feet with thunderous applause as Billy confidently strolled onto the huge stage. He mounted the platform, joined hands with Avery and together they held their hands high in a victory salute. The crowd roared even louder.

Billy waited for several minutes as the crowd continued to show their favor, then he gestured for them to sit down. "Well, good evening and a big hello to you all! You'd a thought I was somebody with all that noise...it's just ol' Billy, folks and say, I'm sure glad you're all here tonight."

Billy pointed to the key TV camera, and continued. "And I'm glad all of you out there have taken the time to tune in, too. I want you to know that this is the biggest audience ever tuned in for anything. Biggest in the history of the world, they tell me. And that's good 'cause what I'm gonna talk about concerns everybody in the world, not just the folks in the USA. Everybody needs to hear this one, 'cause we're all one people on this earth and God wants us to be good folks and get along with each other better and stop the warrin' and the fightin' and make good use of this fantastic world we live in."

The outburst of applause interrupted him.

"Well thank you for all that. But folks, I'm going to ask a little favor of you. Tonight, I'm probably going to say a lot of things that you're gonna like, but I only bought so much time on the airwaves to say them, so please save the yellin' and shoutin' till the end. Then, if you liked what I said, well, I'll give you plenty of time to tell me then. Deal?"

Like children listening to a loving father, the audience quieted down and listened.

"See, it's a done deal. Our side is going to win this election and then we all have to go to work on our country. Work's not bad, you know. In fact, it makes you feel good when you've done a good job. And we've all got one hell of a job to do, so we need to get with it and do it right!

"For the last year and a half, I have traveled, nonstop to many cities and every state in our great nation, as well as to Canada, Mexico, Central and South America. I talked with lots and lots of good folks everywhere I went. I can tell you that I may be the only man alive today who really knows what the people want from our government. I know, 'cause I was out there with you, and I listened to what you had to say.

"As many of you may know, my first college education opportunity was at West Point. I could'a gone there right out of 'Nam, but after thinking about it for a while, I thought I should take a school a little less bent on killin,' so I ended up at GST. See, while I was in 'Nam I learned all the best principals and methods of how to kill and not be legally staging a war. Those generals were experts at getting us killed and gaining no ground. I think some of them are running our country right now."

The audience laughed.

"Seriously, folks. I remembered a lot of that military strategy when I started my own business and I guess some of it works. You see, I do believe that if you're gonna war, you've got to find out what the other side is doing, then figure out how to do it better if you're gonna beat 'em. It's that simple folks. It's called reconnaissance, planning, and implementation. Part of that planning is to give the other side information that ain't true. That's called false information. Oh, they think they've done some good spyin' and got a handle on your plans, but they don't. If you do it right, you don't even let your most trusted generals know the real plans. You keep that to yourself, got it?"

"Well, some of my opponents have said they heard me cry out against NAFTA. Well, truly, I'm for it. But it ought to look like a common market agreement between Canada, Mexico, Central and South America, with no side deals to hold it back. What they've got is the wrong arrangement. Now, we've got a good plan and we're gonna use it just as soon as we open up for business next week."

More laughter. The audience was at ease with Billy.

"You see, if you get the best minds to tackle the problems it always pays off. Let's look at it like an equation: 'Problems' plus 'The Best Minds Available' equals 'Solutions.' Now add 'The Best Planners and Managers,' and you get fantastic 'Results.' And that's what we all want, good results!

"You know my enemy, the opposing political forces—the Republicans and Democrats—heard me yelling about their National Medical Plan and I sure did yell, 'cause it's lousy and I'm a guy that's for health care for everyone. Now, in this new Third Party, we've got a real good health plan and it really works for everyone. Ours is the best and you're gonna hear about it before they do, 'cause it's for all of you!

"They say I never answer the real questions, and they're right. I'm a pretty fair poker player, you know, and I wasn't gonna tell them what I was holding, until tonight, 'cause now it's too late for them to jump on any of these solutions and lie to you and mix up you good folks, but now I'm gonna tell you just what it is that I'm going to do so you feel good about casting your vote for ol' Billy."

The crowd was on its feet yelling, "Bil-ly! Bil-ly! Bil-ly!"

"Hey, remember, this time it's not just Billy, it's William F. Johnstone, that's the name on the ballot for president!"

They exploded again. He stood before them, waiting and smiling that big grin.

"Okay. Okay. Thank you. Now, let me tell you how and why we're gonna win this election. Number one: we all need this Third Party. The other old parties just don't work for the people anymore. They're so mired in inefficiency and corruption, I don't think they'll ever be able work for the people again. And besides, they act like one party... hardly a difference between them. Second: when you vote, I want you to vote for the best person. Vote for the best senator or representative, the best governor or mayor, vote for the best person to do the job. And number three: don't vote a party ticket ever again in your life. That's what happened to the other parties. No substance; just party loyalty. If you just do those three things, then we'll all win the day after tomorrow. And we'll keep on winning after that."

The audience applauded loudly.

"Now let's get back to the facts. They say I won't tell you exactly what I'm going to do when I become your president."

Billy held up a sheet of paper.

"Well, here it is. Here's a list of the most important issues in our nation, and in the world, and I'm going to address each of these issues tonight. Not just some of them—all of them. Because they're our problems and you ought to know what they are and you need to know how I'm gonna fix 'em. See, I've got nothing to hide from you folks. When I'm done talking with you tonight, I'm gonna release this entire list to the media so you can see it again tomorrow in your papers and on TV. You've got the picture. I've got fifteen points to tell you about. It'll be easy for you to remember. Here we go.

"*Number One: Crime.* People, the safety and peace of mind of this country can no longer be used as a political football. It's a very serious and dangerous situation that has been allowed to happen. The crime rate is at epidemic proportions in this country because every attempt to address the issue focused on the wrong things. Failed miserably. I have the studies. They've been finished for a long time now. I know what to do and believe me, crime in our country can and will be eliminated completely, and in very short order, too. That's a promise.

"*Two: High Taxes.* What about NO TAXES? Yep. No taxes. There never should have been this unjust income tax. Our government has been able to put a plan like that in effect for over sixty years, but that greedy bunch in Washington just won't do it. Our big government just keeps on increasing taxes so they can continue to exercise control over the people. Well, I'm going to eliminate taxes altogether and those evil Gestapo bastards at the IRS will be out looking for new jobs!"

Even though they'd been instructed not to cheer, the crowd knew an applause line when they heard one. They erupted with joy.

"Now hold up the noise, folks. All right. *Next: High Unemployment.* How about FULL EMPLOYMENT? And they should've done that one a long time ago, too. Well, we're gonna do it, 'cause everybody needs and wants a job and this great country needs everybody's help. So, when I get into that oval office, you're all gonna get to go to work again and at good jobs with good wages, too."

"*Number Four: The Drug Problem.* That's not going to be a dilemma for this country any longer. As a nation, we're gonna sober up and get to work. No, we're not gonna let drugs cripple this country. It's top on my agenda, and we have a foolproof plan and we're going to take care of that problem, right away.

"*Pollution and the Environment.* This one is killing us all. How long have we been destroying our environment? How in God's name can anyone be against the environment? Believe it or not, that problem began over a 150 years ago. Pollution is still here, and we must deal with it. If we don't, the outside world won't be inhabitable for our children and their children. It's a big problem, folks. But, you know, it's like when you let things go around your house or in your yard. It becomes a mess, then a big mess. Well, we have to clean it up. And that's what I intend to do. No more EPA stalling. And, this is not a threat; it's a fact. All you big corporations get ready, cause you're gonna clean this country up, or else."

"*Number Six: Poverty*. How the hell, in this land of plenty, do we have poverty and starvation? The government continues to control all the little people by starving them, and continues to give away, stockpile, and destroy the food that we grow just to keep commodity pric-es up and use our food to buy favors from foreign countries. These fat cats continue to get fatter. They don't care whether the people of the United States live or die."

The audience erupted with boos and shout in agreement.

"Okay. Now get this and think about it. I just can't imagine breakfast cereal at $4 and $5 a box, milk at $4.00 a gallon, eggs at $2.99 a dozen, bread at $2.00 or more a loaf. It's ridiculous. This must stop! The farmers in this country are paid not to produce food. It's been going on way too long. We all know that we are the best producers of food in the entire world. I want our farmers to get more for their la-bor and investment, but I want them to produce food for our people, so everyone can eat. Well, we've got a plan that will allow everyone to afford to eat. After I'm elected, those food prices will come down, and there will be no more poverty or hunger in this country. And that's a fact, not an empty promise.

"*Number Seven: Education*. Again, we've got a plan here on this one that will allow—no, it will require—every boy and girl in this nation to go to a school of higher learning at absolutely no charge.

None of those life-ruining student loans. It'll be free to all who want to learn, and they'll come out with real skills that they can use for the rest of their lives—skills, not just academic hogwash and certificates. Good, productive and useable skills. It's easy and we'll do it.

"*Health Care.* On this one, our plan is simple. If you're a U.S. citizen and you've got a health problem, no matter what age, it'll be fixed, no charge of any kind, thank you.

"*Number Nine: The Space Program.* It's something we're committed to because we need it. It has brought about great technological advances, and there's even more amazing stuff in store for us in the future. We only live in a little part of this infinite universe and we're just finding out the miracles God has out there for us. Listen, we started the space program right here in the USA, and we're gonna stay on top of it.

"*Ten: Civil Rights.* Here's another one that should never have gotten out of control. How did we ever get boondoggled with civil rights? Hell, we're all born equal and with all the rights promised to us in our Constitution, right! How did it happen? Well, it will get corrected quickly. It's easy. Just to do what's right and treat your neighbor fair. I'll tell you now: I will see that your rights as U.S. citizens are enforced everywhere and on every issue. And if you don't treat all people equal, well look out, 'cause you're gonna hear from me!

"*Number Eleven: The National Debt.* An important issue to us all. When I become president I'm gonna have a lot to do. But can you imagine this? I'm going to have to take on this huge current national debt, too. It's just inherited grief for me. Well, it'll be tough, but understand—no maybes—this is my promise to you all: Within the first 18 months in office, if we all pull together on this one, we will balance the budget. And, if we work real hard, we can actually create a real surplus for the first time in 100 years.

"*Number Twelve: Energy.* We have no lack of renewable energy. We've got the big beautiful sun that God gave to us, and I intend to use its power and get us out of the 'oil scam' business. No nuclear power. The sun is the deal. This one is killing all of us.

"*Thirteen: Immigration.* If you want to become an American citizen, we want you. But you have to come in legally. If you want to be a U.S. citizen you're not going to be in trouble with me. Just do it right. No more illegals. I mean it. I will stop the illegal flow across our borders and coastlines.

"*Number Fourteen: Terrorism.* Well, here's another political football. The world wants terrorism to stop and we know how. Talk, don't shoot and bomb. Talk. Find out what everybody wants. We will stop it. No more terrorism.

"And here's the big one, the last one—fifteen points, just like I promised. *Number Fifteen: The Future.* The reason that I'm gonna take this job as president is for our children, yours and mine, and all the beautiful children of the future. I want to make it safe and sensible for them. We're gonna deal with the real big issues right now. Those issues like world population, communicable diseases, and pollution of the environment, world hunger, world education and world peace. Folks, we must do something fast or all our little U.S. government issues won't matter. As I said before, this planet of ours is a dirty, infected, dangerous mess and the population of the world is growing larger and larger every day. We're running out of room and were running out of time. We've allowed this mess to happen and now we must clean it up for all the generations yet to come. These are the planks in my platform. Solid. Clear and doable. Not at all like the old-guard crap that never gets done. We will do what we promise. Well, what do you think?"

Five thousand people were on their feet. They applauded and stomped and cheered, "Bil-ly! Bil-ly! Bil-ly! Bil-ly!"

He let them go wild and finally calmed them again. "Well I'm glad you like our plans, my friends. And now, I just want to talk to you a bit more about some of these issues we must deal with after we're elected.

By now, you can get the idea. Our country is in real trouble, because most of our infrastructure is breaking down. Bad bridges, bad roads, bad rail system, utilities deteriorated, buildings and whole cities falling down, rivers full of pollution, the air and water so dirty and lethal you shouldn't breathe or drink them. I want to fix our economy, the health of our people, the environment and infrastructure in our country right away. Then I want to take all our good skills and wealth and begin to help the world get on its feet, too. But first we need to set an example for the people of the world. If we can do it here, then they will see that they can do it in their countries, as well."

It is very unusual for several thousand people to become completely quiet. Everything was still in Radio City Music Hall; no coughing, no whispering, no movement.

Billy's voice was calm as he modulated from high verve to a quiet sincerity. "We have to stop destroying our forests and begin to replant the trees we have destroyed. We've got to use less oil by decreasing our dependence on oil and reduce our use of lumber for building houses. There are so many other answers available. Oil and lumber, just like coal, are yesterday's technology. We know how to use the solar energy, and I intend to put those programs into place immediately. No more high-pollution cars, trucks, and trains. We need all-electric vehicles and the creation of the best mass transit sys-tems in the world."

He continued talking to them, no longer sounding like a candidate. He was their friend and elected leader. "And the medicines...well, these powerful pharmaceutical companies, medical associations, and scientific laboratories must stop playing with our lives. There are genetic programs that can halt—once and for all—most of the diseases that are just waiting to wipe us out. I assure you, our medicine is much more advanced than any of you are allowed to know. People, this is not the middle ages when the masses were frightened and ignorant. It's a new millennium and most of you are bright, smart and capable people.

Now let's quit wondering what to do. We've got to wake up and get with it and fix these messes before it's too late for us all."

The crowd stood and applauded even louder than ever.

Billy shouted over their approval. "And now you've heard it all. The political opposition and the media wanted to know all about my plan. Well, there it is and absolutely no candidate or president in the history of this country has ever promised this much to the people and I'll tell you why. They couldn't deliver one-tenth of this to you because they had to take care of so many private, political and special interest obligations. They had to make deals to get elected. So far, nobody in this country's long history has ever truly represented the people fairly, without some sort of greed or obligation being a factor. Well, I don't have any favors owed to anybody. I didn't have to cow-tow to any political machine in any state to get on the ballot, and I've got more money than the next five generations of my family can spend, even if we stopped making money right now and they all started  spendin' it as fast as they could. And that's a lot of money, folks. So, understand: no one can tempt me to sell you out for money. I know what you want. I've been out there talking to you, and I am the right guy to go Washington and get it done for you."

The audience cheered again.

"It's really simple. This country is a big corporation and should be run like a business. If run correctly, the government would have their work to do every day and it would cost money, but they'd have to turn a profit, not generate a big national debt. And they'd have get their work done, not shove it off to the next guy. The government would have to keep the shareholders of this big country—that's you all—happy and continuously deliver those promised dividends. Then it would run like a business."

The cameraman zoomed in for a tighter shot of Billy.

"It's really easy, folks, but all of you will have to work and do the things that need to be done, when they need doing. My opponents are shaking in their boots tonight, and I know that they're all watching me on television, just like you are. Yeah, those ol' boys are scared. They're scared I might just convince the American public that they've been taken for a ride for a long, long time. They're scared 'cause they've always known that I can and will do exactly what I say I'll do. I'll deliver and they won't. They've been hoping that you wouldn't find out that I mean business.

"Now get this, people. I have only one agenda: that's to serve my bosses fairly. And you're my bosses—each and every one of you. Elect me and I'll help you fix this great country of ours. And I'll only need a short time to do it, too."

The crowd rose and roared to a point of near frenzy.

Billy shouted over the clamor. "Listen up, people. Go out to the polls on Tuesday and get everybody to vote on Election Day. Put ol' Billy and the good new Third Party in office and restore this nation to its rightful owners: you, the citizens of the United States of America. And if they don't kill me before Election Day—and that could be a problem, ya know—then I'm confident that we're gonna win this election and we're gonna get rid of that greedy old bunch in Washington. We'll send 'em home to get some real jobs!"

The crowd went wild.

"Good night to you all and may God bless every one of you." Billy stood at the podium for a long time waving to the people. He was sure they loved and trusted him and believed him to be the answer to their future.

Over the airwaves, an announcer spoke over a "Billy for President" slide. "Okay, Americans, this is our chance. We must elect Billy. He will bring the change that all of us want and need. Everyone, everywhere, if you can hear my voice, call a friend, call a neighbor, call someone in your family and tell them to be sure to vote for Billy. If they don't have transportation, pick them up and take them with you when you go to vote. But everyone: please go to the polls on Election

Day and vote for Billy. To put our country back in the hands of its owners we, the American people, must vote for William F. Johnstone for president."

# 10

## PLAN 'A' COMPLETED

The weather was unusually cool for Louisiana on this November day. The clouds in the sky were boiling just as before a storm.

Billy's elite—his most loyal supporters—had been called for a very special meeting. One-by-one, throughout the night and into the early morning, Billy's people arrived at Hurricane House via different airlines, trains or private cars. Each traveled separately. Rob Collings was an expert at special arrangements and when Billy ordered "secret," Rob Collings knew how to make it happen.

Soon-to-be Vice President Avery Harrison arrived first. Impeccably dressed, snow-white hair wafting in the wind, this tall, distinguished, grand old man emerged from his car and was guided inside.

Avery had been and would continue to be Billy's guide dog through the minefields of Washington. When Avery retired from teaching he became a full-time board member of WFJ Polybiotech. Convincing Avery to become his running mate was a wise move on Billy's part. In his forty years of campaign management, Avery's friendly and affable manner hadn't created a single enemy on either side of the aisle.

He'd earned an admirable reputation for supporting the Constitution and the American people. Billy valued Avery's great knowledge and political connections. This man was a friend and a loyal supporter. Avery believed in Billy Johnstone and the new Third Party.

Dr. Charles Gertz, Professor George Osher, and General Alfred Fenwick—three of Billy's oldest and most loyal friends arrived at almost the same time.

Professor Osher had been Charles Gertz's teacher and mentor during Gertz's college days. Osher was a very creative man and a genius in the field of chemistry, as well as biogenetics. Not just an academic, this stout, sour man with the frizzy beard and hair knew how to practically apply his theories. Even now, in his early seventies, few minds like Osher's existed anywhere in the world. As Billy got ideas, it was George Osher and Charles who created the formulas and designed the methods to bring them to fruition. When Charles and Billy teamed up to form WFJ Polybiotech, George Osher was the first to come on board. As tough as he was to deal with, Billy and Charles revered the Professor.

Gen. Alfred E. Fenwick, USMC, retired, had been Rob Collings direct superior and Billy's commanding officer in Vietnam. Billy had saved both Fenwick and Collings from certain death in the prison camp, and the friendship between the three men was extremely strong. Fenwick, generally good-natured, was still a tough military man. As a veteran of both Korea and Vietnam, Fenwick's thinking was influenced by the shift in military strategy he experienced. A youthful-appearing, handsome and fit man of seventy, he looked like a Hollywood-type gyrene. Fenwick was slated to serve as Secretary of Defense. Billy thought, "If you have to fight a war, why have a politician in charge? Use a pro!"

Next came the famous lawyers, Henry Gillespie and Irving R. Penitz. Almost fanatical in their loyalty to Billy and to the new Third

Party, each had been chosen because of his exceptional legal expertise and ability to make things happen legally.

Together with Collings and Barnston, Gillespie, Penitz and the soon-to-arrive computer genius Felix Hansen made up Billy's very secret nine—the "Inner Circle."

The next arrivals were Billy's communications engineer Julio Mondaldo and the bright and aggressive "woman of the year," Sally Hawthorne. In addition to the nine "Inner Circle" members, these two would be added to "The Group," the close fraternity of the new Third Party. These were the people who had loyally and diligently helped to persuade the American people to support Billy for President.

Sally had earned her rep as the girl who could do everything, serving as David Barnston's assistant and Billy's right-hand man. Sally was to become the new Secretary of Education. She had the honor of being the only woman in Billy's secret "Group." Sally undeniably relished being one of his "boys." In the pictures of Billy and The Group on the campaign trail Sally, as the only woman, always netted a double-take. Underneath that beauty was a clever, skilled, and educated mind capable of delivering the goods. She paid close attention to David Barnston. She was a quick study. Sally had become a key player in the making of the president.

The travelers were tired. Even so, Billy demanded they arise early the next morning. "I want everyone there for breakfast at 8 a.m.—they can sleep after breakfast. Dinner is at 7:00 p.m. sharp. Got it?"

They got it. Everyone was used to doing it Billy's way. Each had arrived on schedule and ready to work, though all were worn out from travel, still hung-over and fatigued from the world's biggest party the night before.

As they gathered at Hurricane House the stories each one told about the Big Broadcast and the Big Party further fueled their excitement. The speech from Radio City Music Hall inspired hope in these supporters and the entire nation. Everyone felt exhilarated. The faith shared by The Group was unquestionable, but the confidence in Billy inspired by this event in the hearts and minds of the American people was incalculable.

The big victory party was almost impossible to describe. Everyone who was anyone was there: stars from Hollywood and the Broadway stage, from television and radio; authors and statesmen and scientists and bankers from everywhere in the world attended. But the frosting on the cake was the presence of the long awaited political reinforcements—the staunch, loyal Republicans and Democrats who by the hundreds had been convinced to jump ship, to change parties at the last moment and who now firmly backed and supported their new leader, William F. Johnstone, for President of the United States.

In the morning, just as ordered, they all assembled at the huge breakfast table like good little children waiting for Daddy to arrive.

After a few minutes, Billy entered the room and everyone stood up. He motioned for them to sit down. "Good mornin', good mornin'. How do you like this cool weather? Great, isn't it? The summer was one of the hottest on record, but it's surely nice and cool now. Hope the travel wasn't too rough on you gentlemen, and lady. I always like to travel at night. The world's asleep then, and their thinkin' don't interfere with my thinkin'. Well, enough of my chatter, I'm holding up the show. Let's eat this great breakfast Hilga has put out for us. I'll say the prayer: Lord, we ask that you consecrate this bounty before us and I personally ask that you bless these brave patriots, these men and women of vision and purpose as they strive to heal this planet and its people as you have ordained. May we all find peace and prosperity. In the name of all that is holy, Amen. Let's eat!"

A huge breakfast with everything one could want was before them. For openers, eggs—your way—fixed table-side, with country ham, sausage, bacon, corned-beef hash, lox, cream cheese, bagels, grits, Belgian waffles, cereal, and fresh fruit. Everything was scrumptious! If, by chance, Hilga had forgotten some item someone liked, or if someone wanted something that wasn't there, it magically appeared prepared exactly as desired. Billy always said: "Eatin' is just about the most important thing to a human being, and because we are humans, not animals, we ought to always eat what we want, when we want it, and exactly the way we want it." That was the way it was at Billy's house. Everyone lived like a king and after a while really thought that this was the way it should be.

After a time of earnest eating, Billy spoke. "Tomorrow's the big day, boys, and girl. If y'all have done this thing right, we could start celebrating today. But just for luck and the propriety of it all, we'll control ourselves. You can be sure, I will act surprised tomorrow when I hear the results. We are gonna have one hell of a busy day tomorrow, so we won't work too late. Tonight, it'll be 11 o'clock latest. You all got planes to be on by 10:00 in the morning. Got to go vote in your town, then back on planes to be with me and Avery in the Capital. We'll have a little victory party for just the folks that really made it happen. That'll be two great celebrations in the same week. But that's all right; some of you never have any fun, so you've got it coming. Now, Rob Collings has all the arrangements made. After breakfast, you can get back to your rooms and rest a bit before we get started today."

Billy kept eating. For a little guy, he had a tremendous appetite. Between bites, he chattered. "I can hardly wait for that election. My God, I'm anxious to sit in that chair and get to work!"

Coffee and tea were served. Billy excused himself from the table and left the room. Soon, one by one, the rest of them finished and went to their rooms for a mid-morning rest. Each soon-to-be Cabinet member fell asleep quickly.

They slept soundly because they had been drugged. The delicious breakfast they enjoyed had been loaded with one of Dr. Osher's special sedatives.

As they slept, Drs. Osher and Gertz and two medical assistants went from room to room examining each unconscious person. As part of the examination, a box-like machine was placed over the neck and shoulders of the person for a just a moment. A button was pushed, a whir and click were heard and the results were noted. The machine was removed and the doctors and their assistants moved on to the next room and repeated the procedure until all the sleepers had been examined.

While these procedures were being conducted, Billy was in a hidden planning room hard at work. There were six monitors built into his desk. There was no keyboard. The computer functions were completely operated by voice command. Billy began barking orders in his headset microphone, first to one unit, then another. It was as though he had a large human staff running and fetching files for the answers to his questions.

Rob Collings' voice came over the intercom. He told Billy that Drs. Osher and Gertz had finished the exams and were ready to see him. The doctors arrived and gave Billy a CD disk. Billy put the disk into the drive and shouted a command. One of the screens flickered and came to life. The monitor displayed the health information and fitness status of each Group member. The data file contained previously collected information and included the new health figures that had been gathered just now. This combined information presented the current fitness, future illness potential, and general life expectancy for each person.

Billy smiled at Dr. Osher. "Very good. All of them seem to be in very sound condition. You can't be too careful. At a time like this I need everyone in good health, able to complete the tasks that lie ahead for all of us."

At exactly 4:30 p.m., each of the Group members were awakened, informed that refreshments were currently being served on the library porch and dinner would be served at 7 p.m. sharp. Feeling unusually refreshed, they each quickly showered and changed into their dinner clothes.

The library porch was a covered room separate from the library. The walls of the porch were lined with framed photos and clippings about Billy. You could waste hours learning about Billy's many accomplishments and the famous people he had met during his illustrious career. Part of the outer wall and a curved portion of the ceiling were made of glass panels. Some of the panels were moveable and could be tilted out so that during nice weather, fresh outside air drifted in. The bar was well stocked. In fact, the reputation here was that you couldn't stump the bartenders at Hurricane House. These guys could make any drink. Even if you thought up a concoction on the spot, they could deliver. Hilga provided an array of hot and cold tapas to make it a classy affair.

The Group wandered onto the porch, chatting in twos and threes, casually looking at the wall as they ordered their favorite beverage. Some stared out the windows totally captivated by the spectacular view of the Gulf of Mexico. It had been a long dusty trail on this campaign and a nice drink and a quiet time for these very loyal and hard-working people was overdue.

After an hour or so of talking and drinking they all were relaxed.

That's when Billy made his entrance onto the library porch with his usual flair. "Hello, hello, hello. Everybody having a good time? Great, we'll do some more of this later, but now, if you will, let's go to dinner, boys and girl!" It was that sudden appearance act that put everyone back on guard. Billy always seemed to appear from nowhere. Each often wondered whether Billy was somehow listening to them talk just out of sight.

The members of the Group followed their leader down a hall to an immense, elegant dining room. The dark pecan wood paneling, gigantic fireplace, huge crystal chandeliers and the long, long walnut table all blended together to cast the mood Billy had designed it for: You had been invited to dine with the King!

The table could probably seat a hundred quite comfortably. Only one end of the table was being used for the Group. The single lit chandelier above that end of the table gave a nice glow and allowed the rest of the mammoth room to fade away into darkness. One of the four fireplaces lit the room, crackling and burning. casting a feeling of intimacy in the spacious hall. The table was set seven to a side, with Billy at one end. Suzzanne was to be at Billy's left and their oldest son, Wilhelm, to his right. There was an open seat next to Wilhelm. Everyone wondered who would be sitting in the extra seat. The mystery was soon solved when Tommy, Billy's youngest son, rushed into the room. He was late for dinner.

Billy laughed. "You know, this kid has never, I mean never, come to the table on time. He's the only person in the world that makes me wait!"

Tommy was obviously a little embarrassed by Billy's comment. He wasn't a kid anymore. He was a sophomore in college, a Harvard man. Tommy was home to be with the family in the days preceding the election, and this would be the only event that Billy would allow to interrupt his son's college education. He felt that the whole family should be on hand for this historic event. And besides, it made for a fantastic photo opportunity.

They all remained standing until Billy had seated himself.

"Sit, sit," he called out. "Now, gentlemen and ladies, I will say the prayer: Heavenly father, we all thank you for this most bountiful feast and pray that you allow us continued health and happiness in our lives. We ask that you shine your countenance upon our efforts and help the people of this great nation and the nations of the world to achieve the glorious design you have laid out for us. In the name of all that is holy, Amen."

They all chorused, "Amen."

Billy, as usual, was not through talking and began again without missing a beat, "My friends, on this night, just one day away from fruition and the confirmation of the faith we have all had in this campaign for the presidency, I want to take a moment to again commend each of you on the great creativity, work and sacrifice that you've donated to this campaign, as well as all the hard work of your fine, talented. There's never been a campaign like the one we've waged in United State history. It will definitely be remembered. Our victory tomorrow will mark the beginning of a new world order of peace and prosperity and the ultimate elevation of mankind."

As The Group sounded, "Hear, hear!" in agreement, Suzanne knew that it might take some time for Billy to stop "speechifyin'." As Billy continued, Suzanne nodded to Hilga, and the serving people moved to circle the table with food-laden carts. Suzzanne felt that these people were her guests, too. She knew they were hungry. And she intended to feed them.

Billy was in full oration mode. "...a height and level of human excellence unheard of and heretofore not even visualized by mankind; a peace and prosperity that will shake the history books. Each of us will be named, therein, as *The New Regents* of the American people and we will go on to write many more exciting chapters in that book of history with our many and great deeds." Billy noticed the circling carts and quickly stood up and raised his wine glass. "To you—the brave, the loyal, the dedicated; my friends and true allies—to you, *The New Regents* of the people, I thank you all. Let's drink to the future." Raising his glass higher, the Group raised their glasses, too. "Ladies and gentlemen—to the future!"

The assembled echoed the toast almost as a cheer: "To the future. To the future. To the future. Hear, hear!"

Billy raised his hand for silence and smiled that smile of his. "And as for the present? Don't worry, 'cause starting tomorrow, every-thing's gonna be all right. And that's a promise! Let's eat!"

Scattered calls of "hear, hear" came from around the table and, as if on cue, the sounds of beautiful music drifted in. Slowly, soft lights appeared on a group of string players located in the dark corner of the huge room. On the "let's eat" command from Billy, the food was served up from the carts. Another sumptuous meal prepared under the talented and watchful guidance of Hilga was enjoyed by all.

To many of The Group, Hilga was just one more of Billy's many enigmas. Who was Hilga? Where did she come from? Everyone had wondered at one time or another. She had just the tiniest accent; not enough to betray whether she was Swiss or Norwegian or German. She was a strikingly attractive woman with little gray wisps in the blond hair carefully braided around her head. Her face didn't betray her age. She had to be somewhere in her 50s, yet she had the lithe figure of a young woman still flourishing in her early 30s. There were so many mysteries about Billy, what was one more? What they did know was that Hilga was polite, intelligent, articulate, and very aware of protocol—and she served incredibly good food.

The sweet music drifted throughout the cavernous room. Everyone was having a wonderful time. The Group ate and drank. The conversation was light and animated.

Billy finished his meal. He took a sip of wine and gained everyone's attention. "Sometime early last year, I think, a reporter wrote an article quoting a passage from one of my speeches. I believe it was the speech I made to the auto industry leaders. I tell you now, I thank that man. With that one quote, he gave me the skeleton on which to hang my entire strategy. He wrote that I said that fixing this country, fixing this world is as easy as *A-B-C*. All you have to do is get off your ass and do it. Well, this is absolutely true. I believe what I said, of course. So, when I read that article, a light bulb went off in my brain: *A-B-C*! That reporter inspired me to make a simple plan. For the last year during this campaign, you've all been saying it, too. 'It's as easy as *A-B-C*,' 'cause it is! *A*, we get elected president; *B*, we stop all the crime, corruption and poverty; *C*, we begin to rebuild this country and the economy to become the biggest jewel in the crown of God's world."

Billy's guests put down their forks and knives and burst into applause.

Wilhelm stood up and waited for them to quiet down. "Friends of my father, friends of my family, this great man before us, William F. Johnstone, will make the very best, most remembered and most beloved president that this country has ever known." Wilhelm turned to his father. "Dad, your family and these great friends of ours—now, our extended family—are...Well, we have a present for you, sir."

Billy looked slightly flustered, yet inquisitive.

Wilhelm continued. "If you turn around, father, you will see a picture that will soon become the new icon for America and for freedom throughout the world."

Billy turned his chair around. On the wall above him, a velvet drape fell away revealing a large ornate picture frame. Gallery lights slowly came up on a magnificent oil portrait of Billy. The portrait was done in the style that had been used for all the great, early presidents: stoic yet romantic; Godlike.

Billy turned around. They were all applauding again.

Billy slowly stood up. Turning again toward the picture and then to The Group, he looked at every face. Tears begin to well in his eyes. "I am deeply overcome with emotion. Receiving this gift, this magnificent painting—a gift from you, my wonderful friends and family—is indeed an honor and surprise. I have such great love for you all. I will not forget this occasion for as long as I may live. I thank you. I thank you all."

Billy looked at Barnston and then at Gertz. "Say, I wonder how that'd look on currency?"

They all laughed.

"By the way, how did you do this without me knowing about it? Rob Collings, you're supposed to be up on what happens in my life, and tell me everything. How did you miss this? Oh, oh, I see. You knew." Billy shot a serious look at Collings. "Don't you ever keep anything from me again, for any reason!"

They all laughed, but Rob knew that Billy meant every word.

The festive, happy conversations continued as the remnants of the extraordinary dinner were cleared and replaced with coffee, brandy and desserts. Hilga's crew delivered two tray carts full of every rich, sweet and chocolaty thing imaginable. It was an epicurean's dream.

Billy remained quiet as they all finished their desserts, sipping cognac and coffee. Eventually he broke the silence and spoke in a serious tone. "Gentlemen, and lady, I ask you to bid goodnight to my beautiful Suzzanne, young Tommy, and Wilhelm, and come with me now for that meeting I warned you about at breakfast."

Billy stood up, bent down and kissed his wife. She smiled adoringly at him.

Billy moved over to Tommy and started to kiss him but straightened up and extended his hand. Tommy rose and embraced his father.

The Group said their goodnights to the family as Billy prodded them once again. "Come on now, follow me, we've got work to do. Hope you all have your electronic notebooks, kids; there may be a quiz. If not today...soon!"

Billy and Rob Collings led The Group out of the Great Hall by way of a door built in-between the fireplaces on the wall of the dining room. It wasn't a real secret panel, but it took very careful examination to notice that it was a door and not just a part of the wall. They entered and went down a long hallway, ending up at an elevator. The small door opened to reveal an office-building-sized elevator. The Group entered. As the car descended some noticed that there were no floor number markings. In fact, there were no up/down buttons. More of Rob Collings' good secret stuff.

All of them assumed the same thing. They were headed for the "hidden room." This was going to be a treat. Previously, only the members of Billy's Inner Circle had been allowed in the hidden room.

Rumors circulated in The Group about the existence and location of the hidden room. Everyone was sure that it existed, but the members who had seen it weren't talking. Everyone had his or her own idea of where it was and how it might look.

The elevator car stopped. It began to turn in a circle to the left one revolution and at the same time moved forward on a horizontal plane for a short distance and then stopped. How clever. The location of the hidden room would remain a mystery.

The doors opened and they exited into a vestibule with a plush black-carpeted floor, green and black marble walls with silver trim. No doors. No windows. No stairs.

"Stand where you are. Please do not move," stated Rob Collings.

The lights blacked out. In the darkness, they heard the quiet, ominous sounds of machinery smoothly moving something. The lights quickly came up to reveal a meeting room. The vestibule had vanished and the black marble walls had transformed into a beautiful pink color; the black carpet now a brilliant deep red. Real magic!

Billy led them in. "If you will, please be seated at the place where you see your name."

They all moved forward to a V-shaped table in the center of the room. Billy sat at the point so he could look out to both sides of the table. The wall behind Billy was draped, as were each of the side walls. In the area behind The Group, in the spot where the elevator doors should have been, was a solid marble wall. In the center of the wall was a huge gold, purple, and red emblem with the letters: NWF.

Billy launched. "Gentlemen, and lady, all the secrecy, all the work, all that you have endured these last months has been in preparation for the meeting in this room tonight.

The lights dimmed. A continuous curtain covering the three remaining walls opened silently all around the room. On one wall was a giant "A." Behind Billy was a "B," and to the right of that, a "C."

"This is about the *A-B-C* program that I talked about upstairs at dinner. We are now in Plan A: The Presidency." As Billy continued the huge letter "A" dissolved into a large picture of Billy over a montage including the great seal of the United States, the American flag and the American eagle.

"I have no doubt that we will be elected tomorrow. This, then, is Plan A." The picture of Billy remained as the flag and eagle disappeared.

"Then Plan B." The "B" on screen behind Billy faded into a picture of Billy over the happy and cheerful faces of hundreds of people.

"In this next part of the triad, you will see the total eradication of crime, mental illness, drugs, racism, unemployment and poverty and the immediate return of this country, and its people, to the health and happiness that God has always wanted for us."

The picture of Billy remained. The people disappeared.

The "C" screen changed to the face of Billy over a montage of bridges, rail and building construction.

"And the final phase is Plan C. After our social health is renewed, and with great new strength and hope, we will totally rebuild the infrastructure of this mighty nation so that it will reach its potential and become the eternal envy of the world."

The montage disappeared and only the three huge solemn faces of Billy remained on the three walls. As Billy continued, the faces slowly dissolved into the letters: NWF.

"Each one of you has been chosen for your talents and for the dedication to the principles that will make my plans a reality. You have each been on trial during this campaign and your competence has been examined time and time again. We have used every trick possible in the evaluation of your loyalty to me and to our cause. You have all passed the tests, or you would not be in this room. I have referred to you as 'The Group.' This is true. You are my Group and the very corps that will make these dreams of mine come true, both for America and for the rest of the world. You are a very elite Group—the most elite to be found anywhere—and you are now about to publicly emerge and become the new ruling class of this country. As such, you will, as *The New Regents of America*, assume the duty to care and watch over the citizens and the future of our great new country, as well as all the people and every country of the world.

"As we embark on the next leg of this journey, there will be many domestic and world crises that will confront you. More will be asked of you in the next months than has ever been asked of you in your entire lifetime. Your faith will be tested time and time again. You must not fail me, or your country. It will take the sum total of all that you are—and God's good help—to accomplish this mission and to fulfill your true destiny. I am your friend, your ally, your teacher and your leader. I will expect—no, I will demand—that you commit your lives and your very souls to this crusade. God has given us this opportunity. He has truly caused us all to find each other and come together for His purpose. The elements and opportunity to make great change only occur so often. We are about to come upon a convergence in time and space of unprecedented opportunity. It is His will that we stop the people from defiling His earth and that we stop abiding the sin and sinners that live upon His earth. As we continue in our task, God will support and confirm us in all that we do. Our work cannot be done without God's help, for we only toil and serve for the further glory of God, Almighty. Let us pray together now."

They all bowed their heads as Billy continued.

"God in heaven above, speak to each of us now. Tell us what we need to know and guide us in the right direction in everything we must do. Confirm and reassure us with your divine inspiration, let us each hear your command. Talk to us in the quiet of our hearts and minds. Give us that same word of faith that you gave to Abraham and Moses and Jesus. Let us feel confident that the God of Gods is on our side in this most holy conflict. Great God, please help us all in every way in the challenges we will encounter. Amen. Let each of us remain silent now and have a true communion with God."

The lights dimmed. They were in total darkness and absolute silence. In this quiet, eyes closed, The Group was experiencing something...something not quite explainable. They each seemed to sit taller in their chairs, confident, content, inspired, almost swooning at the possibilities that now seemed very real.

As they opened their eyes together, the room was dark except for a single light on Billy. A warm, indirect pinkness filled the room. The curtains on the walls had closed.

Billy was still standing. "My friends, I feel renewed. God has touched us all this evening with His holy grace. We have His blessings, I am sure. And now, let us lift our glasses in a toast to God's new plan for the future of mankind."

They lifted the glasses of cognac that were in front of each them.

"Turn and, look there," Billy pointed to the wall behind The Group.

They all turned toward the wall and stared at the huge seal.

"That is the future, my friends. N.W.F.: The New World Federation. The entire world obeying *God's Laws* and *The New Laws* of the world, a world beautiful and fit for all mankind, existing in peace and happiness, far beyond this millennium. May we all perform well during the coming months, as our great tomorrows begin to unfold. Drink to the future: *L'chaim!*"

The lights in the room went out. The seal on the marble wall glowed fiery bright as a powerful orchestral theme swelled in the darkened room. A strobe light flashed and the regular lights returned. The seal behind The Group had vanished. In its place was the elevator door.

"Gentlemen and lady, this meeting's over. Collings will show you back to Hurricane House, and I will see you all for an early breakfast, 7 a.m. sharp. Then you're all off to your own hometowns to vote for good ol' Billy. May God bless you all. I bid you a good night."

The Group members slowly moved toward the elevator. As Collings got up from the table, Billy leaned forward and whispered to him. "I just love that. It's like real magic! Rob Collings, you do amuse me."

When The Group members reached the elevator door, they each looked back at the table. Billy was gone; Collings staging completed.

The Group, safely back in their rooms, slept well—thanks to the cognac consumed during the toast in the hidden room—and Dr. Osher's time-release sedative formula.

That night, they each dreamed the same dream. A vision of the future as Billy had described it came to life in their dreams and it seemed God himself spoke directly to them. The voice of God in the dream instructed them each that this was a very private communication. They each were warned not to talk to anyone about it. Their dreams were filled with beautiful images; a fairy-tale wonderful reverie, full of warmth and comfort. Each awakened with even more confidence than before, believing that the world was going be a better place because of Billy's grand plans.

Billy was not present at breakfast the next morning. Collings and Harrison acted as hosts. Everyone wanted to talk about their vivid dreams, but no one spoke or broke the covenant made with the voice. Some of them thought that it could have been a sign, or some sort of prophesy; or merely the after-effects of a "well-oiled," marvelous weekend. All were full of inspiration and renewed faith in their shared cause.

Collings cut the conversations short. He got them into their limos on time and sent them off to their hometowns so they could vote for Billy and the New Third Party.

# 11

## *ELECTED*

Unknown to The Group, the Third Party presidential candidate was already in Washington, DC. Billy, Suzzanne and their two sons had left after the meeting with The Group and were staying in the Presidential Suite at the very elegant Capitol Arms Hotel. It was a nice gesture by the management on Election Day. Billy hoped everyone in the country voted with the same kind of conviction at the polls.

The Johnstone family arose early that morning and enjoyed a quick breakfast in the suite, exuding a quiet happiness laced with a natural dash of anxious anticipation. After a silent meal, Suzanne and the boys slipped away to get dressed for the big day. Billy had a press conference at 10 a.m., scheduled to be held in the suite.

Collings arrived not long after and set up the room, flanking the main entrance to the suite with metal detectors and screening machines before he briefed his security staff and the Secret Service men. Under Collings' direction, two of his armed security guards always answered the door. In the halls, two Secret Service men flanked the door. Closed circuit TV cameras panned the hallways. All of the window glass in the suite had been removed and replaced with bullet resistant glass. A special alcove was erected just inside the main door to the suite. It was made of four-inch steel plate with small one-way glass portholes. It was bomb proof. When a person entered this small security area, an outside steel door locked behind them and bomb detection equipment went to work. Once inside this special bomb-proof enclosure, you'd better be a friend of the Third Party!

Only the major networks and wire services would attend this private press session. A little before 10 a.m., the media began to arrive. Cameras, recording equipment and reporters were all thoroughly checked with metal detectors and the press IDs carefully scanned and verified. Collings took no chances at this stage of the game. Barnston briefed the reporters. All was in perfect readiness. Now, they waited for Billy.

The door opened. Billy shook hands with a few of the reporters in the front and waved his hellos to the others. He had a way of working a crowd so that everybody felt that he had greeted each of them personally. "Well, good morning. I'll make this brief. I firmly believe that we're gonna win. And, if we do lose, it'll be okay, 'cause the rooms are paid for the night!"

They all laughed comfortably.

Billy looked at a small card and mumbled out loud. "Hmm, let's see. Statement first, questions last...okay."

Billy looked out at the reporters and then he looked down, referred to some notes and took off his reading glasses. "Well, this is it. This is the day we've all been working so hard for. This is the day the free people of the United States of America have their bloodless revolution—that's what Jefferson called it—and a damned good idea, too. Every four years you keep the guy if he's done a good job, or fire him if he hasn't. Great idea. Exactly the way it should be. I said should be, 'cause it hasn't been that way for a while. Oh, we get a new Republican or a new Democrat, but both parties have had so much crossover here in Washington that the results remain the same...nothing much ever gets done. Well, that's what we've been showing and telling the people in this country all these months and if they heard us and they believed us, then this time they're gonna get a whole new party that will once again represent the citizens of America. Then we'll see some action in this old Capital city...now we'll see some action. On this important Election Day, I pray that God will bless America and her people with just one more chance to do it better. Amen. Okay, your turn. Go for the throat, boys and girls!"

The hands all shot up together, but Helen Morganstern, the venerable old reporter known as the "Warhorse of the White House," a veteran of more presidential campaigns then any of the others, spoke out loudly. She always had to have the first question, and the press corps respectfully allowed her that well-earned privilege.

"Billy, are you sure you're going to win?"

"Helen, my dear, somehow, I knew you would be the one to ask that question! Well, sweetheart, if it's what the public wants, we will win. Didn't like that, huh? Okay. I'll try again. You'll like this one. To you, Helen, I dedicate this answer and the rest of you can use it if you quote it in its entirety. Quote: 'Helen Morganstern, my old dear friend, we will not only win, but it will be the biggest landslide of any election, in the history of this country.' End quote. You know, that ought to hold you. What else could you people ask in the face of an answer like that? Wait until tonight, when the opposition throws in the towel. I'll give you more then and we'll all have a glass of champagne and celebrate our victory together in the ballroom here at the Capitol Arms!"

Billy had them laughing like an audience for a stand-up comic, but he knew that he had to leave them wanting more. It was the shortest press conference he had ever given, but they did get the few minutes with Billy that Barnston had promised them.

Suzanne and the boys came out and surrounded their father. Billy slipped his arm easily around Suzanne's waist, Wilhelm and Tommy assuming their positions on either side of their father beaming calm smiles for the cameras.

"Well, boys and girls, that's it. You know my message, you've all heard it enough in the last few months on the road with us. Just refer to the quote I gave Helen. Now be good guys and gals and get out of here so the family and I can unwind, tune in the election returns on TV, and I can get back to writing that acceptance speech for tonight's press meeting."

They all laughed again. Every one of the reporters stopped to shake Billy's hand. They all left him with smiles on their faces.

Suzzanne, glowing and ever the hostess, saw each reporter to the door, past Collings' security detail lining the walls. After everyone had left, she turned back to Billy. "May I get you something, sweetheart?" she asked.

"How about a good old chocolate malted? They make 'em great here. And ask for extra malt in mine. Hey boys, want a malt?"

Wilhelm and Tommy were busy watching the election coverage on the six screens set up in the sitting room. Wilhelm, 34 years old, had been Billy's *protégé* since graduating college. Wilhelm was slated to take command of WFJ industries should his father become president. Tommy, six years younger than Wilhelm, was completing doctorates in both business administration and cognitive science at Harvard.

Billy had not moved in time with his sons. To him—and most frustratingly for them—Wilhelm and Tommy were still little boys in need of his constant care, stern tutelage and watchful eye. "Hey, you two. Do you hear me?"

The boys looked up at the sound of their master's voice.

"Wha ... what, Dad?"

"Do you guys want a malted? Okay? Chocolate or vanilla?"

They responded together. "One of each, eh? All right, Suz, that's two chocolate, one vanilla for us guys and whatever you and Hilga want, babe."

Suzzanne ordered the malts from room service and the boys returned to watching the election news on TV. Suzzanne and Hilga went over the notes for the victory party. Billy continued to type on his laptop computer trying to finish his speech. It was the perfect scene of a happy family together at home.

As the day moved along, people again and again attempted to invade the serenity of Billy's quiet domesticity. All afternoon the phone continued to ring. Rob Collings answered and screened each call, but some of the calls had to be given to Billy. Now and then someone came by in person to speak with the candidate.

The afternoon turned into evening. The returns were looking impossibly good for Billy and the Third Party. The suite was now full of people. Every member of The Group was present.

On the various screens around the room, election results came in, the details superimposed over the faces of the TV newscasters: shots of people in the election booths, campaign posters, people in the streets, the U.S. flag.

After a long evening, the final result: Billy had won the election with the largest vote, both popular and electoral, in American history!

In anticipation of Billy's win, Barnston had produced a film tribute to honor Billy's election, which had been distributed to all the major networks and cable companies: clips of the campaign; the great red, white and blue train; the whirlwind airplane tour of every state; all the wonderful moments of the long and eventful campaign were beautifully crafted into one great homage, to Billy.

In the hotel room, there was ecstasy, excitement, and jubilation. Collings instructed Billy and all of the people in the room to follow him down to the ballroom for Billy's official acceptance speech. As they left the suite, the government Secret Service men surrounded Billy and joined Collings' security men in moving the new president safely to the ballroom. Between the Secret Service and Collings' security force there was one armed guard for every three people in the room.

The assembled press had been waiting in the ballroom with several hundred people for many hours. Billy walked through the crowd shaking hands and smiling.

They shouted, "Bil-ly! Bil-ly! Bil-ly!" The noise was overpowering.

Billy mounted the dais and held up his hands for the crowd to be silent. He was the picture of a winner: unruffled; confident; commanding. As the crowd quieted down, he answered a call from the audience. "No. No party tonight for me. I won't stay very long, just want to sleep. You know, five- or six-thousand people—my family, friends and supporters—celebrated our victory with me just two days ago. Some of you were there, and if not, I'm sure you saw or heard about that party. We've had such confidence in our plans and in the American people since the beginning that we knew we were going to win and you know what, y'all didn't let us down. I told you we could do it, and we did it. And we did it well. Thank the Lord in Heaven, we did do it!"

The crowd cheered and cheered.

Billy motioned for quiet again. "The American people are running the show here in Washington now and I'm not waiting until January to go to work. The office of Billy F. Johnstone, President of the United States of America will be open tomorrow morning for business at 9a.m., sharp. I want to hear from all of you. You can reach me by calling 1-800-OUR-PREZ. That's 1-800-654-4439, 1-800-OUR-PREZ, or 1-800-654-4439 or if you forget, just check with the 800-information operator. You can write to tell me your ideas by addressing your letters to President William F. Johnstone, White House, Washington, DC, that's all, don't worry, I'll get it—I think they still exist! The First Lady and I are going to have a little champagne to toast our victory, chat with a few of you, and then we're going to get some sleep. And that's what I suggest for all of you here in the ballroom and all of you in your homes out there across our great nation. We've all done a great job today, so get some rest tonight, 'cause to-morrow we begin to clean house and rebuild this great land of ours, and I'm going to need every one of you to help me do it. No more speeches 'cause from now on, everything's gonna be all right, and that's my promise! And to all our friends and fellow Americans, from my family and myself I thank you for your faith and support. I love you all. May God bless America and protect every one of you. Sleep well, my friends. Goodnight!"

And that night, Billy's family and the country did sleep better than it had for many years.

Just as he had had promised, the next morning Billy was on the line to listen to callers at 9 a.m. sharp. Billy allowed thirty seconds to hear the subject matter from each caller. Working with the efficiency of a telephone operator at the old AT&T, after Billy heard the theme of the call, he would then relay the call to the appropriate future Cabinet member.

Billy had already appointed his Cabinet. They were the elite Group that got him elected, and now he immediately put them all to work. Each Cabinet member would in turn hear more on the subject and forward the call to one of their own staff people. That staff person would enter a synopsis of the caller's comments into a computer terminal, thank the person, and go to the next call. The operation was a giant telephone fulfillment room and the activity and energy was high and the response, because of the media coverage, was fantastic. This was another clever David Barnston idea designed to get major results, and it worked perfectly.

It wasn't necessary for Billy to answer the phones, but the media covered this first day, and Barnston wanted it to look good. Billy and his staff worked from 9 a.m. to 9 p.m. the first day, having lunch and dinner brought in. At the end of the day it was reported that Billy had talked with over 500 Americans himself in the first twelve hours of operation, and he promised the media to be back on the lines the next day for more of the same.

After the first few days, a caller would reach that 800 number and would be automatically patched to special communications equipment that answered:

"This is President Billy Johnstone. I'm so busy that I can't have a long conversation with you right now, and I don't want to waste your time. I've got lots of folks to talk to today, so go ahead and tell me what you think we should do to help the country get better, then push the star button on your phone. That'll show me you're finished. Go ahead now. I'm listening, so start talking."

The caller would say what they had to say and then the "Billy" recording would come back.

"Well thanks for calling. These lines are lit up like a Christmas tree. Now just hold on, I want to direct this to someone who will get right on it for you, so hold on, and thanks for your help. Call me anytime. It was good talking with you."

By using this very efficient phone system, every caller felt as though he or she had personally talked with Billy and then with a Cabinet member and was being given an opportunity to voice his or her ideas for the future of the country. For the next couple of weeks Barnston's news releases were all about "talking to Billy," "Billy reading the mail," "Billy talking to this group and that group," "Billy visiting factories, farms, bridges, highways, the treasury, the Congress, etc."

The campaigning didn't stop. Billy was the news of the day, every day. He was not going to lose any time waiting for the inauguration.

# 12

## *THANKSGIVING*

Not one to stand on ceremony, Billy called the first meeting of his Cabinet. Even though none of the members of Billy's Cabinet had been confirmed by the Senate, they had been confirmed by Billy and that was all that really mattered to him.

The first Cabinet meeting was held at Hurricane House on Thanksgiving Day. Rob Collings personally delivered the invitations and charged each of the new Cabinet members not to refer to this holiday outing as a Cabinet meeting. It was to be "just a Thanksgiving Day with the President-Elect and his family."

All of the new Cabinet members and their wives and children were invited. To further make this appear to be an innocent holiday affair, many important campaign supporters were on the guest list, as well. Billy flew them all to Louisiana for the holiday shindig at his own expense. This was the first of many highly organized, very secret gatherings for Billy's family and friends. Billy never stopped campaigning.

Once again, Rob Collings and his staff coordinated the entire affair with their usual flawless style. The guests arrived before dawn on Thanksgiving Day without fuss or muss for any of the travelers. Of all the Cabinet members, only Sally Hawthorne, Julio Mondaldo, Henry Gillespie, Irving Penitz were unmarried people, but each of them arrived with a guest for this holiday weekend feast. Dr. Charles Gertz was conspicuously absent. The rest of The Group—the married ones—brought children. Fifty-three kids and thirty Secret Service people, Billy's family, the entire household staff, the Cabinet members and their families as well as other guests—some one hundred sixty-five people—assembled for this fine turkey-day celebration at Hurricane House.

Billy ordered them all to brunch at 10 a.m. Barnston did not allow any media to attend the festivities. Instead, he hired a three-man video crew and two still photographers to cover the affair. He promised fully edited video, stills and information releases each day to service the press. Barnston had complete control of the content, eliminating the confusion and intrusion that normally accompanied reporters and their crews.

Billy was in a jovial mood. No politics yet. He played with the kids and acted the part of the great father-image the campaign created. Finally, he rose from his chair and motioned for them all to stand. "Before we eat, I want to say the prayer. Oh God, we thank you for your blessings and the friendship and camaraderie that prevail in this room at this time. May we all serve our God and the people of the United States of America to our utmost capability. In the name of all that is holy, Amen."

Billy remained standing and motioned for the rest to sit. "This, to me, is one of the greatest blessings that we have in our great country. All of us together, one big happy family, celebrating our thanksgiving to God for the bounty that has been bestowed upon us. I will add only one sour note to this otherwise wonderful occasion. I want you each to remember that there are tens of millions of people in our country and hundreds of millions more in countries throughout the world that cannot enjoy living in this kind of style. The poor, the infirm, the homeless—we must, all of us, commit to helping them out of the hell they are currently living in. They cannot help themselves, so we must help them. It is the task of this administration and the responsibility of all of its members to make the American dream real for all Americans and for all people the world over."

As always, his people responded with applause and sincere "Hear, hears."

"Now, my friends, my family, let us eat this wonderful meal that Hilga and her staff have prepared for us. Enjoy."

The amount and variety of food presented was impressive. By Hilga's high standards, though, it was just a good, but not elaborate, brunch. The main table, which looked so large when The Group of only fifteen sat down for dinner not so long ago, was capable of seating one hundred. Now it was flanked with another long table of one hundred. Both were nearly filled to maximum capacity. A full house. This was the way Billy liked to see it.

After they had all finished eating, Billy rose to speak. "Ladies and Gentlemen, I think that, owing to your travels last night and your early arrival this morning, you should all, the children especially, go to your rooms for a little rest. When you awaken, get dressed and please roam about our home at your leisure. Our house is your house, and you will find many things to amuse yourselves and your children."

He turned to Hilga. "At what time shall we all return here for dinner, Hilga?"

"I think we can have it all ready for you by 6 p.m., Bil-, er, Mr. President. But all afternoon there will be some goodies for the children and snacks and drinks for the adults, too. And Suzzanne, I understand that you have some entertainment for the kids at 4 o'clock?"

The children cheered.

Billy continued. "The indoor swimming pool, the libraries, the game rooms, the TV and video room, the covered tennis courts, they're all for you, my friends. Now get some sleep, and I'll see you later in the day for some more good fun."

Everyone was sure that they should make him the king of the world and not just President of the United States.

All the families began to gather up their kids. Given that Hurricane House was so large and everything so spread out, everyone was given a map that had his or her specific room circled in red.

Because Billy thought they were very special, The Group stayed in the very best rooms at Hurricane House. In these rooms, no cost had been spared and the result was true opulence.

Once again, all of the guests, children included, had been given Osher's sleeping potion. It didn't hurt them, and it helped them to get some rest. It also afforded Professor Osher and his team the opportunity to perform the medical examinations on those people that were yet to be cataloged in Billy's computer. These medical exams, as well as those performed on The Group, were designed for the gathering of general health information, which was to be added to the existing computer files on everyone visiting that day. These dossiers were kept on everyone who worked for, or was associated with, the new administration.

Billy wanted to know everything about everybody, and he needed it to be available on-demand. His massive computer system gave him all that information at the touch of a finger. Billy began gathering this data many years ago. Now he had every employee in every one of his companies, worldwide, in that computer. Over the years he had also gathered information about everyone he ever met or even had a casual curiosity about.

As Billy's business grew, so did the GIF, his personal "General Information Files." By using the GIF he could find out everything, from birth to the present moment, about any requested person. No one except Billy and Collings had access to these files.

A staff of fifteen correlated all incoming information and entered new data on a daily basis. The amount of detail on each person was staggering. Photos, fingerprints, voiceprints, blood samples, DNA reports, as well as extensive personal and family information had been gathered on each individual from infancy, to what they had for breakfast yesterday.

Now that he was president, Billy's computer would be linked with all computer systems operated by the U.S. government and even more information would be available to him. But, in many ways, the GIF program was better than the government's files. It was constantly being updated and had much more specific depth.

Early that afternoon, one by one, the guests began to awaken. They were totally unaware that they had been poked, prodded, examined, and cataloged while they slept. They all felt refreshed. Since most of them had never been to Hurricane House, they were anxious to explore this huge mansion and all the amenities it had to offer.

Hurricane House was the ultimate dream home. There were eighty-five sleeping rooms, the immense dining room, an indoor-outdoor swimming pool, a fresh water trout stream and a salt-water lagoon, each filled with fish and crustaceans for the dinner table. Huge hydroponic gardens grew all of the vegetables and herbs used at Hurricane House. The electricity was completely provided by solar, wind, and tidal-driven hydroelectric power. Some distance away from the main house were barns for cows, pigs and poultry—all naturally fed—thus allowing for the freshest of meat, eggs, and dairy products to be provided for the guests. In another building was an industrial style meat and vegetable processing room for Hilga's huge commercial-sized kitchen. All of the food was prepared under her direction. The chefs and cooking staff in her service rivaled those in any five-star hotel.

Hurricane House's general amusement area had everything—a billiards room, bowling alley, a card and chess room, a ping-pong and air hockey room, an indoor rifle and handgun range, and an archery range, all of which guaranteed plenty of fun, even in bad weather.

For the little ones, a large preschool room was available, as well as a huge video arcade and a cartoon theater that played all the best animated shows for the delight of all.

The music and movie room provided plush, comfortable, custom-designed theatre-style tall-backed seating with attached little tables and built-in audio/video controls and stereo speakers in the headrests for viewing films or listening to music. The bar in this room also served soft drinks and snacks. If you couldn't find something to do at Hurricane House, then you really weren't trying at all.

Precisely at 5 p.m., a chime sounded in all the playrooms. It was followed by Suzzanne's pleasant voice over the intercom system announcing that all were to come to the big hall for Thanksgiving dinner no later than 6:30 p.m. The exodus back to the bedrooms began as mothers and fathers began rounded up their children to get them bathed and dressed for dinner.

Promptly at 6:30 p.m., the guests arrived in the big hall to find an orchestra playing bright standard tunes. Two men dressed in Pilgrim garb greeted them at the doors and alternately called out their names. A waiter then escorted each couple or family to the appropriate seats at the big tables.

Suzzanne and Billy walked alone, in opposite directions around the tables, greeting every guest as the servers filled their glasses with water. The carefully choreographed promenade by Billy and Suzzanne brought them to the far end of the tables at almost the same time. Here they were seated in high-backed chairs at a long table situated on a raised dais. With a son on either side they appeared to be true royalty.

The President remained standing as the assembled guests and staff grew silent. "This is the biggest family gathering we've ever had in our home—the biggest gathering of any kind, in fact. Suzzanne and

I are just about to burst with happiness as we see all these wonderful families and all the little guys and gals and all the love you have for each other. I'd like to say the prayer now. Lord, these are the soldiers of your new army. These men and women are going to clean up and rebuild your world. I ask you to shine your countenance on all of us. We thank you for this fine time of fellowship that we are enjoying today and for the good food of which we are about to partake. God, please bless us all and in the name of all that is holy, Amen. My family welcomes you to Hurricane House and wishes you bon appetit. Hilga, let this meal begin."

On that cue from Billy and a sharp order barked from Hilga the orchestra played, the servers sprang to life, and serving carts began to roll around the mammoth tables.

The first carts had huge glass bowls filled with beautiful cut lettuce and greens in a garden vegetable salad served with condiments and some of Hilga's wonderful secret-recipe dressings.

Following behind the salads were the beverage servers. With sixteen carts in use, four starting at each corner of the table, the guests were all served wine or their chosen beverage.

On cue, the first salad plates were removed from the guests simultaneously. The serving procedure was repeated for the main course. This time sixteen giant roaster carts, each filled with carved turkey, glazed ham, sliced leg of lamb and prime roast of beef, fried and scalloped oysters began the march around the tables. In a parade, these meat carts were directly followed by an equal number of carts filled with steaming side dishes of mashed potatoes, sweet potatoes, green beans, peas and mushrooms, carrots, asparagus, stewed tomatoes, corn on the cob, small squashes and quantities of white butter sauce, cheese sauce, and hollandaise sauce to accompany the vegetables.

The diners now understood the huge platter size plates that were in front of them. They could have any or all of the items offered and these big plates were just right for such a feast.

Billy had installed a few novel ideas on his mammoth dining table. Each of these plates corresponded with an induction coil built into the table. Without becoming dangerously hot, each of the plates full of food remained warm throughout the meal. Pressing a button on the side of one's chair illumined a light on the back of the chair and a transmitter registered a bell-tone in the serving kitchen. A waiter then arrived at the side of the guest within seconds. This "waiter alert system" was seldom used by any guest, as Hilga insisted that her servers stand at attention behind the guests so as to observe and anticipate needs before a request could be made. Hilga felt that no one should have to ask for anything at Billy Johnstone's house.

The sumptuous meal finally finished. Everyone was stuffed. As the platters were cleared away, more soft beverages, cognac, port, coffee, and tea were poured. Then, with groans of pleasure from the diners, carts of pumpkin, apple, cherry and mince pies topped with mounds of ice cream or whipped cream were served.

Billy stood up and raised his glass. The room quieted down. "My friends, I hope you are enjoying this fine meal. Hilga has outdone herself. Folks, I want you to meet the lady that keeps this fat belly on me and who plans and implements these great functions for us. It's all her doing, from the kitchen to the game rooms. Hilga is a genius and will be the next White House Executive Chef. She has been associated with me for many, many years. Please thank Hilga Schreyer for this fabulous feast."

The guests applauded in approval.

Hilga waved to them and noticeably blushed.

Billy continued. "Suzzanne and I thank you, too, dear friend. And now a surprise for you all. Right after dinner, each of you is invited to take a moonlight cruise out into the beautiful Gulf of Mexico. After a nice breakfast on board one of our great WFJ ships, we'll have a sport fishing contest tomorrow afternoon. We'll come back here tomorrow night and have a real old-fashioned Louisiana fish fry down on the beach. The first-place winner, for the biggest catch, will receive $1,000 in cash, your fish trophy mounted, and you'll be crowned king or queen of our first annual Thanksgiving weekend fish fry. And we've got prizes for second and third smallest fish, the weirdest fish, and for no fish, too."

Everybody laughed.

"The boats will leave at 10 p.m. tonight. Just pack deck shoes, long pants, a windbreaker and toiletries. You'll find a little bag in your room. If you can't pack it in that bag, don't bring it. And Mom is going along, too, Dad. This is a romantic overnight out in the moonlight, with some fine wine, in your own cabin, with the boat lightly swaying. It'll be a night to remember. And don't worry, Mom, everything's gonna be all right, 'cause we've got baby sitters lined up for all of the kids. This is supposed to be a vacation, y'all. Well, before I talk myself to death again, I'll let you finish your dessert."

Later, all of Billy's guests boarded four shiny WFJ buses and were transported from Hurricane House through the bayous, down the dark two-lane road to the docks. It was a short, merry ride of only five minutes before they reached the Gulf and saw the four, 150-foot cruisers. The ships were silhouetted against the moon and the soft blue lunar light gave the old dock a movie-like appearance. Billy was right. It was an enticing and romantic setting. Everyone excitedly boarded the boats.

The Secret Service, in concert with Collings' security, were instructed to act as stewards, helping the guests with their luggage. Just as when they entered Hurricane House, they were again directed through the metal detectors. The happy travelers noticed the scrutiny and the tight security. It was a bother, but it gave them a sense of confidence, too.

Once aboard, the sleek boats glided powerfully into the moonlit waters. Only a few of the guests remained awake. The Thanksgiving Day party had fatigued most of them, but the dreamy environment of these luxurious boats was stirring. In some of the private cabins on each ship, the lovemaking went on far into the night.

The four cruisers moved effortlessly through the calm waters in a southward direction. After an hour, each boat began to take a separate course to its appointed fishing grounds. Upon arrival at the designated site, the crews set out the sea anchors for the night.

But one of the boats continued to move on. Unknown to its passengers this boat was headed back toward the Gulf coastline. It had charted a new course. North by Northeast. Everyone on board but the crew was sound asleep. It was no accident that Collings had put Billy and himself and all of the members of The Group onto one boat and the Group's wives and single companions onto another.

In the morning, as the people on the other boats started their fishing adventure, The Group was to have a different kind of escapade.

# 13

## THE COMPLEX

The members of The Group awakened the next morning and saw through the windows of the huge yacht that they were in a sort of tunnel, with no idea where they were. Some of those who were part of the Inner Circle knew quite well their location, but pretended to be as curious as their uninformed counterparts.

A steward delivered a memo to each room. It was from Billy, informing them that they should all be dressed and assembled in the dining salon of the yacht by 8:30 a.m. Quickly they dressed and assembled in the salon for coffee, juice, fresh fruit, and Danish and engaged in speculation about the location of the boat.

Billy came into the room. "Lady and Gentlemen, you have been kidnapped and are now my prisoners."

For a moment, The Group members didn't know how to react.

Then Billy smiled. That damned Johnstone humor. With Billy's straight face, you never knew if he was kidding or not. "You are now at the location of one of my most secret experimental laboratories. This is where Dr. Charles Gertz lives and works. You have been brought here today—as part of this holiday vacation—to have a tour of the areas that can be visited and participate in a brief but important meeting. We will be fishing, as promised, by noon. Then it's on to a fine fish fry on the beach tonight. Now, let's all go topside. I'll act as your tour guide for a while. Follow me, please."

The morning sunlight streamed brightly into the tunnel. As they moved along the deck and down the ramp, it grew darker.

Billy continued. "Looking aft, you see water. Can't tell you what water it is—secret place, you know. As you can see, we're in a tunnel. This is the docking area and the little bay out there is deep enough to accept a large ocean-going ship, or even a submarine—the latter of which I don't own. That is, until recently."

The President's remark elicited some nervous laughter.

"Now let's go inside and see the sights."

This was quite a treat. More was being revealed of the mysterious life that surrounded Billy. They all moved down the gangway from the boat and along the dark underground dock. The tunnel was surely big enough for a submarine. They stopped at what appeared to be the heavy metal doors of an elevator. Collings inserted a key in a panel box and opened the lid. He punched in some code numbers and placed his palm on the sensor. The massive elevator doors slowly opened.

As they entered the car, Sally Hawthorne noticed that the elevator doors were at least a foot thick. She tapped her knuckles on them and quickly realized that they were solid stainless steel and were set on tracks behind two feet of concrete. "Blast proof. The place is a god-damned fortress!" she thought.

This man had masterfully prepared for his greatness. He did everything in a big way. Billy was fast becoming a god to many and her dreams of sitting on a throne of power with him were growing stronger and stronger. She felt a little foolish pretending to an adolescent crush on Billy, and wondered if he could keep his composure around her when Suzzanne was at his side.

The elevator stopped and the inside doors opened quickly. They had traveled up what seemed like several floors and were still surrounded by concrete. No windows and only one solid steel door faced the elevator. Sally's curiosity level was high. What really went on in this place?

Collings went to the door, inserted a key in a control box, punched the code and laid his open palm on the sensor. The door did not open. To his left, machinery sounded and a section of the wall opened. Collings smiled. "Cute, huh? We don't want just everybody to get in here, you see."

They walked through the opening in the wall. Inside, a second steel door opened with a swipe of Collings' card and allowed them to enter a large room filled with obviously very high-tech computer equipment.

Charles Gertz was standing across the room. He saw them and ran to greet them. "Billy, Rob, everybody, so glad you came to see me. I have missed you all. I apologize for not appearing at the Thanksgiving fest, but I had to stay on this thing and, Billy, its finished. All set and in production. It's..."

Billy nodded, shutting him up in mid-sentence. "Well yes, Charles, that's good. Will you be so kind as to take The Group on a little tour of this area? Collings and I must leave you for a while."

Charles smiled in agreement.

Billy addressed the rest of them. "Afterwards, Rob will come fetch you and we'll all hike around and see some more. By the way, we've got a nice brunch planned for you, too!"

Charles took over. "All right people, this way, please."

Charles took them to a large table upon which several electronic devices were laid in a row. "As you all know, five years ago WFJ Polybiotech won a contract to produce a special card for the government for use in the National Health Care System. After the 2001 9/11 disaster, the administration wanted to use our exceptional system as a

National Identification Card, which would certify that a person was a valid U.S. citizen, aiding the Immigration and Naturalization Service. As you know, the National ID plan was approved by Congress and the President and millions of these cards have been manufactured and are being distributed. It is quite a special design. Once the card is encoded, it cannot be altered without destroying the integrity of the card itself. It is made of several layers of plastic film. The interior film layers have been uniquely sensitized so that when the card is first activated it is actually exposed to an infrared light and the documenting unit burns in a special new type of bar code. This is the USCBC, United States Citizen Bar Code, and it's permanently etched into these film-like layers. The bar code will contain the social security number of every U.S. citizen."

Charles smugly continued. "But let me tell you a little more about it. This bar-coded card also has a wafer-thin microchip that will soon replace all other personal cards—Social Security, insurance cards, driver's licenses—and other forms of identification. The chip will be able to hold hundreds of pages of information and when asked, will access the National Computers. As you know, all of the major credit card companies are currently being merged into the FCA, the Federal Credit Alliance, which, of course, will be controlled by the government. This same NIC card will soon be used for all credit purchases and banking services that had formerly been handled by the many separate credit card companies. Real system streamlining, eh? Now let me show you how this nifty baby works."

Charles moved to a small unit on the table and inserted a card. "This is a retail reader. It is very inexpensive and is currently being used in banks, retail stores, gas stations and just about every place that currency or credit transactions are used. When you shop at your grocery, for example, it will activate your bank account, withdraw dollar credits, and then transfer the amount required to satisfy your transactions."

Felix Hansen, Billy's computer-wiz, interrupted. "Of course, this is the very beginning of the cashless society that we've all been talking about for years. Hopefully, it soon will be in effect."

"Exactly, Felix. And high time, too, I might add. It will totally eliminate the underground economy, reducing crime in every way and will also make all of our very complicated lives that much easier."

Charles directed them to the next chassis on the long table.

Felix in his zeal continued. "This unit is presently installed in every police car in every city and town in the United States, Canada, Mexico, and most of Latin America. When the NIC card is placed in this unit, it calls up a photo ID and basic personal information, such as Social Security number, name, age, marital status, height and weight, current residence address, telephone number, make and model and license number of your car, insurance carrier, place of employment, work status, your work supervisor's name and telephone number, your closest relative and their telephone number, your doctor, your blood type, and medication particulars, etc.

"Of course, it will report any criminal record status and any, warrants, restraining orders or other criminal information. This is all brought up immediately when the card is inserted in the unit. The law official can also request a list of credit and debit transactions that you may have made over the last seven days. Since you'll have to punch in at work to verify your employment, citizenship and health benefits, and since you'll also be using it for gasoline, public transportation, toll booths, groceries, movies, rentals, etc., this will allow the officer to observe your activity during those previous seven days. These units are plugged into the FOSDCN system. That's the 'Fiber-Optic-Satellite-Delivered-Computer-Network.' By cross-checking the NIC card for any civil or criminal 'flags' that might exist on that individual, anywhere in North—and soon, Central and South America—all that could be known about that individual will be known, almost instantly!"

Felix smiled proudly and added, "And should we ever want to

find you—find your body—then we just reverse the procedure. Your chip has your Social Security number and when it is entered into any computer in the FOSDCN network and an information/location check is requested, the FOSDCN and its eyes in the sky will scan the entire continent—and soon the world, if requested—and find you standing right here, even in this group. Show them how it works, Charles."

"Right. Uh, Sally. Give me your NIC card, please."

Sally fished in her purse and gave the card to Charles.

Charles inserted the card in a reader attached to a computer terminal. The Group watched intently. Very soon, the word "FOUND" appeared on the screen. Charles spoke to the machine: "Location, please."

The computer responded with "LOCATION-CLASSIFIED!"

Charles gleefully answered back. "Right. Quadrant identification, please."

The computer showed a latitude and longitude grid over the Gulf of Mexico and the same "LOCATION-CLASSIFIED!" blinked on the screen.

"That shield will keep our competitors and enemies from finding us. But you can see how well it works. In fact, if we weren't in a classified area it would give the exact location. And I mean exact. The information would include the city, state, address, cross streets, telephone number if there is one, and even tell us which side of the room you're on. We can further identify those who may be with you. It's really awesome, believe me. With this thing you can run, but you can't hide anymore and that's for sure!"

Charles gave the card back to Sally. "And now I would like to..."

Collings appeared and interrupted. "Sorry, Charles. I've got to take them to the next cage in the zoo. See you in an hour for brunch. Don't forget."

They said goodbye to Charles and followed Collings to the other side of the computer area. Collings performed the security procedure and they gained entry to still another solid steel door, and traveled down a long, windowless hall. When all of The Group had entered the narrow access, the door slammed shut behind them.

"Imagine what could happen to you if I left you in this vault. If I didn't like you, I mean." Collings laughed sardonically, delivering a fair imitation of Vincent Price.

At the end of the tight hallway, after another door and more codes, they emerged into an even larger work area. "This is the bioelectric/biomechanical laboratory. Charles could tell you all about this, but he won't because it's highly classified. So, look at what you will as we walk through, but do not touch anything and don't speak to the workers. Be invisible, please."

The place was straight out of science fiction. It appeared as though there were many projects in development, although it was difficult to determine just what those projects might be. Professor Osher approached them as they walked along one of the aisles. Osher was dressed in a white lab coat and hardhat and was intently pouring over papers on a clipboard. He did not see Collings and the rest. They all watched as Osher placed his hand on a sensor and entered an area marked "Biological Contamination Area—Senior Authorized Personnel Only."

Henry Gillespie asked, "What's in there, Rob?"

"Just what it says on the door, Hank. We can't go in there, either."

Irving Penitz quipped, "It's where they keep the bodies, Toddy."

Ignoring Irving's remark, Collings motioned The Group to move on through the security door at the rear of the area, and then down another long, concrete hallway.

Sally squealed with an imitation whine and called out. "Rob! You won't leave us in this dark hallway all alone, will you?"

These comedians were beginning to annoy him. "If I did, you would never find your way out of this maze and you'd suffocate and die and rot." Getting no response, Collings moved right along. "Seriously, sometimes it even confuses me. Billy and Charles are the only ones, I think, who have been in every sector...maybe Osher, too. It's much bigger than it looks and Billy and Charles keep on building more and more work areas."

Felix Hansen agreed. "This is all a first for me. I've only been in the computer laboratory, the dining room, and the meeting room. And I've worked for WFJ for over 14 years. Billy likes to keep his secrets, secret."

Sally wondered just where this complex was located. How far could they have traveled from evening to dawn and in which direction did they travel? She was sure Billy would tell her if she asked him. She believed he never kept her in the dark about anything.

They walked through and around areas called "Nuclear Chemistry," "Laser Research," "Solar Energy," "Astrophysics," "Superconductors," and then past a door simply labeled "Biogenetics." They were all impressed with the immensity of the factory. They soon realized this was how Billy had attained his billionaire status.

The Group boarded a very long, narrow escalator that took them single file, almost vertically, up to another dead-end chamber. Collings put his palm on the concrete and a section of the wall opened.

Next, they passed through a metal door and then suddenly emerged into brilliant sunlight.

They were outside on a terrace. The Group all stopped together and shielded their eyes from the bright sunlight. A neatly attired staff person came to them with a box of sunglasses.

They surveyed the view. It was magnificent. The ocean, or gulf or lake was the backdrop in front of the cliffs where they were standing. Looking down from the terrace it was clear that they were probably more than hundred feet above the water. From this vantage point one could view the sides of the mountain and apparently, what they were standing on was an island or possibly a large rock that came up out of the body of water. Or maybe it was a peninsula.

Looking down, nothing could be seen of the tunnel entrance where they had come in on the boat, just the waves slapping at the rocks below. It appeared to be smooth cliff walls on all sides, with no openings. In back of them and rising another hundred or so feet above, were more ragged rocks blocking the view of what might be behind them. Was it more water or more land?

A voice called to them. It was Billy's son, Wilhelm, waving them over to the outdoor table and chairs.

"He is such a good-looking guy," Sally thought. "I really haven't talked much with him. He doesn't seem to be as on the ball as his father. But, he does own the company now. Who am I kidding? Billy's still the boss."

"Well, Group," Wilhelm called out. "What do you think of the complex?"

Avery Harrison spoke first. "Wilhelm, this is a most amazing place. I've seen several of the other operations that your family owns. All of this very up to the minute technology, the place itself, well it's like going into another time, a visit to the future. Something out of Bradbury or Heinlein, and I'm sure I haven't seen the half of it!"

Irving Penitz agreed. "Willy, I've been your dad's attorney for more than twenty years. In that length of time I have personally reviewed every bit of information that is concerned with his holdings, and I never found a hint of the location of this operation or what it does. It's utterly fantastic. How did he keep it a secret?"

Before Wilhelm could answer, Collings smiled. "Irv, if you ever wondered what it is I really do, well Billy hired me 'cause I know how to make things disappear. This was one of my better tricks, don't you agree?"

Many members of The Group felt as if Collings was always spying on them. And in truth, he was. Rob never allowed anyone to really get to know him. Being detached was part of his job, too, they guessed.

It was his business to make people nervous. Because of that, he was a hard man to like.

Billy arrived at the table and a marvelous brunch rolled out. As the very good French champagne was being poured they began to chat a bit about all they had seen that day. Fine chilled Russian caviar was served with assorted toasts on icy cold little silver trays. That *amuse-bouche* was followed by an intriguing salad and a delicious grilled "mystery" fish. Lastly came a wonderful assortment of fresh fruits. Even though none of the guests knew exactly where they were at the moment, the flavor of this meal hinted somewhat at tropical islands.

Before the meal ended, Billy spoke. "Gentlemen and lady, this is my other world, the place I go to discover new vistas. Few outsiders have ever been here. I am honored to have you as my guests today. I look at your faces now and I see new looks of interest. You are all growing strong, getting ready for the big job. We are the best. And we will do the greatest work ever seen in the history of this great country. We will make achievements only dreamed of a short time ago. You all feel very safe and confident now, don't you?"

They all nodded in agreement.

"Happy and safe and proud of our election win. Well, unfortunately, it's my job not to let you become complacent or smug. Can't rest on our laurels. Should something terrible or catastrophic happen to our country, you are the people that will have to come to the aid of our fellow citizens and solve their problems. Whether our tasks or tests are great or small, that is always in God's hands. Let His will be done. But for now, let us make a toast to our combined health, happiness, and ask our God to give us continued success as we begin this fantastic journey to realize our true destinies."

The brunch ended and one of the stewards took them back through the concrete interior of the complex to an elevator. They traveled down below to the boat, still docked in the tunnel.

When they were aboard the vessel, they were ordered below deck and were told to remain in the main salon until given further notice. Billy, Collings, Harrison, Barnston and Osher were noticeably absent from The Group as the yacht set sail.

After they had been under way for about fifteen minutes, a steward came below, apparently to look in on them. As the steward returned up the steps, the hatchway door stayed open long enough for them to look above and see dark storm clouds brewing in the afternoon sky. The barometer had fallen and the air was calm but becoming cool and clammy.

Julio, Felix, and Sally played poker at a booth near the stairway. They were drinking glasses of whiskey and probably drinking too much, too fast.

Sally turned the music up real loud. She loved the 50s rock-and-roll CD that was playing. It sounded even better to her when it was very loud. She drank shots of Jack Daniels with a beer chaser and got higher with each rocking tune.

Occasionally she'd get up, still holding the playing cards in her hand, throw down some chips, do a couple of sensual turns—bumping and swaying to the rhythm of the music—then sit down and shout "winner" as she threw her cards face up on the table. This infuriated Felix, causing him to swear and pound the table. Julio, however, would just fold his cards and quietly smile. He could care less about winning at cards. Julio was more interested watching Sally.

Gillespie and Penitz sat in the corner, very involved in large water-sized glasses of whiskey and some quiet, serious conversation.

No one noticed Collings descend the stairs. His voice seemed to make them all jump a bit. "Well, I'm glad to see everyone is comfortable down here. Sorry about the 'stay below' order, but the captain tells me we're in for some rough weather. They're all scurrying about up there rigging for the squall. This is definitely the safest place for you to be. The fishing is out, I'm afraid, but there will be plenty to eat tonight at the beach party. As you've noticed, the President is not on board. He stayed behind to finish some work and will fly to Hurricane House later today. He should arrive just about the time we do. In the meantime, amuse yourselves. There are videos galore, plenty of booze and food and stuff to read. Well, you're not children that I have to entertain. I have work to do, too."

Collings poured himself a large glass of whiskey and left them alone once again.

"He certainly is not the genial host his master is, that's for sure," cracked Henry.

The others nodded in agreement.

Henry turned back to his conversation. "Irving, like I was saying, the general influencing of the population is well under way. Welfare will soon be replaced with a new National Works Program. For diligent hard work by both the technocrats and the middle and labor classes, the incentive rewards will issue in the form of credits allowing vacation visits to the great centers of 'Virtual Reality,' i.e., Disneyland, Disney World, Universal City, Las Vegas, Atlantic City, Hollywood, Times Square, Chicago's Old Town, San Francisco, Washington, DC. And as for Denver, Detroit, Philadelphia, Nashville, St Louis, Dallas, New Orleans, Atlanta, Miami...they're all coming online with huge downtown casinos and expanded theme park operations. Fantastic enterprises, Irving, just fantastic."

Irving Penitz took a long draw from his glass. "Amazing undertaking. And the public education—via network TV and cable—is probably the least known and most effective control factor we have. Millions of kids will get the right message every day via cable TV in the classrooms and with the content guidelines in place, soon every form of media will be used to uniformly reinforce the message."

Henry chimed in. "I think we can count on the next generation of citizens to be less violent and more productive. But the crime rate is still high now. Attempts to remove the guns from the citizenry have been almost impossible. More laws and police aren't making a difference, and we can't seem to build enough prisons to hold the huge number of violators. We've got whole tribes of drifters and lawless gangs who have become marauders, committing criminal acts as they please while running from town to town. The police in our country are basically ineffective. Even the military can't keep up with it."

Irving picked up the thread. "Yes. As good as some of the systems are, our real problem is that some people just won't conform. Some of them are true sociopaths. I single out crime, poverty, generational idiocy and basic illiteracy as the biggest problems ol' Billy has to deal with. And that, of course, means we're all stuck with those problems, as well!"

As predicted, the storm arrived. They all stayed below and drank and talked as the boat heaved on through the storm.

Eventually, Collings returned below decks. "We have a message from the President." He clicked on a large wall TV.

Billy appeared on-screen. "Welcome to the open sea. Very unpredictable weather out here, isn't it? Well, I can't join you, but I'm with you in spirit. I would suggest that some of you stop the heavy drink-ing now, so you can enjoy the fine spread you'll have tonight at the fish fry; you'll have plenty to drink then. Tomorrow I'll need your brains fresh and uncluttered. By the way, Irving, I agree with everything you and Henry have been talking about. I'd like to see you both privately in the morning so that I can bring you up to date on some of my plans regarding those problems. Well, *bon voyage*. I'll see you folks tonight."

The screen went dark and the room was eerily silent.

Sally launched the first shot. "Rob, is it necessary for you two to bug everything we do? Will there be no time when we will have privacy?"

Calmly, Collings replied. "Sally—the rest of you, too—try to understand that from the time you agreed to become part of Billy's team, you have been covered by the most elaborate surveillance system ever used, anywhere. In a word, Sally, yes, it is necessary and no, there will not be a time when it isn't necessary as long as you are active in this administration. We are all on probation and will be for a long, long time. Billy's plans call for much secrecy. All of you have become his confidants. Therefore, you must be perfect. It's my job to make sure you remain perfect. So, try real hard, and I will be there to remind you if you fall down. If you were in Billy's position, you would be doing the same thing. Technology allows Billy to sit back at the complex and see and hear what we are doing on board this boat. And he uses that technology. Don't feel bad; he has looked in on the other boats, too, and made a similar broadcast appearance to the people on board. Get used to it. It's the way it is. *C'est la vie.*"

The single boat with The Group on board joined up with the other three vessels and all four boats soon arrived without incident at the Hurricane House docks. The guests had enjoyed a fine day and the festive fish fry turned out to be all Billy had promised.

That evening The Group was very quiet. They didn't even talk to one another. The secrecy and monitoring was fresh in their minds. They each wondered why. They all had the feeling that something was amiss.

The next morning the guests departed. The Group headed back to their respective hometowns to finalize their personal arrangements for the move to Washington.

Billy had ordered that everyone was to be moved into their new residences before Christmas. He wanted to use the high interest of the holiday season to show that his new regime was in place. The media coverage of Billy and his family and friends would certainly serve to eclipse any memories of the old administration.

Barnston had somehow secured agreement from the incumbent president to allow Billy to throw the switch on the big National Christmas tree. This made another mark in the public's mind that Billy was the new President, merely tolerating the old president because of protocol.

David Barnston knew his business. He got the media to cover Billy, Suzzanne and the boys in their hotel suite at the Capitol Arms Hotel. With the fireplace roaring, it looked like the "first family" at home. The hotel had given Billy the Presidential Suite until his inauguration and the press gave Billy more time and space than if he had already been installed in the White House. It was a great Christmas, chock-full of presents for the Third Party.

Billy's New Year's Eve message was the talk of the town, the nation and the world and the global media covered his private party at the Capitol Arms. As the clock neared midnight, Billy went to the bandstand and cued the orchestra to stop playing.

A hush fell over the ballroom.

"No big speeches, my friends and fellow Americans. Just a moment to honor the end of that old political regime. I want to tell you that this coming year will be a bright New Year for us all. It will be a year entered in the history books as bountiful and spectacular. You've sent me to our nation's capital to do a job, a job that hasn't been done here for a long, long time. I promised you a total clean-up, and we all agreed that Americans everywhere want a change in how their government is operated. And now, with the help of God, you're going to get that change."

Billy lifted his glass and with perfect timing said, "Five-four-three-two-one...Happy New Year, my loved ones. Happy New Year, America. Happy New Year, world!"

Billy gave the band a downbeat and they played Auld Lang Syne. Billy and his friends smiled and laughed and sang in the New Year.

This was the start of a great and glorious new chapter for the people of America.

# 14

## *INAUGURATION*

Billy waved from his bright, shiny presidential limousine as the crowds on Pennsylvania Avenue cheered him on. No sight of the protesters or anti-government signs that had lined the streets in past inaugurations. The people were happy with Billy's election, and they showed it.

Billy recited the oath of office and was sworn in on the Capitol steps, just as all of the Presidents of the United States had been before him. As Billy announced his final affirmation to "preserve, protect and defend the Constitution of the United States," the crowd exploded in thunderous applause and cheers.

Billy stood at the podium, looking out on the huge audience assembled below him for this momentous occasion. He felt he was exactly where he was supposed to be. "My fellow Americans. This is the most important day of my life. I have just made the most sacred pledge any American can make. A moment ago, you—the people of the United States—witnessed as I pledged to serve my country to the best of my ability before the Chief Justice of our great country. But, you know, people, when I go to work I want my bosses to personally hear my promise to do good work, and I want it said in my own words. So now I'm going to face you, the people of America—my employers, my bosses—and in addition to the traditional oath, I'm going to declare my own oath of office, and I'm going to use some of the eloquent words used by our founding fathers in their original commitment to our emerging nation."

Billy took a step back, looked up, and then stepped forward looking directly into the camera facing him. "I, William F. Johnstone, do now pledge my life, my fortune and my sacred honor, and with full belief in and a firm reliance upon God and the protection of His divine providence, I do now agree to discharge the duties of my office to the best of my abilities. I now stand before you, the people, and gratefully and humbly accept the great honor of being President of the United States of America. May God almighty bless my efforts."

The crowd roared their approval making it difficult for Billy to be heard.

"You know...You know...Every four years since this country was founded, some man just like myself, has dedicated himself to the honorable and responsible task of helping to govern and guide the people of the United States of America. Some of those men entered this high office in times of peril. Most met with tremendous problems during their tenure as president. Some died—or were even killed—before they could accomplish their missions. None of them started with a clean agenda. Much of what a new president has to deal with on his first day in office are tasks left undone by his predecessor. My job, as your president, will be to bring this country and its people up to their greatest potential, to help us all become, once again, America the beautiful; America, the home of the free and the brave. America, a place where the rugged individual and his good enterprise can still make a difference. America, where hard work and good ethics will pay more than crime and irresponsibility. A caring America where men and women know the benefits of being good mothers and fathers and which will once again create moral families producing fine, decent citizens for the world.

"Yes, my friends, this America, this great country, is in a very big mess. But we can fix it. You sent me here to do this formidable job and with every ounce of strength that is in me, with God's help, I will succeed in accomplishing that task for you, the wonderful people of the United States. God bless you and God bless America!"

The crowd in front of Billy roared their approval and millions of people all across North America roared with them. The people believed their new President wouldn't pull any punches.

Billy and Suzzanne waved at the people and shook hands all the way down to the limousine. As the big car moved forward in the motorcade Billy waved to the crowd wearing his biggest Teddy Roosevelt grin and thought, "Now it all begins. Onward, to the next step."

That night, Billy was more like an emperor than a new president, presiding over the inaugural ball with Suzzanne as his lovely empress, and the ladies in waiting, Hilga and Sally, quietly basking the glow of this special occasion.

It was the first royal ball in Washington in a long time, and Billy wanted it to appear majestic in every way. It was his private belief that stored deep in the DNA of the American people was a longing for a king, a monarch that gave them the wonderful pomp of royal-like events, immersing the people in the opulence and affluence they believed was the true American dream. Billy intended to give them what they wanted. The ballroom reflected the American fantasy of royalty depicted so often in entertainment: military in their finest dress uniforms, ambassadors in swallow-tailed coats and crimson sashes, the Queen of England—replete with crown and jewels—and the Duke of Windsor in full regalia. All of the men wore white tie and tails and only the service help wore tuxedos and black tie. The women's gowns were among the most elaborate and expensive creations ever seen at any affair. A full orchestra played for dancing and another band performed for the fabulous floor show which featured the brightest lights from Broadway and Hollywood.

Again, David Barnston delivered. This first inaugural ball was televised in its entirety. For three full hours, the public watched their new administration having fun. Thirty minutes each hour was solid back-to-back entertainment. The rest of the hour, roving reporters interviewed the guests and offered commentary. Again, the commercial time was sold with all the profits going to feed the hungry. In reality, this gala was sponsored by the new Third Party and was intended to be the continued selling of the new President and his administration—just like cars and beer and cereal. The event was touted as having one of the greatest worldwide audiences in the annals of television.

By the end of the evening, when all of the guests had gone home and viewers in millions of homes throughout the world had turned off their TV sets, everyone knew that they had been to or were part of a fabulous party. This, then, is how the fairytale began.

Early the next morning on his way into the Oval Office of the White House, Billy motioned for his agenda secretary to follow him in and handed him a note. "Here's a list of my Cabinet appointees, Mr. Bobling. Call them now. I will see them for our first meeting in one hour!" Billy then plopped his briefcase on the floor and sat in his chair behind the desk.

"But Mr. President, what about the Senate? They haven't approved any of these people. Is this to be logged as an informal meeting? And it's very short notice, Mr. President."

"First, Mr. Bobling, my personal secretary talked to each of them yesterday. They will all be here. The ones that aren't here are fired! Next, I really don't care what the Senate says, these are the people I want on my team, so they're in! I'll deal with the Senators after I come back."

"Come back? Where are you going? These surprises, Mr. President, you must maintain an agenda. There are certain practices, sir. I realize you're new, but I don't know, I'll have to alert..."

"Goin' away right after the meeting with my Cabinet, Bobling, and I'll be back sometime tomorrow."

"But, Mr. President, I am charged with documenting your whereabouts..."

"That's all anyone needs to know. By the way Bobling, I don't like explaining myself to you. Just do want I tell you to do, and then please record in your log that my first official act was to fire you. Don't be here when I come back."

The agenda secretary's mouth dropped open. He backed out of the office and closed the door.

Billy had personally selected the most brilliant and capable people to be a part of his new administration. This first Cabinet meeting would be unofficial. It was to be a no-work session. They would just talk and get to know one another.

Everyone stood when Billy entered the Cabinet Meeting Room. They remained standing until Billy sat down.

"I will make this short. Today, I want you to work with some of the veteran White House people. They will help you prepare the day-to-day systems that you and your personal staff will be using. They will show you around the White House and familiarize you with your new surroundings. I want you to review your staff selections. Your final staff choices will be entered into the computer systems and official badges and credentials will be printed and issued for you and your people. I will be gone the remainder of the day, but I expect to see you all tomorrow morning, completely outfitted, oriented, and ready for work. I sincerely welcome you all to what will be the most exciting time of your lives. Thank you. This meeting is over."

The President shook hands with each of his Cabinet members and withdrew from the Cabinet meeting room. He walked back to the

Oval Office and found his son, Wilhelm, pacing in front of his father's desk, waiting for him.

"Father, may I speak with you?"

"Of course, son, but make it quick. I have to go." Billy sat on the front of his desk.

"Why was I not appointed to your Cabinet or some other government position?"

"Well, it's quite simple, son. I need you to run the family store. It was my decision alone, and I think I'm right. Disagree?"

"Yes, I do. You know that running the company is just a front job. Charles certainly could handle it. I'm not in charge. Your loyalists still take orders from you and Charles, and always will. I'm not allowed in and don't have clearance for any of the Top Secret areas. Am I not to be trusted? Why haven't you allowed me to actually run WFJ or be involved with this new government?"

"Here goes the truth, Will, and I hope you're ready for it! You drink too much and at the wrong times. Then you talk too much about the wrong things and to the wrong people. You have always made sure everyone knows that your dad is the owner and the boss. Instead of pulling your own weight and gaining your own respect, you've used our kinship to impress people, to get girls to like you. In short, young man, you still have to grow up a bit before I'll put any part of my company—or this country—in your hands. There it is and there it stands. I can't move from that decision until you, not me, make some changes."

Wilhelm was furious. "So, I'm still a kid, am I? Can't be trusted in the 'big man's' world, huh? I do everything you ask of me. Everything! A drunk, a braggart..."

"Willy, stop it. I don't have time for this nonsense. I have to go." Billy started for the door. Wilhelm grabbed his shoulder and turned him back.

"Oh no you don't. You're always too busy to talk. You stay until I'm finished."

Billy pulled Wilhelm's hand away and shoved him.

"Why you old..." Wilhelm swung at Billy. Billy blocked the swing and threw a punch that landed square on Wilhelm's chin, knocking him down. Billy stood glaring down at Wilhelm.

Two Secret Service men burst through the door with their automatic pistols drawn.

Billy shouted at the men. "Get out. This is a family squabble. And stop eavesdropping."

Billy reached down and helped Wilhelm to his feet. "Now look, boy. You do some hard and fast thinking before I come back. Any more acts like this and you'll be barred from the White House—not by me, by my staff. Get it together. I'll be back tomorrow. We'll talk again."

He hugged Wilhelm. "I love you, son. We need to fix these bad feelings and get on with the work ahead for both of us." He let Wilhelm go, grabbed his briefcase and left the Oval office, still shaken.

In the hallway, he was joined by Collings and the Secret Service. Not a word was spoken.

They left the White House by a ground floor exit and walked briskly across the lawn to the waiting Air Force One helicopter. Billy waved the Secret Service men aside and ordered the pilot out of the copter. The head of the Secret Service Protective Detail protested Billy's decision, but Collings interceded and the President's orders were followed. The pilot stood down and a man in civilian clothes entered the cockpit. Billy and Collings got on board and the copter roared off.

After a brief flight, the copter landed at a private airport. Billy and Collings disembarked, shook hands with a new pilot and walked a short distance to a small, unmarked private jet. Within minutes, they were airborne.

Less than two hours later, the plane touched down on a private airfield on the Gulf Coast of Mississippi. The President and Collings stepped down from the jet, walked to the edge of the airfield and into the wet brush to a waiting Land Rover.

Collings drove a short distance cross-country to the beach. There, a small powerboat stood anchored and ready. The two men got into the boat and moved out into the water. Soon, the little boat rounded the coastline and moved out to approach a much larger boat. Billy climbed aboard as a crewman used an electric hoist to lift the small boat from the water and secure it to the moorings.

Billy went forward to the pilothouse. The big diesel engines roared to life and the cruiser moved away. In less than an hour they came to an inlet and the boat glided into the tunnel entrance in the rock face of the shore. They were back at the Complex.

Billy and Collings left the boat and walked up the long dock to the elevator. Once inside, the car quickly moved up six levels and the doors opened to a large, well-furnished apartment. From the window, there was a beautiful view of the glistening waters of the Gulf of Mexico.

Billy took off his shoes and began to disrobe. "All right, Collings give me half an hour to shower and dress. Gather the rest of the men, and we'll meet below decks at 1500 hours, sharp."

Collings saluted, said "Aye, aye, Cap'n," and left the room.

Billy opened a large walk-in closet and got his robe and slippers. He entered the bathroom, closed the door and started the shower. The phone rang. He was immediately irritated. He grabbed the receiver from the shower wall.

"Hello! Sally? How the hell did you get this number? Doesn't matter—it'll be changed after this call. What do you want?"

Billy listened. "Inner Circle? You mean The Group? Well, now get this, lady. I invite whomever I want, whenever I want. I'll let you know when you can travel with me...Yeah. I... If you can't control yourself, then I will...Take it easy. Of course, you're important to me. I'll be back tomorrow. Do your homework and settle down, will you? By the way, whoever gave you this number is in a world of shit with me, and I will find out who it was. In the future, mind your own business and don't get anyone else in trouble! Got it?...Good-bye, Sally."

He hung up the phone and continued his shower, talking out loud to himself. "Good God, this bitch is driving me crazy. Sex. That's what it's all about. Just sex, and that's all. She's great to be with, but if she doesn't back off, she's gonna be history."

After a good shower and shave, Billy dressed. He pulled on his suit coat, put his digital recorder in the inside pocket, took a quick look in the mirror and dashed out the door.

The boardroom inside the Complex was buzzing with activity. The Inner Circle was assembled at the conference table, each person facing a computer monitor. On the wall were three huge TV screens with the letters N-W-F.

The doors burst open and Billy made his entrance. Everyone stood up immediately.

Billy started in right away while walking across the room. "Success can only be accomplished with precise timing, gentlemen. This particular chain of events may never happen again."

Billy sat down in his chair. "Monday morning, I meet with Congress in Washington and then with the heads of all media in New York. Later in the day it's back to DC with the Joint Chiefs of Staff. I will need each of your plans before I leave at 0300 hours. Don't delay my departure. Tell me what you have, so far. Media?"

Barnston stood up. "Mr. President, everything is in order for Monday's media meeting in New York. Julio Mondaldo and his staff are ready."

"Good, and the plan for the Congress, Vice President Harrison?"

"Right. We are still discussing the numbers. Most of us felt that to fool with the Congress all at one time might arouse unnecessary suspicion. Instead, we've dealt with each member individually during this recess period. They'll be assembled again as a whole body tomorrow. So far, we've gotten to over seventy percent of them. But be rest assured, the full operation, the entire Congress and staff, will be completed before the end of the opening day, tomorrow."

Billy smiled. "Okay! And the military, General Fenwick?"

"As the Secretary of Defense, I've ordered the Joint Chiefs of Staff to assemble. They are, of course the first, and then every man jack down the line to the rank of captain. We've got our end well organized and will be ready tomorrow, Mr. President."

"Excellent. Ah, General Fenwick, I'm placing the expansion operations and the total design of that affair under your supreme command. You will answer only to me."

General Fenwick saluted. "Thank you, sir. I'll take care of contingency plans in all sectors. I will personally direct all operations, as ordered, sir."

"Okay! I assume that the internal plans will include dealing with our governors, mayors, chiefs of police, heads of the major corporations, etc., and that will all be accomplished by the end of the week as ordered?"

"Affirmative, sir," General Fenwick replied.

"Barnston, you will personally handle and direct the news media right from the start."

David Barnston nodded yes.

"Professor Osher, Mr. Surgeon General?"

"I have notified the AMA, the CDC, the WHO and the CPB. The heads of those organizations will meet with me tomorrow. My staff and I will handle them directly, sir."

"Where is Charles?"

No one answered.

"I see. Well then, gentlemen, if you handle all as planned, we can avert catastrophe. With God's help, and some good work by all, this will still be the most beautiful springtime any of us has ever seen. Now, do what is to be done. The fate of America is in your hands. Do not fail me! I will turn this meeting over to the very capable hands of Vice President Harrison for final discussions. I'm off to find our elusive, mad scientist, gentlemen."

The men chuckled at his remark.

The President and Collings left the room and went to an elevator to begin the long ride to the most bottom regions of the Complex. Once there, they walked down a long hall to a solid stainless-steel door. Collings punched in a code and pressed his open palm on the reader. Billy also followed the security procedure and the heavy door unbolted and opened. They entered a reception area.

The guard on duty asked for further identification. Satisfied with their credentials, Billy and Collings gained entry and walked to the right of the guard station to another heavy metal door. This door required iris and voice identification as well as number codes and palm prints.

The door didn't open.

An emergency horn sounded its "oog-gah, oog-gah" and a loud alarm bell rang. A recorded message in Dr. Gertz's voice came from a wall speaker. "Your code identification and palm print do not match. You are not known to this system. Security police at this level and throughout the complex have been alerted. WARNING: Remain standing within this yellow floor area for your own safety. Lasers have been activated. Movement of any kind may result in injury or death. I repeat: WARNING: Remain standing within this yellow floor area for your own safety. Lasers have been activated. Movement of any kind may result in injury or death. I repeat. WARNING: Remain standing..."

The disembodied voice droned on.

Billy shouted at the guard. "Shut that goddamned thing off!"

The guard obeyed. The bells, horn and recording stopped.

Billy rushed to the security desk. "I suppose everybody goes through this. Give me the phone and connect me with Dr. Gertz's office immediately!"

Billy waited. "Another damned message. He can't be disturbed?"

Billy slammed the phone receiver on the desk, then shoved it in the guard's face gesturing wildly. "Listen, Fred. You punch in...What's that emergency code, Rob? Yeah, 4873...and then Gertz's extension number, got it?"

Fred, noticeably nervous, followed Billy's instructions.

Billy listened as the phone rang and then connected.

Dr. Gertz answered and Billy shouted. "Charles. What the hell is going on? You weren't at the meeting. Rob and I just tried to come in to see you and that goddamned laser system almost blew us away. What do you mean by locking me out? Talk to me, Gertz!"

Whenever Billy called Charles, "Gertz" he was plenty mad. It made Charles mute. The more Billy yelled, the longer it took for Charles to regain his composure.

Charles attempted a response. "B-B-Billy, calm down, please. Please stop shouting. I am sorry for the trouble. Th-This is standard procedure, here." Charles took a deep breath. "When the entrance to section 'R' is in use, all five remaining entryways are closed off. I used the section 'R' entrance. Nobody's codes will work. No one should come in here when I'm working on this stuff, anyway, right? I put a big sign on the outer door. Di-Didn't you see it? You-you and Rob told me to ma-make it top secret and let no one know what I was doing. I've done what you asked. N-Now you're mad at me?"

Billy cooled down. "Okay, okay, old boy. You're right. May we come in now?"

"Billy. Billy, now don't get angry again, but it will take me over thirty minutes to unseal this area and almost the same time to close it again. Is it really that important?"

Billy let out an exasperated sigh. "No, no, it's not. Just one question. How far away from completion are the IA units? We need them as soon as possible. And the LOES systems, too!"

Charles relaxed. "I have the IA prototypes in final testing now. They should be in production by tomorrow morning and shipped late Monday night. The LOES units are being produced as we speak and are being shipped as they come off the line. I'm on schedule, Billy. May I go back to work now?"

"Yes, Charles. Please don't forget that I need you for that Cabinet meeting tomorrow at the White House. You are a Cabinet member. I can excuse your absences after this meeting, but you must attend tomorrow."

"I'll be there. But, could you have somebody remind me, please? I lose track of time in here. This is more social calendar than I've had in twenty years. I'm oblivious to all that, you know."

"Yes Charles, I know. Great job. We're all impressed with your work. Back to it, man." Billy hung up the phone. Doing business with all these "absolutely necessary" security safeguards sometimes made Billy wish he were in a 'kinder gentler' industry.

"Rob, let's get out of here. We've got places to go and people to do!"

The return route reversed Billy's arrival: boat to boat to Land Rover, then by jet to DC, and by helicopter to the White House.

The President and Collings walked across the lawn and entered the building at the lower level. Several White House aides and Secret Service men were there to meet them. All silent; no questions asked. Billy and his right-hand man climbed the stairs to the President's living quarters. Billy bid Collings good night.

Suzzanne greeted Billy at the door like a husband who had stayed out too late. She'd been waiting up for him since he called her during the flight. The coffee and cookies were out. That was her signal. Billy was going to get some talk, before he got some...

"Hel-lo, ba-by." He kidded with her. "Did ya miss your big bopper?"

"Good to see you happy and smiling. What have you been up to? Got a girl I don't know about? Make another million?"

"Only one girl for me, honey. I've got other fish to fry than makin' more millions. Besides, we got plenty of millions. Now, I'm just lookin' down from the top and working on stayin' here."

"I'd be careful. Could make a loud noise when you fall."

"Not gonna happen, ba-by. We're in this house and we're not leaving for a long, long time. Believe me!"

"Uh-huh. You're a silly man, but I do love you. How 'bout some coffee and cookies and a chat with your loving wife?"

"Hot coffee. Mmm, that sounds good. Fix it up, while I get into my robe."

In her youth Suzzanne was the sexiest woman Billy had ever seen. Now, this still well put together woman was strikingly beautiful and emitted all the femininity Billy could stand. He loved Suzzanne with all his heart and soul. She was the only woman he had ever truly loved. He trusted this human being. Trust had always been tough for Billy, but his relationship with Suzzanne had been solid from the beginning. He'd always had faith in her. Never had a doubt.

Billy sat down at the table. "Okay, Suz, how was your day?"

"Well, as the First Lady, I formed a committee to review the Arts Councils in the U.S., Canada, and Mexico. I suggested to my committee that we form an International Arts Council that would unite us with similar arts organizations throughout the world. You know my mantra, education through entertainment...."

He had forgotten how brilliant she could be. "I should marry you." He gave her a gentle kiss on the cheek, and turned his attention to the cookies. "How 'bout the wife and mother report? How's Tommy doing? When did you talk with him last?"

Ignoring him completely, Suzzanne went on. "...and I may need your help with Congress to get the funding and avoid authorization issues." She could see he wasn't really listening. "Hmm. Tommy's doing fine."

Suzzanne got up and poured another cup for herself. "Maybe you would share some of your day with me. I haven't a clue what's going on, but it feels bad. Are we in trouble? War? Depression? What's going on?"

"Suzzanne, you know I can't tell you. But I should let you know, it could get real nasty. You and the boys and I will be extremely safe. Now, don't worry, 'cause everything's gonna be all right, and that's a promise, baby!"

"Save that tired campaign line, Billy, 'cause if it's not gonna be all right, I want to be the first to know about it! Hear?"

Billy knew he was in for it when she got that wrinkled-brow look.

"Billy, I'm worried. I don't like you not trusting me. You've always told me everything. Everything."

Suzzanne's anger had finally erupted. "Just because you're President of the United States doesn't prevent you from talking. Ronnie shared with Nancy and FDR talked it over with Eleanor, and Bess knew...."

"Now stop. Harry did not talk with Bess, or ask Bess, if he could drop the atomic bomb, and I'm not going to be baited into talking about what I know I can't talk about. So, drop it baby, or I will tear off your clothes and remind you how babies are made. Maybe I'll even show you exactly how we made those two boys. Okay?"

Suzzanne stuck out her tongue.

"That's it. Now you're in trouble."

Billy lunged at her. She jumped up squealing and laughing. They ran around the room in a mock chase. She let him catch her. Billy picked her up in his arms and gently carried her to their bed. They embraced and made love like kids in heat.

Billy was happy to be home. He thought to himself, "The best kind of sex is with someone you really love and trust. Suzzanne is the best."

Next morning Billy lingered in bed, waking up slowly.

Suzzanne, already up, read the morning paper. She ambushed Billy with reality as he came out and gave her a quick squeeze. "They're finding more cases of that H2P5 virus, Billy. The Post says that there are outbreaks in New York, Detroit, Miami, New Orleans...Oh my god...in Galveston, Mobile, L.A., Seattle, Vancouver, Toronto. All of our port cities, Billy. This is bad. Billy, are you listening to me?"

Calmly, Billy replied, "May I read that when you have finished, dear?"

She handed him the page and made her comment. "A front page story with 'HUNDREDS DIE IN MAJOR CITIES'—'EPIDEMIC ON THE RISE' as a big, bold headline. Banner headline. That's pushing responsible journalism just a bit, isn't it? Are they trying to cause a public panic? Billy? Billy?!?!"

He looked up from the newspaper. "Yes, yes. Irresponsible. Very bad reporting. I'll put Barnston on it and get them to tone it down. Shouldn't be front-page stuff. Not to worry, my dear."

Suzzanne started at him incredulously.

Billy looked her straight in the eye. "We are very aware of the virus. I mean it. Don't worry. We're getting all the details and plans are under way to deal with it. In fact, I have a Cabinet meeting this morn-ing and that very issue is at the top of our agenda."

Billy got up from his chair and laid the paper on the table. "Got to shower and get my very satisfied ass on the road." He bent over and kissed her tenderly and whispered in her ear, "Can I please wait for at least one day before we try that again? Two in a row might kill me, baby!" Billy quickly disappeared into the bedroom.

Suzzanne picked up the paper and said aloud, "How the hell did the news of that virus become a front-page item?"

Billy put on his overcoat, and joined the waiting security detail in the hallway, worrying to himself, "David's got to squash those stories. We've got to get a handle on this virus thing quickly—like today!"

# 15

## *THE CABINET*

7 a.m. on Sunday. An agreeably crisp morning in the nation's capital. The city was quiet. On a normal Sunday, Billy and Suzzanne might have gone to church and then enjoyed a wonderful brunch together. Sunday mornings had always been time for them to be together.

But today, Billy had called an emergency meeting of his Cabinet and that trumped their ritual Sabbath gathering.

Billy exited his living quarters and walked briskly down the White House hallways, flanked by Secret Service agents on either side. He passed the staff officers, smiled and nodded good morning to each of them. Though he acted professionally cheery, the Secret Service detail noticed that something was on the President's mind.

Billy was content. But he wondered, momentarily, whether this was all going to be worth it; whether a nice, quiet life with Suzanne might make more sense. He shook it off. He was in this thing with both feet now. No turning back.

Billy reached the side door and entered the Cabinet room. All of the members were present, even the usually absent Dr. Gertz. Billy nodded at Charles and smiled quickly at Collings. He knew that Rob had made it a point to get Charles to this important meeting.

This was the new Cabinet's first opportunity to work together. As much as Billy had looked forward to putting his new brain trust in motion, he worried that even this great and talented team might not be able to handle an issue of this magnitude.

Billy cleared his throat and addressed the Cabinet. "First, the rules for this meeting: You will note that there are no microphones on the table and no stenographer. In this Cabinet's book of records, this meeting will have never occurred. No official meeting until the Senate accepts you. All of you came in via the Metro, and you'll leave the same way. I don't care what you tell your friends and family about your absence from them today, but you were not at the White House and there was no Cabinet meeting. It never happened. Got it? Let's get started. Chart, please."

A wall projection screen displayed the words "TOP SECRET."

Billy clicked the remote control, changing the screen to a map of North America.

"I know you're wondering about the purpose of this meeting. Unhappily, in these first days of our administration, we have been presented with the most dangerous crisis that has ever befallen this or any other government in modern times. We face a scourge greater than earthquakes, floods or atomic war. Plague, ladies and gentlemen. Plague."

A nervous murmur glided through the room

Billy clicked the remote and the video wall map of North America displayed pulsing red markers near city names. "New York, Cleveland, Detroit, Chicago, Miami, New Orleans, Corpus Christi, San Diego, Los Angeles, San Francisco, Portland and Seattle. All of these port cities, according to the CDC in Atlanta, are presently in an unrestrained infectious predicament—that's a 'pandemic' in regular parlance. The rapidly spreading H2P5 virus that you've heard about over the last few years is the root cause. These major port cities are in serious danger and the local and state public health officials are asking for Federal help. We need an emergency response plan. Now!"

He clicked again and orange markers pulsed near several more cities on the screen. "And these areas—over thirty-five of our major inland cities—are now reporting multiple virus cases. This virus is spreading at an alarming rate. We are not alone in this crisis. Canada, Mexico and most of Central America are experiencing the same problem at a slower rate. The CDC is presently compiling a list of cities in our neighboring countries, and you should have that information delivered to you within the next few hours. I have a full day planned tomorrow with the media in New York, at the Pentagon, and on Capitol Hill. Tomorrow, I will ask Congress to approve temporary martial law for these troubled cities and will then direct the military to begin immediate planning in hopes that this thing can be contained as quickly as possible. Here's the bad part. This crisis is no longer a secret, as most of you already know. Today, in the Washington and New York papers, this virus issue is front-page news. Secretary Barnston, how did this happen?"

David Barnston was unapologetic. "When the media smells a story, they lose all sense of propriety, Mr. President. Yes, they did come to me first. The editors personally assured me they'd wait at least one more day so we could get a handle on this thing. Obviously, scooping the other media was more important. Now it's all over TV and radio..."

Billy was on his feet and pacing. "David, I want you to get to every person that controls a media outlet and let 'em have it. I want them to take the steam out of those stories. Tell them they've violated Federal Emergency regulations and that I am personally very angry with them and they risk being shut down if they don't cooperate immediately."

David shot a look at Billy. "We can do that?!?...We can do that." David started scribbling notes.

Billy was fuming. "I want the owners of every media outlet—movie guys, too—to meet with me in person tomorrow in New York

City. If it prints or talks or moves, I want its owner's ass in a chair at that meeting in Radio City tomorrow. Every goddamned one of them, got it? And if they resist, or are too busy, have the FBI arrest them wherever the hell they are in the world and haul them to New York."

David Barnston gathered his notes and jumped up, heading for the door.

Billy grabbed his shoulder, spun him around and held tightly onto his arm. "And David." Billy looked him straight in the eye and spoke in a low tone of controlled anger. "You get a press release out there. The government is involved now. There is a prevention for this virus. Vast quantities of the antivirus serum are in production. It'll be available for public inoculation very soon. Get ahead of this, man. Now." Billy let go of him.

Barnston quickly left the meeting.

Billy calmed down a bit. "Now, lady and gentlemen, there is some good news about this situation. A few weeks ago, a group of U.S. scientists, in cooperation with others throughout the world, developed a serum for this virus. Not a cure, but a definite prevention. As deadly as this H2P5 virus is, if you are inoculated before you contract it, you will survive. Inoculations for all of you will occur today. Dr. Gertz and Professor Osher will take care of each of you here in the Cabinet room, right after this meeting. Arrange for each member of your staff to get inoculated, by tomorrow. Check with our doctors today so that we can get your families in for shots sometime tomorrow, as well. This is serious business, people. I don't want to lose any of you to this terrible virus. Follow through with my instructions and get those inoculations."

Billy clicked the remote. A bar graph on the screen displayed the virus's growth rate over the last two years.

"Look at this chart and remember it. This is where the enemy is located. This is the real picture."

Billy motioned for a stack of envelopes to be distributed to the

Cabinet members. "Each of you must digest the data in these envelopes. I need recommendations from each of your departments when we meet again, tomorrow at 11 a.m. I want bottom line answers from each of you. No time for discussions or arguments. I need real, ready-to-go plans. Don't be afraid of being right or wrong. Nobody has the correct answer on this one. Use your fertile imaginations. We'll select the best of the methods for solving this crisis tomorrow. We have to move quickly. By Wednesday, the chosen plans must be implemented. Millions of people in North America are counting on us."

Billy sat down and looked at each member of his Cabinet. "This virus is a killer. It's highly contagious. Get going on this and let the doctors begin the inoculations. I want you back in here working as soon as possible. Talk about it. Get those very expensive brains working. I need answers, and I need them quickly. This meeting's over."

Billy walked out of the Cabinet room and hurried back to the Oval Office. Billy plopped into the big chair behind his desk and swiveled around. He sat quietly for a few minutes, looking out the window. He prayed that he was going in the right direction. He knew this thing was huge and could get out of control if not handled precisely.

Coming back to reality, he picked up the phone and asked Hilga to meet him in the Oval Office.

Hilga, now the White House Executive Chef and Assistant to the Chief of Protocol, was a very busy lady, but the request from Billy made her drop everything. Since coming to run his personal household, Billy had called on her a few times. Hilga rushed to the President's office.

"Good morning, Mr. President. Is everything all right?"

"Cut the President stuff, Hilga. I've just come from a Cabinet meeting. The die is cast. And...Well, I'm a little concerned."

For Billy, talking with Hilga was almost like talking with Kurt, and he needed that sounding board now. He could speak freely with Hilga. They were somehow on the same wavelength. She understood more about the motives behind Billy's plans than anyone; even more than Gertz or Collings.

Billy got up and opened a door in the wall.

Together they entered the "silent room." This was the only place in the White House that was not and could not be bugged. It was totally sound-proof. Billy's security people "cleaned" it three times every day.

From the mini-bar inside he made drinks for both of them, then sank into the large plush chair beside Hilga.

Billy, relaxing, spoke quietly. "I'm Okay, Hilga. Just a little unsure...just a little."

Hilga understood. "Probably a lot unsure, Billy. Remember what Kurt taught you? Investigate. Make a plan. Initiate the plan, and don't look back. Have confidence that you're right. Have faith in what you're doing. That will carry you through. Just do it, Billy!"

Billy sighed. As usual, Hilga's invocation of Kurt's words calmed him. He closed his eyes.

Hilga sat patiently nearby, watching over him like a mother.


Billy thought of Kurt, remembering that first meeting at GST when the old German snapped at Billy. "Vell, are you just curious, or are you a man who vill do somesing?"

"What do you mean 'do something'? Why the questions? Who are you, anyway, the Gestapo? What's your name, old man?"

Kurt laughed at this young man's audacity. "Hardly zhe Gestapo, mein herr. Please do not be offended, young man. Permit me to introduce myself. My name is Kurt Rheinlin, and I am alvays interested in talking about serious issues. But I am more interested in talking mit a man who vants to take action—not just talk."

"Okay. You talk. I'll listen. If you make sense, then conceivably you'll be my life's inspiration and maybe I will act. So, talk. Why can't we get this country and this world to stop repeating history and come to some sort of sensible order?"

The old man accepted the challenge. "It is really qvite simple. Zhe rich und powerful maintain a position of control over zhe people. From generation to generation zhey carefully arrange marriages, land purchases und zhey create businesses—real vealth. Und zhey protect it. Zhey acquire vast fortunes to pass on to zheir offspring. Zhis ancestral vealth und zhe power zhat goes mit it, generally, but not alvays, is improved upon by zheir heirs und zhe prozess of zhe conzentration of vealth und power continues. Zhe rich get richer on zhe backs of zhe poor. Zhey alvays have, und zhey alvays vill. But you see, zhe poor, because zhey are poor, alvays vant more. Zhese poor, zhese malcontents, from time to time, rebel und upset zhe plans of zhe elite. Zhey sometimes overthrow zhe rich und zhen try to redistribute zhis shtolen vealth among zhemselves."

Kurt paused, and looked at Billy.

Billy was expressionless.

Kurt continued. "Zhen, even mit zheir best-laid plans, zhe poor fail to really become zhe rich. Zhey don't understand zhe responsibility. Zhe vealthy always endure, und zhey alvays resume power, und zhe status returns to normal. Zhen zhis ancient prozess repeats troughout all of history. Real vealth und power are permanent; can never be eliminated. Zhe poor remain zhe poor, *ad infinitum*."

Billy interrupted. "So, the little guy is wrong. Right?"

"Ya. No. Ya. But understand. Zhe poor have never been right. Zhey only thought zey vere right. Zhis is zhe annoying und recurring problem for zhe men who are really in power. Zhe common man is qvite dependent upon zhe rich man, und some of zhe common men play zheir part in supporting zhe rich and powerful as instructed in zhe creation and transfer of vealth to its rightful owners, as zhey should do. Though, in reality, most of zhe average people are unproductive, irresponsible, und bothersome. In the end, zhese people are very unnecessary."

"People? Considered unnecessary?"

"Ya, but I'm not saying zhat about all of zhe people. Just zhose who are mithout doubt unnecessary. Zhose kind of people, vhy should zhey exist? Only zhe people zhat contribute value should continue on. Zhe vones who are zhe best in every vay. Zhey are zhe important ones. Zhe rest are only dreck. Zhey cannot survive."

Billy was angry. "Dreck? You're nuts, old man! You talk crazy. Some necessary, others not? Keep some, but not the others? And who—Heil Hitler—would choose these 'best'? And what would you do with the remainder? Kill them?"

"No? Ya! Maybe. A very good qvestion. Vhat vould you do?"

Billy hesitated. He sensed that this could be a trick question.

"I couldn't make that decision. I'm not God. No man could—or should—decide who lives or dies."

"Vell, if you are not Gott, zhen I don't think I can discuss zhis any furzher mit you. I have vork to do now. It has been very interesting. I thank you, mein herr."

Kurt got up and turned away from Billy.

Billy stood up, too. "Wait. Wait! Hold on a minute. I'm not done yet. Remember Hitler—you've heard of him, I imagine. He tried to determine who should live and who should die and it didn't work out so well for him, did it? The world didn't like that at all and they put him out of business for trying to play God. So, killing all the people that don't work or can't work or are poor or sick or...Well, that's just not the answer. Not at all!"

Kurt stopped. He turned and slowly walked toward Billy, staring deep into his eyes.

"Hitler? I vill not discuss him. He is dead und vhat he did is dead mit him! But you agree, mein herr. Ve are discussing real problems, und mit any problem, zhere are qvestions. Und if you can create zhe qvestions, zhen zhere vill be answers! Und you, mein herr, must find zhe answers!"

Billy pressed him further. "Please sit down, Mr., uh, Rheinlin. From what I've read this is the same problem that has baffled mankind throughout history: too many poor, ignorant, immoral, infirm and nonproductive people always getting in the way of—and making trouble for—those who want to work, those who can work, those who are law-abiding and decent. It always seems that the finest of the population, the ones who want goodness, peace, productivity, love, and social order for the further advancement of the human race are impeded by these people and..."

Kurt turned back. "You are on zhe right path. I must continue my cleaning job."

"How long will it take you to finish your work?"

"Two hours, or so."

"I'll help you. Then it'll only take one hour. Maybe we could grab a beer and talk some more? Okay?"

Kurt laughed. "Yes. Vell, you have zhe enthusiasm and apparently you're not afraid to vork, so how can I refuse your help? Vhat is your name?"

"William Johnstone. Billy, to you."

"Billy? No. Vilhelm. Now, use zhis mop und start over zhere. You must do good vork now. Not just fast vork. Good vork, you understand, Vilhelm?"

Kurt was only 68 years old, then. His white hair made him look a lot older. Kurt Rheinlin had worked for the college since 1949. He was German, from the little town of Bergensdorf. He told Billy that he used to teach history at GST. Billy wondered why he worked as a janitor.

That afternoon Billy chattered on about everything that came to his mind.

Kurt sized Billy up. "Young man, you know a bit of history and philosophy. You might even become quite a brilliant thinker who vill go on to form his own opinions and viewpoints on zhese issues. I vonder if you really vant to hear what I know, vhat I have seen in my lifetime, or are you just a bright boy looking for amusement?"

They finished about 7p.m., locked up the cleaning equipment and walked down the steps and out of the building.

Kurt motioned for Billy to follow him. "'My place. I have some books I vant you to read."

The night air was cool. It was autumn and the fallen leaves crunched under their shoes as they walked briskly across the campus against the chilly wind.

Billy noticed it was cold inside Kurt's house. Kurt turned on the living room lights. Everything was neat and clean. Billy saw that the room was furnished with a collection of fine antique furniture. The walls were covered with bookshelves from floor to ceiling. No pictures. No paintings. Just books.

Kurt knelt down, started a fire in the fireplace and an order into the air, "Hilga. Come here, please."

A very attractive young blonde woman appeared. Billy judged her to be about his age.

"Some glasses of beer und etwas zu essen for us, please."

Hilga smiled at Billy and went back to the kitchen.

Billy perused the bookshelves. "Wow. Some of these look like first editions. You have an amazing collection of books, Kurt."

"So, you like my library, young Vilhelm?"

"Yes. Yes, I do."

Hilga returned rapidly with beer in cold mugs, a bottle of schnapps and those little German glasses that make that good, lethal liquor go down so quickly and easily. She also delivered an expertly arranged tray of cold meats, pickles, crackers, and cheese. Billy looked her over again. Hilga was beautiful.

Billy and Kurt talked on and on, late into the night.

As the sun came up, Billy brought them full circle. "Okay, so why doesn't man address this sustainable population issue? Problem's been cited often enough. Why no solution, no answer after all these years? You said if one can pose the question, there is always an answer, didn't you?"

Kurt smiled. "Ya, Vilhelm, I did. You see, men are often not very smart; und most times, zhey also lack zhe courage to do vhat is known to be zhe right thing to do."

Kurt continued. "An example: Zhe rat. Zhe rat is very smart. Vhen rats are killed by force—aggression—Zhe remaining rats increase zheir numbers in order to replace zheir losses und to defend zheir position against an enemy. Vhen zhey are killed by a lack of food—by starvation—zhey decrease zheir numbers in order zhat zhe colony may survive."

Billy's face reflected his intense concentration.

"Man, on zhe ozher hand, is stupid. He has no sense of collective survival. He continues to breed in spite of his circumstances, vhezher he has food or not. Just imagine how zhe vorld might look today if Stalin or Hitler had completed zheir plans. Zhey eliminated millions of zhe population. Churchill und Roosevelt—veak moralistic leaders—stopped zhem. Zhey got zhe entire vorld to oppose Hitler and Stalin. Churchill und Roosevelt too, had plans to usurp control."

Billy couldn't pull this together in a way that allowed him to perceive Kurt as reasonable.

"You know, Billy. Stalin und Hitler acted just like zhe rat. Zhey did vhat zhey believed needed to be done."

Billy was on his feet, fuming mad. "What kind of Nazi claptrap are you spouting here, Kurt? You really think Stalin and Hitler were right to murder millions of people in the name of their twisted ideology?

No. No. No! After all you've said, Kurt, you can't make me believe that you really mean that. This is some kind of test, right? I don't buy it! You don't just sit down and contrive methods to kill all the people who don't fit into your little sociological, theological, and political plans. You just don't do that!"

Kurt stood up. Over six feet tall, he towered over Billy. "Vhy not?" Kurt said flatly.

Billy looked up, wide-eyed.

Kurt's blood pressure rose. He spoke in a strained, a low tone of controlled anger. "Zhese misfits are, zhey have alvays been, zhe curse of mankind, und zhere is only one vay for zhem, zhey must be eli—ah, zhey must be, ah, dealt mit, und, uh, examined und a decision made, zhen..."

Kurt looked up and trailed off. Hilga caught his attention.

Kurt took a step back. "I am very sorry, mein herr. I have had too much to drink and have said too much. I am very, very tired now and I must sleep."

The coldness of Kurt's response sent chills up Billy's spine. Did this thoughtful, intelligent man really believe genocide was the answer?

Billy stayed put. "No, Kurt. Man can't do what you suggest because, unlike any other living things, man has the ability to love and to care, and should not kill. When a man kills another man with malice and forethought, he's destroying his own humanity. If mankind does what you are suggesting, the end result is only evil and corruption. Kurt, listen to me. God said 'thou shall not kill' and any man who believes in what God has commanded, well, I think that that man is better off for his belief!"

Kurt's tiredness disappeared and his fire returned.

"You think Gott said 'zhou shall not kill,' und zhat vas zhat, eh? Vell, in fact, vhat your good book says is 'do not murder,' und furzher, zhat you can kill. It's all right to kill, if zhe great Gott of zhe universe commands it. Don't you see, Vilhelm. Man invented Gott. Everysing in zhe Bible uttered by Gott, man thought of for him to say. Man put zhe vords in Gott's mouth. Gott is zhere to make man's lust und avarice, his cruelty und carnage appropriate under certain conditions. Again, look at Churchill und Roosevelt. Zhey told zhe world zhat Hitler und Stalin vere gottless monsters und murderers. Yet Churchill und Roosevelt brought zhe nations of zhe vorld togezer, in Gott's name, to vage zhe horrible murder of millions of innocent people for zheir holy var. Zhey caused millions to die just to kill zhe monsters!"

Kurt raged on. "Monsters? Who vere zhe monsters? Do you know about Dresden, Berlin, Tokyo, Hiroshima and Nagasaki? No, Vilhelm, vhen man commits his vile acts against man in zhe name of Gott, it is all very right and zherefore it cannot be wrong!"

Billy was in a quandary. "So, you are saying that acts of violence committed by man against man sanctified by God are justified as necessary because they are allegedly under the auspices of divine approval? And from Hitler's and Stalin's point of view, then, their actions were justified. They were right because the Allies were interfering with God's plan."

"Correct, Vilhelm, continue..."

"And Hitler intended to conquer Russia and Europe and then the entire world—all with God's approval. Hitler believed his success was sanctioned by God, and that made his actions acceptable; right. From Hitler's perspective."

"Ya, ya, you're beginning to think now. Keep going."

"But the Allies had their own version of world dominance—in the form of democracy and capitalism—and they decided that the socialism, communism, nationalism stuff was not right for them and so they decided to wage war against those who believed differently— also with God's approval."

Kurt jumped in. "As man has alvays done! If you can get enough people to believe in vhat you believe in, you can create a strong dogma and mit zhe proposal zhat 'Gott is mit us' you vill alvays assume zhe position of being right, even if you happen to be morally wrong. Vhich leads us to zhe ongoing philosophical question of 'vas is right, und vas is wrong, und vhy?'

Billy started to speak, but Kurt cut him off.

"No, no, no. I'm sorry. Please do not answer, Vilhelm. Not now. You have vorn me out. You vant to know all zhe answers to all zhe qvestions, and you know most of zhe questions. Unfortunately, you think I know all zhe answers. Vell, I don't. You vill have to find out some of zhe answers for yourself."

Billy had found in old Kurt the classic guru—the "true teacher." Kurt, on the other hand, had discovered in Billy the dream of his lifetime—the perfect student. Billy had a brain that reasoned much like Kurt's. They both were able to absorb an endless stream of information, debate it, use it, and eagerly ask for more. This new friendship and the never-ending trading of ideas continued for many years.

Hilga sat quietly in the "silent room" watching Billy sleep. He occasionally muttered words and phrases. Hilga had seen this trance-like effect come over him in the past. She waited patiently for Billy to emerge from his dreams and reverie.

When Billy awakened, he blinked his eyes and got up shakily. He instinctively poured himself another drink.

Hilga decided to be blunt. "You've been thinking about Kurt again. You look even more scared than before. What are you afraid of, Billy? Are you worried that what you're doing won't work? Or, that it will work?"

With some hesitation, he answered. "I've taken a lot on my shoulders, Hilga. A whole lot. Millions of people will either live or die because of my decisions. I must be right. My actions must be correct. Am I right, Hilga? I need to hear it from you."

"Billy, Billy, Billy. Think about it. You sincerely believe that you're right, don't you? Then you know this is the only course of action that will solve the problem and make it better for all the people."

Hilga spoke firmly, now. "You already know what to do. Just do it!" This has to stop. You should not be asking me to confirm your decisions. You are our leader. Your intentions are good. And therefore, all of your decisions and plans are right. Act. Don't doubt."

Early the next morning Billy arrived at the Capitol. Inside the rotunda, he stopped for a moment and looked up at the depiction of George Washington, flanked by Victory and Liberty, ascending to heaven in the fresco above. How many presidents in crisis before him, he wondered, looked upward at *The Apotheosis of Washington*; former commanders-in-chief seeking inspiration and strength, steeling themselves before going into a struggle with Congress.

His spiritual battery charged, Billy abruptly turned and, with six Secret Service men at his side, walked across the lobby and moved swiftly down the hall to the Congressional chambers.

Inside, the joint session of Congress was about to begin. The Speaker called for order and the roll started the roll call.

Without announcement, Billy made his entrance. He was almost all the way down the aisle before he was noticed. Members of Congress, stood up one-by-one stood as he approached the lower podium. Billy walked up the steps to the microphone and interrupted the roll call.

"Mr. Vice President, Speaker of the House, ladies and gentlemen. I know that it's unusual for the President of the United States to appear here unannounced. I apologize. I have an issue of such importance that I want you to hear about it right now from me and get to work on..."

One of the legislators, Senator Applegate, shouted at Billy. "All due respect, Mr. President, but we do have procedures for the introduction of new legislation, even from the White House. I object..."

"Don't lecture me on how to get things done. You got no legs to stand on there. Ladies and gentlemen, this is not some bill I want to get passed. This is a national emergency and our country needs some definite action today on a very serious, life-threatening problem. I need your attention and immediate help!"

Senator Applegate stood with mute with his mouth open.

Billy directed his reproach. "Now sit down, Senator Applegate, and start taking notes! Ladies and gentlemen, this is serious. No time for *Robert's Rules of Order*. Hopefully, the media hasn't gotten wind of my appearance here, yet. I've ordered the Capitol building to be completely closed and sealed. The Marine guards and the Secret Service are now on permanent duty and will not allow anyone into or out of this building without a pass personally signed by myself or Vice President Harrison. No one but Congressional members will be admitted into these chambers during this special emergency joint session. All pages are to be escorted out of this chamber immediately."

Secret Service and special security collected the pages and remaining staffers and lead them out of the chambers. The legislators were stunned more by the unannounced intrusion and the manner in which Billy addressed them, more than anything else. Loud calls of protest and objections gathered attention.

Ignoring them, Billy ascended to the upper podium and motioned for the Speaker of the House to vacate his chair. Billy remained standing, looking down at the growing disruption. He banged the gavel.

Billy shouted. "Order. Order, please. Order.

They quieted themselves and listened. Billy gave the Senators and Congressmen much the same overview he'd given the Cabinet.

"About three years ago, a virus called H2P5 was identified. There were a few isolated cases throughout the country. As a routine measure, the CDC in Atlanta began tracking individual cases of the disease and the exact locations of each occurrence. Then, there were only twenty-three known cases of the H2P5 and those occurred in only a few areas in North America. Hardly anyone noticed. Not long ago, the number of cases started doubling each month. The number of cases has grown exponentially. not just here in our country, but in Canada, Mexico and Central America. Our scientists and fellow scientists throughout the world initially did not believe that the H2P5 virus fell into the highly contagious category. That has changed. Now these scientists have concluded that we are dealing a modern plague; a pandemic."

The legislators' chatter roared.

"Gentlemen and ladies, please." Billy banged the gavel on the block again. "You must hear me now. Please listen very carefully. As of today, each of you will have a member of the CIA or the FBI assigned to be with you twenty-four hours a day until this crisis is over. This is for your safety and protection from those who might want the details of the information you are receiving and, quite frankly, to prevent you from talking to any unauthorized individual. This is a deadly serious situation!"

The chamber fell silent.

Billy's voice took on a somber tone. "I'm sad to report that Senator Hutlings, Senator Stromend and Representative Belquive died this morning from the H2P5 virus. And many more of our friends and colleagues are ill and will also die. There is no known cure at this..."

A mixed stirring of voices in the chamber signaled alarm.

"Listen, this is very important, I want you to know that our scientists have developed a preventive inoculation. If we act quickly, it can save millions of lives."

The legislators grew silent. They looked up at their new commander-in-chief, listening intently, respectfully

"I was informed this morning that this virus has reached epidemic—no—pandemic proportions. We must act immediately. Therefore, I formally move that this joint session authorize and approve—unanimously, without objection, debate or delay—a temporary state of total martial law throughout the United States and its territories, effective immediately, and to continue until such time as this deadly pandemic is under control."

A great cry of protest erupted.

Senator Applegate, visibly sweating, stood again, shouting nervously above the crowd. "Mr. President, Mr. President, Mr. President! I know I speak for my colleagues. I know you're eager to get things done here in Washington, as you promised so often to the people in your campaign speeches. You may have forgotten, sir, just how this country is run and the limits of executive branch power. Your sudden appearance here and your motion are out of order and I, for one, object. I urge my colleagues to join me in moving to table this motion. We can accept all the information you have for us today and recess for deliberation. I think we all need some time to review the details of what you've just told us before we conclude that this motion should be approved. Martial law? That's not a simple matter, Mr. President and I suggest that you..."

Billy leaned over the edge of the Speaker's desk and slammed his hand flat against its wooden top. The room was immediately quiet as he shouted: "Sit down, you old fool."

Applegate steadied himself as Billy bellowed.

"Under these circumstances, the rules have to change here and now. We have a crisis of unbelievable scope; greater than any nuclear threat, greater than an invasion of our shores, greater than anything we have ever encountered as a nation or as a people. There is no precedent for comparison. There is so little time left. We must get ahead of this thing. And there is absolutely no time at all for your nonsensical pointless politics. I will not waste one minute more on your...Are you willing to risk the lives of millions of innocent people? For a debate? No, Senator. I'm running this show. Decisions need to be made quickly and effectively, by one administrator, not deliberated by a goddamned committee."

Several members stood and shouted their objections with clenched fists.

Senator Applegate leaned against his desk, then stood up straight again, yelling, straining, struggling to be heard. "Mr. President. Mr. President! Hear me, sir!"

Applegate steadied himself again. Perspiration visibly dripped from his face, and the collar of his shirt was soaked through. "You cannot do this. We will not let you exercise this kind of power. You cannot..."

The Senator suddenly stopped speaking.

The chamber became quiet.

Senator Applegate grabbed his head and fell forward onto his desk and then rolled off, falling to the floor.

Billy yelled, "Get a doctor for that man! You, Congressman, or Senator, whatever, you over there near the door. You! Get up and get the Surgeon General in here, now! Hurry, man.

Billy banged the gavel again. "Please! Please, people! Everyone stay away from Senator Applegate. Don't anyone touch his body or clothing! Get back. Get back away from him!"

All of the legislators were on their feet and in full panic.

A distraught member stood up and shouted out. "Mr. President. Mr. President, are we all to be held here as prisoners?"

The other legislators answered in chorus. "Hear, hear! Hear, hear!"

Billy banged the gavel again and again. "Ladies and gentlemen, please. I want order."

Billy took a breath. "We have all pledged to protect and serve the people of this country. I guess we are all technically prisoners of the problem. Listen, people..."

Billy was interrupted by Dr. Osher, the Surgeon General, two doctors and several medical attendants, all wearing full hazmat suits, bursting into the chamber. Osher went to the stricken Senator. The medical team stripped off Applegates shirt and connected him to a defibrillator.

The chamber hushed as Osher and his men valiantly attempted to revive the Senator.

Osher called out. "Mr. President. I'm sorry, but there is nothing we can do for him. It's the virus, Billy. Senator Applegate is dead."

There was a collective gasp and then stunned silence.

Billy looked up at Collings in the gallery, then to Osher on the floor near the fallen Senator. "Dead? Dead?!? Are you sure it's the virus, George? Here?"

The legislators started to pull back toward the exits.

Billy, banging the gavel, shouted. "Order. Order, please! Sit down! No one leaves!!

The legislators returned to their seats as the medical team packaged up Senator Applegate and his things into hazmat bags.

Billy calmly but firmly continued. "Ladies and gentlemen, a true loss to us all. My sincere condolences and sympathy go to his friends and colleagues, and of course to his loving family and friends. Robert J. Applegate was a good and loyal American. He served his country well. Let's have a moment of silence for quiet personal prayer."

The medical attendants put the corpse of Senator Applegate into a black body bag that was marked ominously with yellow letters "H2P5." Quickly and silently, the medical team gathered the bags and the corpse and left the chamber.

On their exit, Billy pronounced, "Amen. And now, Ladies and Gentlemen, at the risk of sounding cold and heartless, we must continue."

Panicked murmuring grew.

Billy shouted, "Please, my patience is running out. His is not the only dead body you will see before this is over. Many of you today were asked to get your inoculation for the H2P5 virus. Now you know why and what it's all about. Those of you that have not been inoculated, you must leave this chamber at once and get those life-saving shots. Please follow one of the Marine guard's out now. Your life depends on it! A special clinic has been set up downstairs and the Surgeon General himself is directing the inoculations. You know whether you have been inoculated or not, so just get up and go now. Don't delay.

A few members got up and nervously looked toward one of the Marine's with his hand up in the air.

"After you've finished I want you back here in these chambers. Now get going and get back here as quickly as possible, we all have work to do. The rest of you shut up and listen to me!"

Like little schoolchildren, they quieted down. Billy had their complete attention.

"The H2P5 virus outbreak is spreading at an alarming rate. Major populations in New York, Miami, and Los Angeles are well into early epidemic stages. We've been able to keep this news quiet until it hit the news, yesterday. We must act before more information is leaked, or we will have widespread panic.

As Billy continued to speak, Collings and several Secret Service men entered the chamber, splitting off down each aisle. They distributed to each of the legislators, large envelopes marked "TOP SECRET." Newly inoculated members trickled back in, returning to their seats. Everyone opened and studied the material in the packet.

"Detailed inside these envelopes is the plan. You can see from the information in the first two pages why I need your immediate approval."

Calm, ordered, cooperative discussions ensued from various members. The demeanor of the legislators had changed. Billy had turned this traditionally politicized and argumentative body of legislators into a corporate board of directors. They recognized him as Chairman of the Board, and now he campaigned for their votes.

Billy looked at his watch. "So, there it is, gentlemen and ladies. I believe you have the whole picture. I have spoken with the heads of WFJ Polybiotech and all of the major medical and pharmaceutical houses throughout the nation. As we speak, the anti-virus serum, the dispensing equipment, protective clothing, etc., are being manufactured, prepared and readied for shipment across the continent. All of the medical companies have pledged full manpower and materials. They will provide everything necessary to get this done. It's a grim picture right now. But with the very good plan you have on your desks and your immediate cooperation for the ratification of martial law, we can save the lives of millions of North Americans. We must act here and now, or the devastation will be on our heads."

An ominous silence permeated the chamber.

Then, scattered applause gradually grew into a solid sound of unanimous approval. Billy had won them over. They were only human, and they were afraid. Those who might have wanted to fight with him or to be uncooperative had acquiesced to the obvious logic of the plan he had presented to them.

Even on the eve of war, this joint legislative body had debated and deliberated the merits of each option. But on this day, Billy changed legislative procedure for all time. He became the absolute boss. President William F. Johnstone would be remembered forever as the only man in American history to have taken complete and absolute control of the United States without opposition.

Without notice or formality, Billy descended the Speaker's podium and helped gather the necessary signatures from the members of Congress on his Emergency Martial Law bill. In a short time, he turned over the meeting to Vice President Harrison and left the congressional chambers. His job there was done.

Step one was now complete.

Billy sailed down the stairs with Collings and the Secret Service men running to keep up with him. In the tunnels beneath the Capitol he quickly got into a subway car and headed for the White House. Upon arriving, he took the elevator to the second floor and entered the Cabinet meeting room. It was exactly 11 a.m. Just as he had ordered, the Cabinet was assembled and in action.

The President called the meeting to order. "Everybody take a seat.

I want you to carefully examine again each and every person on your staff. You only want to keep the very best. We need the profiles of these very best and your recommendations for in-depth security evaluation immediately. Please give this information to Secretary Penitz so he can crosscheck it with the National Computer. This will be the final verification that you have chosen the right people to be working with you on this thing. This is very important."

Billy sat down. "Now, concerning your ideas. I'll review each of your proposals. We'll discuss and finalize the usable ideas at tomorrow's all-day meeting, and integrate them into the existing CDC plan. That meeting will be here and will start at 7 a.m. sharp. You have your instructions, people. I'll see you tomorrow."

As the Cabinet members continued their work, Rob Collings, Julio Mondaldo, and David Barnston put on overcoats, picked up their briefcases and quietly followed the President out of the Cabinet room. The four men got on the private elevator and descended to the ground level. They exited the White House and hurried across the lawn to board the Presidential helicopter. They were bound for New York City.

As they flew north, Billy and Barnston prepped Julio regarding the meeting with the media scheduled right after their arrival. The trip to New York took just under an hour.

They landed on the helipad at Rockefeller Center. With the Secret Service men in tow, the four men went inside the adjoining building and were met by a few of Mondaldo's staff. Julio gave two huge briefcases to each of them and informed his staff that they would all learn more details in a few minutes at the meeting. The Group moved to the huge, private meeting room that "General" Sarnoff himself had designed for just such secret rendezvous.

Inside the meeting room, seated shoulder-to-shoulder at three very long tables and in chairs lining the perimeter of the room, were the owners and CEOs of all the major print, filmed, and digital media. The atmosphere in the over-crowded room was strained, everyone talking loudly over one another. Each of these very powerful leaders played the part of the big media mogul with anger and indignation. They were trying to cover up an intrinsic curiosity and apprehension regarding this emergency meeting with the President of the United States.

The speculation grew. More government intervention? More new media laws? Why the word "emergency"? And what are all the Canadian and Mexican media people doing here? Why is the President, himself, attending this meeting? Why the armed guards? And just what was this virus thing?

Billy burst in followed by Collings, Barnston, Mondaldo and several their staff people.

The President seated himself and called the meeting to order. "Good afternoon ladies and gentlemen. Thank you for all responding to my call for this very important meeting. I have just left the Congress in a closed emergency planning session. This morning, in a joint session, Congress voted unanimously to invoke martial law in every state and U.S. territory during this terrible crisis."

Billy stood up. "This 'virus thing,' as I just heard it referred to, is probably the greatest calamity ever to hit the modern world. It is real. It is vicious and deadly and if we don't stop it, this virus will kill millions of people very quickly. I hope you do hear me. Many millions of people from Canada to South America are in danger. We're talking plague here, people. A huge pandemic! The United States military is sealing all ports of entry and all borders. I assume all of you were inoculated this morning. Is there anyone in this room that has not received the vaccine?"

No one responded.

"Good. Now, please look over the envelopes marked "TOP SECRET" in front of you. We're hoping that the media will save the day, here. I need your full cooperation. We want you to immediately route the source of all lines of communication to New York City. As of today, there'll be no more local news broadcasting or local newspaper reporting. All regional radio, television, cable and newspapers will be temporarily shut down. All TV and radio news and all programming will be produced and originate from New York and will be distributed via satellite. One national newspaper will be produced here in New York and its content transmitted via Internet for printing and distribution by all newspapers throughout the continent. This is the very heart of the plan. Do you understand me?"

They all shouted at once.

Billy gestured for quiet.

One of the print moguls continued shouting. "What are you saying? Shut the papers down? How dare you even propose such a plan? Our advertising losses will be unbelievable. And, Mr. President, as you well know, the news, all the news, must remain uncensored, unrestricted and available to the people. No government intervention or control, ever, and under the provisions in the Constitution, in the First Amen...."

"Sit down Mr. Undermeir."

The man remained standing.

"I said sit down!" Undermeir complied.

"Now all of you listen to me. Obviously, none of you can read. The basics of this problem are outlined in the first paragraph. The details, if you need them Mr. Undermeir, are all in the report! This is serious!"

Billy hurled a folder at Undermeir. "We are all about to get wiped out by a plague of epic proportions, people. This isn't a movie! I told Congress this morning that this virus situation is more dangerous than the threat of atomic warfare or national invasion. We need the people to be calm and follow instructions. We don't need you inciting them into insanity."

Billy calmed himself a bit. "Now, I don't want the media of this country in the government's hands forever, gentlemen. But we cannot risk one wrong, misplaced, or sensationalized story from you guys, or we'll have a national panic. You're not rational or trustworthy, especially in a national crisis, and truthfully, we just can't rely on your judgment or your word under these circumstances. Selling papers and tickets, getting the best ratings...making money won't matter if this thing gets sensationalized and the people are out of control. We'll all be dead."

He had their attention.

"You have absolutely no integrity and you know it! I want to do this with some sense of cooperation, some teamwork. But if you don't play ball with me, I will use the military to close any or all of you, by force! Gentlemen, the government will have total control of the media during this crisis, not on just some issues, but on all form, world-wide content and delivery methods and schedules. Total control. Got it? We are your new editors. Your 'free press' and its previously unreliable and wild journalism will cease until we alleviate this 'virus thing.'"

"Now, Julio and David and their people will go over the details of the plan with you. Knowing that you folks always agree with any-thing and end up doing whatever you want, I'll leave you with this thought. I will not tolerate the slightest bit of interference or insubordination or disobedience from any of you. I want and need your cooperation, but I remind you that during this crisis you, too, will be under martial law. If I get friction of any kind, there will be no discussion, no explanations, and no apologies. Oh no, gentlemen, I don't have time for that. This is more than war. So get this: Any individual, big or small, who violates these orders will be arrested as a traitor and shot by the first soldier I can find. This is not an idle threat, gentlemen. Have I made myself clear?"

The media owners nodded in numb agreement.

"Now get on your phones. Call your offices and speak with your operating managers. Top-secret government documents will be arriving by messenger within the hour. These couriers are armed members of the CIA and FBI and will remain on your premises as security guards during this situation. Your people are to consider this a national crisis and follow the emergency security guidelines outlined in the documents. Your top management and a small number of support staff are to immediately seal themselves in their offices. they are to use only the private telephone codes in the instructions for all communications.

"CIA and FBI agents will remain in your offices for protection and enforcement. Individual agents are assigned to stay with your people day and night until this is over. You give your people two hours to assemble their best people and have those people digest the courier's material. Instruct them to end the rest of your people home without discussing the nature of this crisis. Tell them you'll speak again later and that they must follow the instructions in the packets to the letter.

"Gentlemen, you are now operating under Federal orders. This building will be the source of all news to the public, starting with today's evening news broadcast.

Billy stopped for a moment to let this sink in and then he continued. "Accommodations are being set up for you here until we have a handle on this situation. You will not be going home or out of this building for some time, so get used to the idea. I want the network and independent media across these countries to shut down normal operations by 6 p.m. EST. Understand? Get busy and make those calls!"

These once powerful executives jumped to work like office boys and began to make their calls. The room buzzed with activity. Billy watched them and tried to pick out the potential troublemakers. As a backup to his first-hand observations, the meeting had been videotaped from the time the media moguls had entered the room and tape would continue rolling after Billy left. Even the restrooms, hallways, and sleeping areas were bugged. Billy knew that media people really could not be trusted . It was vitally important to know who was who in this group of megalomaniacs. These people could be dangerous. They all needed to be watched very closely.

Billy and Collings walked up the stairs silently, each deep in thought.

As they approached the helipad Collings finally spoke. You know that it will require one or two of them being made an example of in order to impress the others. It should be done today, in front of the rest, to be effective."

Billy agreed.

Collings pulled out his cell phone and said, "Review the videotapes," and gave a coded order.

The two re-boarded the copter and flew back to Washington.

Billy's mind was racing now. Second down, goal to go. As the copter touched down at the Pentagon, they saw General Alfred Fenwick below them waving.

Billy and Rob alighted and walked briskly toward their old friend. With hearty handshakes, the three Inner Circle members greeted each other and strode toward the entrance of the building. Inside they boarded an elevator that descended to the War Situation Room.

General Fenwick had met with some of the leaders in a briefing session that morning. He stayed after the meeting to be on hand to help the doctors and medical attendants coordinate the virus inoculations of the top brass. In another part of the huge building, the inoculations of the remaining high-ranking military and civilian personnel were well under way.

When the President, Collings, and General Fenwick arrived in the War Room, the officers were all chatting and joking among themselves, still unsure of the severity of this crisis.

The President entered. All rose to attention and saluted.

"Thank you all for coming. Gentlemen, we are at war. We're about to wage a war with the worst plague ever seen on this planet. Some of the best and greatest people of our nation have died from this ugly scourge. As you know, Generals Klondiens, Sevrhine and MacAlaney died in the last twenty-four hours. It could be any one of us next."

"As of this morning, we're under martial law. By unanimous agreement of the Congress, I alone, as commander-in-chief, am in charge of and the Absolute Commander of the Army, the Navy, the Marines, the Air Force, the Coast Guard and all reserves of military and every police force in this country. Through diplomatic channels, the governing bodies of Canada and Mexico have given their asset to my assuming command of the militaries of Canada and Mexico."

The U.S. military acknowledged their Canadian and Mexican counterparts, and nodded their heads in agreement.

"My word and my decisions will be obeyed during this crisis. There will be no infighting; no insubordination. The penalty for violation of my directives during martial law is immediate death. No court martial. Immediate field execution."

The huge situation room screen lit up showing the names of commanding officers and the rank and file beneath them.

"Each of you must create a command line starting with yourselves and descending to the rank of Captain. One command line for each of you and—most importantly—you must secure extreme loyalty in this chain of command. There is no margin for error in your evaluation of these people. You and you alone will be totally responsible for their actions. They must be willing to die for you, for me, and for their respective countries. Any other profile will not be acceptable and will put this plan in total jeopardy."

Billy got up from his chair and walked to the other end of the long table. "I have created a top command team whose combined knowledge of how to wage this kind of war is far superior to any group, anywhere. Gentlemen, allow me to introduce your new War Council. Your Supreme Allied Commander, General Alfred D. Fenwick and his Allied commanders, General Benson of Canada, General Gorjez of Mexico, General Parsons of the U.S. and from Canada, Admiral Norstrum, Admiral Panto of Mexico, and our U.S. Admiral Mancey. They will brief you further on the details of this operation. Supreme

Commander Fenwick's word is my word, and my word, gentlemen, is now the law. General Fenwick?"

Fenwick and his Allied command group immediately started briefing their subordinates. The room was alive with activity.

Billy stood up, smiled approvingly at the work in progress, and quietly walked to a corner of the war room. He dialed a number on his cell phone. "Charles, Billy here. Daily report: Barnston and Mondaldo are with the media guys in New York. I'm at the Pentagon and General Fenwick and his boys are addressing the Allied chiefs now. Congress is in place. Avery is handling the disaster plans in a closed session. It's all working, my friend. The plan's afoot!"

Billy and Collings took the elevator to the underground subway and headed back to the White House.

When they reached the Oval Office, Billy asked for his messages. He perused the notes quickly and set them in a stack on his desk and turned to Collings. "Long day, Rob. Ol' Billy is dead tired."

Billy walked to his chair and flopped down.

"Mr. President, I suggest you get to bed. Don't stay up and work. Get some rest. It's what I intend to do. You really do need some sleep, Billy."

"Good idea, old buddy, good idea."

The phone rang.

"And then again, maybe not!" Billy lifted the receiver. "Yes … okay, show her in."

"Suzzanne? Sally? Hilga? Or…"

"Sally."

"Get some rest. You're too old to keep that many women happy."

Collings gave a tired salute to Billy and left by the side door as the other door opened for Sally Hawthorne.

She made a grand theatrical entrance right up to the front of Billy's desk, stopped and looked down at him with an almost cartoonish sultriness. "Whatcha got planned for the evening, big boy?"

"Well, my little chickadee, the Prez is tired. I'm going to bed."

"Billy, I want to be with you. When are we...."

He put his finger to his lips and frowned at her while pulling on his ear.

"Why don't we take a walk, Sally?"

He took her into the very small "silent room." Billy turned a switch and the sliding door closed, starting a whirring white noise.

Billy seated himself in one of his plush chairs. "This is a 'silent room.' Sally, you can't just walk into the Oval Office—which, by the way is always bugged and videotaped—and announce that you want to be with the President of the United States. Extremely bad form, my dear."

"So, is this where we have to do it from now on, Billy? This little room with just chairs? What's that whirring noise?"

"That device makes it impossible for our conversation to be successfully recorded, even if they—whoever they are—could get a bug in here. Hope this tiny room is okay for you, my dear, 'cause it's here or nowhere, baby."

Before he had finished his statement, Sally had removed her clothing and was standing naked before him. She unbuttoned his pants and kissed him passionately on the mouth. It was obvious that this little room was going to be just fine.

Outside, away from the sensual pleasures that were occurring in that little room, the battle against the plague had begun.

# 16

## *THE CRISIS CONTINUES*

The next morning all media reported on the spread of the deadly H2P5 virus throughout North America, describing it as a full-scale epidemic. In a matter of hours, the entire world knew of America's great troubles. William F. Johnstone, President of the United States, was scheduled to speak on the crisis at noon that day. Every radio and television station worldwide carried his message.

A concerned but confident Billy spoke to the cameras. "My fellow Americans. What you have been hearing on television and radio, and reading in the newspapers is absolutely true. A very dangerous and deadly virus is spreading throughout North America. Please listen to me, now. What I have to say will save your life and the lives of those dearest to you. Help is on the way.

"There is serum that will prevent this virus. Everyone, every-where, can receive this inoculation at no charge. A Federal resolution was unanimously passed by a joint session of Congress today allowing us to open massive field inoculation centers in every city and town in North America. The largest public and college arenas have been selected to be used as inoculation centers. In the smaller towns, the armories or high school gyms will be used.

"Again, there is no cost to anyone for this inoculation. It is free! But let me emphasize that everyone, without exception, must be examined and treated at one of these inoculation centers. All of your local doctors, nurses and health technicians are now working at these centers. This is a highly contagious disease We must all cooperate in order to stop it.

"Congress has approved invocation of immediate martial law for the entire United States and its territories. Canada and Mexico have also enacted martial law. This means that we can call upon the vast resources of all armed services, the military reserves, state militias, the police, sheriff's and fire departments, as well as the National Guard to help in this major crisis.

"For the remainder of today, regular programming of all kinds will be suspended. Do not go to work or to school. Do not leave your homes or make phone calls unless absolutely necessary. You must stay indoors. Listen for further instructions that will be broadcast on radio and television. Follow those instructions exactly. Don't panic. With God's help, we will survive this terrible plague. Thank you. And may God bless you."

The newspapers distributed in all of the cities were reduced to just four pages—a one-sheet folded in half, with no advertisements. On each of the four pages large, bold type screamed at the public to turn on their television sets for inoculation instructions. In order to maintain local identification, the newspapers used their own mastheads. A single editorial space under the banner headline featured four-column pictures that graphically displayed the horrible devastation caused by the H2P5 plague. The message was the same in every city, but the editorials were localized for impact:

*DEADLY VIRUS PLAGUE SPREADS IN ILLINOIS*

*PEORIA (NDN) A killer is on the loose. Thousands of men, women and children are dying in every county in Illinois from a plague-like virus. The city of Peoria has been hardest hit with over 800 struck down in just two days. The deadly H2P5 virus has caused this unprecedented epidemic. The great cholera outbreaks of the last century did not cause nearly the number of deaths that this indiscriminate killer is wreaking throughout North America. Even the famous black plague of Europe was kinder.*

*All the world is stunned by the devastation this virus has wrought upon the populations of the United States, Canada, Mexico and now, even Central America. But citizens are to take heart, for there is prevention if everyone acts right away. The Center for Disease Control in Atlanta, Georgia and the Surgeon General's office both urge the general public to get to one of the Federal Inoculation Centers for an examination and immunization immediately. The CDC warns that delay in getting the inoculation could mean certain death. Immediate inoculation is the only prevention for this deadly plague.*

*President Johnstone has urged all citizens to stay tuned to their televisions and radios in order to get the exact instructions for how and when to go to the inoculation centers.*

*PLEASE DO NOT DELAY.*

*YOU MUST GET INOCULATED TODAY!*

*A list of the Federal Inoculation Centers in Northern Illinois can be found on page 2 of today's newspaper. Turn on your television and radio now! Further details will appear on television. Stay tuned to all local television stations.*

*YOU MUST FOLLOW ALL FEDERAL INSTRUCTIONS.*

The newspapers, billboards and radios endlessly instructed the public to watch their television sets. An attempt to comfort the public with well-produced television, radio, and cable messages stressed calmness and order and told the people exactly how the inoculation procedure would operate. Day and night the broadcast repeated:

*Do not leave your home until you are so ordered.*

*Keep your family together and indoors.*

*Do not visit with friends or neighbors.*

*No physical contact with anyone.*

*Keep your television and radio turned on.*

On the television, a simple quadrant plan for each neighborhood displayed, street by street, which areas were next to go for inoculation. The messages also stated the rules:

*Drive or take public transportation to your inoculation center. Go through the main entrance to the Registration Desk. You will be issued an ID card and instructed where to go.*

Short television programs aired continuously to give the people an exact view of what to expect at the inoculation centers. The public was told that before receiving their inoculation they would be sanitized to eliminate any contamination on their clothing. They were shown how a harmless ultra violet light would be used for the disinfecting process.

The TV coverage showed people entering the decontamination areas and then, unharmed, the smiling faces coming out of the booths. They were told that if they had the H2P5 virus, they would be immediately inoculated and then transferred to a quarantine area where they would remain for a few days until the virus had been totally arrested. As the television announcements continued, viewers saw how their local arena had been set up with beds and food facilities, transforming these giant entertainment centers into efficient quarantine areas. The good food, the friendly nurses and pleasant surroundings made it all seem quite homey and safe to the citizens.

The announcements explained further that those who didn't have the virus would just receive inoculations and then be allowed to return home. Bed rest was recommended for at least one week following inoculation.

The television messages played for ten minutes out of every half hour. The messages were graphic, yet friendly, and continually stressed that order and cooperation must prevail:

> Help your neighbor. Help your family. Help your country.
> Do not panic. Be cooperative. Everyone must be inoculated
> to prevent infection and spread of the virus.

Normal programming vanished. Carefully selected movies aired to entertain and occupy the public; comedies, cartoons and family films made during the thirties and forties. They were classics, with basic themes reinforcing the togetherness and cooperation of the American people in times of crisis or moral dilemma. These old chestnuts were perfect propaganda gems and demonstrated what our great country could do during a national emergency. There were no commercials. No talk shows. No live news.

The inoculation announcement was the same on radio. Only positive, bright music and old-time radio shows were broadcast. Even on the Internet the music was of an older, gentler time.

Barnston called upon a handpicked corps of actors, writers, directors and technicians to use the new science of "synthetic acting."

Quickly, the people got to see icons of the golden age of movies: John Wayne, Elvis, Bette Davis, Fred and Ginger, Humphrey Bogart, Clark Gable, Spencer Tracy, Bing Crosby, all in their prime and performing in brand new films. No matter that all of them were dead. Using the available computer magic, these greats lived again on the silver screen. One by one, the old propaganda pieces were removed from scheduling and replaced by these new films. Audio editing and voice synthesizing allowed the old radio stars like Hope and Skelton, Benny and Burns to perform again in new and exciting radio programs about "The War On the Plague."

Very quickly, David Barnston had mounted the most complete and effective entertainment/media blitz since World War II.

The inoculation centers continued to operate twenty-four hours a day. The majority of Americans cooperated. Most people had enormous faith in Billy and his new Third Party administration. Despite an innate fear, most believed Billy could handle this awful crisis and save them all from a very imminent death.

The newspapers, radio and TV broadcasts, the Internet, magazines, billboards, posters, sound trucks and moving signs shouted the message. With more and more people being inoculated almost everyone in North America knew about the virus plague. Television showed lines of people in front of the inoculation centers. The people were obedient and orderly. Interviews with those who had received the inoculation showed scenes of sincere gratitude. It seemed like everyone was involved and wanted to get the inoculation. This single event, albeit deadly, had galvanized the entire nation once again.

Barnston had done his homework. What Marshall McLuhan had said about the then new medium of television was correct. Television was the "God Box" and whatever the TV said, the people believed. Barnston banned commercials and replaced all programming with hour after hour of reports on the plague, juxtaposed with carefully crafted entertainment reinforcing the 'solidarity' propaganda. People listened, became interested, and absolutely believed what they were being told.

Soon, the newly named *National Daily Newspaper* expanded to include more content and the local mastheads disappeared.

"How to" stories that ranged from getting to the inoculation centers to managing businesses and home life during the crisis, to funeral preparations and memorial services were very helpful. Daily, the media continued to scream at the public with one frightening, stirring message: "Get Inoculated Today ... or you will die!"

President Johnstone's administration, the military, the media and the people all worked in concert to end this terrible blight. In the process of having faith in the future, many people went beyond trusting Billy; they began to adore him. He was their Messiah.

As time went on, some people began to wonder what had happened to their parents, their wives and husbands, relatives and friends, those who had remained behind in the quarantine sections of the inoculation centers. Where were they? Were they getting well? Were they alive? Why hadn't they come home? These people wanted to know and once again the TV told them how to find out.

*CALL THE H2P5 VIRUS INFORMATION LINE*
*TO CHECK ON THE QUARANTINE STATUS OF*
*A FRIEND OR FAMILY MEMBER.*

*CALL TOLL FREE: 1-800-HOPEFUL*

The bank of 800 numbers allowed people in every city to check on the condition of family and friends who were quarantined. Computer systems tracked the source of each call and routed the caller to the appropriate message line.

The telephone message remained the same for the first four days:

*Because of this epidemic, hundreds of thousands of people*
*are ill. The person you have inquired about is in serious*

*condition and under quarantine. Please call again tomorrow for a further update.*

On the next call to the Toll Free line, the message changed:

*Because of the epidemic, many thousands of people are dying. The person you have inquired about is on the critical list. We are sorry to report that there is a possibility they may not recover. Please call again tomorrow for an update.*

Finally, on the last call the message was:

*The H2P5 virus is the worst plague ever set upon mankind. Millions of people have died and possibly many more may still die. We are sorry to report that (person's name) died last evening at (time) and because (person's name) was so horribly ravaged by the highly contagious H2P5 virus, the body, clothing and personal effects of (person's name) was cremated as ordered by Federal law. Please watch channel 31 for instructions and suggestions on how to prepare an appropriate memorial service for (person's name). Please accept our sincere condolences. May God bless and give eternal rest to (person's name).*

On Channel 31 the bereaved were told to use a picture or some personal artifact owned by the deceased individual as an icon. They were told to go the family's place of worship and hold a memorial service for the deceased. By contacting a funeral director, the icon could then be buried or encased in a small vault so the departed could be remembered for all time. For those who couldn't afford to buy these services, a booklet was offered: "How To Perform A Free Memorial Service."

Barnston had thought of everything.

A week later, at 2 a.m., with Billy and Suzzanne sound asleep in their bedroom at the White House, one of the bedside phones rang.

Billy awakened from a deep sleep and groggily reached out for the blinking light. It was his private number.

"Now what?" Billy picked up the phone and answered in a quiet, but firm voice. "Hello."

"Billy, I've got to see you." It was Sally Hawthorne.

"In the morning. It's been a long hard day...need to sleep."

"No, Billy, you can't put me off this time. I must see you now. Privately. We need to talk about the details of your Plan B. Now. This is an emergency. Everything depends on my speaking with you... tonight. Where will it be?"

Sally! Billy was wide-awake now.

"Use your entrance pass and meet me at the lower level in the subway at the Capitol, at the Number Two stop. Give me thirty minutes. I'll be there!"

"Billy, come alone. No Secret Service or Collings. No one. Just you. Understand?"

"All right."

He hung up the phone and immediately dialed Collings.

"Collings here."

Billy told him of his conversation with Sally.

Collings said he would leave immediately and plant a bug in the subway car that Billy would be using. He suggested that Billy carry a microdigital recorder in his coat as a backup.

As Billy dressed, he wondered just what this wild woman had on her mind. If he had only listened to Rob and not hired Sally... Oh well, that was yesterday. Now he had to deal with her.

Billy ordered his Secret Service guard to follow him only to the subway entrance of the White House and to stay there with two of the Marine guards until he returned. He told them that this was a high level secret meeting and that was all they needed to know.

The subway car traveled down the rail and as it rounded the bend to the Number Two Capitol stop, Billy saw Sally and a man in an overcoat beside her. The car came to a halt and Billy got out.

"I told you no one but you, Billy."

She was angry.

"Bob Harvey, Secret Service, Mr. President. I have two more operative and four Marines at the top of the stairs. What are your orders, sir?"

"Thank you, Mr. Harvey. This is a top-secret meeting. I want you and your men to seal off this entrance from the topside. Remain on duty there until you hear from Eddie Carlton, the chief on duty. Eddie is on channel 63."

The guard saluted and went back up the steps. Billy looked at Sally and gestured for her to get into the car. He followed her into the seat and started the car in motion away from the entrance.

After moving a short distance, he stopped the car and turned to Sally. But, before he could speak, Sally snarled at him.

"I told you no one. How many people know we're here?"

"Just the Secret Service, Sally. I can't go to the bathroom without them following me and you should be bright enough to know that!"

"Well, this is important Billy, I think what you are broadcasting to the people is probably unnecessary. Maybe the H2P5 virus isn't as bad as they say. Maybe it isn't a plague. Maybe there is a cure. I don't know all of the details, Billy, I just need the truth."

Billy thought to himself: 'Emergency.' This was just another one of her little, hysterical maneuvers. Totally made up to get him alone with her. Alone. Hell, half the Secret Service and the U. S. Marine guards knew about it. This girl was becoming a nuisance.

Billy cleared his throat and gave her a stern look.

"Sally. First, I want you to know that this nonsense must stop. I am a married man and the President of the United States, not your personal gigolo. You'll be in big trouble if you ever do anything like this again."

He had insulted her and she became incensed. "Don't flatter yourself. All I want from you is some truth. Why is this terrible virus suddenly spreading out of control? I must know."

Before he could answer, Sally's demeanor changed from aggression to pleading. "Oh, Billy, be honest. Is it really a crisis? Are you taking advantage of this to gain more power? You must tell..."

"Stop it. Where did you get these ideas from? Talk!"

He was angry now. "Get this quick, woman. You are playing with your life here. You don't just wake up the President of the United States in the middle of the night and tell him that the government has made an error in judgment and then get off by pulling an 'I'm just a stupid little girl' act. Now you tell me where you got these absurd ideas. Now, while you still can."

"All right, all right." Sally took a breath and a quick survey of the surroundings. "You know that I've been seeing your son, Willy. You do know that, don't you? Well, he told me he's overheard things about this Plan B; things that you haven't told The Group in any of our meetings. Secret things. Billy, you don't' talk to me anymore. You won't see me..."

"Was Willy sober when he told you these 'things'?"

"Well, we were both drinking. But I wouldn't say he was drunk."

"Willy has been drunk ever since the day I told him why I wouldn't have him as a member of my Cabinet. We had a very violent fight—a fistfight. Sally, Willy harbors a lot of deep hostility toward me. He's not very happy with me, and I'm not very happy with him. Now, what exactly did he say?"

"Billy, you're scaring me. What will you do to Willy and me? God, don't let Collings hear of this. I'll just disappear or have an accident. I'm sure that man is evil. I know he hates me..."

"Please, Sally, control yourself. You're paranoid. Collings is not hateful or evil. He is just a very dependable man who does what he is ordered to do. What you're saying is irrational. What has caused you to say these things?"

Billy grabbed her arms tightly.

Sally shook with fear. "Willy said that you planned—or maybe he said, what if you had planned—to take advantage of this plague...Oh, I don't know. We talked so much. I guess we were drunk. Maybe it's just all bullshit. I'm confused..."

Billy could smell the liquor on her breath now.

"Pure bullshit. It makes no sense. Sally, you're really loaded. So, what else?"

She sat upright and looked him straight in the eye. "He said that you wanted to be the king of the world and that nothing would stop you and that he and I, all of us, would be killed and you would enslave this country and...I left him dead drunk on the floor at my apartment. He had been raving on for hours..."

"All right now, Sally, listen to me. I want you to stop seeing Willy for a while, and I want you to stop drinking, especially in public. You could become a problem and I can't afford you as a problem. You must remember who you are. You are a Cabinet member and the Secretary of Education in the Government of the United States. Sally, don't make me ask for your resignation."

She sobbed like a child.

"Oh, Billy, I'm so sorry for this. Can you forgive me? This is so stupid."

Billy put the subway car in reverse, heading toward the Capitol entrance. "Yes, I can forgive you. I can forgive you both."

Billy helped her out of the car, kissed her on the forehead and lightly smacked her bottom. "Get out of here and don't talk to anyone. This meeting never happened. Get a cab and get that young lout out of your apartment. Go to sleep. I'll talk to you tomorrow."

When the subway car reached the White House, Collings was the only one waiting on the platform. He gave Billy a helping hand from the car.

"You hear it all?"

"Yes, I did. Give me the recorder, Billy, we may need it someday."

"You might be right. My son could become a problem. You know, I hate to say it, but he is not reliable at all any more. The drugs and alcohol. We have to get him into a good dry-out program, and Sally, well, she needs to stop drinking and shape up!"

Collings, in a rare moment of compassion, grasped Billy's shoulder and quietly advised his friend. "Sally may have a substance abuse problem, Billy, but as cynical as I want to be, I don't think her intentions are bad. Still, like it or not, you've got to give her up, Billy."

Sally arrived at her apartment building, paid the cab driver and hurried inside past the doorman. She was still confused. Was Billy telling the truth or had he just outfoxed her? He was certainly a very smart man and capable of lying. Something didn't ring true. Why did he jump out of bed to meet her? Was he really hiding information? She had to know the truth.

The elevator door opened, and she was in her apartment. Wilhelm was still passed out on the floor near the fireplace where she had left him. Sally quickly her appointment calendar and decided that she could cancel everything except the Cabinet meeting at 7 p.m. that evening. Maybe this would give her time to find out more, if there was any more. It was 3:45 a.m. Time to wakeup Wilhelm and find out what he had to say when he was sober. She wasn't going to let little Willy off the hook quite so easily.

She looked at Willy as he slept. He was regally handsome, but so immature.

"Willy! Willy get up. Willy!"

Wilhelm rolled over and sat up, staring at her with a glassy look in his eyes. He shook his head, got up on his feet and quickly headed for the bathroom.

"Coffee!" he shouted as the bathroom door shut.

"Coffee it is, my dear."

Sally went to the kitchen and turned on the automatic coffee maker. It burbled to life and the dark liquid poured down into the pot. She got a jug of orange juice and tray of Danish and bagels from the refrigerator. Breakfast.

Wilhelm came out of the bathroom, approached Sally and gave her a warm kiss on her neck. They sat down at the table. Wilhelm gulped down the hot black coffee, and then looked up at Sally. "You're the best thing that's ever happened to me."

Sally smiled faintly.

He could see something was not right. "I got pretty drunk last night. Did I say or do anything I shouldn't have?"

"Oh no, Junior, not much. You just told me that your father, the President of the United States, was using this plague for his own ends, wanted to kill us all and become the king of the world. I believe that is how you put it. Other than that, Willy, we just had a quiet intelligent conversation."

"What...?" He grabbed his head with both hands. "Wow. I was really out of it last night!"

"Now the bad part, Willy baby. You got me so convinced and suspicious with your ranting and raving and swearing and bragging that 'you ought to know, 'cause I'm close to The Inner Circle' and all about how you knew things that I would never know! Well, Willy dear, I panicked. I believed you. So I called your father and got him out of bed and made a real fool of myself by accusing him of all that nonsense. Oh Jesus, Willy, why did you tell all those lies?"

Sally knew the word "lies" was Willy's big button.

"What makes you think I was lying, Sally. I do know things that you don't know, and you never will."

"So, what is the truth, Willy? Aw, you're full of shit!"

"Do you know what the Inner Circle is?"

"The Group, of course."

"No. The Inner Circle came before the 'Group.' They are Billy, Avery, Collings, Gertz, Barnston, Fenwick and Osher. The "Group" only happened during the political campaign. Way back in the beginning it was Billy and Charles. Then he added Osher, Barnston, Collings, Fenwick, and Harrison. They have maintained that Inner Circle for many, many years. The "Group" is the Inner Circle with the addition of Julio Mondaldo, Irving Penitz, Henry Gillespie, Felix Hansen and little Sally Hawthorne. And it doesn't include me, Sally, honey baby, and if you hadn't been bedding down with my Daddy, you wouldn't be included, either."

Sally ignored his slur.

"So. These Inner Circle guys have been around for a long time. Years, huh?"

Wilhelm nodded and mumbled yes with a mouthful of danish.

"And this whole Billy for President idea came from...?"

"From Billy, you idiot. And it was all supported by his Inner Circle. Billy progressively acquired the other talent as he went along. He has formed quite a formidable coalition."

"So, you told me that he intends to become the king of America and the world and that this plague is not as bad as reported?"

Wilhelm stood up. "No, no, no! Stop quoting a drunk. I probably said that as clever as they all are, it could be exploited. And that Billy has always has acted more like a king more than a president—or a father. Don't. Don't go blowing this out of proportion."

"But Willy, what if you're right? It would take a genius to make a plan like this work, but what if it was? Look at the benefits if you could turn a mild epidemic into a pandemic. You'd get control of Congress, the media, and the military with no opposition and you would have a very tight rein on the citizens under martial law. But why? He can't keep the country under martial law forever. What could he really be doing?"

"You're nuts, Sally. God, I want you to stop this. You know they have your apartment bugged. Knock it off or we're both gonna be in a lot of hot water. I was drunk out of my mind. Now just shut up with all that stuff. It's totally crazy."

"Don't worry, I have a private company that debugs here every day. I know they rebug it."

Sally looked up at him. "Willy, what if I'm right? Is there anyone in that Inner Circle that you've ever seen or heard of to have words with your father or disagree with him? Any friction? Think, Willy. Anyone?"

"No. You've got to understand something. These guys who have been with Billy over the years are more loyal than his family. They would die for him. They never, ever fight with him. They are his men; body and soul."

"Willy, if you knew he was doing something bad, I mean monstrous, something horrible to control the people, wouldn't you try to stop him?"

"First, even though I'm furious with him right now, I'm just like the other guys. I think he's a very special man, maybe even the greatest man in a hundred years. I can't even conceive of him doing anything that wrong."

Sally stopped being the investigative reporter about to make a kill. She could see that Wilhelm's loyalty for Billy was strong. She would lay off—for now. But a drunken man's words are sometimes truthful.

"You're right, Willy. This is a dumb conversation."

Sally ended the conversation, just in case the place really was bugged. She reached under the table and delicately fondled him. "Carry me to bed, cave man. I need more lovin'."

Willy smiled, picked her up, and carried her to the bedroom.

As Willy had sex with her, Sally thought to herself. "I'll go to an inoculation center, and I'll see what's really going on. When Willy finishes, hopefully he'll go to sleep as usual."

As predicted, he did finish, rolled over, and promptly went to sleep.

Sally stayed awake for a while. As Wilhelm slept she looked at him and whispered out loud, "You're not that bad, honey. But you're not your father."

Sally rolled onto her pillow and decided to sleep.

# 17

## *THE SUSPICION*

Sally awoke at 9 a.m. Wilhelm was snoring soundly. Leaving him asleep in bed, she got up, showered and dressed in casual clothes. She shoved a small digital camera/recorder into her purse and quietly left her apartment.

The world outside was very much awake. The inoculation centers hummed, busy with the processing of endless lines of people. It was bitterly cold, aggravated by a stinging drizzle of rain.

Sally was chilled to the bone, hung over, and in no mood to drive. She hailed a cab in front of her building and gave the drive directions to the big inoculation center in downtown DC.

The morning traffic moved slow and steady.

As the taxi pulled into the parking lot of the Balder Sports Arena, Sally noticed all the tow trucks hauling cars, vans and pickup trucks from the parking lot.

"How strange. Wonder what that's all about?" she thought.

Sally paid the driver and walked to the main entrance. A continual stream of humanity lined up outside and stretched around the massive arena. The people moved slowly toward the building. Most of them were tightly clutching handkerchiefs or had filter masks on their faces.

Instinctively, Sally reached into her purse and found the micro-filter mask that had been issued to her at the outbreak of the H2P5 epidemic. She wondered if the mission she had undertaken this morning was going to be safe. She countered that thought by remembering that she had already been inoculated. Just in case, she put on the mask. With renewed bravery, she walked past the slow moving lines into the entrance of the arena and up to one of the reception desks.

The attendants on duty were all dressed from head to toe in white anti-contagion suits replete with gloves, full head masks, and air tanks. Sally showed an official her government credentials and asked where the she could find the inoculation center director's office.

As she walked to the director's office, Sally noticed that the people were very calm and orderly. Sally entered the office and once again identified herself to a white hazmat-garbed receptionist.

A tall, middle-aged man, also dressed in white protective clothing and mask, greeted her warmly. "Secretary Hawthorne. How nice to meet you in person. I'm Dr. Victor Jennings. I'm the director, here, at the Balder Center. I apologize for not having a better office to receive you in. We've had to do this all very quickly, you know. Everything's very Spartan here, and very busy. What can I do for you? Come to look around the operation?"

"Well, yes I have, Dr. Jennings. I know you're busy, but do you have someone who can show me how all this works?"

"I can do that, Madam Secretary. You'll have to get disinfected, first. And then change into some of these protective clothes."

"Is that really necessary? I have been inoculated, you know."

"Oh, yes. As your doctor undoubtedly told you, you'll need a booster shot in about six months. You see, the H2P5 virus is a very stubborn strain. It seems to have the desire to grow again in some people and we're they're still working on getting a handle on its mutations. The boosters help you build up an immunity to the existing virus; on the other hand if you are exposed again, it's possible to fall sick just as though you have never been inoculated. It's all very complicated. Please, Secretary Hawthorne. It's for your protection."

Dr. Jennings took Sally to a large cabinet-like unit located in the back of the office. "If you'll just step in here, please."

She was apprehensive. "What in the world is this?"

"Oh, it may look like a big stainless-steel refrigerator, but it's actually our decontamination unit. It uses ambient air exposed to a strong ultraviolet light and swirls the air around inside the unit to disinfect your skin and clothing. It's quite harmless—except to the virus! The procedure takes only a few seconds. If you will, please step inside."

Sally complied. Dr. Jennings closed the door after her.

Inside the cabinet, a bluish light came on and then the rapidly moving air swirled around her. She felt just a slight pressure.

After thirty seconds the door unlocked and Sally stepped out. Dr. Jennings opened a sealed package containing one of the white anti-contagion outfits. With his help, Sally was suited up. He placed the headgear with a clear plastic front over her head and secured it to the suit.

"Doctor, I'll be taking video pictures of what I see and recording our conversations on this little camera as we go along. Okay?"

The doctor nodded his approval.

Sally and Dr. Jennings walked to the front of the arena and approached one of the registration desks.

Jennings gestured. "This is where they start. Each person gives his or her name and social security number. Then, by placing their hand in this little device, a scanner takes a full palm print and quickly removes a little blood. The information and blood sample are scanned by this machine and sent via satellite link-up to The National Computer for a complete analysis. The person is then issued an ID card, which has only their name on the surface. Their social security number is imprinted internally in the bar code. Next we'll go to the Assessment area."

Sally remembered the bar code cards. They were exactly like the ones that Charles had showed her at the Complex. How odd!

They moved down the hall to a bank of machines. People in lines were placing their ID cards in these machines. Each stood anxiously waiting for the results

Dr. Jennings commented. "Next, the individual stands in line to wait for the results of the computer analysis. They put their card into one of these machines. The internal bar code signals the system to imprint a specific Assessment category onto the card."

He stopped one of the people and showed Sally the card.

"The imprinter machine has coded a 'B' on this card. That signifies that this person does not have the H2P5 virus. All 'As' and 'Bs' are directed to the inoculation areas on the floor above us. Shall we go?"

"What is the difference between 'A' and 'B,' Dr. Jennings?"

"There is not any specific distinction. It really is just a way of controlling the traffic. There are more people uninfected than there are those that have the virus, you know."

Sally saw a sign on the wall in back of the counter:

*YOUR KEYS MUST REMAIN IN YOUR VEHICLE.*

*ATTENDANTS MUST KEEP THE PARKING LOT ORDERLY AND FREE OF CONGESTION!*

*PUT YOUR KEYS IN YOUR VEHICLE.*

—*Federal Order.*

"Well, that answers that question," she told herself.

Sally viewed the hundreds of people quietly doing exactly as they had been instructed. "The calmness and order here are quite remarkable, Dr. Jennings. Everyone seems to be very cooperative. No panic. No sign of the normal human selfishness. They're following instructions without any objections. Or am I just seeing it at a good time?"

"No, not at all. It's like this most of the time. Never the confusion associated with crowds of this size. Everyone wants to live, you know!"

They walked up the stairs to the first level of the sports arena as Jennings continued his narrative. "Up here, as you can see, the floor is sectioned for 'As' on this side and 'Bs' on that side."

Situated between the "A" and "B" sections were the shiny stainless-steel decontamination booths. People were going in the front doors and then, shortly afterwards, exiting out the doors on the backside. According to their designations, they moved into the long lines of those waiting to be inoculated. The flow was continuous and the pneumatic doors opened and closed with a slapping sound.

At either end of the banks of decontamination units, small treatment booths had been erected. There were hundreds of them fitted along the semicircular hallways on both sides of the arena. Because these enclosures had been made from the pipes and curtains of the arena's convention display stock, it made for a gigantic, brightly colored emergency room.

The lines of people waiting for inoculation were staggering. Dr. Jennings and Sally moved past the huge lines toward the "A" side and stopped at one of the booths.

"Let's stop in here, okay?" Jennings suggested.

They entered the curtained area. It was about ten-by-ten in size and had an eight-foot long banquet table on the far side of the entrance. There was another, narrower table on which sat a large gray device marked "Inoculator." Various bottles and cotton swabs were all neatly laid out. The table arrangement made an efficient L-shaped operating area. In the corner was a large trash bin filled with hundreds of used vials. On the floor, under the tables, were many green plastic shipping boxes. Looking closely, Sally saw that one box was marked "H2P5-C In vitro," another "H2P5-S" and the last "H2P5-I."

"Dr. Jennings, why are there three types of serums being used?"

"You are very observant, Madam. Secretary. The computer doing the analysis has also done a health diagnostic work-up on the individual. Based on the blood sample, the person's present physical condition is assessed. The computer calculates the prescription and the dosage for this three-part inoculations accordingly. Watch and you'll see how the procedure works."

A white-garbed medical person helped a man take off his shirt. The man was instructed to lay face down on the table. His head was placed in a sanitary paper covered cradle. He was told to relax and not move.

Dr. Jennings continued. "We position him so that the head stays in alignment with the spine. Then this person's ID card is placed in the Inoculator unit. The information on the card automatically tells how much of each medication is to be administered. The device is now placed on the patient, the proper position is located using a laser beam, the button is pushed and, quickly and painlessly, the inoculation is completed. It's pneumatic, you see. This device allows us to handle hundreds of people very efficiently."

"Uh-huh. Very, very quick! I had it done to me, too, but I couldn't see how it operated."

Sally noticed that the injection device bore the name of WFJ Polybiotech as the manufacturer. A quick glance at the green boxes on the floor showed the WFJ Pharmaceuticals logo. Both were companies owned by Billy!

The medical attendant wiped some alcohol over the injected areas, the patient got up and was told to dress outside. The next person was called into the vaccination area.

Sally announced, "Total time: less than two minutes from undress to out, I would guess."

"You are exactly right. And some of the assistants can do it in less time than that. We are processing an enormous number of people in this center alone. Without the computer titration and this remarkable injection device, it would be very impracticable. Imagine having to do the blood work-ups, make a decision as to how much of each serum to use and then administer three separate shots. With the many thousands of people we are handling every day, the task would be totally impossible. The virus would get ahead of us in no time. Thank God for technology."

Sally and Dr. Jennings left the inoculation booth and walked back down the hallway. Sally shot pictures of the lines and treatment booths with her digital camera. After taking one photo she noticed that the picture had captured part of a concession stand.

"Remarkable," she thought. "This huge inoculation operation is going on in a sports arena. Well, after all, it is quite a circus!"

She laughed at her little joke.

Sally addressed her tour guide. "Yes, it's all very well thought out. What about those that do have the active virus? How are they treated, Dr. Jennings?"

"They are classified as 'Cs', for contagious, and are on the lower level hallways. Because of the concentrated numbers of active virus carriers, I don't suggest we go down there!"

"I want to see it all, Dr. Jennings. Let's go."

Jennings shrugged his shoulders and reluctantly motioned her to follow. They went down the steps to the main level. Dr. Jennings went to a cabinet and picked out a small tank of sterile air. He attached the tank to Sally's suit and connected the hose to her mask.

As they continued their journey down to the lower level, Dr. Jennings explained. "You must use the auxiliary air supply while we are down here. Let me turn the tank on for you. This air will last for about 30 minutes. It's sterilized and has been treated with a special disinfectant that mixes with the filtered ambient air to help arrest any virus that you might encounter."

Sally noted that the lines of people in the lower level seemed to be as large as on the top level. It was very congested. As they passed in between the lines, she noticed that all of the entryways—the portals into the arena proper—were boarded over and sealed with plastic sheeting. Each portal had a "No Admittance" sign and an arrow pointing to the right. Following these arrows, they came to the back of the arena, where a huge temporary wall had been erected with doors marked with the numbers 1, 2, and 3.

The double line had split into three lines. Sally assumed that a similar wall and doors existed in the hallway on the other side of the arena. A white-garbed medical official with a bullhorn monitored each line. There were four other men in white with American flag patches on the left arm of their outfits. Each of these guards had police batons in their hands, machine guns on their shoulders, and holstered 9mm automatic pistols.

"Why the heavy artillery, Dr. Jennings?"

"You probably didn't notice them on all levels when you came in. We do have many armed guards throughout the building—enough to give an attitude of control and quell any disturbances that might occur. I don't mind having them here. In fact, it's a comfort knowing they are here."

"Uh-huh. What happens behind the doors?"

"Behind each door is a double bank of decontamination booths, like the one you used in my office. Every person is first decontaminated and then inoculated as you've just seen. They are then sent into the interior of the arena to stay under quarantine for several days."

Dr. Jennings directed her to look at the two large-screen TVs that were telling and showing the people in line what was about to happen to them. A narrator informed the visitors that 200 people at a time were allowed to enter the decontamination units. The video cut to a shot of visitors coming out the doors of the decontamination units and then showed them being inoculated in the prescribed manner. Then the people were directed to the interior of the arena, where the cameras panned back and forth covering the entire area.

The main interior of the arena had been converted into a field hospital. Beds had been erected in the seating area as well as on the arena floor and several catering trucks were dispensing food to the people. The atmosphere was calm and happy. The audio/video announcement continued, over and over.

Dr. Jennings assured Sally, "Inside we have the capacity to house thousands during the necessary quarantine period. Unfortunately, Ms. Hawthorne, I am not permitted to take you any further. Those medical assistants who have been assigned to the quarantine area actually live in there. They will stay inside until this crisis is over. There is no traffic back and forth and, with a contagious epidemic of this type, I think that's good policy, wouldn't you agree? Now I think we should go back upstairs."

They traveled back down the hallways past the lines of "Cs" and up the stairs to Dr. Jennings' office. Sally took off the hooded suit and thanked him for his courtesy.

As she was leaving, Sally snapped a few more pictures and noted that, at every entrance, stairway and desk, there were armed men in white contagion uniforms.

The situation in the inoculation center seemed to be just as it should be. Sally went outside to wait for the cab. This little excursion had her mind working overtime. She was reeling with imagined conclusions and conjecture about what she had just seen.

In the taxi, on the way back to her apartment, she continued to think about her tour. Sally's thoughts were always processed with questions first.

"Why am I so paranoid? Why do I always have to question? Was what I've seen the real truth? I have to stop that kind of thinking. It was real and it was being handled in a safe and correct fashion. Maybe Billy was right. Maybe I am nuts!"

It was nearly noon when Sally arrived back at her apartment. Wilhelm was gone.

As a matter of habit, she turned on the TV. It blared:

> *Go to an inoculation center immediately. You must get the H2P5 Virus examination test and inoculation. Watch your TV for instructions. Your life depends on getting the inoculation!*

Another announcement followed:

> *If you need money for transportation, get to the nearest H2P5 VIRUS inoculation center and receive $20 in cash. Go now to the nearest inoculation center as instructed. This epidemic is serious. Do not delay. You must get inoculated.*

Then a very menacing message:

> *You are violating Federal Law if you have not been examined and inoculated for the H2P5 Virus. You are also breaking the law if you fail to report to the authorities anyone who has not had the vaccination. You must report all people who have not been inoculated. It is your duty as an American Citizen to call the Federal Crisis Hot Line and report all violations of this Federal Order. Call 1-800-555-5764. These unvaccinated people need your help now. You will save the lives of your friends and family by reporting them. Act now. Call: 1-800-555-5764.*

"My God. It is a real epidemic." Sally thought. She was angry at the way she had treated Billy last night. "He is an extraordinary man! Without his courage, his organizational skills, and his ability to take over this horrible crisis, millions of people would be dying. I have to apologize to him and beg him to forgive me!"

Sally was exhausted and decided that a little nap would be a good idea. She set her alarm to ring at 5 p.m. so as not to be late for the nightly Cabinet meeting. She quickly fell asleep with the television on.

As Sally slept, the TV continued to deliver its messages to the people.

# 18

## *THE INVESTIGATION*

The daily Cabinet meeting was held at the White House at 7pm. Every second day, the President was scheduled to chair the meeting as "crisis" conferences. On the other days, Vice President Harrison presided over the meeting.

Tonight, Billy would be there, and Sally wanted to see him before the meeting. This would be an opportune time to talk with him about what she had seen earlier that day at the inoculation center and to sincerely apologize for her rudeness.

Sally telephoned from her office in the White House to Billy's secretary. The President was in. She was connected.

"Hello, 'Miss Madness.' How was your day?"

"Fine, Billy. I went out to the inoculation center at Balder Arena today and had a very interesting tour with a Dr. Jennings. I have pictures. Wanna see?"

Billy answered her with sincere interest. "Sure, come on over. I have a few minutes between appointments."

Billy hung up and rang Collings. "Rob, Sally went to the Balder center today, took a tour and some pictures...She's on her way over to my office."

In a few minutes, Billy's secretary showed Sally into the Oval Office. Billy got up to greet her and kissed her lightly on the cheek.

"What have you been up to, Mata Hari?"

They sat on the couch.

"Well, after last night's episode...Billy, I sincerely apologize for all that. I was a little drunk, you know. I wanted to put all that nonsense to rest. And in the process, I think I became better informed about the operation in general. I think I'm the only Cabinet member that has actually gone to one of these inoculation centers. I got some great pictures—which I just gave to David Barnston—and he's going to have them projected for the Cabinet meeting tonight. I found out so much about how this is being handled, it's...."

"Whew. You're running full speed ahead, aren't you? Slow up and try to put a bottom line together for me, will you? Want a drink?"

"Thanks, but no."

Billy got up and poured a drink for himself.

Sally continued. "I discovered today that you and Charles designed all the stuff that's being used to operate these inoculation centers. Very fortunate for WFJ, isn't it? You'll make even more millions. I didn't like was that I wasn't allowed to go into the quarantine area. Dr. Jennings' reasons seemed a little lame, but I suppose he was just following orders, eh?"

Billy sat back down with his drink, and took a sip. "First, all that inoculation 'stuff,' as you called it, is being provided below cost. WFJ will not make a penny. I think we'll probably lose a lot of money. That's a fact, my dear! As to the quarantine area, I think the doctors over there try to keep the in-and-out traffic at low levels. Makes sense, doesn't it? We are dealing with a highly contagious and deadly disease, you know. At any rate, you seemed to have had a very good fact-finding mission. I'll mention your field trip at the Cabinet meeting tonight and maybe you can share some of your observations and pictures with the rest of us."

"I would be honored to do so, Mr. President. I know you think I'm a nut case. I liked what I saw today. The inoculation center was very neat and well-organized. Very calm. The people were cooperative. It's not at all what I imagined the public's response to an epidemic would look like. Is there something I didn't catch, Billy?"

He laughed. "You just won't quit, will you? It's well organized because I organized it. I'm very good, you know, and the citizenry have cooperated because of the good work done by David Barnston. The information campaign he created is very thorough and effective. David knows human nature quite well. No, my little curiosity cat, you didn't catch any ulterior motive, because there isn't any. The good news is we are making real progress in containing this virus and we're saving millions of lives every day. Felix tells me that the National Computer reported that if we continue to operate as we are, we can probably have this thing wrapped up for all of North America within the next ninety days, or even less!"

"How many people are dying, Billy? What's the mortality rate? Is it high? And what are they doing with all of the dead bodies? It could tax another end of the system. Could be a big mess, don't you think?"

"Sally, I haven't heard the bad news on this thing, yet. Let's bring it up at the Cabinet meeting tonight and see what kind of report we get."

He looked at the wall clock. "Listen, I don't mean to rush you out of here, but I have to meet with Walter Manning from the Auto Laborers Union. Walter has been very helpful in coordinating things in the big cities. Out you go. I'll see you in a little while."

Sally smiled demurely obediently left the Oval Office.

Billy picked up the phone to call Collings but before he got the receiver to his ear, Collings came through the other door.

"This is a great test of our system, Billy, but that ditzy broad is pissing me off with her snooping. What do you think we should do with her?"

Billy put the receiver down and looking Collings in the eye. "Forget about it."

"Right." Collings was not happy and shrugged his shoulders in defeat. "You're the boss. I still think we should use the NIC satellite tracking system to keep an eye on that young lady and continue to replace the bugs in her apartment, on her videophone, cell phone, and in her car. I'd like to know whether this is her own curiosity, or someone else's. What do you say, Billy?"

"Surveillance is your call, Rob. If it's necessary, put your snoops in action."

The Cabinet meeting that evening was productive. Sally's photographs were of great interest to everyone, and she was the belle of the ball with her first-hand commentary.

Sally asked about the mortality rates and body disposal. The statistical answers on the numbers of dead and dying came from Professor Osher and were substantiated by Felix Hansen, but the details of the body disposal were sketchy and definitely not to Sally's liking. She insisted on more.

Sally was a bit upset. "Cremation? Is that the only way? Where is it being done? How are the bodies transported?"

Professor Osher continued to explain. "Well, I don't know of any other way to do it. We've a huge number of dead bodies to contend with, a rapidly decomposing mass of virus-ridden flesh. Normal embalming and burial would be very dangerous, if not impossible, to accomplish without contamination. Death is never palatable, Ms. Hawthorne. I can you see you don't have the stomach for it. You'll discover that, much as in any war, it becomes a routine occurrence, as it has during this crisis. I might add that, historically, in times of plague, the burning of the dead was the only sure way to stop the spread of disease."

Sally persisted. "You'd think that with all your great scientific inventiveness, Professor, you might have come up with something other than carrying dead bodies to funeral pyres as they did in the middle ages."

Billy shut Sally down. "Sally, I think you need to drop this subject right now. Professor Osher and his staff have explored all the possibilities. This is not a subject for debate at this stage of the game. Let's go on to something more positive, ladies and gentlemen."

And they did go on, but Sally had been cut off; told "no." You did not tell Sally Hawthorne "no." Curiosity and anger fueled her over-active imagination. She couldn't hear the rest of the meeting. Her mind recalled the old newsreel footage of Auschwitz and Buchenwald, where the bodies were carted out like cordwood and piled high beside the crematoria alongside mountains of clothing and glasses and teeth. Try as she might, she couldn't believe that Billy, or any of them, could have fallen into that kind of horror scenario. Yet, with the death figures that Osher had reported, she conceded that something had to be done with the dead. It was obvious that funeral homes and morgues couldn't handle the load.

What did they do during wars, she wondered. That was something to research. But this wasn't war. What were they doing with the dead bodies of the plague victims? Why wasn't it done in public view? The lack of details was driving her mad. She had to go back to that inoculation center tonight and find out what they were really doing and how it was being done. She wanted to leave immediately. Suddenly her daydreams were interrupted. The Cabinet meeting was over.

Sally almost raced out of the White House. She got to her car and started out for the Balder Arena Inoculation Center. As she drove, she made a plan. She would act like she was part of the "C" class and go through the entire process, get inside the quarantine area, take pictures and watch for someone to die and see how the body would be handled. She would follow the removal of the body and see what really happened.

Sally smiled to herself and thought that maybe she was a little overly dramatic. For some reason, she was acting like Charlton Heston in Soylent Green. She hoped that she wouldn't have to ride in a garbage truck to find out the truth. She had to go through with it, no matter what.

As she turned into the parking lot at the arena, Sally noted that the traffic was a lot heavier than earlier in the day. She found a parking spot and, not obeying the sign, she locked her car and kept the keys. Sally didn't like anyone telling her what to do.

Inside the building, on the lower level, the lines were long and dense with people. It looked like it would be a long wait, but Sally was determined. The line moved a bit faster than she expected and before long she could see the doors marked 1, 2 and 3. She clicked off a few pictures and spoke quietly into her camera/recorder. "The line is moving up, but in order to get inside the main arena, I need a 'C' class card. My 'A' card won't get me past the doors."

She looked up and down the line for an answer. She spotted an old woman in line who had the necessary "C" card in her hand. Sally spoke authoritatively to the old woman. "Your card please, ma'am." The old woman gave Sally her card.

"This is the wrong card, ma'am. I'm sorry, but you'll have to go back upstairs. Just ask them again for a card. I'll keep this one. Thank you."

The old woman obediently left the line and headed back toward the stairs. Sally was thrilled. She had the "C" class card that would get her inside the quarantine area. The line was slowing. It appeared as though the attendants were counting the people in the long line.

Sally continued her dictation. "About fifty or sixty from each line are allowed to enter the doors and then the attendants slam the doors shut and slide large bolts across all three doors. I wonder why they lock the doors? Oh well, I'll find out soon enough."

Sally was in the next group being counted. That group was ordered to enter the #2 door. Inside, it was like a maze. A turn to the left, then to the right and finally into a large room. On the left side of this area were the stainless-steel decontamination cabinets she had seen earlier that day. She quickly counted nearly one hundred of them. They would enter the cabinet and then exit to the interior of the arena for inoculation and quarantine. The people were being ordered to stand in front of each cabinet and were told to await the order to enter. The doors automatically opened and the order to enter was sharply called out.

Sally started up the steps to enter the cabinet. Suddenly someone grabbed her arm. She turned around. It was Collings.

"Let me go, Rob. I want to see what's going on inside the arena."

"Sally." The look in his eyes was severe. "Come with me. Now!"

She sensed that she should follow his direction without debate and gave up any idea of struggling with Collings.

He dragged her roughly, back through the main doors and down the hall and up the stairs. When they reached the parking lot, Collings stopped and calmly spoke. "Give me the keys to your car."

Sally fumbled in her purse and found her keys.

"Where are you parked?"

She told him and they went to her car. Collings drove. He clearly did not want to talk.

Sally broke the silence. "Why did you do that, Rob? You had no right to stop me. How did you find me? Where are we going? Talk, dammit."

Collings pulled the car violently to the curb.

"Now you listen to me, you meddling bitch. I didn't want to hire you the first day I met you. You're trouble to Billy, to this country, and to me. We are headed back to your apartment. Billy will be there, and you'll find out the rest of the story very shortly. Now shut your mouth or I'll knock your teeth in!"

They drove on in silence.

Rob and Sally entered the building through a side door and took the stairs to her apartment.

Sally nervously fumbled with the keys in the lock. Finally, she unlocked the door and the two of them entered the apartment. Collings closed and bolted the door.

Just as Collings had promised, Billy was there. He stood with a glass in his hand, talking to Wilhelm, who was seated on the couch.

"Well, well, well. Got her in time, did you? I guess that's a blessing, although we've yet to confirm that thought. Sit down, Sally, we've got some real talking to do."

Sally seated herself beside Wilhelm.

"Now. First, let me tell you that Collings just saved your life. You were about to enter one of the LOES chambers and you would have been instantly disintegrated!"

Sally's mouth dropped open.

Billy intended to shock her. "Oh, I see you don't comprehend what I'm talking about. Understand, all of those people on the lower level— the one's that have the 'C' classification—they have the virus and they are being killed! There is no cure, Sally. Only prevention. Get it? No, you don't. It's too much, too soon."

Billy began to pace and spoke to her quietly and carefully. "Not quite a year ago, we discovered that this H2P5 virus was highly contagious and also it was concluded that there was no cure. Once you contract it, you die. Scientists worldwide began to work on an antivirus serum. My people at WFJ Polybiotech began to prepare the delivery equipment necessary to deal with a gigantic outbreak of this virus. The CDC told us that hundreds of thousands had already been diagnosed as having the H2P5 virus and the death rate, according to the computer models, would grow exponentially into the millions in a very short time. We were faced with the most fantastic dilemma ever known. Under these circumstances, the possibility that the human race could be totally wiped out was very, very real!"

Billy moved to the DVD player on top of Sally's television set. "Let me show you what really happens in the LOES machine."

He punched the button and the TV screen came to life. The video was titled: "The LOES-I MACHINE—Operation and Effect."

Sally saw a stainless-steel cabinet just like the one she was preparing to enter when Collings stopped her. The video showed a very sick person, obviously suffering from the H2P5 virus—covered with sores and in an extremely weakened condition—being helped into the LOES chamber by two white-suited men. The door on the demonstration unit had a vertical pane of glass the full length of the door. An attendant pushed a button on the machine. The man inside opened his mouth and, with eyes wide in terror, he literally melted away. Then a spray of fluid washed down the inside of the cabinet, the interior light came on and the door automatically popped opened. The camera tilted down to the drain in the floor and back up the walls. There was nothing left of the man or his clothing. The complete and total disintegration of the man's body and clothing took only about thirty seconds.

Sally gasped, horrified."Oh, my God..."

"Yes, that could have been you, my dear. Now you understand why I said that Rob Collings saved your life. Please compose yourself and listen. You see, if we killed the people and burned their bodies using conventional methods, we would face the same management problems that Hitler encountered during the Holocaust. Even though our motives are certainly different from those of the Nazis, we have some of the same logistical problems. For example, the killing of the individuals, the transportation of the dead bodies, and the safe, efficient disposal of the bodies are..."

Sally stood up and shrieked. "You are Hitler. You're monsters. You're sick and depraved. How could you even think of...?"

Billy calmly walked over to her and smacked her across the face with a force that sent her falling sideways into Wilhelm's lap. "You keep your mouth closed until I'm done. I'm tired of your incessant interruptions. You never have facts, only raw emotion. Now shut up and listen!"

Sally was in total shock. With terror in her eyes, she slowly sat upright on the couch.

Billy continued. "Sally, I'm going to try another tack with you— some different words that, hopefully, will help you understand this problem."

He was pacing again.

"I want you to imagine that you are the President of the United States and that your advisors have told you that this H2P5 virus epidemic was still growing and would reach pandemic plague proportions very quickly if nothing was done to stop it. And then they tell you that a vaccine has been discovered that can save those who are not yet infected, but those that have, or will contract the virus are definitely going to die. There is nothing that will save them. Well now, Sally, you ask these scientists how many will die, and they tell you millions. You, of course, ask them how will they handle all those dead bodies, 'cause you've read your history books and to allow dead bodies to lie around will produce even more lethal diseases. And then the science guys tell you that with this plague, it will probably become worse than just decomposing dead bodies. They tell you that each of the people that die from this virus will become a great big Petri dish. The virus goes on living on that dead flesh and that whole mass of dead flesh grows more viruses and becomes a huge deadly mass. You quickly realize that this is a problem that no one has ever had to deal with before. You ask for more advice as to what to do and how to handle this crisis."

Billy stopped and looked directly at Sally. "The scientists go away and come back with some very shocking answers. They give you their recommendation: Mass diagnosis by computer and immediate inoculation on a scale never before attempted—immediate mass disposal of the dead and infected by laser disintegration in order to eliminate the spread and further mutation of the disease. They further instruct you that no cure has yet been found and that we must use a very exacting test to see if whether a person is infected and, if they are, eliminate them humanely and immediately to prevent their suffering, and thereby also prevent the spread of the disease."

Sally's face had frozen into a dazed look of astonishment.

"You're horrified, aren't you, Sally? 'Genocide,' you think. No, my dear. We are not killing particular individuals, groups, or races of people for some racist, religious, or political reason. What we are doing is called euthanasia. We are humanely, painlessly and safely preventing millions of people from suffering a very painful death, and by using this process, we are saving millions—maybe the entire population of the planet—from absolute and certain death."

Billy paused to sip his drink

Sally spoke to him in a cautious and quiet voice. "What if you are killing people who could recover, who could get well?"

Billy screamed at her. "THERE IS NO CURE! Don't you get it? If there were even the slightest hope that even one person could recover, we wouldn't have taken this approach. As of this date, NO ONE—do you hear me—no one has ever recovered. They all DIE!"

Sally trembled, but again weakly asked, "Are the scientists continuing to try to find a cure? If they do, will you stop this terrible thing you are doing?"

Billy regained his composure and drew in a deep breath. "Sometimes I wonder whether you will ever use any common sense to temper all that expensive knowledge you have acquired. Sally the answer, of course, is yes. Clearly, if a cure is found we will stop the killing."

Wilhelm stared intently at his father. Finally, he blurted out. "I was right, Dad. You've engineered this whole thing."

Billy was let down. "Willy, have you heard anything I've said?"

"Of course, I have, Father. I'm not condemning you with that statement. It was a compliment to you. I admire and love you even more. I'm just amazed at what you have done. I understand the issue and that no one else must know. This must be kept quiet."

Billy interrupted. "Yes, son, it must. Allow me to tell you both what would happen if the general public found out. Panic. Rebellion. Civil disorder of the highest magnitude. And for what? It wouldn't alter the facts and millions would still die. No, you both must never talk, even among yourselves. From this day on you will be watched and followed. Your apartments and phones will be bugged. Your whereabouts will be monitored. For as much as I love you both, I cannot under these circumstances trust you. When this is over, soon I pray, well then..."

Sally spoke angrily. "Billy, you're a mass murderer and I think that this is monstrous, and..."

"Now, I don't want to call you names or slap you again, Sally, so slow up. I want you to understand something. Last year, when we designed this plan with the former president, we all agreed that anyone—get this now Sally—anyone outside of the top people who are directing this program, anyone who might find out the details, whomever they might be, would be killed immediately. Not put on trial or given a talking to—killed! Collings is capable of following that instruction, and he can do it here and now, if I so order. I have intervened on behalf of both of you for the last time. I am in a most difficult position because of your meddling, Sally. Emotion says try to inform you and save your lives. Reason says you're both dead. Don't push this issue with any more of your crap, Sally!"

Sally and Wilhelm were both speechless. They sat on the couch and stared blankly at the wall as Billy walked to the liquor cabinet and poured another glass of scotch for himself.

"I suggest we all have a drink and let everything sink in."

As they sat there, Sally and Wilhelm thought it over. They believed Billy. And the public would have believed him too, if they had known the facts. But sadly, the real truth was still hidden from them all.

# 19

## *PLAN 'B' COMPLETED*

Billy's "Plan B" was operating just as he wanted. For over a year, the media had dutifully reported that a mystery virus was causing deaths in various parts of North America. But most of the public thought of it as another news story, just a terrible problem that would not personally hurt them. Now it had become a lethal plague.

The H2P5 virus was an efficient and deadly disease. It caused immediate sickness to those who drank or used contaminated water. Anyone who contracted the virus became nauseous and soon projectile vomiting would occur. Then the individual would become dizzy and frontal headaches would begin. Within two days they would suffer from blurred vision, profuse mucus emanation from the nose and severe and uncontrollable salivation. They would finally become so weak that total bed rest was needed. By the third day, their arms and legs would swell with acute edema and infection and ulcerated open sores would appear on their bodies. There was no way to reverse this condition. No one lived more than four days.

The media announcements stated that the virus was slowly

spreading, that an epidemic was imminent. These announcements in turn caused the public to become alarmed. The news sources continued to let it be known that a cure for this deadly disease was being sought from the worldwide scientific community.

The fear of plague was an ancient ghost. Everyone wanted to live, so they obeyed the government's orders unfailingly.

Sally's intuition regarding Billy's Plan B was, in fact, absolutely correct. It was a lie, and even though she knew some of the truth, that truth that Billy had told her was, of course, just another lie. The real details of his "Plan B" and the artificial plague were to be known only to Billy and the members of the Inner Circle.

Billy had carefully designed the H2P5 virus epidemic as a plague that would become a huge, yet controllable national crisis and pandemic. He used the media to make the public believe that he and his Third Party would be able to solve this public health disaster promptly and with minor losses.

It was a brilliant contrivance and Billy was confident that this huge national calamity would insure him firm and enduring control over the government, the media, the military, and the people.

As the days moved forward, this phony plague worked with frightening results, and the people bought the lie without protest. Billy was a planning genius. He had created a mystery and wrapped it in an enigma. The secrecy was so tight that only a few would ever know the truth.

Billy considered his new Third Party an opportunity to deal with even larger issues. It was more than just being President. He knew that as President he would finally have the opportunity to put his theories and plans for mankind's social reconstruction into action.

David Barnston had contrived a clever plan to use the media to gradually shape the public's awareness of the H2P5 virus. Barnston knew that over time and with careful handling, the media systems would ultimately sow the psychological seeds of fear into the general public. Little by little Billy and David had created a massive crisis situation that seemed quite natural and spontaneous, and the public bought it.

During the year that Billy campaigned for President, Collings had his very capable "S Class" operatives moving about North America creating one H2P5 virus outbreak after another. There were just enough cases to keep the media reporting the horrible death details on a weekly basis.

Barnston maneuvered the media with deft precision and made sure that the press was fed only the most graphic pictures, videos and extremely lurid details for their articles. The results were that each report and newscast allowed the public to have a close-up look at the dead and dying. What they saw wasn't very pretty. The media reports usually stated that a cure was in sight. It was that promise alone that gave the public just enough comfort and complacency to put it out of their minds. They listened and looked, but they still didn't get excited until the "plague" was publicly announced. Barnston's psychological preparation had paid off. Billy was right on target when he said that the people of America could easily be controlled. As in times past, they obeyed all orders and quietly allowed this treacherous government to selectively kill them.

Before Billy and the Inner Circle had embarked on their "Plan B," Professor Osher and Dr. Gertz had reformulated the original natural strain of H2P5/4 virus and added a few new touches. It now became H2P5/4B, with quicker results and even more horrifying deaths. It was premeditated murder and Gertz and Osher had concocted a most efficient method for death. It was in fact, absolutely foolproof.

Neither of the strains of H2P5 had ever been contagious. The virus had to be injected or ingested in the body to become deadly. Professor Osher had devised a very clever method to distribute the virus. He personally instructed Collings' S-Operatives, showing them how to place the H2P5 virus into various drinking water systems in the selected cities. Osher deduced that apartment complexes, hotels, dormitories, military bases, etc. would be the best venues to gain the desired controlled terror results. By adding small amounts of the H2P5 virus directly into the water mains that fed these heavily populated dwellings, and by using random-day insertion patterns, the S-Operatives were able to produce the appearance of a highly contagious disease.

Because the targeted dwellings had large concentrations of people, the residents would begin to talk with one another when a crisis occurred. An outbreak of disease in these buildings would become the topic of conversation and therefore raise immediate alarm. Since the H2P5 virus dissipated in the water after thirty minutes, when tests were made by health officials no trace would ever be found. Cleverly, Osher speculated that not everyone would drink or use water during the period that the virus was active in the water mains and therefore not everyone in the building would become infected. Gertz and Osher felt that by using this methodical system, the stories of an airborne, contagious virus would come about and further hide the real source of contamination.

During the latter part of Billy's election year, Collings had ordered his S Corps to expand the pace. Gradually, hundreds of people contracted the virus. The increased numbers and the incidents occurring in multiple cities continued to be worrisome in appearance. Slowly, the H2P5 virus became a recognized problem and progressively caused greater public concern.

After Billy's election, the "plague plan" went into high gear. Barnston began to intensify the reports that the H2P5 virus was extremely contagious because of the very horrible effects of the new H2P5/4-B formula. The H2P5 virus appeared to be every kind of contagious disease that anyone had ever heard of. It was a horrible, ugly plague and now the media informed and warned the population of its dangers.

With a blanket over his legs, Billy sat upright on his bed in the White House watching and listening to the TV:

*The H2P5 virus is highly contagious.*

*Wash your hands after touching anyone, friend or family.*
*Wash all fruits and vegetables.*

*Boil all water both for drinking or bathing.*

*Cook all meat and poultry to a well-done condition.*

*Do not share drinking or eating utensils with anyone.*

*Do not kiss on the lips or with the mouth open.*

*Do not eat in restaurants until further notice.*

*Do not allow anyone to spit or sneeze around you.*

*Stay tuned to this station for further details.*

Billy clicked off the TV. Suzzanne was out attending one of her committee meetings, so Billy picked up the phone and called Hilga's room. "Hilga, want some company?"

As he walked toward Hilga's rooms, he was inspired and became anxious to read and compare Kurt's letter with his own.

Hilga greeted him at the door. Billy motioned for her to come with him. They walked to the Oval Office and Billy went directly to his private safe, opened it and took out two envelopes. He directed Hilga to follow him into the Silent Room.

He closed the door and plopped into a chair. "Hilga, make us each a drink."

"Those are the letters, aren't they Billy? After all the months since Kurt died, I think you must read these letters."

In Kurt's stead, Hilga opened Billy's envelope first. Hilga carefully slit the envelope and took out the page. She read it aloud: "Title: Mankind's Moral Dilemma and the Only Solution. You've gone right to the heart of it, haven't you, Billy?

*My Dear Friend Kurt:*

*When great numbers of people in any society begin to suffer such moral and physical degeneration that, for whatever reason, they are not able to care for themselves and their communities, or to care for and prepare their children for the customary social obligations necessary for a civilized society, they therefore become a blight on that society's future. It is then incumbent upon that society, using the highest compassion and greatest concern for the dilemma of that society, to remove the misfits from the general population by any means possible. This assistance to nature must continue to be done until the society becomes healthy, productive, and balanced once again.*

*Only by employing this final answer to this unmistakable dilemma, can mankind once again pursue the pleasure of living in true harmony with nature and God.*

*—William F. Johnstone.*

Hilga handed Kurt's envelope to Billy. "Now, Billy, read what Kurt wrote to you."

Billy opened the envelope. He felt the very good paper and once again saw Kurt's bold, thick handwriting. Unlike his own typewritten letter, Kurt's handwritten, informal correspondence had no title. Before allowing the words to register in his mind, he held the paper and thought lovingly of Kurt. Then he read aloud:

*Dear Wilhelm,*

*The last answer to your big question has always been simple: Those that are inferior and impair the growth of a society must, because of their inferiority, be removed without remorse, quickly and efficiently.*

*In fact, those who break the laws of society and will not work to help the society must be also be removed. Not jailed or reeducated. Eliminated.*

*Those who are not healthy will eventually die. And since death is a part of life, how or when they die is of no importance.*

*For mankind, staying alive has and always will depend upon the survival of the fittest.*

*You realize now that the only good use for your accumulated knowledge and natural insight is to become a true leader of the people. You are the man the world has been waiting for. Your destiny has been preordained. You are the man who will make it happen.*

*All my love forever,*

*—Kurt Rheinlin*

"The answers are the same, aren't they, Billy?"

"Very close. But the old man had a more colorful and concise way of putting it, didn't he?"

Billy had finally become the "man" whom Kurt had looked for. Billy had only one agenda, not just talking about making the world better, but actually making it better. It was all perfectly planned.

The "contagion" story had been fabricated, and David Barnston knew it was just the sizzle that would make it all work. David and Billy were very capable and cunning manipulators and the "plague" was one of their biggest and best fabrications.

From the beginning, Plan B had been a premeditated stratagem designed to eliminate the undesirables that Billy knew prevented America and the world from moving toward their natural potential. Billy had predicted that the "plague" would become the most effective cleansing the world had ever experienced. It was an efficient method of human sanitization and provided a means of total domination over the people. For the first time in history, an oppression of the people would not be met with resistance.

This well-put-together plague scenario allowed Billy the opportunity to gain ultimate power during a seemingly desperate national emergency. Billy was able to wrest all of the safeguards and controls from the Congress, the military, and the media. Billy had them under his spell and now he had the public positioned to depend on the President and his government as never before.

Many of the port cities, such as Seattle, San Francisco, Los Angeles, San Diego, New Orleans, Miami and New York, had been target-ed for the phony infection to further set the stage for a full-scale pandemic. Federal orders were issued to immediately close all ports of entry to the United States. Martial law had been ordered and approved by Congress. The President had declared a state of national emergency and called in the military, National Guard, reserves, and police in every city to manage the crisis. A great plague had seemingly fallen upon the citizens of North America.

William F. Johnstone now possessed the greatest Presidential authority in history. He was, in fact, the absolute ruler of North America.

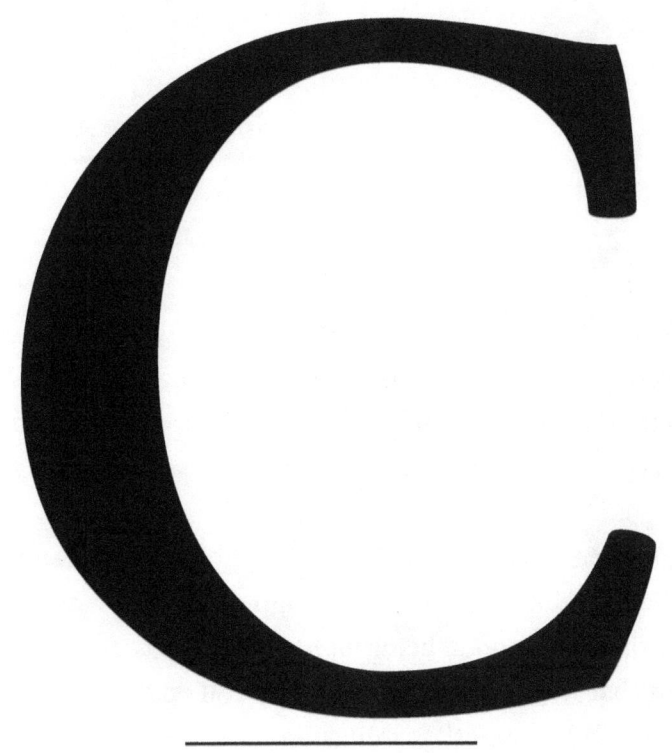

# 20

## THE CLEANSING

After his recent confrontation with Sally, Billy was worried about the disclosure of facts that he was forced to make to her and Wilhelm. Collings tried to convince Billy that even if those two now knew more of the story than they needed to know, the real truth was still safely hidden.

Billy's great deception had experienced the acid test with Sally and Wilhelm and it had passed with high marks. Sally might not have approved of the methods being used, but he was sure that she was convinced that it was, nonetheless, a very real epidemic.

But now Billy had other things on his mind. He returned to the Complex. He needed a private meeting with Charles Gertz and all of the members of the Inner Circle.

Once inside the Complex, Billy descended by elevator to the bottom-most level. The elevator doors opened to a long hallway. At the end of the hall, near a heavy metal door, he opened a box, entered some code numbers and put his hand on the palm sensor.

The "Access Approved" signal appeared, the door opened and Billy entered another long passageway. The door automatically closed behind him as he moved to the manned security station. Codes, signatures, palm prints, iris scans, voice ID, and then down the hall through a final door. He was in.

Billy entered the very heart of the busy, very secret WFJ Polybiotech manufacturing facility. Here, hundreds of technicians operated strange, sophisticated electronic equipment, making the area look like a scene out of a sci-fi movie. The workers labored day and night to produce vast quantities of the vicious and insidious tools of death needed for Billy's "plague."

Billy approached a supervisor "Where is Dr. Gertz?"

"In his office, Mr. President."

Billy knocked on the door. Above the lighted "No Admittance" panel, a speaker barked: "I told you I wanted to be left alone. Go away!"

"It's the President of The United States."

The door opened.

"Billy...goddamn. You made it! You're the President."

"Yeah, yeah, Charles. Quit screwing around!"

"I mean, I haven't seen you for a while. Uh, how long has it been?"

"Try four days, Charles. You've got to get out of this hole once in a while. You're starting to lose touch with reality again. You need to go upstairs and get some sun and fresh air."

The two entered Dr. Gertz's office. A large flat-screen computer monitor hung on one wall. Below it, on the cluttered desk, were a keyboard, a microphone and several little TV screens for the elaborate security system. The place was a bewilderment of files, papers, blueprints, and odd bits of "stuff."

"Charles, do you know what day and month this is?"

Hesitantly, "Is it before or after Christmas?"

"Right. Seriously, if you can't get out, Charles, at least turn on the news on the private channel from time to time."

"Billy, I get my National Newspaper every day at breakfast, all three pages. I read all the shit that's news to print."

"Okay, then.... Let's just leave that where it is. We have to talk seriously. I'm gonna need one hell of a lot of coordination here in a very short period of time. Have you got the Arrestor/Controller production under way?"

"Oh, yes, yes, I do! I was just reviewing the progress, Billy."

Charles approached his computer and spoke a command to the microphone.

"Gertz. Top Secret File: 4-356-8. Show now."

The big screen lit up and displayed columns of facts and figures.

Charles gestured toward the screen. "As you can see, all of the equipment production for the plague scenario is up and running on schedule. Want to see one of the new Arrestor/Controllers at work?"

"That's what I'm here for."

Charles spoke a command and closed the computer display. He motioned Billy toward a big safe-like door located in the wall in his office. Charles inserted a security card in the door, put his palm on a sensor, whispered a few words in a wall microphone, and the door unbolted and opened. They entered another part of the huge underground facility.

"Is the new unit as good as the prototype?" Billy asked.

"It's outstanding. Let's go to the test area and I'll show you."

They walked down a corridor to a glass enclosed room. Inside, several men were being put through various physical tests. On the outside wall near the window, Gertz picked up a telephone. Inside the room a lab technician answered.

"This is Dr. Gertz speaking. I want you to immobilize one of the volunteers. Use Level Number Two."

The technician removed a small handheld device from his belt holster, aimed it at one of the men, and pushed the button. The test subject stopped in his tracks and fell to the floor.

"Level Number Two, Billy. Immediate unconsciousness. The two MMEAs–the 'Multiple Micro-Electrode Array'—implants in the back of the ear in the mastoid bone—one array on either side—vibrate with an astounding effect. This controller unit broadcasts a signal on a low frequency radio band that excites the MMEA. With the setting at Level Number One, the MMEA vibrate. A mild sound impulse occurs in the ear, causing the subject to become dizzy, disorientated, docile and very cooperative. Should it be necessary—say, if the subject becomes violent or decides to use his willpower to resist Level Number One—then the operator can increase the sound wave to the second level, causing unconsciousness, as you've just seen."

Feeling the pride of his work, Gertz continued. "Now let me review that with you, Billy. Level One shocks the nervous system into disorientation. Increase it to Number Two, and we get unconsciousness. If it is increased further, to Level Number Three, immediate death should occur."

Using a microscope, Gertz showed Billy a box of tiny, clear, glass-like pieces. "These MMEAs are manufactured to precise specifications and will all receive the same radio frequency. As you can see, they are smaller than grains of sand and are kept in-vitro, and when injected in the mastoid bones they open to form clusters and become quite remarkable radio receivers."

"The Controller Unit is directional—point and shoot—or for a group it can be widened to omni-directional. The MMEA can also be activated by a special FM radio broadcast signal."

"As you know, all radio station transmitters are being set at the same frequency. In an emergency, a rebellion, or the like, we will be able to control a whole city's population, if necessary. Give me your old controller, Billy, and take this new one with you. Who knows. You may need it."

Billy removed the prototype Arrestor/Controller unit that he had been carrying in his pocket. He held it side-by-side with the new model. It was just about the same, except the new model had a button marked "IC."

"Charles, I know that everyone in The Group has been implanted with the special Arrestor MMEAs. But the IC button on this unit—does this stand for the Inner Circle? Have you implanted us, too?"

"No, Billy, not you and me, just the rest of the Circle—Rob Collings, too! I've used a separate frequency, last resort sort of thing. Only you and I will have these special IC capable units. Rob has a unit with a 'G,' Group button."

"You are a very sneaky man, Charles Gertz. How in the world did you get to Collings? Well, I guess you have your ways, don't you? I suppose that IC button should make me more comfortable. You're sure I'm not implanted, Charles?"

"Absolutely not, Billy. I'll show you."

Gertz turned the controller on Billy and pressed the button.

"Charles, quit fooling around! Say, I don't know if you've tried it on full power—I mean to kill—but let me tell you it does work. Collings used the prototype on Sen. Applegate at the Capitol building, and he dropped like a fly. It was amazing. Right there in Congress. It looked like a cerebral hemorrhage and they bought it hook, line, and sinker!"

Charles was impressed. "Hmm. Interesting. We've only used Level Three on lab animals, so far. I'm happy to hear that it works on humans. Anyhow, to continue, as you already know, during the mock immunizations, the MMEAs are injected by the pneumatic gun housed in the Inoculator units and then..."

Billy patted Gertz on the back. "Okay. Okay, Charles. It's all a marvel of technology. You and your people have done a great job. And yes, I do understand this system. I designed the original plans, remember? Now, Dr. Forgetful, I assume that the Inoculators and support supplies are in full distribution."

Slightly embarrassed, Charles hoped to impress Billy with his progress. "Oh, yes, they certainly are, Billy. We have produced and shipped more than enough to get the major cities started. We make shipments two times every day. Rest assured, Billy, we will continue to manufacture 'round the clock and will soon be creating big inventories of all stocks and equipment. The LOES-100 units have been installed in the major cities and are operating now. Everything is going according to your plan and, with these new Arrestor/Controllers, in conjunction with the radio stations that Julio Mondaldo is presently retrofitting, you will be able to restrain even the most uncooperative citizens... should you ever need to do so."

Billy looked at the unconscious body of the test victim and gingerly fingered his Controller Unit. He began to speak, talking to the air, not to Charles. "Ah, yes, yes. What we are doing is absolutely incredible. Soon we will have eliminated the dregs of humanity and will have an entire world free from greed and avarice. No more violence or crime or criminals. No more war or famine. It will be a wonderful world brimming with citizens who are always able, always creative, always willing to work, always productive. A world filled with people who will want to love and work and play in genuine harmony with each other. People who will never be ill again, and whom, very soon, we can assure that death will never visit them again. It will be a brave new race of people who are happy, civil and fruitful. All thriving under one great government...and one great and benevolent God."

Billy abruptly stopped his inspired sermon. "Charles, I want you up in Washington on Monday without fail for that Cabinet briefing. And now, you and I have a meeting with our Inner Circle."

Billy and Charles left the test area, took the elevator up to the next level and soon arrived at the private IC meeting room. In attendance were all members of the Inner Circle: David Barnston, Rob Collings, General Alfred Fenwick, Professor George Osher and Vice President Avery Harrison.

Billy began the meeting. "Gentlemen. We have much to do tonight.

First, Professor Osher, my good Surgeon General, you and Dr. Gertz have created the humane elimination techniques that are now being used during our plague scenario. I have just read the daily reports and your systems are operating better than we anticipated. I thank you both for your good work.

"And Mr. Barnston, as Secretary of Communication, you have been put in charge of getting my messages to the people. Your results are better than I ever imagined...a really fine job, David. Currently under your command is Julio Mondaldo, our Director of the FCC. Mondaldo has the task of dismantling the existing local broadcast machinery—but saving all the necessary transmission equipment, of course. David, I know that your work is ongoing, but can you give us a little update as to what is happening at this time?"

Barnston stood up. "I certainly can, Mr. President. Much of your initial directive is well under way as we speak. All of the radio and television studios located in every city in North America are being destroyed. All radio and TV programming will now originate via satellite from New York City with the broadcasts delivered through local unmanned transmitters in all cities throughout the country. All video production will be done at the selected studios in Los Angeles and New York and the finished product, after approval, will be beamed via satellite for network broadcast to all local cities. By changing the production centers and mode of delivery, the media as we knew it will no longer exist. All communications will be totally controlled by the government. All broadcast personnel, save the new Federal News people, are being eliminated. Even the garage and basement production types will be gone and all storehouses of raw film, magnetic tapes, CDs DVDs, all camera and recording equipment, all broadcast and theatrical equipment, sound systems—everything is being confiscated and warehoused or destroyed. After we have selected the best and most loyal of the support people, all engineers, high-level production, management and technical people will also be eliminated.

Mr. President, within ninety days, your original mandate will have been accomplished."

"The emergency transmitters, David, are they being put in place?"

"Yes, sir. First, understand that Julio and his crews are under the assumption that we are retrofitting these transmitters for a special, top-secret emergency broadcast channel. Julio will see that the radio and TV transmitters, dishes, and antennas will be kept in place. He is convinced that central broadcast and local distribution is a genius idea and actually thinks he invented it. He very much approves of the addition of the special computerized server equipment installed in each transmitter location. This will enable each transmitter, in an emergency situation, to be tuned to a higher frequency and used to activate the implanted MMEA for general public control. It's all on schedule."

As Barnston reported, the computer screens in front of each member displayed the drawings and floor plans of some of the transmitter areas. "The newest, most modern FM equipment will then be installed in Julio's newly constructed transmitter houses. Each new location will become a very fortified bunker, completely surrounded by high-walled heavy concrete walls and ceilings. As I indicated in my recent memo to you, after Julio's people have done the transmitter retrofitting, other crews will come in after him to raze the actual broadcast studios and management offices. This systematic plan of building and razing will continue and very soon we will control all communication in North America with all production and transmission originating from New York City!"

Billy made a move on the keyboard in front of him. The images on the computer screens at each member's desk quickly changed.

Billy took over. "Very, very good David. Now, on to the daily reports, gentlemen. The H2P5 virus has been constantly represented to the public as an epidemic. The people have been made to believe it is a pestilence of biblical proportions. They are being identified, classified, implanted or eliminated, day and night, and have accepted the inoculation ruse without question. All Americans now pray to God each day and hope that our government and the scientists of the world will quickly find a cure for this disease. Gentlemen, psychologically, the people are primed for our next move."

Billy paced, moving back and forth in front of the IC members. "As you all know, we've been able to rely on the majority of the propaganda set in motion after World War I and World War II. In fact, those several administrations may have had something like this under discussion, although I doubt that they could have figured out how or mustered the nerve to pull it off. The CIA has used a virus to cause chaos and social conflict among certain Third World countries and on a few domestic minority groups. But our H2P5, the Osher/Gertz formula, is much more dramatic and effective. The previous administrations fanned the fires of AIDS and let it be known that there were many viruses that had the potential to become not just epidemics, but pandemics. Measles, polio, tuberculosis, Ebola, bubonic plague, cholera, anthrax, smallpox, SARS and the bird flu—they all had their fifteen minutes of fame. These very contagious diseases were always hot words with the government and the media. The scare-then-cure, then scare-again tactics were merely a sociopolitical football bounced around from administration to administration. That kind of propaganda was designed to keep the public nervous and hanging on to the hope that the government would protect them or save them from those imagined epidemics. To be fair, it did give the past administrations some degree of control, but they never had the guts to follow it through."

Billy stopped his pacing. "The ignorant, misinformed and confused public has been educated to accept whatever the U.S. government might tell them regarding outbreaks of disease. So far, that blind American trust and respect for good ol' Uncle Sam has paid off for us. The old boys always talked about a final solution, but we're doing it!"

Billy walked a bit more and then stood behind Professor Osher and put his hands on his shoulders. "My Surgeon General, in cooperation with the CDC in Atlanta, has quietly conscripted the best, most loyal, licensed doctors and nurses in North America for immediate aid in the treatment of this plague. General Fenwick has secured the cooperation of the military. Huge field centers under U.S. military control in every city are in operation, handling public inoculations. After the purge and mass implanting is completed, we will begin a clean-up stage that will use all hospitals, clinics, health facilities and our M.A.L.U. elements to service the leftovers."

With a slightly wild look in his eyes, Billy continued. "This, then, is the first chore in the cleansing of the world. I have created a totally controllable, yet seemingly supernatural epidemic that can be started and stopped whenever I want. Now this 'God-sent' plague will run rampant, spreading throughout North America as the media shouts the news of the life-saving government inoculation centers. Everyone is being tested and inoculated. They believe they must have the inoculation to remain alive and prevent the spread of the virus. Congress, without opposition, has passed my request for martial law as well as the mandatory Federal Inoculation Law, thereby allowing us absolute control over arrest and punishment. Now it will be against the law if you don't get implanted, uh, I mean inoculated."

Billy took a breath. "The governments of Canada, Mexico and the countries of Central America have ratified similar national legislation. Under these great humanitarian circumstances, our military will be allowed to come and go across foreign borders without any questions. I assure you, much will be accomplished during our kindhearted invasions of these countries."

Every eye in the room was focused on Billy. They were quite used to this frantic genius and awaited his next inspiration.

"If anyone, at any level, resists my orders in any way, the penalty will be death. My Plan B must continue to appear as a national— and growing international—emergency. Secrecy and obedience are mandatory. Soon, we will change the face of this epidemic. Mr. Barnston, your media plan has generated great public anxiety and concern, but before long this message must begin to have a definite ring of hope; the sound of human salvation, David. And, I think that the Surgeon General should personally announce on television that the FDA, the AMA, the Centers for Disease Control, World Health Organization, etcetera, have unanimously affirmed the effectiveness of this new 'preventative' inoculation. Use charts, graphs, comments from the scientists, whatever is necessary. Make it real convincing."

Billy changed their computer screens again, this time to an image of a pie chart.

"Felix Hansen tells me that our National Computer predicts that over ninety percent of the population will obediently and peacefully get their inoculations as ordered. When we near this ninety percent figure we will offer a further incentive to bring in the rest of the population. I will personally announce that the U.S. government will offer $500 in cash to anyone helping any aged or infirm person to get to an inoculation center. After a period of time, as a cleanup of the ones that won't comply, we will offer a $1,000 cash reward to anyone reporting those who have not obeyed the Federal Inoculation Law. This will set the whole nation looking for the remaining few violations. Then we will begin using the plague scenario to implant and eliminate the unfit and unnecessary and quickly move through Canada, Mexico, Central America and then into all of South America. The U.S. will be perceived as heroic in its efforts; then Europe and the rest of the free world will become 'infected,' allowing for our plans to fall into place very quickly."

"Bottom line, gentlemen? We will use this *faux* plague worldwide to finally eliminate the scum of humanity. The criminals, the useless, the unfit will disappear forever. The world will become better, the people will become better, and God will be happy with us all. This is my plan and it will be done!"

Dr. Gertz was on his feet, for he knew that Billy was about to go over the edge and would become quite manic if not interrupted. "And an excellent plan, too, Mr. President. And may I add that all doctors, everywhere, feel that they have become part of the most massive public health operation ever, a true heroic effort to save mankind. I suggest that David continue to issue information revealing that the H2P5 virus is in fact far more communicable than previously thought, but, of course, that the scientists feel that a cure is in sight."

Billy took the cue from his old friend and returned to his chair. "George, would you report how the inoculation process is currently operating?"

Professor Osher stood up and the computer monitors followed his speech with facts and pictures. "It really is working in the field, far beyond our dreams. Let me review: An individual enters the inoculation center and states his social security number to the reception clerk. That social security number is then entered into a terminal. By placing the person's hand in the Documentor, a blood sample is taken along with full hand and fingerprints. This information, together with the social security number, is then transmitted via satellite link to the National Computer Center, where the information is disseminated and run against existing files in the computer. First, a positive identification via the social security number and fingerprints is made, then, based on information found in that individuals 'Life-File,' the computer uses a special program to evaluate the worthiness of that individual. It then transmits the decision, with a classification, back to the inoculation center. In less than five minutes, the Documentor unit receives the transmission from the National Computer and the information is laser-etched onto a National Identification Card. The machine prints the card, and this becomes the Inoculation Card that the person takes to the appropriately designated area for treatment."

The computer screens displayed a picture of the Inoculator unit as Professor Osher continued. "Next, the person is directed to one of the many inoculation stations. Inside, the doctor or nurse instructs the individual to remove all clothing covering the upper torso and to lie face down on the examining table. The doctor inserts the Inoculation Card in the unit and positions the Inoculator over the person's neck and shoulders, makes simple alignment adjustments and, with one push of the button, the ID chip and the MMEAs are firmly set in place. The person is also injected with a reversible sterilization serum, as well. The card is ejected and the deed is done."

Osher turned and faced everyone. "Our security system reliably monitors the doctors. There is no medical equipment or medicine in the Inoculation Centers. They can only use our diagnosis, our medicines and our equipment. All diagnoses and instructions for the classifications come from the National Computer. After the computer issues the instructions, that same NIC card—when inserted in the Inoculator unit—will report by wireless connection to the National Computer that the process has been completed. If a report is not made within thirty minutes of the card being issued by the Documentor, military security officers using satellite GPS track the issued card and immediately find and investigate as to why there has been a delay in performing the scheduled inoculation process.

Osher stopped for a moment, anticipating their questions. "Since the doctors are permanently housed in the Inoculation Centers and cannot leave until the 'crisis' is over, we have control. Upon completion of this phase, most of them will be eliminated."

Osher clicked and the screens displayed samples of the issued NIC cards. "This is the *A-B-C* rating and what each means:

"The 'A' Cards are classified 'AS-Skilled.' The Inoculator will give them the Arrestor-1 MMEAs, an S-ID locator chip implanted deep in the shoulder muscle, and a reversible sterilization serum.

"The 'B' Cards will be classified 'RW-Worker,' and will get the Arrestor I MMEAs, the W-ID chip implant and reversible sterilization serum."

"'C' Cards are classified 'C-LO' and receive immediate death via the LOES machine. By the way, LOES stands for 'Laser Oxidation Elimination System.'"

Osher switched the computer screens to a diagram of a single LOES unit. "As we speak, these LOES-1s are being shipped to foreign countries throughout the world. The smaller LOES-1 units are easily installed in any doctor's office in less than an hour. Later on, as the 'plague' appears in full force, we will of course be exporting the LOES-100s, Inoculators, Controllers, MALU units and all the necessary supplies and parts to these countries as the worldwide Adjustment is put into operation."

Osher switched to diagrams of the big LOES-100 units. "Here at home, the LOES-100s are being ganged together as necessary to do the job in each city. They are in operation day and night in the mass inoculation centers that we've set up in major arenas, gyms, and armories throughout the nation."

The display switched again. "The medium range multiple units— the LOES-12s, 24s—will be used here at home and abroad in clinics and hospitals for "booster shots" during the final cleanup."

Osher finished with a video of the LOES unit in operation.

"Gentlemen, I assure you, these LOES machines are quite humane, no pain at all. The person is killed instantly and the body, including clothing, shoes, eyeglasses, dentures and all personal belongings, are vaporized into a fine powder by the lasers. These units also auto-clean as they flush the ash remains into the sewage system. The LOES unit reports to the National Computer that complete extermination has occurred and the eliminated person's name is erased from the National Computer files, and from that moment on that individual never existed. The entire process takes less than one minute from start to finish."

Dr. Gertz took over. "Computer surveys and projections tell us that a very large percentage of the people will unfortunately be 'Cs. In the story given to the assisting doctors, we are telling them that anyone who has the active H2P5 virus is doomed to die slowly and painfully and during that dying process they will definitely infect many others. They are convincingly told that, if unchecked, the 'plague' would then accelerate and continue to spread and that presently there is no known cure. Only the inoculation of those who do not have the virus or the prescribed euthanasia of the infected, via the LOES machines, will be acceptable procedure. We've carefully selected only those who understand and approve of euthanasia. They've accepted what we've told them as the truth!"

Osher interrupted. "Yes, and in my briefings with these doctors, all of them believed our story completely. To reinforce the severity of the situation, we've instructed all doctors and health officials to wear white anti-contagion suits with special breathing units. They are shown training films with actual field results on a daily basis. They are completely impressed that the prescribed euthanasia of an infected person is not only a good and humane idea, but must occur immediately to keep the virus from spreading. These videos have been prepared with varying story formats, but the themes remain consistent."

Dr. Gertz jumped back in. "The doctors make no decisions. During the process, they see and hear nothing. The LOES units produce almost no sound. The machines handle hundreds and hundreds of people. Within a short time, the doctors, nurses and health officials become quite indifferent and uninterested in the actual procedure. They are kept quite busy. Just like battlefield surgeons, they cease to have any feelings of remorse for what they are doing. In addition, let me say that the LOES units, Inoculators, the terminals and readers, were all under secret testing and in production for over a year before the 'plague' began and these machines function flawlessly."

Professor Osher continued, "And, as you have ordered, Mr. President, infants, children, all those up to the age of twelve will be spared. Of course, those young that are crippled or have disease will be killed. After the purge, we will closely examine the remaining young people on an individual basis to see whether they are fit to be part of our future. We are currently operating the inoculation centers well ahead of your guidelines, Mr. President. Now it's up to you and David to continue making the 'plague' announcements palatable, meaningful and effective in order to maintain control and avoid panic. We are well equipped and prepared for any contingency."

The screens dissolved into a map of the world.

Osher concluded, "In the near future, Mr. President, in the foreign scenario, we will be using a quiet method for the Adjustment of the governments. Vice President Harrison and his people are now employing Mr. Collings' high-level S-Operatives. By going through foreign diplomatic channels, they will appear to be innocently warning the leaders and the elite of these nations that the 'plague' will most likely migrate to their countries and an epidemic will occur. As a precaution, our operatives will direct these leaders and very special people to our own doctors and they will be immediately 'inoculated.' These foreign leaders will be told that the U.S. government is prepared to graciously provide our doctors and health officials, as well as the terminals, readers, and satellite linkup to our computers for diagnosis and the Inoculators, serums and the LOES units for immediate treatment in their countries. They will be assured that the U.S. will be there to assist them in every way. These Special S-Operatives will also begin to create the 'plague' scenario in these foreign countries by using the same plan that was used here in North America."

Billy concluded the meeting. "Professor, Doctor, your reputations for genius have certainly not been exaggerated in the least! Gentlemen, at long last, we have a good and final solution to the ills that have troubled mankind throughout his history."

# 21

## *THE NEW LAWS*

Later that night, Billy and his Inner Circle were flown back to Washington. Charles Gertz remained behind at the Complex to direct the further production of "plague" materials.

The next morning the President and a few of his Inner Circle were taken by car to the National Computer Building that housed one of the lighting fast computer machines. The President had come to tour the newly renovated facilities and receive a demonstration of the Classification and Law system.

The Director of the National Computer Operations, Felix Hansen, led the tour. Hansen was in high spirits. "Mr. President, gentlemen, good morning. Today we will show you one of the high-speed computers and demonstrate just how this great network of machines is presently handling the crisis. Then I'll show you how our National Computer Network will operate after the crisis, for the future care and benefit of all mankind. First, I want to give you a little background information on why we chose to use this particular type of computer for the impartial diagnosis and selection needed during the epidemic."

Felix directed them to a wall chart. "This computer is a seventh-generation machine. Simply put, this very advanced machine operates in many ways like our brains. It allows for parallel processing of information and, instead processing information displaying results serially, its memory system has the ability to remember, recall and compare, just as our minds do. This computer uses very rational logic and has been programmed to have total internal control of these processes. It can learn and make decisions like a human brain. After we installed the operating programs and started the machine, believe it or not, it quickly made very useful suggestions and began to have an artificial life of its own."

Hansen sounded like a proud parent. "The Computer assisted us in the formulation of its own program, based on the original parameters given, of course, and it has demanded copious amounts of information since it first began to function. Since we initiated its operation several months ago, we have continued to feed it data, day and night. It wants more and more information. Just like our human brains, we compute much better when we have more, not less, knowledge. And so it is with this machine. This is the most advanced form of AI—artificial intelligence—that exists in the world today. Because it has great cognitive capability, it is almost able to think—in a limited way, of course. It has been given a huge amount of data, primarily individual dossier parameters that have taught it to make the very moral and fair judgments that we needed during the evaluation period of this crisis It was designed to entirely replace the hesitant, confused, biased and otherwise fallible decisions that were previously made by man, about man. It has an accuracy ratio of one error in every three billion calculations. Much more consistent and superior to man's own very emotional, contradictory, and untrustworthy brain. 'Big Baby,' as we call her, is currently being filled with the sum total of man's legal experience. And with these extraordinarily designed legal programs she will become the new American Justice System for this millennium and the next. And probably, for all millennia to come."

Felix clicked his handheld controller and a curtain on the wall opened to reveal a large window. The men crowded together and got close to the window. They were looking into a darkened room. In the center of the room, all alone, was a huge glowing, bubbling, oscillating sphere-shaped tank.

Felix beamed. "She's quite a sight, isn't she, Mr. President?"

Billy whispered. "Astounding, Felix. Absolutely astounding! This, then, is the backbone piece of machinery of our great plan. This is the digital marvel that will provide resolution to the matters of conscience that have cursed mankind for thousands of years! Finally, pure, exact, unbiased justice!"

Felix continued. "Quite so, Mr. President. Unadulterated, precise and impartial. This is just one of eight separate Supercomputers. They are all alike in every way. For security reasons, each one is located in a separate geographic area in the United States, in a highly secured underground bunker. An expert operating team monitors each of the locations. If one of the Supercomputer's should fail, any one of the other machines in the network can take over the failed computer's tasks, or they are able to operate as a super virtual computer operating from disbursed locations. In the event of a national emergency, such as we have now, where lightning speed and massive capacity are required, all eight machines can be linked together to make one gigantic Super Virtual Computer. I have personally designed most of the operating programs being used during this plague crisis, and I am quite proud of the remarkable reliability it has produced. In order to be correct, and fair, we are using an evaluation program that is based on the moral and ethical criteria developed by the attorneys, Henry Gillespie and Irving Penitz. The program, of course, includes special guidelines as set forth by our President. The results, we believe, give us the ability to identify the very best citizens. Drawing on the immense information that has been gathered on every man, woman and child, those selected to survive will be the individuals whom we feel are the most capable and useful in the rebuilding of the infrastructure of our hemisphere after the purge."

Billy allowed himself an indulgent moment of self-satisfaction. Felix understood what needed to be done and had executed Billy's plans thoroughly and expertly. These thoughts warmed and satisfied Billy. "We are very lucky to have Felix Hansen on board. He understands exactly what I wanted done and he's done it."

The relatively recent decision to bring Felix into the Inner Circle had been a very wise decision.

Felix clicked the handheld controller again and the curtain closed on the Supercomputer. On the wall, a projection screen lighted up showing a series of numbers.

"I want to call attention to the fact that, since before the turn of the twentieth century, every agency of the federal, state and local governments has been gathering and filing information on the citizens of North America. In 1949 that information was taken from manila folders in hundreds of thousands of filing cabinets. This data was then systematically entered into computers and converted into electronic files, spawning an entirely new phrase and job title: 'Computer Data Entry.' Since the late forties, all of that data has continuously been upgraded, checked, and crossed-checked against the constant flow of new data that continues to pour in from banks, insurance companies, lending institutions, doctors, lawyers, schools and colleges, hospitals, churches, utility companies, telephone companies, cable companies, newspaper and magazine subscriptions, rental agencies, transportation companies, employers, the IRS, the SEC, the FBI, CIA, NSA, all sorts of bureaus of vital statistics, licensing divisions, casinos and many, many other information sources."

Hanson, gasped and pulled in a deep breath before continuing. "It is an enormous amount of information, gentlemen, and we've gathered trillions and trillions of bits and facts on hundreds of millions of people. With current technology, all of these individual data dossiers are quite easily aggregated into the National Registry, and that data is available to our Supercomputers, and cross-checked with the old and new data repositories, on a daily basis. Our 'Big Baby' knows everything about everybody and has given us the ability to have better and quicker access and more accurate files on every citizen who has existed in the last one hundred plus years. It is the very best people information system in the world and it continues to grow!"

Felix clicked to another chart. "We currently have very accurate activity information on over 95% of the population of the United States and 85% in Canada, Great Britain and Europe, 75% in Australia, some 55% in Mexico, and a little less in Central America, and thanks to the Germans and Juan Peron, an amazing 65% in South America. Now, we've just hacked into China's and expect to get around 50% of the Chinese population tabulated, and that's a lot of people. In Africa, India, the Middle East, and the Pacific Rim countries we have very low general population data, but we are currently entering all of the national, state and local government officials, the corporate people, the rich, the scientists, educators and clergy. What is missing everywhere are the rural, aboriginal and tribal figures, but I'm told, they don't matter. All in all, here in the United States we know more about the people of the world than any other country."

Felix clicked on another graphic representation. "Here's how the classification program is being used during this crisis. We've had excellent data available to construct our A and B files. The 'As are the highly intelligent, the gifted and very creative, the best managers and leaders, and the 'Bs are the most skilled and responsible workers in North America."

Felix surveyed the room to make sure everyone was still with him. "Until recently, the 'As' and 'Bs' were all been mixed in with the misfits, the 'Cs', as we call them. Without 'Big Baby', the job of culling out the good from the bad would have been totally impossible. We have pictures, fingerprints and DNA, as well as very up-to-date and complete profiles that include family histories, residences, education, jobs, etc. We pretty much know who's who. We know what job skills they have and what they can produce. We know of their social and behavioral habits. We know what they have done in the past and can pretty well predict what they will probably do in the future and whether they are, or can be, productive, law-abiding citizens. We know everything about their parents, grandparents and even their great-grandparents and what, if any, these predecessors might have contributed to society in their lifetimes. We know whether any of their relations were criminals, had mental illness or congenital defects, were social dissidents or radicals.

Felix switched to another slide. "We're using C.A.R.E.—our Computerized Anthropological Review/Evaluation—as the base in the operation of 'Big Baby.' We are able to link up all of these Supercomputers, eight of them operating as one, directly with the 700 inoculation centers and find, sort, evaluate and conclude who the very best people are at a current rate of about, oh, 29,000 complete classifications per hour. And that includes the time back and forth during transmission."

Irving Penitz interrupted Felix. "The bottom line is accuracy. Because of the computer's accuracy, it is easy to make the selection of only those who are law-abiding, well-educated, in excellent physical and mental condition, creative and highly skilled. These selections get an automatic 'A' rating and become immediately eligible for the 'RS' class. Those with good social and work skills receive the 'B' and are rated 'RW' class and are allowed to live productive lives as long as they perform well. They could someday be reclassified and thereby be eligible for 'RS' class. Those who are honestly homeless or jobless but who are skilled—even the disabled and the aged, if they are functional and skilled—they, too are given a 'B' rating. Conversely, those individuals who are currently in prison or those who show a record of crime or have had criminals in their family tree, the ones that won't work, the totally disabled, the very aged, those with a record of civil disobedience, the mentally ill, those over the age of twenty who are still illiterate, the substance abusers. and the indigent become bona fide losers. They get a 'C' rating by the computer and are immediately exterminated. Now, we are telling everyone that they need to get a 'booster' shot in six months. By then we will have gathered more information on the surviving population and by using more date with our more sophisticated algorithms, we'll run new evaluations through the computer. The results of this second evaluation will weed out those marginal cases."

Penitz summarized. "Gentlemen, this harvesting and analysis of data is the most exact and accurate evaluation of human behavior that has ever been attempted and will clearly benefit of mankind. The people receive impartial decisions, completely based on the documentation from their own Life Files. No mistakes. No misgivings. No guilt or remorse. Absolutely perfect justice!"

Irving Penitz placed a small green leather-bound book in Billy's hand, "Mr. President, the very first copy pressed of *The New Laws for Mankind*. Gentlemen, each of you will also receive one of these fine first editions before you leave today."

The title line and dedication were deeply embossed in gold leaf on the soft green leather. Even though it was thin, the volume looked and felt like it was as important as the impressive title made it sound. It was designed to be small enough to fit neatly in any shirt pocket or purse. Pentiz read aloud:

# THE NEW LAWS FOR MANKIND

# GOD'S COMMANDMENTS FOR LIVING

and

# THE NEW WORLD FEDERATION MANIFESTO

*Appreciatively Dedicated To:*

*The President of the United States,*

*William F. Johnstone*

*Presented in The Year of Our LORD
Two Thousand and Nine*

# GOD'S COMMANDMENTS

*I am the Lord your God: you shall have no other gods before me.*

*You shall not make yourself a graven image, or any likeness of a thing that is in heaven above, or that is on the earth beneath, or that is in the water under the earth; you shall not bow down to them or serve them; for I the Lord your God am a jealous God, visiting the iniquity of the fathers upon the children to the third and fourth generation of those who hate me, but showing steadfast love to thousands of those who love me and keep my commandments.*

*You shall not take the name of the Lord your God in vain: for the Lord will not hold him guiltless who takes his name in vain.*

*Observe the Sabbath day, to keep it holy, as the Lord your God commanded you. Six days you shall labor, and do all your work; but the seventh day is a Sabbath to the Lord your God; in it you shall not do any work, you, or your son, or your daughter, or your manservant, or your maidservant, or your ox, or your ass, or any of your cattle, or the sojourner who is within your gates, that your manservant and your maidservant may rest as well as you; therefore the Lord your God commands you to keep the Sabbath day.*

*Honor your father and your mother, as the Lord your God commands you, that your days may be prolonged, and that it may go well with you, in the land which the Lord your God gives you.*

*You shall not murder.*

*Neither shall you commit adultery.*

*Neither shall you steal.*

*Neither shall you bear false witness against your neighbor.*

*Neither shall you covet your neighbor's wife; and you shall not desire your neighbor's house, his field, or his manservant, or his maidservant, his ox, or his ass, or anything that is your neighbor's.*

*THESE WORDS THE LORD SPOKE TO MOSES AT THE MOUNTAIN,*

*FROM THE MIDST OF THE FIRE, THE CLOUD,*

*AND THE THICK DARKNESS, WITH A LOUD VOICE;*

*AND HE ADDED NO MORE.*

# THE MANIFESTO

## OF

## THE NEW WORLD FEDERATION

*All Humankind Will Hear and Heed This Proclamation:*

*The Adjuncts To*

*God's Commandments*

*All decisions made by The National Computer must be obeyed.*

*Posted Work Rules in places of employment must be obeyed.*

*Everyone must work six days each week.*

*Everyone must maintain good personal habits and attitudes.*

*No one may borrow or beg or barter goods from another person.*

*No social disorder or prolonged illnesses will be permitted.*

*Everyone must maintain well-behaved households.*

*Three violations of any of The New Laws will result in Elimination.*

*Failure to report violators of The New Laws will result in Elimination.*

*Violating God's Commandments will result in Immediate Elimination.*

Irving concluded. "So, there you have it, gentlemen. *The New Laws: God's Ten Commandments and The New World Federation Manifesto* as written by you, Mr. President. These constitute the great *New Laws*. It is a majestic document designed to guide the way for our people to live lawfully in peace and harmony. But, as it is fairly decreed, to break any of these laws is to invite death."

Billy added, "Three strikes, and you're out of the game!"

Jumping back in Penitz continued. "Every city, county, state and federal statute book in North America is currently being taken from the shelves and burned. They are totally obsolete. These old law books were based on the archaic and fallible system of individual trial by judges and peers, using precedent to evaluate so much conjecture and argument to reach a consensus. Possibly the worst concept of justice in all of history. Not trustworthy or honest, but utterly corrupt and, ultimately, very unfair."

Irving wildly thumped the *New Laws* book. "In order for the people to have faith in our government, the original Constitution of the United States has only been changed in one spot: that of Presidential powers. Now, all *New Laws* will be approved by the President. The Supreme Court of the United States has been allowed to remain intact. This justice body will be purely symbolic and will only act as an advisory board to the President—a safety valve between the Computer and the people. There are no more state's rights. All state, county and city legislative and judicial bodies will be dissolved. These *New Laws* and our innovative computerized system of justice will allow a concise and understandable methodology of fairly managing the people so that they will live in peace with each other. Actually, the people are responsible for governing themselves. Everyone will be educated in the meanings of *The New Laws,* and therefore each person will be able to monitor all other persons for any violations of the laws. Theoretically, no major disobedience should occur."

Irving dropped his voice to his normal, low, persuasive level. "However, if anyone—private individual or official—witnesses a violation of *The New Laws,* a complaint must be filed. These filings can be made through the interactive TV units in every home, or by cell phone or videophone, or at any of the government field terminals. The complainant will not remain anonymous. To see a violation of *The New Laws* and not report it is in itself a violation. Everyone, therefore, will be watching for violations and will accurately report them. To make a false report is punishable by immediate elimination. Therefore, the public will be quite careful and accurate in their reporting of violators."

Irving used the remote and changed the display on the large wall screen. "The computer will accept all filings as honest and will make all decisions based on the content of the report as filed. If a false complaint filed by anyone is found to be false as a result of differing testimony of three or more corroborating individuals, it means immediate death for the perpetrator of that false filing. Mistakes will be made in reporting violations. The computer is able to ascertain an honest blunder and will judge accordingly. 'Big Baby' is capable of compassion, you know."

He continued. "These new civil statutes are based on hundreds of years of socio-legal experiences, and Felix Hansen himself has designed a very efficient 'civil law' program for our 'Big Baby'. Civil cases that used to tie up courts, judges, prosecutors and lawyers for months and years can now be adjudicated by our computer in minutes. Here, let me show you how it works. Will one of you step forward to this terminal and file a complaint? Just imagine some civil problem that in the past you would have taken to the police department or small claims court. Just step up and speak clearly to the computer, please."

Billy walked forward. "If you don't mind, I would like to test it."

"But of course, Mr. President. I would be honored."

Billy thought for a moment. Then he spoke in a quiet, ordinary voice at the computer screen. "Your honor, my son's bicycle is missing."

The computer answered.

"Please state your name and NIC number and describe the bicycle in detail: make, serial number, color, age, condition, value, when it was last seen and at what location."

The requested questions were displayed on the terminal screen.

Billy hesitated and then responded to the computer's requests. "It was a Wheeler Roadmaster, color blue, less than one year old, in good condition, worth $690, don't know the serial number. It was last seen on Tuesday, August 23 of this year on the porch of 1932 West Elm Tree Street in Washington, DC."

As he spoke, his answer was displayed on screen as a response to the appropriate question.

The computer spoke again. "Please confirm that the answers displayed on screen are correct and then give a list of any persons, anywhere who at any time, may have seen this bicycle. Also, include any prime suspects and state whether you want to formally accuse them."

Billy gave a list of people who could have seen the bike. "And as for suspects, your honor, I have one. Irving R. Penitz. But I do not accuse him."

As an aside to the others, Billy said, "Just playing it safe. I want it to be the computer's problem if Irv's guilty, not mine."

They laughed at Billy's joke

The computer screen responded with a comment. "Please wait!"

Within seconds the computer spoke again. "Thank you for waiting, Mr. Johnstone. We will attempt to reach the names on your list and will interrogate each of them. An all-points bulletin with a description and picture of the bicycle will be issued to the local Constables of your Neighborhood Surveillance Squad. They will be looking for the bicycle. We will all do our best to have it returned to you. But if we are not successful, you will be issued cash credits to obtain a replacement bicycle. Thank you, Mr. Johnstone and have a good day, sir. Next case, please."

Penitz explained. "Now, that could have been a car or suitcase or television set or any goods. As the investigation continues, the complainant will be required to provide serial numbers, photos, anything to aid the system in finding the missing goods. This computer program is able to do the work of a major police force. With roving TV surveillance, street-by-street TV surveillance, house-by-house interrogation, electronic bulletin boards, live constables and everyone in the area looking for the bike, it will be found. Now let's assume that, as was suggested by Mr. President, that I stole the bike and, through investigation, I am discovered by the justice system."

Irving typed something using the keyboard. "As you can see, a warning order is issued to the violator of *The Laws*—me. It would be sent to me by government delivered paper mail, email, displayed through the interactive home TV units, and sent by computer voice via telephone to my home recorder unit, and cell phone. My employer would be notified in the same manner. No one will ever be able to say that they have not been duly contacted and fairly warned. In this case we are talking about grand theft and, even though I must return or replace the bicycle, I have committed a major violation of *The Laws*. That will count as one violation, and it will remain on my record even though I may have made full restitution."

Proudly, Irving continued. "Upon committing a second violation of any of *The Laws*, the violator will be cited again and cautioned that there will be no further warnings. The penalty for a third violation of *The Laws* is arrest and immediate execution. Everyone has been implanted with locator-style ID chips during the virus inoculations, and the guilty party could run but, not hide for long. The satellite network—our 'Eyes In The Sky'—is able to track the implanted ID chip even through 30 feet of solid concrete and steel. The public will quickly learn that to transgress *The Laws* is not only futile, but also deadly. In addition, because this justice system is interactive, it can be accessed from the home, workplace, anywhere. Anyone can ask the Computer whether a situation is a violation of *The Laws* and find out the answer very quickly."

Irving signaled for the lights in the room to be turned on. "Soon we'll begin the education of the masses of this hemisphere, so that moral and intellectual understanding of the reasons behind *The Laws* will be learned by everyone. We will show the people how these solid principles, enforced by the people themselves and adjudicated by the impartial and very effective New Justice System Computer, are ultimately the fairest way for mankind to live peacefully with one another. This method is a swift, impartial and self-governing legal system for our citizens and, unlike the old ways, it will be very fair and efficient. Well, Mr. President, how do you like what you've seen?"

"I like it very much, Irving. I sincerely believe that God himself could not have created a more charitable system of justice for mankind!"

# 22

## *THE FINAL PURGE*

On the outskirts of Washington, DC, a small group of the very loyal "RSS" (Regent Senior Security) class operatives gathered for a meeting. These were the same men who accomplished the clandestine mission of inserting the H2P5 virus into the water systems of cities throughout North and South America. The "plague scenario" was well under way, and Collings had recalled these talented RSS operatives for a very secret meeting. They had been told that they would be given instructions for a new and very important mission. There were just thirty-six undercover RSS agents in this special force. They wore civilian clothing and, although small in number, they alone had caused the viral epidemics throughout North America.

They waited, as ordered, for Collings in the sitting room of a large suite in an old hotel in downtown Washington.

Collings entered the room and the men all rose to attention. He gave them no greeting and sharply called the names of twenty-four men who obediently stepped forward.

Collings stepped around the chosen men and, without warning, aimed two IA Controller units on the remaining twelve agents. The Controllers were set on setting number two, stunning the men immediately and causing them to fall where they stood.

Collings was in no hurry. The years of methodical killing allowed him to take his time as he ordered the remaining agents to search the unconscious bodies and remove any identification or papers that might possibly be incriminating.

"You twenty-four will now head up new teams and will immediately be dispatched to South America to quickly perform the same operations you have done in North America. I have been carefully monitoring all of you. You were good at your jobs. These men were not and will no longer work with you."

He handed them each an envelope.

"Memorize your target cities and then return the paper to me. You will each be assigned new operatives and leave today. The locations for the contagion in these cities are to be your decision, but I want heavier concentrations and more occurrences, got it? Big and fast. Europe is next. Do it right and you'll be rewarded. Screw up and you'll be on the spot just like these jerks. When they wake up I will reassign this bunch to some hard RW work."

Collings retrieved the city lists from the twenty-four men and ordered them to leave the building.

Using a portable air tank and a pneumatic gun, Collings quickly injected each of the unconscious men with a concentrated solution of the H2P5-4 virus. After inserting the virus in the last of the men, he sat down, lit a cigar and patiently waited for the virus to coarse through their bloodstreams.

Soon, the faces and hands of the unconscious men began to swell. Their skin became discolored and sores began to form. They would all appear to have died from the virus but, to make sure, he set his Controller unit on level number three and quickly killed them. The unfortunate RSS agents died quickly and painlessly.

Collings packed his equipment into its case, left the hotel and calmly walked down the street to his car. He started the engine and as he drove away he out his cell phone. Calling to the nearest inoculation center, he reported that he has just found a group of dead people in "decay condition" and requested an immediate pick-up. Collings gave the address of the hotel and location of the suite. One of the LOES disposal trucks was dispatched to the hotel. The bodies of the dead RSS operatives would be oxidized very quickly. Like hundreds of thousands of other people, they, too, had simply ceased to exist.

With this deed done, Collings knew that the truth about the plague still remained secure within the Inner Circle and a chosen few. A possible weak link in this chain of mendacity had been made whole once again.

Throughout the country, the ones marked as the "RW" (Regent Working) class had become the main labor corps throughout the inoculation. They were clothed in royal blue uniforms. On the back of these uniforms was the insignia RW and below it the assigned job title, such as RW Medical, RW Transportation, RW Clerical, RW Transportation, RW Labor, and so on.

Because so many people were involved, this color coding and titling made it easy to spot and direct the RWs and aided in the general organization of operations. While setting up the necessary equipment and keeping the supplies transported to the inoculation centers, these hardworking RW laborers became invaluable and were the very backbone of the entire operation.

Professor Osher and his "RSM" (Regent Senior Medical Class) staff had handled the training of the RW Medicals very well. The RWs were very devoted to this valiant human effort, and just like the general public, they wholeheartedly believed that the plague was real.

The RS Medicals, who had better education and skills, became the administrators and managers, directing the RW Medicals. RS Medicals were the doctors, nurses and major health care attendants and wore impeccably clean white uniforms with "RS Medical" and their specific job title clearly printed on the back.

The RS Medicals had read the federal guidelines and had seen the "plague" training videos. They worked each day with total and complete belief that the immediate disposal of the dead bodies and the elimination of all living infected individuals via the LOES units were very necessary. They knew it was the only way to stop the spread of the virus and manage contamination. That is what the guidelines said, and that was what they believed. Therefore, these dedicated professionals did exactly what they were ordered to do.

From time to time, certain doctors, nurses and scientists would question whether the virus was really as contagious as they had been told or whether the procedures were effective or necessary. These individuals usually contacted their superiors about their doubts or curiosity. There was little discussion. These matters were always referred to the "RDS" (Regent Domestic Security) office.

The red-suited RDS had a standard, immediate, very effective reply to such inquiries. The complaint was heard. The individual was ushered into a side room of the RSS office, shot with an Arrestor and quickly oxidized in a waiting LOES machine. Neat and effective—that individual's questions no longer bothered anyone.

As medical practitioners or workers discovered that many of their colleagues just turned up missing, they were told that the person in question had been transferred. Satisfied, they would quietly do their jobs as ordered. They remained unquestioning and obedient and followed all of the guidelines to the letter. To not question became an unwritten rule. Failure to follow the many exacting and demanding regulations set forth by the Third Party Administration were, in the final analysis, as lethal as the plague itself.

In every city throughout North America, the mass inoculations continued. The huge human herd was swiftly being thinned out. The misfits, the crippled, criminals, the old, and the unproductive were systematically and effectively eliminated. All of the prisons were emptied of their inmates. Crime and homelessness were wiped from the streets. Retirement communities and nursing homes became barren; those who had been waiting to die were helped across the veil. Hospitals soon transformed into apartments, as they no longer housed the sick. The sick, too, had been put to death. The plague, as Billy had designed it, was performing its merciful carnage at an alarming rate.

As millions were being inoculated, the truth of the plague remained a secret from the public. Of the untruths that the media were telling the people, "Trust Your Government" was the worst lie of them all.

But these small sins didn't slow the advance of Billy's plague. He was determined to cleanse the world and make it as beautiful as he thought it should be. Many more would die to fulfill his savage dream of perfection.

Even the Inner Circle didn't know the full extent of his plans.

Soon, Billy decided to hold a press conference to inform the world of his progress. It would originate from his new Federal Communications Center in New York City. But instead of an audience of the very rich and influential this time, he wanted the huge Music Hall auditorium to be overflowing with people—ordinary people from all walks of life. The order came down from Billy to open the doors wide until the auditorium was filled with Mr. and Mrs. Average Citizen.

Again, the entire world tuned in to this important broadcast. But, this time, they would hear a new Billy. His manner and speech had changed. All of the "good old boy" phrases and Billy's normally friendly and affable attitude were gone.

This was the Billy they would see and hear from now on. Serious. Resolute. Imperious...the Boss!

Many years before, old Kurt had told Billy that he might be the savior for whom the people had long awaited. Kurt had been right on the money. The multitudes, who for generations wanted and needed a great sovereign, were about to welcome their new ruler. But even these enthusiastic subjects demanded that their new king give them a good and bountiful future. With a blind faith so fervent and full of passion, they wanted action—not words.

Billy was ready for them. As he approached the podium, he could felt the anxiety emanating from this tired and very worried audience. These people had been through an immense amount of tension and fear during the plague crisis. Their sense of dependency upon him, and the raw urgency to hear some positive news from him, was not lost on Billy. This insight gave Billy one of those rare opportunities to say the right thing at the right time.

"My fellow Americans and citizens of the world. I am speaking to you tonight to give you an update on the health crisis we are experiencing here in North America. In addition to my job as President of the United States of America, I have been given another job, that of Supreme Commander of Allied Forces and Crisis Operations during the massive inoculations to prevent the spread of this terrible H2P5 virus in North, Central and South America. Millions of people have been saved, but many, many lives have been lost in this battle. Many more, I am sorry to say, will die before this terrible virus has taken its full course."

The audience murmured understanding.

"But, I have good news for you!"

The audience became very quiet.

"Because of the extraordinary cooperation and the good sense shown by the people of the United States, Canada, Mexico, Central and South America, and the very excellent work accomplished by all military and health care professionals everywhere, real progress is being made. I am happy to tell you that we are winning this war against the H2P5 virus in every city, state and country throughout the Northern and Southern hemispheres. The worst plague ever to assault mankind is being dealt a vigorous and heavy blow by our Allied forces with an impact that will quickly and effectively end its expansion and end the horrible death it brings, once, and for all times."

The audience began to applaud, but Billy raised his hands, and with that command they instantly fell silent once again.

"There are still many problems. Hundreds of thousands of people in the United States, Canada, Mexico, Central and South America have not heard my words. They have not responded to my requests to get the H2P5 inoculation. You must understand that those who are not inoculated make the potential for reoccurrence of this epidemic a very frightening reality. Everyone, everywhere, those who can hear the sound of my voice, must listen now. As President of the United States of America and as Commander in Chief of all Allied Forces and by the emergency powers vested in these offices, I hereby deputize every person who may be listening to this broadcast. You are now a legal extension of each of our governments. Your duty will be to assist the United States and your respective countries during this crisis situation."

The crowd was quiet.

"And here is how you will be able to serve. You must help me find the people who have not been inoculated. They may have the virus or may soon get it. Talk with every person that you come in contact with each day. Ask them if they are inoculated. They must verify to you that they have been inoculated against the virus and, further, they must confirm this statement by showing you their Federal Inoculation Card."

"If they will not give evidence by showing you their FIC card, then it is now your appointed duty, as deputized citizens, to see that these people get to an inoculation center very quickly. The old and crippled ones that can't get out must be found and helped. Those that cannot read or write or are so poor they do not have television or radio; these are the ones that must be given the vaccine for this horrible virus. And listen to this: any person, and I mean any person, who will not cooperate with you is a violator of federal law. If they refuse you, then you are to go to a phone and call 911. You'll get immediate help from the authorities. Each of you listening to this broadcast must help me find these people or this horrible disease will continue to kill."

Billy paused to allow these thoughts to register on his audience.

"I have asked Congress to authorize cash rewards for your help, so watch your televisions for the details. The troubles we face are not over. I am sad to report that thousands of people are today becoming infected with the H2P5 virus, and that in Africa and other countries around the world a real and serious pandemic has begun. But be clear: first, we must stop the virus here at home, in the Americas, and we must stop it now!"

The TV camera closed in tight on Billy for the home viewers.

"Remember: We, as free Americans, have always answered the world's call for help and mercy."

The camera pulled back to show Billy standing in front of the many flags of the Allied Nations.

"Now hear this order: As Supreme Commander, I am asking for all branches of active and reserve American, Canadian, Mexican, Central and South American military personnel to immediately report to their command centers for deployment to designated areas to help combat this plague. I will tell you now that I will not stand for any violation of the imposed martial laws by anyone—civilian, or military. We are in a state of war. But we must conduct ourselves in a law-abiding and civilized manner."

Billy spoke quietly. "Those of you who are watching and listening to this broadcast tonight, hopefully, have been inoculated. You are now, immune to the H2P5 virus. Please understand, the rest of the world is now facing the same dangers that we are enduring. The U.S. Congress and the governments of the Allied countries have unanimously agreed to commit our combined resources, both military and medical, as the virus spreads to other countries. Therefore, I am now further asking the civilian and business sectors to help us provide whatever else may be needed to help eliminate this virus for all times."

The camera zoomed in and tightened on Billy once again.

"I am counting on you men and women of the private sector, so get going right now and let's show all the nations of the world your great spirit and willingness to help in this very real war against this evil virus. My friends, please continue to have faith in the Almighty and we will win this war. May God bless each one of you. Good night."

The audience "of the people" quietly filed out in the auditorium.

On TV and radio, there was no commentary following Billy's speech, just a new public service announcement:

The President has ordered that anyone who reports the location of any person who has not been examined and inoculated for H2P5 VIRUS will be entitled to a cash reward for service to the Allied movement.

> **BULLETIN:** *ALL MILITARY PERSONNEL ARE TO REPORT TO THEIR OFFICIAL COMMAND CENTERS AT ONCE!*

Following the next movie, an even more ominous message:

> **Notice:** *By order of the President of the United States and Allied Countries of North America, all people are warned: You must show proof of H2P5 VIRUS inoculation when asked, or be arrested!*

> **BULLETIN:** *ALL MILITARY PERSONNEL ARE TO REPORT TO THEIR OFFICIAL COMMAND CENTERS AT ONCE!*

The messages played day and night, over and over.

The majority of the population in the Western hemisphere had responded to the President's first request and had dutifully been inoculated. But some, perhaps because of disbelief, or because they were sick or old, did not or could not comply. Now, after arousing their cooperation and deputizing the entire population of the United States and Allied countries to find these people, results were absolutely guaranteed.

People that lived in very remote areas and could not hear the government proclamations posed yet another problem. To achieve maximum results, a massive movable cleanup plan was conceived and put into effect. Special mobile squads were formed to comb the mountains, forests and deserts of the very remote regions of all countries. These Federal hunters were able to locate last few uninoculated humans and determine whether they were "fit to live" in Billy's new world. The familiar methods of evaluation were used. If, however, the person was not listed in the National Computer, the investigator, using a government issued set of guidelines, would decide on the spot whether that person would live, or die.

The resolute inoculation crews traveled in well-equipped mobile all-terrain units. For efficiency, each of the large MALU trucks had two LOES-12 machines installed inside. The custom-built trucks opened up in three directions and further expanded to form the main inoculation clinic, as well as providing living quarters for the eleven members of the MALU team. An attached air-lock structure acted as the quarantine or killing area.

The big engines of the trucks operated on hydrogen fuel cells. Inside the MALU truck itself was a self-contained electric system that operated entirely on electric power if it was available. If electricity was not present, power was provided by large solar panel arrays on the roof surfaces, and by four large wind generators atop tall telescoping masts. During the daylight hours, solar and wind generation regenerated the hydrogen fuel cells for the trucks engines, and, as the sun waned in the late afternoon, the wind generators continued to charge the system battery banks, allowing for full time operation, day and night, without the aid of fossil fuels.

The MALU had a sophisticated communications system that could transmit and receive data via satellite to the National Computer Complex, ensuring that the general information gathering and *A-B-C* inoculation assessment remained consistent. The homing device for the MALU was tracked via global positioning at Allied Command Headquarters. Locations could be accurately identified within two feet, anywhere in the world.

The MALU units could withstand severe combat explosions. They were bulletproofed to repel even armor-piercing shells. The RS Medical staff consisted of a doctor, medical nurse, a nurse-interpreter in charge of PR, an electronic communications person and six RS combat/assault soldiers. They were all under the direct command of the RS Field Military Officer. All personnel were armed with 9mm automatic pistols, pepper spray, and Arrestor units.

The six-man combat/assault team was uniformed with riot helmets, batons and shields, including full-body Kevlar covering underneath their army fatigues. They carried tear gas, concussion and fragmentation grenades, 12-gauge combat shotguns, MP-5 rapid-fire sub-machine guns, as well as Monocular Night Vision Devices and 4 Multi-Purpose Assault weapons.

To see these soldiers was to know that each was capable of meting out destruction and death very quickly, even to large numbers of attackers. One of these warriors was on guard, near the entrance door to the MALU truck, day and night. The other two men on duty were located at opposite corners of the vehicle. The three reserve crewmen remained off-duty, dressed and equipped on full alert in the air-conditioned underneath-barracks of the big truck.

Each of these military men had been selected for their training and competence. They were respectful and extremely courteous. They had been schooled in public relations and crowd control and were expertly prepared for assault action. They were very obedient, very methodical, and very well behaved, yet each could be extremely cruel and totally inhuman when necessary. These men were skillful killers. Without hesitation, they could ruthlessly maim or destroy anyone who posed a threat to the MALU unit or to any crew member.

Mexico, as well as Central and South America, posed the biggest problem in the total purge of undesirables. Scant records, if any, were available in most villages, making the inoculation process very difficult in these countries. But Billy wanted everyone, everywhere, to be examined. So, the search went on

On a typical day, a huge MALU truck would roll into a Mexican town or village just like a traveling show. The people would turn out to see the big red, white and blue-trimmed truck. The black letters "MALU" on the doors made no sense to them, but the local people never seemed to be disturbed by its arrival. In fact, the citizens were very excited to see this big truck from the United States.

To the MALU crews, the procedure had become quite routine. All they had to do was take the truck to the town square and the people would come. The locals would gather around and watch with curious interest as the massive truck unfolded and was set up. It was as though they were watching a circus tent being raised. They waited patiently as the "Quarantine" air structure was inflated. When the wind generator masts telescoped up into position and began to spin, the PA system chattered to the assembled villagers in colloquial Mexican, and the people drew in even closer.

Good day, ladies and gentlemen. We are here on behalf of the Allied Nations of the Northern Hemisphere, the United States, Canada, Mexico, Central and South America. There is a very dangerous sickness spreading throughout the Americas and it is now in your village. We are here to treat those of you that are ill and help prevent the rest of you from becoming sick. Please form a single file line now and come into the truck so that the doctors and the nurses can give you the medicines that will help you. You must see the doctor and get the medicine. It is the law. If you do not get the medicine you will get very sick and then you will die. If you refuse to cooperate with us, you will be arrested, so please cooperate. This is painless to you and very quick. After you receive the medicine, if you cooperate, every man and woman will be given fifty pesos. Please line up now! Attention! Attention! Please line up now!

The message continued to repeat in an endless loop:

Good day, ladies and gentlemen. We are here on behalf of the Allied Nations of...

The doctors and the nurses in their gleaming whites stood smiling at the entrance to the truck and beckoned the people to come up the steps and inside. If anyone was hesitant, the presence of the heavily armed soldier stood out as something familiar and convincing that they all seemed to understand. The lines, as always, moved quickly as soon as the people heard and understood the statement about the pesos. Hundreds of people were processed each hour.

The inoculation method was the same. Billy's basic inquisition criteria remained immovable. It was altered only slightly to fit the cultures of these small Mexican towns. Once the infirm, the old, the sick, the crippled and the mentally retarded entered the truck, they never came out. The farmers, and those who had useful skills were spared if they were healthy, productive and without a criminal record. All were implanted as As and Bs and entered into the National Computer.

Late every night the inmates from the jails and patients from the hospitals, clinics, nursing homes, and mental wards were walked or carried down the streets to take their turns in the voracious death machines, their lives reduced to a yellowish powder.

The huge, windowless, inflatable red, white and blue air-structure attached to the back end of the big MALU truck was lettered on three sides in English and Spanish:

*DANGER-QUARANTINE AREA-NO ADMITTANCE*

The copy below the sign explained in detail why the sick people needed to be detained and placed in isolation.

Two armed soldiers on the corner sides of the "Quarantine Area" sat quietly in umbrella chairs with their automatic rifles across their laps. They were calmly reading and listening to portable music while sipping canteens of juice or water.

Hour after hour, the loudspeakers continued to recite the provocative invitation as the procession of the doomed continued to move into the MALU. Every day, efficiently, methodically, without incident, more than a third of the people in every town and village were willingly and unknowingly slaughtered. On average, it took the better part of two or three days to process all of the people in these small towns.

Generally, locals didn't challenge why others were detained in the Quarantine Area. But there could be problems when the MALU unit left town. When hundreds of people in the Quarantine Area were not released, many of the townspeople would become quite suspicious. Timing for the MALU departure had to be very carefully planned and kept very quiet.

The MALU crews usually waited until after midnight to leave. The office area of the truck could be put in order during the evening, but the air-structure had to stay inflated until the last moment. Once the structure was deflated and quickly packed, the truck and its crew had to get under way, right away.

Prior to leaving, the MALU field officer would give a special packet to the Priest and mayor of the village. Inside this envelope was a list identifying those people who had perished from the plague and an explanation of why they had been cremated. This "farewell package" was a well-written explanation detailing exactly what had been done in their town and why it had been done. Included in the package were letters from William F. Johnstone, President of the United States of America, and a similarly appropriate letter from the President of

Mexico, who was also a Secretary of the Allied Nations. Each of these presidents empathized with the living and expressed sorrow for the deceased, giving personal prayers for the dead and large, including autographed and framed pictures of both leaders.

The packages were written in both Spanish and English. Great pains had been taken to illustrate to the local leaders how the letters and photos from the presidents should be displayed to the public. There were separate pamphlets included containing suggestions for religious memorial services and how to generally help the people in dealing with their grieving and loss. It was all very neat, professional and believable.

But not all of the people could be fooled all of the time.

Occasionally, the MALU units met with some resistance from the locals. Because of the quick disappearance of so many people and the fact that it occurred under very unusual circumstances, anger and outrage toward MALU crews was not uncommon. Sometimes the MALU personnel encountered civilian reprisals as mild as cursing and rock throwing and at other times as violent as an armed assault. If the townspeople were so foolish as to fire upon a MALU crew, the death count in that town increased very rapidly.

Generally bored from having little to do, the over-trained MALU assault teams eagerly waited for reprisals to happen. From time to time, they even provoked the uprisings. An armed and aggressive rebellion gave these MALU assault teams the opportunity to break the monotony and return fire, and they almost always went too far and killed not only the armed, but also many of the unarmed people. The bodies were wrapped in paper body bags, taken inside the quarantine area, and disposed of quickly in the portable LOES machines.

Because of the occasional violence that created by the MALU trucks, the units operated in wide concentric circular geographic patterns. The MALU inoculation units were strategically placed in these concentric circles around the center of every town, with each unit 150 miles from the next MALU unit. The plan was to head off trouble by working the widest possible geographic area. It was thought that this would eliminate the possibility of enraged survivors who might decide to travel to a nearby village to tell the people what had happened in their town.

By using this radius-style routing for the inoculation plan, little resistance occurred after the MALUs left a town. Remorse and sorrow in these little towns and villages almost always reversed any serious ideas of rebellion.

Radio, TV and newspapers were also being controlled in Mexico, Central and South America. Everyone was rapidly discussing tales of the "Plague." The people heard the stories and quickly accepted that their fate might be death. After all, it had always been God's way that some should live and some should die.

And so it was. God's will (and Billy's plan) be done!

# 23

## THE RATIONALE

No one, not even those closest to him, thought to question Billy's plans. No one ever openly talked or debated with him asking whether it was right, or moral, or even whether what he was doing was a good idea. No one challenged his apocryphal rein and tight control of the government, his strict *New Laws* or his absolute rule over the people. The reason: They thought he was good; they trusted him unconditionally.

Even though Sally continued to love Billy the man, she felt that he had gone too far in his plans to control the people. She didn't approve of what he was doing. She didn't know the exact details, but she intuitively knew it was wrong. Sally Hawthorne loved a mystery, and this one still didn't add up. She talked privately with members of The Group and the Cabinet. She began to challenge everything, especially the strong military that Billy was using in the inoculation centers.

She was smart enough never to talk publicly against Billy. During her investigations, Sally realized that no one seemed to care about moral issues. What was occurring in the world appeared to be a natural event, and far beyond man's capabilities to correct. A huge majority of people seemed satisfied that some must die and some would live. But Sally was curious. She had to know the truth.

Even though her relentless investigation had resulted in some insight, she had little substantive evidence or facts. Sally knew the more she kept looking, the more trouble she was creating for herself. Still, she had to know more about what was going on. Was there a hidden agenda that she hadn't discovered? If so, what was it and why?

Sally compiled the details she had. She had formed a sort of conclusion. It was very weak on real evidence, but she decided to see Billy, pose questions, show her modest proof and, as was her style, demand some answers.

She was going to play bluff poker.

Sally called Billy at his private number. "Billy, Sally here. I need to talk with you. Alone...today."

Slightly perturbed, Billy responded. "What's up now, Sally?"

"Time to talk about the future. I've gathered a lot of information, pictures, tapes, etcetera, and before I go any further, I want you to see what all of this looks like, Billy. I think I know the real truth about what you're doing. Pick me up in your car in front of the Lincoln Memorial at, say, 6 o'clock?"

"Sally, I thought we had an understanding. You still bent on making trouble for yourself?"

"No, Billy. I'm not looking for trouble. But I do have some stuff that I think should be seen by your eyes only. It's important to me and to you, Billy. See you at 6, then!"

The light colored, four-door sedan with private plates pulled up in front of the Lincoln Memorial at exactly 6 o'clock. The back door opened. Sally slipped into the seat and was warmly greeted by the President of the United States. The rear passenger area of the car was closed off from the front seat. Dark bulletproof glass intensified the sense of privacy.

"How are you, dear? You look very tired. You're working too hard. You need to play a little more. Too much devotion to office."

Sally ignored him. She handed him a large envelope filled with papers, tapes and pictures. Steeling herself, she spoke. "It's taken some time to piece it all together—to find out what's happening, or at least what I think is happening. It leads to some startling conclusions. I don't like what I've found. The taped interviews back up the paperwork. You keep it all. There's only one copy and you've got it. I'm not a blackmailer. No one knows the results of this study but me and, of course, now you."

She looked at him. She couldn't see any reaction.

"Billy, why are you doing it? I still don't understand your real intentions. Why are you doing this to our country, to our people, and now to the world? Why are you killing all these people? It looks like murder, Billy. There are more sane and humane ways to gain control of the people. What are you hiding? What terrible power do you want over our lives and why? Tell me the truth. I don't want to assume anything. I need to hear the truth from you."

"Sally, Sally, Sally. You just won't quit, will you? You are so very good at what you do. I wish I could have had you on my team years ago; maybe today you would understand all of this. But now, I'm afraid, it's too late for that."

Sally straightened, uncomfortably.

"You've just got to know it all, don't you? Even my wife doesn't know anything about this. And, best of all, she doesn't question me. But you, Sally, well, you ask a whole lot of questions. So, you think this plague is a fake and you want to know, if it is, why we did it? Why are we killing all those people without any apparent reason?"

Sally looked at him, sizing him up.

Billy kept going. "Well, first, it is a contrived epidemic. And there are reasons. Since you're bound and determined to know everything and get yourself killed, I'll tell you."

Billy cleared his throat, pushed into the corner of the seat, crossed his legs and, with a big sigh, started his comments with a quiet and paternal tone.

"I'll begin at the beginning, Sally. I want you to understand everything. Throughout recorded history, the world has always been a mess—crime, disease, starvation, natural disasters, wars, you name it. Most of the people just existed throughout their lives, struggling with no hope that the future would be any different, without enough skills or resources or answers to make life much better than it had previously been. History shows us that the human struggle was generally quite futile. The true advancement of mankind was terribly slow and filled with many setbacks. There have been many times when things have gone badly for mankind: insurrections, wars, natural disasters, plagues, starvation...But somehow man has always endured his plights and, in a feeble way, he survived. Mostly, emerging the better from his hard luck. Sort of a forced progress."

Sally listened attentively.

Billy continued. "Today, the troubles are getting progressively worse for man. The population has exploded. It seems to be a very bad trend. For many years, I've watched the worldwide situation worsen, and I assure you, Sally, the end of days was in full runaway mode— really moving fast. About fifteen years ago, I began some careful study and calculations and it became sadly obvious to me that the usual balance of nature had precariously tilted and, theoretically, it appeared to me that nature might never again return to its proper balance and might just continue to deteriorate year after year. I ran my theory by some very excellent brains and surprisingly these people were all in agreement. What they came up with was shocking. They concluded that 'the end of the world' was not just some religious fable. These very learned men told me that the end was occurring now. Can you imagine, Sally? The end of the world—the end of life on earth—happening in our lifetime."

Sally wasn't sure what to make of this.

Billy didn't let up. "You see, natural, ecological and sociological processes are intertwined and a real change was taking place in the wake of our rapidly advancing technology. More and more people were being locked out of any reasonable part of the future, if there was to be a future, that is."

Sally listened with full interest, but wondered where all this was going.

Billy continued his diatribe. "Today, nations all over the world are searching for peaceful coexistence. Throughout history, mankind has experienced puritanism as well as decadence in his hunt for the 'right' way, the 'moral' way. But that kind of philosophical thinking is, of course, merely ideological perception, for 'true' morality can really never be found. Moral principles are always motivated by ethnic or religious tradition, or contemporary style, or even a provincial state of mind. The people of the world, as they've continued their search for this elusive 'morality,' have become quite amoral. Anything goes—and not just in the U.S. The world is crazy, too!"

Billy began speaking very fast. He leaned over to Sally and began gesticulating wildly. "Our young people are suffering from moral ignorance. They haven't been taught the genuine difference between right and wrong and so, they are either, one—idiotically moral, or two—immoral and idiotic. Since neither of these qualities, even at the highest or lowest levels, has ever been a very successful social trait, frustration sets. Because neither high nor low morality, as a dogma, ever works for very long, we now have rampant amorality. Then what? Nobody knows for sure what to do, or how to do it, or whether it's right or wrong, so they become frustrated and soon…They do nothing. Apathy. This country and most of the countries of the free world have been suffering from apathy for a very long time…the people are lost."

Billy's near maniacal attitude frightened Sally.

Billy was just getting started. He continued his tirade. "The parents of our recent generations have been obsessed with 'material gathering.' Because of their selfish focus on 'things,' they've failed to teach their children the true and original rules for living. These incompetent mothers and fathers, these keepers of our future, have become idolatrous. They haven't learned that the answers to the mysteries of life aren't contained within the commodities that they desire, consumable on demand. They can't buy this kind of information off the shelf."

His frenzy subsided. "To live a good and productive life requires personal discipline, a philosophy—real truths. Those are things that can only be nurtured by teaching and by the consistent example of a role model—a mother or father or guardian who possesses integrity— parents that really care for their young. Only then, by using daily applications of discipline, understanding and love, are we able to teach our young, by our example, the right and proper way to live in God's world. This living illustration then, becomes the acceptable way of living for each of our offspring. This new and good and correct attitude becomes part of our child's lifelong character and personality. The child grows up to be a good and productive person and therefore creates good people of his or her own, *ad infinitum*."

Billy took a breath. "Character, integrity and morality form the backbone, the very core of solid social order. One must have a belief in some sort of God, something supreme, an entity more than man, plus a true recognition of and respect for nature and all of its power and beauty and, finally, a person must believe in total submission to these invisible and immovable forces. Man must return to living in awe of God and nature in order to rediscover man's relationship with man. This kind of belief requires intention and caring, parent to child, teacher to child, person to person."

Billy's fire returned. "But with all of the need and greed in today's world, the belief in something greater than our own personal wants is virtually nonexistent. Our preposterous penchant to acquire 'things' is nothing more than idol-worship. The current population doesn't understand morality so they choose not to have any. God is forgotten and thought of as a fake, or God is considered as ineffective and unnecessary because He won't deliver on demand. These people don't even know they need God. They are truly ignorant.

"The parents of these current generations have forgotten their real jobs. They were put here on earth to teach their children to be dependable and accountable and responsible for the future of the world. These parents have acted as spoiled children, not responsible adults. They consume everything and want more and more, and if they don't get it—just like children—they pout and withdraw and whine and demand and accuse, hoping to finally be given what they want, when they want it.

"Our recent generations have been taught by selfish parents. Those children will not be the ones to protect and preserve; they will just waste and want more. We have a population full of godless, dangerous ingrates, none having learned patience or compassion or respect. Our present world population is not functioning appropriately and not acting as the appointed stewards of God's world. Because they do not know how to act responsibly, they will suffer even more, and what is worse, because of them, the succeeding generations may perish altogether. Life is short and very unforgiving. Nature is always the ultimate winner. But, there is an answer, a method for correction: a true and final solution."

Sally's eyes widened. "You know, Sally, the ability to observe and analyze the results of social change previously required hundreds of years of study. Now, for the first time in history, we can recognize this change, think about the change, and do something about it, even while the change is occurring.

"The world is currently producing vast numbers of unskilled, uneducated, unfeeling people and, because technology is our ruler—not nature and God, as should be the case—those who are not technologically oriented are being shoved to the side. These unfortunates cannot be integrated into the system and so they fall back, again and again, into an ever-growing pile of obsolete, starving, out of work and depressed people. These leftovers are genuinely frightened. They cry and snivel and whine, yet, in reality, they have had the same opportunities to become educated and skilled and discover a good life, just as their ancestors did.

"But because of the lack of parental guidance, personal life planning, sound education and adherence to the traditional ways of living, they are caught in the circumstances of their times and they can do little about it. These are truly the lost generations. Their socio-genetic deficiencies have brought about a strange new impassive, nonproductive breed of humankind and for these ill-fated, misfit generations...there will be no future at all!"

Billy spoke louder and faster and with even more intensity.

"Sally, Sally, can you imagine that in some parts of the world, millions of humans spend each day, full time, just searching for water and wild vegetation in order to live, just to live for one day, Sally? Exhausted with their rigorous daily task, these people do not have the strength to plant or harvest, or to dig wells. They are steadfastly and industriously starving, generation after generation. Elsewhere, millions more starve using the ineffective methods of slash and burn agriculture. Millions more are trapped in the mega-population cities of the world, where they, too, are starving and dying from drug abuse, crime, malnutrition and disease."

"These worldwide indigents suffer from ignorance and illiteracy and lack the skills and ability to keep up with the world's technological progress. All in all, the third world, the free world and all of the people of the world are creating a legacy that will, ultimately, only mean failure for them and their progeny—a slow, agonizing and very stupid death. Believe it, Sally, 'cause it's true!"

Billy smiled in a transcendent way at the distraught look on Sally's face. "Be not afraid of the truth, my dear. You see, during the study we undertook, we found that this malaise was steadily growing throughout the world. This spiraling increase of useless people would—if not checked—continue to multiply at a disastrous rate until the worthless would eventually outnumber and choke off all of the potentially good, productive and decent people of the world."

"My analysts discovered that unbelievable numbers of the aged, the sick, the homeless, the mentally infirm, the unskilled, the drug users and criminals had increased in greater proportions than we ever imagined could happen. Just how or why this staggering amount of aimless, corrupt and sick people has grown beyond the natural balance is yet to be understood, but the facts are there. Oh, Sally, we are in big trouble!"

"So, you see. This lack of natural equilibrium was rapidly killing all chances for the future of mankind. For the first time in history, the real end of the world was more than a religious proposition; it was about to become a horrible reality!"

"Several of us decided to do something about it. We formed a secret circle, a think tank, and began to throw all sorts of solutions at the problems. Science and technology, via the computer, have thankfully afforded us the ability to gather and sort huge amounts of data. Using this distillation of historical and current information as a base of knowledge, we spent a great deal of time in discussion and study, struggling for answers. Soon the data demonstrated that a natural common denominator continued to appear in every study we made.

"You see, Malthus and Darwin—you remember them, don't you, Sally? Those old boys were definitely on the right track. But they both reached incomplete and, therefore, erroneous conclusions. They probably would have arrived at the answers we discovered, if either of them could have lived a hundred years longer, or they had the use of a modern computer. The problem is not just being able to feed the masses, like Malthus proposed, or seeing that the fittest would survive, as Darwin concluded. Today, with the availability of large quantities of better food, a real understanding of nutrition, miracle medicines and modern health care, mankind is definitely stronger and living longer. The number of births has steadily grown larger than the number of deaths.

"What are we to do with the ever-expanding number of human misfits? Alongside the decent and productive people, these others continue to be born and breed and survive because of all this technical abundance. The weeds in the garden are choking the growth of the good, healthy, industrious people. What to do...what to do?"

Sally was about to speak but Billy sucked up a fresh batch of wind and hurried on.

"Well, we found out what to do. We identified the major problem that mankind had always been forced to live with and had never considered as changeable. Man had never postulated that this natural misfit situation and its inherent sociological problems should or could be solved. Man just coexisted with the natural contradictions as he always had done; put up with the inconsistencies of his fellow man and nature, and take the good with the bad.

"We, fortunately, live in a time when man looks upon his society and surroundings as something that can and should be changed whenever he thinks it is necessary. For the first time in history, mankind has the ability to alter his environment in almost every possible way. Man is not God, but Man has learned to do many things to help himself and not wait for God's intervention."

"The big question that has tormented the human race forever: How can man effectively and fairly educate or humanely eliminate the dregs of society and thereby make way for a more pleasant, productive, and better world? A big problem, and one that certainly has always demanded a final solution. But what was the answer? Was there an answer?"

A chill ran up Sally's spine. She finally understood.

"Sally, it came to me in a flash one day as we were studying and researching these very complex socioeconomic population problems. The answer was, of course, very simple. We learned that every time man attempted to change his world, the backlash became worse than the original problem. *Ergo*: Don't fight nature, allow nature to prevail—go with the flow."

"I won't bore you with the details. I presented my theory to the boys at the think tank."

Billy's intensity continued to grow. He spoke to Sally in a whisper. "We discovered that Nature has always had its own population problems, but there was a natural and very consistent way in which all plants, animals, and insects managed their herds or packs or colonies. The sickness, lack of food, group and individual aberrations, predators, they all seemed to occur the same way in nature at all levels. We discovered that there was even a common denominator for the natural management of all living things, but, because of man's intervention, his tampering with nature, the animal, man, wasn't getting enough group management from these natural paths: disease, war, natural disaster, and so on. Mankind desperately needed an equalizer that could eliminate the burdens of the 'human herd' by removing those people that were weak or had inferior traits."

"Elimination, I proposed, would deter the continuing procreation of bad strains of people and further provide for the stable and natural expansion of the herd. Our research, of course, showed that man himself has always been man's only true predator. No other species on earth can destroy or prey on man. We looked into the past, to history, in hopes of finding new options for the future. We explored mankind's oldest calamities as we looked for new methods to help thin the human herd."

"Famine? No, man is now capable of feeding everyone on earth. That he doesn't, of course, is also part of the problem."

"Natural disaster? Who can tell when or where disasters will happen and besides, man has become expert at recovering from floods and hurricanes, earthquakes, and the like."

"War? No good either. Man has finally advanced his warfare techniques to such an efficient degree that the mortality rate due to war, is so miniscule that it is no longer a practical solution for thinning the human herd."

The teacher in Billy had come out. He sincerely wanted Sally to learn, to understand.

"Sally, do you know how much we are really animals? After millions of soldiers were killed in World War II the reproduction rates, worldwide, in the late 40s and early 50s, went sky high. Instinctively the human herd manufactured newborns in greater numbers than had died during the war causing the 'baby boom'..."

Sally nodded and sat dumbfounded as Billy continued his zealous dissertation.

"Just like all animals, insects, all living things, we react to the forces of nature in the very same way. If losses occur by force, the reproduction cycle shortens, fertility increases and more of whatever, or whoever is needed is produced to fight off the adversary and to allow life to continue. If losses occur via starvation, the reproduction cycle slows down and we get less reproduction, the herd or colony doesn't increase in size and those remaining are therefore able to survive.

"We knew we were not the first people to notice the human population problem or to make an attempt to correct it. Throughout history some have tried to cleanse the great human herd of its ills for various reasons. Their attempts were crude, awkward, and cruel. In the end, their efforts didn't last long, nor were they very effective.

"No, we had to develop a plan that could make a real and lasting change worldwide. It had to work quickly and efficiently, without permanent emotional damage to the human herd and, in the end, it would have to be something great and uplifting with visible results. An obvious purge or oppression, using force, has always caused the people to rebel. Organized resistance then occurs and, in the end, the persecution becomes counter-productive. Genocide has been tried, and the history books are full of details of the failures. What we needed was a plan that would cause the people of the world not to be horrified, traumatized, and rebellious such as they were during the Nazi Holocaust or Stalin's purge of the people. I'll admit, for a while the problem seemed impossible.

"But wait! What about pestilence, I thought? Maybe! Although, it seemed that man was able to cure any disease that had been thrown at him during this last century, it did seem like it could be a possibility. We needed a disease that was big and yet controllable so we could kill only those who deserved to die. And so, with some extremely good brains involved, we devised a plan that would finally be able to right the imbalance of our world. The answer: The H2P5 Virus, an actual pandemic."

Sally interrupted, muttering, "...not just a contrived epidemic...An artificial plague!"

"Yes. Yes. You've got it. See, our final conclusion was that we should imitate nature and create a huge 'naturally occurring' crisis. Great in size, but one that mankind could endure and could seemingly emerge as the victor. Even with the huge loss of even billions of people and the expected suffering from this human tragedy, at the close of our contrived catastrophe, mankind will feel good about it all, because he survived."

"We were certain that the people would actually feel elated about living to tell the tale of a plague and, in the end, feel as though they had personally prevailed over this enormous natural catastrophe. They would be able to look forward, bravely, to the future, with true hope and renewed faith. They'd be able to forget and forgive this unexpected calamity. After all, it was nature—God himself—that they would be forgiving. They would accept all of their losses as part of life, tighten their belts and thank the Lord they had survived. The idea was perfect!"

"We had to create a totally manufactured and controllable plague and do it as quietly and quickly as possible. We developed our Plan A get elected, get into the power position and Plan B, well it's working very nicely, as you well know. After all, we're not killing Jews or Blacks or Christians or Communists or Muslims. Our computers select who will live and who will die and it's all based on the genetic health and genuine usefulness of the individual. Think of the utter simplicity, Sally. Even you will have to agree that it is quite intelligent and fair. There are no ugly memories. No visible death. No bodies. No fuss, no muss, no bother. All neat and pretty. And that, my dear Sally, is the end of the story. Now you know it all!"

Sally had been waiting for him to She could barely speak. She whispered frantically. "Billy, you're mad. I-I can't allow..."

Billy had a maniacal look in his eyes. "Slowly now, Sally. Slowly. Think! Don't just react. Did you hear any of what I just told you? Do you understand? No. Somehow, you still have the audacity to sit in judgment of me."

Panicked, she pulled back away from him as far as she could, staring at him. "You're insane. Completely and overwhelmingly evil. You're psychotic. You're playing God, deciding who should live and who should die. How can you..."

His anger flared, and he raised his fist in the air. "Cease, woman! Take a different tone with me. I'm playing God only because God has allowed me to conceive of the idea of playing God!"

Sally froze.

"As a matter of fact, this game is just about over for you. That kind of outburst is senseless. I can't, or should I say, I won't bring back the dead. They're gone for good. For the good of all mankind!"

Knowing that she was dealing with a madman, she tried to force calm on herself. Sally spoke quietly. "Okay. Okay. Our country has been repaired and you can't erase what you've done to the people and now you're going worldwide with this fake plague and there'll be even more death. The nations of the world seem to be welcoming your help. You've succeeded, Billy. But where will this take you? Don't you have any remorse? Have you no fear of God at all?"

"Until God tells me differently, Sally, I feel that I'm helping him out here. The world needs just what I'm giving it. A good clean bath!"

Sally mumbled, stunned. "And then you'll be the absolute ruler of the whole world, Billy?

"One government. One God. One leader. It makes infinitely more sense than the multinational, multi-religious, committee-ridden crap that has existed before. This is no longer debatable. It's already set in motion. It's all but done now."

Quietly and with great sadness, Sally concluded, "Then there is no point in discussing this any further, is there?"

"Absolutely none. Now let me tell you how your life will be from now on. You will resign your Cabinet post tomorrow. I will be sorry. The Cabinet will be sorry and the American people will be sorry to lose such a talented and devoted leader. We'll tell the public that you are very ill and then you will withdraw from public life. You'll be well taken care of, I assure you. If you weren't so good in bed...You know what I could do to you. No more trouble, Sally, 'cause on my oath, I'll put that beautiful body of yours in a LOES machine without a second thought. From now on you are a dead person just waitin' to be buried. As of this moment, you're gonna transform from an outspoken and biased little girl to a reclusive, quiet lady, and my secret mistress. You'll never be heard from again. You are now under house arrest and will not leave your apartment building, ever. Your living area will continue to be bugged, day and night. You are my private prisoner, Sally, and I will be your only visitor."

He touched her gently on the cheek.

She didn't move; afraid to breathe.

"How sad. You could have had anything you wanted. But now, Sally, you're finished."

Billy stopped abruptly and picked up the telephone receiver next to his armrest. "Drive to Ms. Hawthorne's address, please."

Billy punched another button to get an outside line and dialed a number. "Rob, Billy. Key in the scanner on Sally Hawthorne. Set the warning signal to activate if she leaves her apartment. Meet me at Sally's right away...Yeah. She's gone too far this time.... No, just surveillance. I want her to stay alive. God knows why...Please, Rob, no arguments. Just do as I say.... No, I've got her with me, and we're on our way to her apartment now."

For Sally Hawthorne, the tan sedan had become a Black Maria as it rolled on into the night. Sally had gambled, and this time she had lost her freedom.


At her apartment, Sally and Billy sat quietly waiting for Collings to arrive. Neither of them talked. Sally was frozen in fear. Then came the dreaded knock on the door. It was Collings. He and Billy went immediately into the kitchen, leaving Sally alone in the living room. She sat in the semidarkness of her apartment, staring out the window at the dreary, cold, night view of Washington, DC.

Her mind was a jumble, and she was terrified. Billy had disposed of her in a most cruel way. Had he killed her, it would have somehow been welcome. Why hadn't he killed her? Just to keep her as his sex slave, she supposed. Funny. Being his lover had been an acceptable idea since the first day she had met Billy, but to have him impose this imprisonment on her, with no choice, was rape.

Sally was sure that death was what Collings was suggesting to Billy.

When he came through the door, the look in Rob's eyes was enough to kill. She didn't care about her job as Secretary of Education, and she wasn't going to worry any more about what was going to happen to her. Sally was calming down and becoming strangely resolute. Her old courage returned. Her anger was welling. Deep inside herself, Sally knew if she was fortunate enough to stay alive, she'd find a way to do something to stop Billy. For all his talk of high principles, the methods that Billy was using were murderous. Only God had domain over life and death. Not Billy Johnstone.

In normal times, a resistance movement could have been formed or she could have gone to the press and disclosed all. She could have exposed him to the world and stopped him. But sadly, the Third Party controlled all of the media.

How could she mount a citizen's resistance movement when the only people remaining after Billy's plague were those whose lives had been spared? He was a hero. No one would be angry enough to mount a rebellion. They were all very busy being safe and productive and happy. All were glad to be alive and blissfully looking forward to the future. No one would see a reason to rebel. There was no government oppression, no dictator to hate. The people simply would not care. They would not believe her story. The genius of Billy's plan was that it seemed there were no loopholes.

Still, she reasoned, there had to be others out there just like herself. People who, if told, would understand and appreciate the monstrous immorality of it all. But where were these people? Who was she kidding? Did they even exist? In reality, even if they knew, they still wouldn't care! Billy had won, and the people had lost.

Sally was shaken from her thoughts by Billy's voice shouting from the kitchen.

"Sally. Come out here, please."

Billy's face was stern and his demeanor frightened Sally.

"Everything I told you in the car will be done. Your house arrest begins now. You will not leave this apartment again, ever. Someone from Collings' office will talk to you tomorrow to schedule your needs. I will see you in a few days. Goodnight, Sally."

The President and his man departed.

# 24

## *TODAY THE WORLD*

And so, the world was getting better. It was all just as Billy wanted and maybe even a little more than he had expected. The people of the United States, Canada, and all of Latin America were cooperating with the vast inoculation for the H2P5 virus.

The old, the infirm, the criminals, the homeless, and human misfits of all kinds were quietly and efficiently eliminated. The tons of yellow death-dust that the LOES machines produced were simply washed down the sewers into the rivers and into the sea, and with it several generations—countless millions of people—quickly and quietly disappeared.

Processed day-in and day-out by the hundreds of thousands, the huge human herd of the world was expeditiously becoming lean and healthy once again. Only the best survived. It was truly a good, tidy and final solution. It was the most effective, acceptable, and unopposed mass killing in the history of man.

As planned, the plague spread throughout South America, Africa, Europe, Russia, India, China, Australia, Japan and the Pacific Rim countries. Billy promised the illuminati, the world leaders and elite of all countries that the United States and its Allies, Canada and Mexico, would be there to help them fight the H2P5 Virus. They all accepted the help Billy offered. And they all ceased to function as independent nations. Quickly, each become part of Billy's New World Federation. Each country operated under the direct authority of the United States of America and its powerful ruler, President William F. Johnstone.

Every day methodical international operations moved forward in each of the countries. All U.S., Canadian, European and South American passenger airlines were turned into transport planes, loaded with RS doctors, nurses, technicians, Inoculators and LOES machines. Cruise ships and ocean freighters were conscripted to carry the necessary fighting men and the thousands of MALU trucks for the massive inoculation and elimination of people worldwide. The movement of massive loads of equipment and supplies and the thousands of now-seasoned health officials and military personnel were effectively coordinated with amazing control and precision.

The research and development phase was over. North America was the proving ground for all the techniques now employed abroad. The inoculation was an enormous nonmilitary invasion and occupation of every country on the planet. It was a war that Billy would win without the destruction of property—without bullets or blood or dead bodies.

For many years, Billy and his Inner Circle had planned, in great detail, the actual coordination of this huge undertaking. Soon, the Allied Nations would be renamed the New World Federation. As each country signed the NWF Concords, they lost control over their nations.

In country after country the inoculation progressed much as it had in North America. Millions and millions of people disappeared. The vanished were the useless and nonproductive. The good and useful survived the plague; the rest were quietly killed as country after country fell under the ruthless march of the New World Federation.

Ironically, the world didn't seem to mind, and the people appeared to be healthier and happier for it all.

The foreign media were quickly taken over by the New World Federation military. The current, local management of these propaganda machines was eliminated with lighting speed. Julio Mondaldo's radio transmitters rapidly added a global reach to Billy's insidious network of control. The wrecking crews followed and the old newspapers, radio stations, and TV stations were soon a thing of the past.

After the inoculations in these countries, many governments experienced an extraordinary change. They all began to use common administrative precepts. They governed their citizens in a very similar way. Each nation used one central Regent, who in this time of great crisis, controlled everything in that nation's government.

Kings, Presidents, Prime Ministers, Chancellors and all national government leaders acquiesced (just as the U.S. Congress had done) and willingly agreed to give exceptional powers to this "temporary" Regent. Those who hesitated, immediately got the "virus" and were in the way no more. These *New Regents* of the nations of the world were under the direct control of the Allied Commander, U.S. President William F. Johnstone and his New World Federation.

Of course, it was much faster and easier in those countries where freedom and liberty had not solidly existed. The authoritarian governments were the most eager to cooperate. Even though the officials might have sensed the true objective behind the inoculation, they did nothing to deter the work of the Allied Health Forces. In fact, leaders of the more tyrannical countries enthusiastically joined the process and never objected to the methods being used. After all, it was a dangerous plague that required harsh action. The great and powerful United States of America was directing the operations, so it must be necessary.

Even though many billions of people died during the worldwide epidemic, no one cared, or if they did, they didn't care very long.

They all accepted that the plague was something natural. It bound them together against a common natural enemy; an enemy, through determination and great providence that had been beaten. The people believed that they had won, and that the virus had lost. They were happy to be alive and did not suspect any wrongdoing.

After receiving all the help and guidance from the great United States of America, most citizens of the world gained a feeling that their own country had somehow become another state of that glorious American republic. All had faith in the new streamlined style of their governments and in the wonderful future that was unfolding. And, still, no one knew the truth.

The arrangements for this international "invasion" were expertly implemented with breathtaking efficiency by General Fenwick's handpicked NWF military staff.

The LOES elimination method continued to be used during the international plague scenario. Again, massive inoculation centers were set up in all of the major cities, and as planned, those that were old or useless or diseased or criminal were automatically "processed" first.

The MALU trucks with their portable LOES units rolled to the jails, hospitals, and asylums and quickly dispatched the sick and unworthy. In the end, large portions of huge metropolitan populations were systematically eliminated in a matter of weeks.

The processing was a little more difficult to accomplish in the rural areas and in the less developed countries. The only media available were the infrequently published newspapers and a few scattered radio stations. This lack of reliable media made it difficult to alert populations who couldn't read or afford TVs and radios.

In Third World countries, only a handful of the ruling elite needed to be contacted. Because no social security numbers or population classifications existed, Billy's on-the-spot guidelines became the deciding factor in most of the principal cities. Using quick interrogation, these simple regulations determined who was productive and skilled, and who was worthless. Once again, as in previous times, a single man had the power over life and death.

In South America, Africa and elsewhere, the MALU trucks became quite effective in the little towns and villages. Initially, the problem of gathering the people from the rural areas, the remote hills, jungles, and regions that were a far distant from the main cities proved to be a difficult task. But Billy's ingenuity knew no bounds, and after a little creative planning, he gave his directors of Third World operations a very effective and rational design for the purge.

In these provincial territories, the people did not have a modern media to alert them, so it was decided that the use of word-of-mouth communication would be the only way to bring in the rural populations. Traditional and local religions would be the conduit used to reach the natives. A corps of messengers was sent out to tell the people that a great religious experience would be occurring very soon. They were told to go to a special area that had been selected for the event. It was declared that everyone, the old, the young, the sick and crippled must attend this gathering. Miracle cures for the ill and blessings for prosperity, health, and long life were promised.

The site was to be as central to as many of the small villages as possible and would be located in a large open area. When the people came to the site, they saw a huge air structure. This portable building had been designed with a beautiful temple-like edifice, one consistent with the theme and decor of the local religion. A ten-foot high, razor-wire fence surrounded this balloon temple. Armed guards dressed in local attire were posted at each of the entrances around the circumference of the area. The entry portals were artistically modeled using the colors, style and symbols of the indigenous religious cultures. When fully inflated, the huge temple was over 250 feet in diameter. It was quite impressive and appeared to be able to hold thousands of people.

There were twenty portals set in the sides of the massive air-structure. Long lines of the faithful waited to enter the "temple" to receive the promised blessings. The people were instructed to enter a portal and walk down a long maze-like corridor and, in doing so, directly into one of the 150 LOES units located in the center of the building. None of the people ever emerged. Every two minutes hundreds were being "processed" in these death temples. Thousands of people per hour quietly, painlessly and anonymously were permitted to meet their own particular God, on Billy's terms, of course.

The lines of people continued day and night. Indigenous spiritual music played throughout the area and special RSS agents dressed as religious leaders and shamans loudly chanted and prayed in ritual attitude, creating high fervor and encouragement among the faithful. Billy gave specific instructions to find and eliminate all tribal leaders, priests, and shamans. This order was strictly followed, for Billy felt that the old pagan ways should be destroyed for all time. This method of killing was so efficient that entire cultures and religions were eradicated wholesale.

Billy determined that the people of Third World countries contributed nothing to the world in general. His edict, "Screening is not necessary. Historically, these people contribute nothing; they are not useful and cannot support themselves. They take up space, use up food, water, and oxygen. For their own good and the good of the planet, most of them should be eliminated."

As this was being done, Billy imagined it made God very happy.

# 25

## *THE EXECUTION*

The days turned into weeks, the weeks into months as Sally Hawthorne sat alone in her apartment. Billy came over to use her body once or twice a week. Sally began her imprisonment with a strong dislike for Billy, and that dislike slowly turned to revulsion and contempt. Now, she hated him.

Sally begged Billy to allow others to visit her. After a while, he agreed, but only those on his prepared list were permitted to see her. Billy warned that these visits would stop if she ever divulged the details surrounding her "retirement" or why she was confined to her quarters. Sally knew his surveillance was flawless, and without opposition, she obeyed his command.

Wilhelm came to visit her occasionally. Julio Mondaldo and Felix Hansen came over periodically. She had to endure their happy tales of how well the war on the plague was going. The endless card games, the drinking, and the dull conversations with "the guys" were slowly driving her mad.

Sally was frustrated and constantly daydreamed about doing

something to stop Billy's campaign of murder. She desperately wanted to fight Billy and his monstrous lies, but she had no ideas, no one to help, and no way to escape her imprisonment. Billy was quite creative and efficient at killing. Sally's incarceration would be a slow and cruel death. She was humiliated and depressed. But still, she was thankful to be alive.

Billy had elevated governmental lying to a high art. He gave the task of marketing *The Laws* to Irving R. Penitz. With his oily-slick, yet somehow charming personality, Penitz became the Third Party spokesperson educating the people on the details of *The New Laws*.

In order to be fair and to make the population aware of how *The New Laws* would operate, Henry Gillespie, the Attorney General, collaborated with David Barnston to launch a huge campaign to inform and educate the public.

Billy and his IC had spent years planning the reorganization of the world. Every aspect of each operation had several parallel operations in progress at the same time. Billy's genius for design allowed for major redevelopments to occur in a very short time.

In every place of business, in every factory and warehouse, *The New Laws* and *The Rules for Workers* were posted on large metallic plates. Citizens could now read and learn about the prevailing codes that governed their lives. Millions of copies of *The New Laws Handbook* were published and sent to every household.

Special television and radio programs were produced to discuss *The New Laws*. In addition, "800-number" telephone lines and Federal web sites allowed anyone to find out exactly what *The New Laws* were and how they were to be used by the people.

David Barnston produced Irving's daily television and radio broadcasts. These programs were inserted in between the worldwide new reports regarding the "Plague." The programs were part college seminar, part talk show, part entertainment, and part historical documentary.

Billy ordered Avery Harrison and Henry Gillespie to, occasionally, share the spotlight with Penitz. This team of Inner Circle members was charged with making the program both entertaining and educational.

David Barnston pulled together the very best of the remaining TV producers, writers, and directors. Together they made the government infomercial an exciting daily event.

Guests from all walks of life appeared on the show each day, giving the program an ever-changing, variety-style format. The same half-hour show was aired four times between 8 a.m. and midnight, then repeated four more times in the middle of the night. Viewing of the program was mandatory. Everyone was forced to watch "The TV Show."

The implants in each person allowed sensors in the new interactive cable boxes to make verification monitoring quite simple. Utilizing the "Citizen-Management" computer, a person's location and viewership was quite easy to confirm.

All work stopped for one half hour as everyone watched the show. Every industry, office, retail, and recreational facility had television sets that automatically tuned into "The TV Show."

One of the first issues that Penitz explained at the beginning of each broadcast was "Why You, Your Family and Friends Must Watch This Program!" He encouraged and appealed to all citizens to report those who did not watch "The TV Show." A saturation schedule of programming and compulsory viewing would exist for ninety days. At the end of this time, Billy felt that all citizens would probably be aware of *The New Laws*. Thereafter, the schedule was reduced to only three times each day for two more months. "The Hour of Penitz," as the brave came to call it, played morning, afternoon, and night and was on everyone's daily agenda.

The shows were very well-produced and were actually entertaining. No one seemed to mind. In fact, after a short period of time, the TV "hook" was driven in so deep that everyone forgot it was mandatory government viewing, and no one wanted to miss the next episode. The conditioning of the citizens was now in full bloom.

The penalty for violating *The Laws* three times was now quite clear to the public. The punishment was death. The method of execution was yet to be explained to the people, but Billy had a disturbing kind of genius for these things. Soon, the public would learn of the method of execution, but for now, during this *Law*-learning process, there was amnesty for any violation of *The Laws*. No was arrested or executed. For now, they would joyfully and dutifully tune into "Uncle Irvy's" delightful program, "You and *The New Laws*."

The title should have been, "How to Reconsider Everything You Ever Knew About Freedom, Fairness, and Justice, Follow What We Tell You to Do, and Look Like You're Enjoying It So You Can Survive Under *The New Laws*, Or Else"-TV program.

After three months, Billy announced to the people: "Being a fair man, and a man of my word, as of midnight tonight, *The New Laws* will have full force and effect on everyone, everywhere. Each of our *New Laws* for living will now be enforced to the maximum."

Billy's now famous, "three strikes and you're out" slogan became the watchword and the dread of mankind. If arrested for a crime or violation any of *The Laws* three times, the penalty was death.

For the first few days after amnesty, no one became a violator. The world waited for the names of first "three-time losers," and everyone wondered if the punishment would be as severe as Billy had promised.

Because man is capable of error, even repeated error, less than two weeks after the announced enforcement of *The New Laws*, the media reported that several three-time offenders had been apprehended and taken into custody. The TV gave the details of how, for the first time, a computer had fairly and justly convicted these violators.

The execution of these people was to become a history-making broadcast, and would be beamed via satellite to every household on the planet.

The world watched the ominous title on the TV screen: "EXECUTION TODAY," and waited with fear and trepidation. Soon, the title dissolved to Billy seated at his desk in front of the NWF emblem. "Good evening, my fellow citizens. Tonight, it is my sad duty to call for the execution of two men and one woman who have broken our *New Laws*. The offenders were warned each time they violated *The Laws*. They knew that they were committing crimes against God and society but, apparently, they decided to commit those offenses without fear of reprisal."

The three violators appeared onscreen naked and with their backs to the cameras, standing in front of large stainless-steel chairs. Regent Police Guards entered the room and forced each prisoner to sit in a chair to which they were then strapped. Billy's image appeared in the upper-right portion of the screen. The camera focused on each prisoner's face as that person's name and offense were displayed at the bottom of the screen.

Billy was the narrator. "This is Lois Kartcher. She is 39 years old and violated *God's Commandments* three times. She is guilty of stealing from her friends and, therefore, stealing from society. She wanted more, even though she had plenty. She stole food and jewelry from retail stores and personal property from her neighbor's house. The sin of greed will be the cause of her death.

"Next is a young man to whom God has given much. He had a wonderful life ahead of him. His name is Robert Neilson. He is 19 years old, and he killed a man and stole that man's UWC card because he thought he needed more 'things.' Robert forgot that the Universal Workers Card can only be used by its owner. The sin of stealing caused him to murder. He has violated two of *God's Commandments*.

"The last is Charles Billings. He is 25 years old, in good health, has a good mind and was quite able to work. He apparently has some valuable skills, but still he refused to work. He stayed at home in his parent's house while his family worked hard each day. He demanded that his family feed and take care of him. Charles was cited three times and warned that he must go to work. When his father pleaded with him, begged him to go to work, Charles hit his father with a baseball bat, killing him. Charles will die for breaking two of *God's Commandments*, murder and dishonoring his father and mother. Further he has violated *The New Laws* by his refusal to work."

"Criminals? Yes. Evil? Oh, no. These are not evil people. They are people just like you and me. But they are people who didn't believe in the fair-mindedness and integrity of *The New Laws* that now govern our wonderful society. Maybe they did not believe they would be punished for their crimes. Who knows? Only God in Heaven knows the truth of their actions. Tonight marks the beginning of public executions, which will be aired when necessary. My hope is that this is one television program that will soon be cancelled.

"Months ago, the members of the Justice Council and I discussed the traditional, quick, and humane methods available to us for the execution of criminals. Since violation of *The New Laws* by anyone, is in fact, an obstacle to the growth and civilization of our society, it was decided that humane methods were not options for offenders of *The New Laws*. After doing some research, I decided on what I believe to be an appropriate method of execution."

Billy continued, "Our desire, and I'm sure the desire of all people everywhere, is to eventually eliminate crime of all kinds. Everyone must obey *The New Laws*. To repeatedly break these laws means certain death to any violator. No excuse. No trial. Just death. Everyone must be impressed with the need for full compliance and total adherence to *The New Laws*. This is what we all want for our society and why we have decided to use this particular method of execution for these people.

"You see, this type of punishment will deter crime because the offenders will be executed by a very unhurried and painful method. Not a quick or humane death, but one that is premeditatedly vicious and that, hopefully, will be long remembered. Tonight, you will watch this horrible ordeal. And as you see the pain, you will positively realize that unless you obey *The Laws*, you too could end up like these sad people and be doomed to die a slow and horrible death. I assure you that would be a most wasteful and tragic end to any of your lives.

Billy paused, looking down for a moment and then straight into the camera. "Not to be able to fulfill the potential happiness that God wants you to have is a waste of the life He has given you. Good people, you must watch this now. As devastating as it will be, you must watch. Your TV sets are locked onto this channel and cannot be switched off. To attempt to turn off your TV will also be a violation of *The New Laws*, and you will be cited as a violator.

"Watch now and remember what you see. Remember, that but for the grace of God and your good sense in obeying *The New Laws*, one of these people could be you. And now, let the execution begin.

Billy's image disappeared from the screen.

The guards left the room and the white-masked RS Medical Technicians, dressed in long white lab coats and surgical gloves appeared. The shiny stainless-steel chairs sitting on the stark-white tiled floor eerily reflected the light.

A small table was positioned in front of the female prisoner. Her head had been firmly strapped to the chair. The back of the chair was then titled slightly and the prisoner's mouth was pried open and two ratchet-style dental props were used to keep her mouth from closing. An RS technician deftly pushed a large rubber tube down the prisoner's throat and into her stomach. Attached to the top end of the tube was a clear plastic funnel. The TV camera zoomed in closer as the technician poured several small, slimy fish into the funnel. These little fish slid easily down the tube, through the woman's throat and into her stomach.

The attendant pulled up on the tube, allowing the esophagus to close, trapping the fish in her stomach. The funnel was removed, but the tube remained in her throat and mouth so that she could not regurgitate. The technician secured the tube with a surgical clamp and moved on to the next prisoner, repeating the process.

Billy spoke over a wide-angle shot of all three prisoners.

"Live Candiru, so-called Amazon vampire fish, have been forced down the throats and into the stomachs of these condemned criminals. The Candiru are blood eaters and are particularly fond of soft organ tissue. They can exist inside a person for quite some time, and until they are fully engorged with blood. they will continue to eat. Adding to the fish's discomfort, the human body heat and digestive acids of the stomach will further irritate them and force the Candiru to attempt to chew their way out of the stomach. Since they have also been starved for several days, the Candiru will emerge from the stomach and will swim about in the torso and burrow again and again into the heart or liver or lungs as they continue eating the human innards until their voracious hunger has been satisfied. The condemned will die slowly and very painfully by internal hemorrhage."

The lights in the execution room dimmed. Three solo spotlights illuminated each chair as the TV cameras focused on each prisoner. Only the groans of the prisoners were heard. On the lower portion of the screen appeared the ominous message: "Obey *The New Laws*...OR DIE!"

The vast worldwide audience watched in stunned silence as three human beings squirmed and writhed in excruciating pain. They could not scream because of the tubing in their throats, emitting only garbled moans and cries. The terror and tears in their eyes and the moaning as their innards were gnawed apart was seen and understood by everyone.

After waiting for what seemed like an eternity, two of the prisoners appeared to have passed out. A technician checked each of the prisoners, then an RS Doctor came forward and examined each of them. Finally, and mercifully he pronounced them all dead. These criminals were the first to be executed by this most cruel and inhuman method, a type of death that no one would ever forget.

Billy spoke again, an unseen voice as the camera held steady on the remains of the three lifeless bodies slumped in the chairs. "They are dead. May God take their souls to heaven. These first violators of *The Laws* are with us no more. Do not try to remember their names, for their brief existence here is best forgotten. Do remember how and why they died here today. I beg you, do not violate *The New Laws*. Please live good, productive. and decent lives. Be kind and fair to each other. Bring true happiness and joy to your families and be ever mindful that to break *The New Laws* is to offend God and all of mankind and will be punishable by a slow and horrible death. Remember, too, that I sincerely love you and pray to God to bestow His blessings on you all. Good night."

No one would ever forget this first public execution. They would return to their daily lives with vivid memories of the horrors that they had been forced to watch. Clips of this first execution would be inserted into every news program throughout the coming week. The people would all desperately try not to violate *The New Laws*. Billy had impressed them. No one wanted to die like that!

Sally was appalled and revolted at what she had just seen. She was screamed out loud at the television. "You bastard! You dirty, evil bastard. How can you do this? No judge? No jury? No defense? Just a set of pompous guidelines? Allegations from spying, meddling, self-righteous people! It's monstrous and unfair! All the thousands of years that man has tried to find a fair system of justice and this is the end result—a computer? Will no one stop this man? Can no one fight him?"

She began to sob. "Does anyone know the difference anymore? Does anyone care? Is there no courage left in the world? Or is everyone afraid, like me? Oh, God, please deliver us from this evil!"

Sally prayed to God until she fell asleep.

The next morning, Billy called Henry Gillespie to meet with him Oval Office. "What response have you heard regarding last night's execution, Henry?"

"Without a doubt, Mr. President, the entire world and this country in particular were shocked and very impressed. The message is firmly ingrained in the people, I assure you. No one wants to die like that."

"Sadly, I agree. Henry, you have been acting as my Secretary of State and you've done good job, I might add. Well, I want your resignation from that post, as well as your personal recommendation for a replacement. As of this moment, I officially appoint you to act as my Regent of the Holy Doctrine. It's the first such post, I might add, in all of American history. There can be no separation of God and Man. God's commandments must rule. I need you to hear of my plans for international religious unification and realize how accurately these plans correspond with the true words of God."

Billy sat down at his desk. "Henry, most of the great conflicts, the wars throughout history, have been fought over how man should perceive and obey the Creator. Under this new administration and with your help, we will begin another historical first: the worldwide belief in one God. A God that everybody knows, everybody understands, everybody loves, everybody trusts, and everyone obeys. Worldwide belief in one God is a must. What we are accomplishing in the rebuilding of the nations of the world is a true act of benevolence. We must have world unity and devotion to one God. Remember: He that will forget God, will also forget his benefactors! Religious oneness will reinforce our New World Federation. All of mankind must approach God uniformly in order to learn what He expects from each of them. They will learn to obey the one God and will confess their sins and allegiance and have total fidelity to the one God. And, if they disobey

*God's Laws* I will quickly help them out of this world and into the fiery depths of Hell!"

Gillespie stood up. "May this mission be blessed. Amen. With humility, sir, I accept this new and important post, and in the company of heaven's assistance I will help you remove the infidels, the heathens, and the nonbelievers. I pray that God almighty will show his countenance on this holy crusade, Mr. President."

"Thank you, Henry. I know I've picked the right man for this most important job. I want you at the State of the Nations telecast next Wednesday. It'll be a very important time for us, and I'd like you to do the introductions before I speak to the world."

With the same brilliant planning Billy had employed during the Purge, Billy was about to change the way man related to God.

Conflicts around the world had completely stopped. There was no more war, crime, hunger, or disease. The land in every industrialized country was becoming unpolluted and bountiful again and now, as Billy unfolded this new strategy, for the first time in history mankind would have no more religious doubt.

Peace and happiness were found everywhere, and the people of the world were content and productive. It was surely the way that God intended it to be.

The people who had survived the plague followed the instructions of their new superiors without fail. In this newborn world, a period of higher moral standards had begun. No one resisted following this new uprightness, but then, why would they? Almost everyone understood the benefits of being moral. It made sense. It was logical. As Socrates had so aptly pointed out: "Only an utter fool would desire anything less."

The media continued to produce inspired messages about the future as an exciting reconstruction commenced throughout the world at a level greater than had ever before been imagined.

The surviving population of the world knew they had been lucky.

They believed that they had been chosen by God to survive the plague and they were most eager to work hard to build a better world. The people sincerely wanted to make a bright new future for themselves. Even though the people now had fewer freedoms, as long as they did what they were told, life was very good for them.

Roads and bridges were repaired in record time, and the new highways and elevated structures were of ultramodern design, speedily built in vast numbers. Maglev rail systems were installed and the old-style trains were scrapped. Local transportation was modernized as all-electric buses replaced the stinking old diesel buses. Modernized public transportation of all types dramatically reduced the dependency on fossil fuels and the old utility companies had disappeared. The old internal combustion cars were traded in for wonderful, brand new electric cars. Solar and wind power were made available to every home. Very effective ecosystems were being installed in all houses throughout the world and buildings everywhere were remodeled to be safer and energy efficient.

The National Computer's Justice System replaced judges, lawyers, and courts. Most of the lawyers, judges, and legislators were deemed unnecessary and uneducable. They were classified as Cs and eliminated in the purge.

Ad agencies, as well as the need for the advertising of consumer products, was totally unnecessary. The ad people were eliminated. Certain brand name items were selected by the government in order to inspire a comfortable, familiar feeling for products available in the market place. The people had three or four good brands of everything they needed, and all other competitive brands disappeared. The era of competitive consumer goods was over. Corporate competition no longer existed. Retail rivalry wasn't necessary when the people themselves controlled the quality of the products.

Gigantic Federal Super Centers were built to replace the former regional shopping malls. Huge new building expansions created mega shopping and entertainment centers with even more luxurious atmospheres. Now the public could shop and obtain just about anything that could be imagined with better quality and polite, efficient service.

From groceries to household goods to furniture and automobiles and clothing, it was all found beneath one immense and dazzling roof. These Federal Super Centers were constructed in every city, making the new mega-malls convenient and accessible to everyone. Hundreds of thousands of freestanding retail stores, strip malls, and discount stores were demolished. The land upon which they stood was rapidly turned into new housing developments, mini-parks, or recreational areas.

Office buildings transformed into apartment complexes. Old bank buildings were turned into theaters, libraries and mini-museums. The downtowns became cultural centers. Slums were destroyed and acres of asphalt parking lots were plowed up and landscaped to become beautiful parks for the people.

All of the criminals had been killed. The prisons had been razed. Police departments were reorganized and those gun-toters and blue bullies of the past were considered by "Big Baby" to be socially and genetically flawed and were exterminated along with the criminals. The old type of law enforcement was now unnecessary.

Very few people dared to break *The New Laws*. If someone did violate the laws, everyone—the entire population—would be there to discover the problem and catch the offender. The people were living in true harmony, peace, and security.

People were proud again. They got dressed up to go out. Manners came back in vogue and everybody liked being called "Mister" or "Miss." The war of the sexes was finally over. The boys were boys and the girls were girls again. The renewed understanding and appreciation of the differences in the sexes made it exciting and wonderful to be alive. There was love and harmony everywhere.

Entire industries changed and new technologies developed

overnight. The health and safety of the people were considered for the first time as most important. Corporate profitability did not exist. "The People" came first.

Mankind was just beginning to learn how to be a good steward of God's world. Rivers and lakes were cleansed and made bountiful and safe again. The production of unnecessary toxic chemicals was stopped and healthful, natural substitutes were found for just about everything. Industrial and agricultural pollution ceased to exist and ecological conservation of every type was put into effect. Only the best and safest methods of production were allowed and, for the first time, cost was not an issue.

The destruction of the rain forests stopped. Logging was reduced and reforestation mandatory. All human efforts were focused on the continued cleanup of the world, and an ongoing ecology plan was put into effect that would benefit the people of the future. Life became as it should have been. Everything, everywhere, was bright and clean and new.

Bankers and tax collectors ceased to exist. Taxes and tax accounting were no longer necessary. The CPAs—corrupt dinosaurs from a system that hadn't been successful—were also eliminated. The insurance companies, banks and all of Wall Street had been disbanded. Financial investment was unnecessary.

Capital for start-up and day-to-day operation of all types of business was provided and managed by the New Government of the People for the benefit of the people.

For the first time in history everyone, everywhere had a job that was enjoyable, a car, plenty to eat, and good place to live. All human deprivation had simply vanished.

Billy, with skill and great creativity, successfully merged communism with capitalism.

All over the world the people eagerly accepted Billy's New World Federation and *The New Laws*. Billy pushed more and more domination of the people and still they did not rebel. But, why would they? The people were happy.

This feeling of bliss did not exist everywhere. There was a soundless, rising discontentment from those who had not been inoculated during the purge. Even though the MALU units had operated quite efficiently on a full-time basis, there were still tens of thousands of people who had not been "adjusted." Many of them had just slipped through the cracks. Some were missed by accident and some because they had intentionally avoided being inoculated.

Even though those who had been overlooked in the massive cleansing were not aware of what was secretly happening, they had become paranoid. They really didn't know why, but they were quietly afraid.

Oddly enough, even some of the people who had been processed also began to feel uneasy. Though they had survived the plague and received Billy's new prosperity, in some, the usual feelings of happiness and optimism were missing. Something was wrong. They could work and love and play, but intuitively they sensed that something was missing from their lives. It was just a feeling, more than some-thing that could be described. It gnawed at them.

After the plague, with all of the new order, no one wanted to discuss such feelings in a philosophical way. As wonderful as the world appeared to be, *The New Laws* still made for very dangerous times. To talk of misgivings or doubts might cause too many questions to be asked. If these private conversations were overheard, sometimes a person would be accused. A consistent attitude of caution and a pretended happiness and indifference prevailed. This attitude probably came from an old survival logic: "Remain calm. Be thankful you're alive. Enjoy what you have, and don't talk too much!"

But that quiet gnawing continued to grow within some of them. An indefinable yearning, a restive fear of the unknown, and an instinctive sense of uncertainty were still there. But, in these times, no enemy could be identified. Who were they to be against and for what reason? Everything was really good, so why should they question whether anything was right or wrong? Who cared, anyway? After all, it was an accepted fact that everything was all right and life was better than it had ever been.

They heard this propaganda every day. Billy told them everything was all right and if Billy said it was all right, it must be!

# 26

## GOD SPEAKS

It was to be another big media event, and it was again scheduled to take place in New York City at Radio City Music Hall, in the old RCA building. The venerable theatre was now called the Main Hall of the New World Federation Communications Center. All of the remaining media experts had been summoned to produce Billy's "really big show" in the massive auditorium.

The people of the United States and the world would again be gathered in front of their televisions and radios to hear and see their exciting, charismatic leader tell them of his great plans for the future of mankind and the New World Federation. It was nearing Billy's second year in office and because of the Plague crisis, this would be his first real State of the Nations address. Every channel on radio and television was locked in. It was mandatory that everyone view and hear this momentous event.

As the leaders, celebrities, and notables from around the world arrived and were seated in the huge auditorium, the broadcast commentators described for viewers and listeners the thrilling background of each of the dignitaries. The cameras cut and panned over the audience on the main floor and each of the four balcony levels of the great hall, always returning to the gigantic New World Federation emblem hanging from the topmost arch of the massive stage.

One of the commentators spoke. "And what a night it is. Every face in this audience is a familiar face. Luminaries from all walks of life and every country in the world are here. We haven't received any advance briefing as to the issues that President Johnstone will cover in this address, but the White House has hinted that we will not be bored with the usual statistics and dry rhetoric of a State of the Nations report. Also, today—and what a surprise it was—the Secretary of State, Henry J. Gillespie, resigned his post, on camera, and without explanation left the podium. The President's Press Secretary then introduced President Johnstone, who came to the platform with the good news that he was now appointing Henry J. Gillespie to the newly created post of America's First Regent of God's Doctrine."

Suddenly, the house lights dimmed and the news commentators stopped talking. With exciting drum rolls, followed by nine trumpets precisely playing the familiar "Ruffles and Flourishes," the mammoth cascade front curtain moved upward, revealing the stage. The production had begun.

Situated in the center of the stage was a unique carved, clear glass lectern atop a large platform draped with sparkling gold cloth. The NWF insignia was etched on the front panel of the lectern. The tall swagged curtains were a beautiful, rich shade of purple, trimmed in gold.

The stage lights dimmed and the inspirational voice of Henry Gillespie filled the hall. "Ladies and gentlemen, the President of the United States of America, William F. Johnstone."

A one-hundred-piece orchestra played the familiar "Hail to the Chief." In the dim auditorium, six bright spot lights focused on the center of the stage as Billy, dressed in an immaculate cream-colored suit, ascended high in the air on a platform that rose from the floor revealing an enormous gold and white staircase. The music continued playing as Billy slowly descended the stairs to the lectern. The audience was on its feet, cheering and applauding wildly for this very theatrical entrance. Billy basked in the spotlights and the approval of the audience for a few moments and then raised both hands for them to stop. The applause subsided and the audience sat down and quietly waited for him to speak.

"People of the world, I give all of you greetings from my house and family and from my country and the people of the United States of America. On this occasion, my first State of the Nations report, we Americans have decided to share with our relatives in our vast world family the joy and blessings of this past year."

The stage darkened and Billy was brightly lit by all of the spotlights.

"As we all know, the world has finally become safe from the deadly H2P5 virus. That horrible plague cost the lives of more than three and a half billion people over the last eighteen months and nearly caused the entire human race to be annihilated. Life on earth could have very easily ended for us all. But this was not what God wanted for us! No, my friends, God wanted the human race to survive, so he gave us the strength, the resolve and the ability to combat this plague, and we did survive!"

The audience erupted in cheers and applause.

"In this new millennium, God wants man to prosper and to live a more bountiful life than ever before. It is His plan for all of us to be happy. It is His plan for us to have plenty to eat and to be healthy. He wants no crime, no wars. No conflict. Great God in His heaven above loves us all and wants us to love Him and follow His word. For those who honor and obey Him, His treasures are generous and great. For those who disobey His word, who don't abide by His laws, the punishment for them is the immediate death of their body and their immortal soul. You must understand. God's requirements are simple, if you desire to lead a good life.

"But remember that His first and most important commandment is: 'Thou shall have no other god before me.' He is, and must be, the one and only God you pray to. We need the one genuine and only God, the great Lord of this world and of all the worlds of the universe. We need him to come into our hearts this very day with His message of love and commitment.

"Listen and hear, O' people throughout the world. Let us now pray to the Almighty, together. Oh, Lord of hosts, God of our fathers, tell us now what we should do to maintain your favor. Give us insight, Lord, give us direction and help us to find our way to do your will. We need to come together as a one-world family, Lord. You and you alone can help us to be united in our praise of you. Our ancestors, too, have defied you and blasphemed you. You punished them by scattering them throughout the world. We have struggled these thousands of years to come together as one family of people again. Forgive us Lord. Allow us to repent and to pray and honor you as our one true God and to live in peace and harmony with each other to enjoy the blessings you bestow upon us. Talk to our hearts and minds now, Lord. We beg you, great God, speak to us and tell us what you want us to do. Answer us, God. We pray to you, talk to us now and answer our prayers. Give us your will..."

As Billy droned on, a bright light began glowing behind him. The spotlights faded out as the backlight became brighter and brighter, until it seemed as brilliant as the sun. The audience in the auditorium was almost blinded by its brightness. To the television viewers, the light became so intense that even with the camera lenses stopped down as low as possible, little else could be seen. It was frightening and not at all natural.

Billy was wound up like a tent preacher. "Oh mighty God, speak to us, give us a sign, come into our hearts and minds with your commands.

Talk to us, Lord. Show us the way, oh ancient God of gods, tell us what you want us to do. Let your voice be heard..."

At that moment, Rob Collings, hidden in a control booth high in the dome of the auditorium, looked out upon the stage and pushed the master dimmer control for the light in back of Billy. The lamps extended to their full blinding brightness. Collings then pushed the start button on the console and a digital audio deck came alive, the volume up to full, as the sounds of an ethereal choir flooded the theatre.

Collings inserted a key into a switch and turned it sharply to the right. He then pushed the lighted button on the console marked "Level 1—Auditorium." The audience, the orchestra, the stage technicians and house staff instantly reacted to the 'Multiple Micro-Electrode Array' or the MMEA that had been implanted in all of them. At Level 1, the broadcasted radio waves caused the MMEAs to vibrate, causing rapture. The people became instantly disorientated and fell into semi-consciousness.

Billy intoned, "Great God, let us hear your voice..."

Collings pushed a lighted button designated as "Level 1 World-wide." He waited for a count of thirty, then pushed the next flashing button marked "God."

Radio transmitters throughout the world responded instantaneously, activating the MMEAs implanted inside the heads of the world's population.

Billy pleaded. "Speak, Lord. Talk to us." Then he became silent.

With their television sets glowing brightly, the great population of the world began to swoon in unified ecstasy. For the first time in history, the people of the world listened to the authority of God's word. It was a strong, but quiet inner voice they heard. God was speaking to every person in the world and each of them was able to hear the voice of God in his or her own native language.

*Hear me now, you sons of man. I am your God. I enter*

*your hearts and minds so that you will know my power and will obey me. Over and over I have visited my wrath upon you. You resist and ignore me. You defile and abuse all the good that I have given you. Do you not remember how I caused you to be scattered across my earth unable to speak or understand each other and how I flooded the earth with water to cleanse away the sinners?*

*Now, again, you have seen my anger and punishment. Yet from this pestilence I have spared some of you and allowed you to emerge unharmed from this great plague of death. This is my last warning. You must serve me as I demand. The laws that I gave to Moses and the people of Israel are the only laws. I am the one God of this earth and no man may worship any God before me. I am not Jesus, or Muhammed. I am not called Allah. I am God and all else said by man is blasphemy.*

*Hear my words and follow my laws or I shall destroy you and your world for all time. Observe my commandments and heed the words of him who is my prophet. I give unto you now a son of man, whom I have chosen to lead you back to my ways and to beautify my world. You must obey this leader as you would obey me, for my word will come through him. You will see my mark upon him. Revere and submit to this anointed one who stands before you now.*

*You must all learn to speak one language so that you may clearly understand and know my word.*

*Your priests have told you that they have spoken with me and know my mind. They have lied. The prophets of old have lied, for this is the first and only time I have spoken to man. I command you to destroy the churches and temples of the liars. Grind them to rubble and dust.*

*Do as I command and I will surely speak with you again. Repent and make atonement, for joy and glad tidings are at hand. Soon I shall make a new covenant with you and thereby remember your sins and transgressions no more.*

The voice stopped. There was stillness across the planet. The people of the world were motionless for quite some time. Then the realization of what had happened became apparent to everyone, everywhere. God had spoken to Man and every person in the world had heard His words.

The TV cameras slowly panned over the audience in the Great Hall. They centered on Billy and slowly circled around him. He stood still, looking straight ahead as though he was in a trance. He had changed. His black hair had turned snow white, and his face was tanned and seemed to have an angelic appearance. It was an awesome and overwhelming sight.

Most of the audience was motionless and quiet. Some were on their knees praying and many were crying. The others remained still in their seats, staring in a semiconscious daze.

This was the miracle that Mankind had prayed for and asked to happen for thousands of years.

Sally had fainted just like the billions of people worldwide who had been watching this event. She awakened to see the television showing the people of the world recovering from shock. She, too, was stunned. Not just from the rapture or the voice of God, but from her suspicion of what had really happened.

She railed and raged out loud at the TV "Billy Johnstone, you dirty, filthy, evil man. You've done this to us. You've violated our minds and bodies and made us your slaves. You are the ruler of Mankind. You have become God! Someone must oppose you. Even a cat only has nine lives. You're not immortal, Billy, you can die!"

Suddenly Sally was overtaken with a feeling of hopelessness and fell to her knees. "Oh, God in heaven. I take an oath. I will find a way to get out of this prison, and I will destroy this evil man! I promise, dear God, I will do it!"

# 27

## *REBELLION BORN*

A few days later, Sally was still wondering just how, or whether, God had spoken to her and all of the people at the same time. She had followed the "miracle" on the TV. It was driving her crazy.

Then it came to her. Sally remembered what she had discovered about the "Plague." That knowledge was why Billy had put her under house arrest. She had learned that the survivors of the plague, the As and Bs, had been implanted with what she had assumed, was some sort of chip identification. But now it was clear that she and the entire world were implanted with some sort of device that could create a physical effect and transmit a voice message directly to the auditory center of their brains.

The swooning—the sensation in her head—it was quite real. She was sure that it was more of Billy's high-tech gadgets that had caused a very impressive virtual reality. Sally had indeed heard the voice of God. Logically, she was quite sure it wasn't the voice of God and suspected that it was just Billy, playing God. How dare Billy do this to her—or to anyone? She wondered if the devices were implanted in everyone's head?

Of all the things Billy had done, this was the most vile and insidious. To use mankind's innocent love of God, to put words in God's mouth, meant that this monster—William F. Johnstone—had no humanity, no sense of morality and absolutely no integrity. In his zeal to help mankind, Billy had become depraved and horribly obsessed with his power.

Sally, spent with rage, fell back exhausted onto the couch. She slept for hours.

Sally awakened with a start at the sound of a whirring motor coming closer and closer to her head. Quickly, she sat up and turned toward the noise.

It was only Marguerite, her cleaning lady, using the vacuum cleaner.

Marguerite saw the shocked look on Sally's face. "Oh, I am so sorry. I did not want to wake you, Meez Sally. Do you want me to stop?" The vacuum cleaner continued to run as Marguerite sat on the couch beside Sally.

"Meez Sally, I need to talk to you. You have always been so kind to me. Please tell me, did you, too, hear the voice of God? Did he speak to you? Everyone, everywhere heard the voice. It was a sign from God, oh, *mi Jesus*, a miracle. But, Meez Sally, Marguerite did not hear the voice. God, he did not speak to me."

"Yes, yes Marguerite, we all heard the voice." After a moment, Marguerite's words sunk in, and Sally did a double take.

"Wha-what did you say?"

"The voice of God, I did not hear it. Oh, I will not go to heaven. God must be angry with me. The end eez near, the plagues is upon us. I am so afraid!"

Sally tried to comfort the old woman.

"Marguerite, calm down, everything will be all right. Are you sure you didn't hear God speak?"

"No. Not a word from God to Marguerite and, Meez Sally, I am so frightened, I have not got the virus shots they wanted us all to get and now the televisions say they will kill me. I am..."

An idea flashed in Sally's brain. "Marguerite. *Silencio!*"

The noise of the vacuum cleaner continued. Sally leaned toward Marguerite's ear and whispered. "You did not get the virus shots, and you did not hear God?"

The trembling woman shook her head no.

"Listen. You are safe with me. I will tell no one, you understand? And you too, must never tell anyone again or it will be big trouble for both of us. Would you like for me to help you, Marguerite?"

"Oh, thank you, yes, *Senorita*. I am old, and I live alone. Don't let them get me. Oh, I must turn off the sweeper, Meez Sally."

Marguerite started to get up from the couch.

Sally grabbed Marguerite's arm. "No, no, leave it on and sit here."

Sally hoped that the sound of the vacuum cleaner would make the audio bugs incapable of hearing their conversation. She kept Marguerite positioned in front of her, blocking the video camera view of her mouth and that of Marguerite's. Sally had to move quickly now, so as not to arouse the security guards' attention.

"I want you to take a message to a person, a friend of mine, and I do not want anyone to know. Do you understand?" Thinking quickly, Sally decided to embellish the story to make it believable for the old woman. "He is my lover, and he is married, so you must be very careful. Do you understand what I'm saying, Marguerite?"

The old woman nodded yes. A smile came to her wrinkled face. The gleam in her wizened eyes confirmed her complete understanding of the request.

"Thank you, Marguerite. I don't want you to ever speak to me about this again. It hurts and upsets me too much. I will give you a note and his address. Will you take it for me? Please, I will keep your secret if you will keep mine."

Marguerite agreed.

"*Si, si, Senorita.* I will do it."

Sally concluded dramatically, "I never want you to talk to me about him again. Oh, I love him. I am so miserable." Sally thought she was doing a pretty good job of soap opera acting.

Marguerite offered a hanky.

"Now please get back to your work, Marguerite, and I will tell you more after I have rested." Sally rolled over and hoped she could dream up a plan.

Sally couldn't sleep. She lay there, thinking. There must be others like Marguerite. She had yet to meet these latent rebels, but her thoughts were of nothing but Billy's destruction. This obsession was slowly driving her mad. Sally knew she had to take a chance. She had to do something to stop Billy.

Sally tossed and turned and then suddenly sat bolt upright. Finally, an idea emerged. She remembered that during the planning meetings, Julio Mondaldo had sometimes not been in agreement with the programs Billy was proposing. Julio had spoken enthusiastically of freedom for the people, and he'd sounded like he meant it. Julio had thrown in with Billy because he believed that Billy and his New Third Party stood for the solid principles first proclaimed during the Third Party campaign: "A better America and a better world for all people."

But after the election, slight contradictions of purpose began to surface. Billy, like most politicians before him, had simply lied to everyone. Sally recalled dinners with Julio. Even though he dutifully reported the progress of the Third Party, he spoke compassionately about the plight and sorrow of the people. One night, Sally had seen Julio with tears of disappointment and quiet anger as Billy's control over the government and the people grew stronger and more obvious. Maybe Julio knew the plague was a sham, but he was in too deep to stop it. Or maybe he was a loyalist. Whatever the truth might be, Sally had to risk seeking his help.

After some thought, she wrote the note.

*Julio—*

*I need your help. Billy has placed me under house arrest at my apartment. I'm not allowed to tell anyone about my predicament. I must gamble on our friendship and trust you with my life. I've wanted to talk with you about this for some time, but my apartment and phone are bugged. The very kind woman who brings this message to you knows nothing of my circumstance. She is just a cleaning lady whom I have asked to take this envelope to you. I hope to God she is able to safely make the delivery! Please come ASAP. Bring a notebook with you so we may talk without being overheard. Be very careful what you say when you arrive! I look for-ward to seeing you, my friend.*

*Sincerely,*

*—Sally Hawthorne*

Later, that afternoon, Sally gave Marguerite an envelope with the note enclosed. Julio's address was printed clearly on the outside. Again, she cautioned the old woman not to let anyone know about her errand. Sally and Marguerite had promised to keep each other's secrets, and she hoped that the old woman would be loyal to romance and Sally's pretended liaison.

About 7:30 that evening, the phone rang. The sound startled Sally from her daydreams and from the writing she was doing about her imagined "resistance" movement. She put down her laptop and pushed the button on the videophone.

"Sally, it's Julio."

She pushed the button again so Julio could see her. "Hi, stranger, whatcha up to?" she replied, trying to remain calm.

"Are you accepting visitors to the convent, Sister Sally? Like about 9:30, maybe?"

"I'm going nowhere fast. Come on over."

"Great. See you about 9:30. Bye."

Sally was elated and frightened at the same time. Anxiously she wondered. Was he a friend? Was he coming to her rescue? Or would he be part of another trap for her?

Sally stashed her notebook computer in a safe place and straightened up the apartment. She put a couple of bottles of white wine in the fridge to chill, and made a late evening snack tray for the two of them.

At 8 o'clock the door buzzer sounded.

Sally jumped. It couldn't be Julio. He wasn't expected until 9:30.

Sally opened the door.

It was Julio. Before he could enter the apartment, he threw his arms around her and kissed her on the neck, whispering in her ear. "Pretend I'm Billy. Act natural and watch what you say!"

"Oh, B-Billy, Billy, I'm so glad to see you..."

Sally closed the door and took Julio's coat and hat and threw them in a chair. She turned off the door lights and led him quickly to the living room couch where she embraced him once again. Continuing the pretense, Sally cooed. "Billy it's so lonely here. Why do you stay away so long?"

Julio mumbled his fondness and showed her an index card and pretended to passionately kiss and fondle her. The card said:

> *Continue to pretend that I'm Billy. We're getting out of here. I have figured out how to beat the monitors. Just follow my lead. First, we'll have a little wine and then we'll go to your bedroom and pretend to make noisy love. Just be natural and follow me. Don't worry, we'll be ok— Have faith! –Julio.*

Sally got up from the couch. "Well, big boy, shall we have a little wine and something to eat before I do you in?"

"Oh, yes. I'm starving, baby."

"Good. You take the wine to the bedroom, and I'll get the snacks."

Sally was impressed by Julio's impression of Billy. It was really very good. The bedroom. What a clever plan. It was the only room in the apartment that did not have a bug or video camera. Billy never liked the idea of someone watching him make love. But the hallway to the bedroom was bugged for sound and that was why Julio wanted "noisy love" to occur.

For half an hour, they did just what Julio had ordered. It wasn't, to Sally's pleasant surprise, pretend. They really made love and he was good at it! When they had finished, Julio showed her another card:

> *Sally —I liked this part of your rescue the best. Now I will play back a recording of our love making while you put on some jeans—a heavy shirt—hiking shoes and a winter coat. Put only a few toiletries in your pockets and nothing else! Next card when you've completed this one!—Julio*

Sally began to dress as Julio turned on the recording. Julio pulled a turtleneck dickey over her head and piled that wonderful red hair into a stocking cap. She looked at him quizzically. He smiled his neat, confident smile and, even though she didn't know exactly what he was doing, she trusted that it was all right. After she was dressed, Julio shut off the recording.

"Are you trying to kill me, Sally Hawthorne? I'm going to get some more wine for us, my sweet. I'll need the energy just to keep up with you." He gave her another card:

> *Sally—I'm going to rig the video cameras in the living room and kitchen. I will come back and dress and then we will go! You're doing great!—J.*

Julio quickly returned to the bedroom holding the wine he'd poured for them in the kitchen. He put his pants and shoes on and pulled another turtleneck on himself. Sally watched as he put something on each of their pillows and started the recording again. Looking at his watch, Julio grabbed Sally by the arm, and they boldly crawled down the hallway to the kitchen.

Sally's apartment was on the third floor. Julio had brought a knotted rope and secured the end of the rope around the pipes under the sink in the kitchen. He opened the window and dropped the rope, motioning for her to follow him. Slowly, Julio and Sally moved down the rope. On the ground, they ran quickly to the parking lot and got into Julio's car.

Julio pushed Sally to the floor, fired up the engine, rolled out of the parking lot and down the street. Neither of them said a word. Julio grinned at Sally. Her face was frozen in terror.

"You're out, Sally Hawthorne. You're free. I have helped you to escape. Do you not have words of thanks for your rescuer?"

Oh, I do, I do. But how did you do all that? And why aren't we being tailed by the 'eye in the sky' right now?"

Julio explained to her how he had tipped the cameras up a little and how the recorder playing in the bedroom would divert the security. Then he began the details of where they were headed.

Sally was absolutely thrilled with Julio. He had it all—intelligence and bravery. She felt quite secure with this man.

Julio told her how he had been putting little bits and pieces of Billy's operation together for some time and how he had been meeting, one on one, with a few other people who seemed dissatisfied with "Billy-World." Tonight, he told her, they were going to form the very first resistance group.

"Sally, I want you to speak to these people. Tell them everything you know. They'll be impressed that two of Billy's highest have quit him and now want to oppose his tyrannical government."

A resistance! Sally had been looking for them, waiting for them and now, somehow, they were all being brought together. Maybe she had found a way to stop Billy. These few rebels were just what Sally Hawthorne needed. She was no longer alone.

Sally and Julio were about to make the first sounds that would be heard from the peoples' resistance. Late that evening, the light of freedom and truth beamed bright and, with Sally's help, this little group of greenhorn guerrillas would soon learn the awful truth of Billy's plans. Sally spared no details.

Though these people were frightened, they were eager and available. Surely, there were more non-implanted humans left in the world?

Those who had not been "adjusted" gradually began to come together. Maybe it was because they sensed they were different from the rest. The people without the implants were different all right. They had not obeyed the Federal Inoculation Order. Without fault, they had become outlaws and just as disenfranchised people have always done, they reached out and formed little cliques and slowly began to talk to each other about how they felt. When they talked and questioned one another, it was always with some degree of suspicion and trepidation.

They weren't political dissidents, they were federal lawbreakers and because of their circumstance these people could become a resistance movement. All that was missing was guidance with a defined purpose and the courage to show them the way. Sally and Julio explained to them that there were many more of them and how even a small group could wield great opposition to an oppressive government. They quickly learned that Sally and Julio were well informed and had the courage to lead them.

At the close of that first meeting, a genuine resistance group had been born. These people now understood what had happened to them, as well as their fellow countrymen. They believed that this evil should be undone. They wanted to stop Billy and help regain freedom for all people. All hoped that the resistance would grow.

Now it was up to Julio and Sally to teach them how to fight that hideous strength that had taken control of the world.

But unknown Sally and Julio, or to anyone, Billy was about to implement the next part of Plan C.

# 28

## PLAN 'C' COMPLETED

Billy was President. He had acquired absolute control of the government, as well as the people. His Plan A and Plan B had been just as easy to accomplish as he had promised. Now began the final scenario of Billy's Plan C, in which he would dictate and control how mankind would live and conduct itself for all time.

Billy called a meeting of the Inner Circle to be held in the hidden room at Hurricane House. The members of the IC arrived on schedule. Rob Collings greeted them and directed each one to follow him to the library bar for a few drinks before Billy arrived.

Acting as temporary host, he explained, "Billy will be joining us soon, gentlemen. Enjoy a drink. O'Malley here will mix your favorite brand of poison. He'll make 'em like you like 'em, boys. He's a master chemist."

Collings moved around the room and talked with each man. He stopped to speak with General Fenwick and in hushed tones asked, "Alfred, do you have any updates on the activities of those suspected rebels?"

Looking around the room to assess if they were being overheard, Fenwick replied. "Yesterday, about noon, we monitored a conversation that two of the suspected rebels were having in a small park near the Fowler building in downtown DC. With that bit of surveillance, we learned where they planned to hold their first resistance meeting. It happened last night. I immediately sent an RSS surveillance team over to that building and set up cameras. The meeting went forward as they'd planned. We watched them gathering. From the way they were talking, I don't think many of them had a clue what was really going on. The conversations had little, or no details. It was just grumbling. Not much of what you would call rebel talk, just grousing and wild distrust. We ran identity checks and continued to watch them. Only a few of them were not implanted, and I didn't think they posed any problem, at all. That is, until our little Sally Hawthorne showed up!"

"Sally? That's impossible. She's under house arrest. She can't leave her apartment building without the scanner knowing. Are you sure?"

"Rob, I've got the videos. It's her. She didn't show up on the scanner system. I don't have a clue how she's done it...But let me finish. So, Sally came in and gave them a fast, stirring speech and, even without charts and graphs, they got the whole picture about the fake plague and ID implants. She told them all about it. Rob. She's good! She galvanized them into a real resistance force, and she did it very quickly. Now they have knowledge and a reason to fight, and we've been identified as the enemy. But here's the worst news: Julio Mondaldo has joined them, and they appointed him their official leader. I tried to pick him up on the scanner, but he's off the system, too! Between Julio and Sally, they have all the inside information. Julio is smart, Rob. He knows how to take us apart!"

"Julio against us? I can't believe it!"

"Rob, we're not as invincible as Billy thinks we are. We had secrecy on our side, but it was only for a little while. If the truth ever got out, well, it would be a few of us against the population of the world.

We'd all be dead and that's a fact. Remember what the people did to Mussolini!"

They moved away from the rest of the members.

"Julio's a pretty smart guy, Rob. The very first thing he did was to divide the group into four parts. Then he assigned a leader for each group. He told them that they were going to move the meetings to a new location. Julio must have suspected that we were monitoring the area because he spoke in a very loud voice. Then he made them all huddle around him so the video cameras couldn't see him and used a small writing tablet to conduct the rest of the meeting. Then he ripped up the paper and burned the pieces. He's changed their method of communication, too. Haven't got a clue on that one either. Julio has encouraged each of the new resistance members to find others to join them. The meeting only took about twenty minutes and then they dismissed the group. I can tell you this, Rob. They're looking like a real underground movement."

"But you arrested them, didn't you? You got there in time."

"Uh, No. We didn't get them. Here's some more bad news. By the time I personally got wind of what was going on and dispatched an RSS squad to the location, they'd finished their meeting. We kept scanning them and viewing them on video as my troops rushed to the site. Then, right after the meeting, as the rebels left the building, all of them disappeared off the scanner system. How the hell we lost track of Julio, Sally and twelve people, with eight of them implanted, I'll never know. They just blipped off the screen. Vanished."

"What do you mean, 'vanished?' You know that's impossible! And why didn't you jump on this? Why didn't you send your men immediately? I don't like this, Alfred."

"I did react immediately, Rob. I just told you. Listen, man, by the time my guys got there all of them were gone. I called for a net on the entire area and sent a squad to Julio's and Sally's apartments, and to the addresses of those we had identified. We found evidence at each place to show that the individuals had packed up. They were all long gone. This thing must have been planned for some time because it went off without a hitch. I've ordered men stationed at Sally's apartment and at Julio's place and at all the other places, as well. Not to worry, Rob. I've got a full court press on this one. We'll find Julio and Sally and the rest. We're using an all-points nationwide alert to get them. But, I'm sorry to say, so far nothing has turned up."

"Not good, Alfred. How could you have let this happen? We've got to find these people. This could spread."

"Rob, I didn't let it happen. It just happened. Christ, you guys are the people that built that damned scanner. If it failed, don't blame me. I've got the engineers pulling a full system check on it right now. One of them thinks we could have an intermittent glitch on the satellite; another thinks that somehow the names and numbers of those we want to locate have been removed from the Registry Computer. Hell, I don't know! Listen, I'm really concerned about this. I think we need to bring Billy and Charles in."

"No, I don't think this is the right time. I'll personally handle it. Don't let anyone on your staff mention this to Billy. He has enough on his mind right now. I want you and your people to stay on top of this. Keep the ID numbers on Sally and Julio and those connected with them on the satellite scanner system. If they make one mistake, we'll find them. I want to know what you know, as soon as you get the information. Got it?"

The drinks flowed. The talk among the men became louder. Late, as usual, Billy entered the room.

"Gentlemen, let's go to work."

The men followed him down the hall to the elevator and descended to the hidden room.

Each took his proper seat at the V-shaped table. Billy remained standing as he spoke. "Once more into the breach, dear friends, once more. We have accomplished much, yet there is still more to be done.

We have paved the road for this next millennium and truly have an enormous beginning toward a wonderful and peaceful global village. The results are everywhere. We've achieved this not by oppression, but by logic, for man can only live peacefully with rules that he can understand and believe in. To force the control of his thoughts and behavior is only to encounter man's very natural resistance to despotism and to incur all of his righteous fury as he naturally rebels against his enemy."

Billy looked at them, one by one, and became very serious. "We, however, have created an atmosphere of hope and have given the people daily circumstances that positively reinforce the ideas that we wanted to sell them. We have convinced them that all is well in their lives. It can be assured, without doubt, that the people willingly accept, in every way, whatever out leaders tell them."

"Our predecessors accomplished much of this control and acceptance work for us. They created a conditioned response pattern in the people. However, their cumbersome and contradictory attempts to make more and more trivial and useless laws in order to manipulate society simply primed the way for us. The myriad of stupid issues that were given to the people year after year, century after century, just left the citizenry bewildered. They didn't want more frustrating decrees followed by inconsistencies and non-results. They wanted answers."

Billy pulled a cigar out. "Well, here we are. We've given them answers—our answers—and the people seem to like it!"

Billy lit his Cuban cigar and continued the pace. "They will keep obeying *The New Laws* because they have been programmed to do so. You see, for years, before we came into power, the people quietly believed that someday, someone would lead them out of the frantic and chaotic world they were living in and when that happened, only the good, law-abiding citizens, would be favored by this new leader."

Billy took a long draw on the cigar, filled his lungs, and exhaled the spicy smoke. "Now, God Himself has spoken to the people and told them that I am, in fact, that very leader and that I am 'the way and the light.' God has told them that they are to 'obey me as they would obey Him,' and now they're happy and have no fear of the future. They feel safe and secure. Our new administration has become the paternal monarchy that the people have always wanted and needed."

Billy placed his cigar neatly in the ashtray. "Our removal of human dross is not like the purges of the past, not like the Holocaust of World War II, with its terror and sadness, followed by hatred and vengeance. The people of the world do not suffer any guilt or sorrow for what has happened to their fellow man during this nasty, but necessary, plague."

Now he spoke like a tragedian actor. "No widows' tears or orphans' cries, no dead men's blood or pining maidens' groans. No war. No bodies. No oppression—no oppressors."

Billy laughed. "They think that the Almighty Himself has done this to them to make them strong. They think that those who have lived through the plague are the most fit. They believe that they have prevailed against the awesome, but just, forces of God and nature. They have survived, and they feel righteous about their survival.

"It's true enough—we did select them using accurate data. So, they are the best, the most capable, the strongest, and the fittest. Therefore, these survivors are entitled to all that the future, and God and I will give them. Gentlemen, by reducing the numbers of the world's population by more than three and one-half billion people we have eliminated the natural misfits. We now have the very best specimens of humankind that have existed in all of history, and they realize and accept without qualification the principal rule for living well: If you work, you eat...and if you work hard, you can eat more and if you don't work, you die!

"They will no longer be troubled with all of the petty problems that have gone before them. Each of them now has a chance to excel in his or her chosen field and will be given every opportunity possible to grow and improve. Gentlemen, we have cleaned God's house for him. We've gotten rid of the vermin and the horrible human garbage that has accumulated through the years. What is left now are good people with a true understanding of peace and harmony and a new awareness of the responsibility of being good stewards to God's earth and loving brothers to each other. Many things have changed and many things more will change in order to make our society and the societies of all the world the greatest triumph of the ages."

Clearing his throat and shifting to a business-like manner, Billy stopped and gestured to the walls of the hidden room. Appearing on the three large screens were the letters U.W.C.

"As we speak, the United States, all of Europe, Australia, Canada, Mexico, Central and South America, China, Africa, India, the Middle East and the Pacific Rim countries have replaced their currency with our Universal Work Card. The UWC has been totally accepted by the people and has become most effective as an incentive."

Billy turned to Avery. "Mr. Vice President, will you take over now and explain to us just how well the new UWC system is working?"

"Thank you, Mr. President. The survivors of the H2P5 'plague' have been reclassified by the National Computer. Using a job rating from R1 to R1000, we have created a workable caste system based on the present skill levels of each individual. From this point on, each individual's work performance can move him or her up or down."

"...or out!" Billy declared.

"Rrr-right. As we know, all currency in all countries has been withdrawn from circulation. To hold cash or coin is now a criminal offense. The UWC, the Universal Work Card, was issued to each person as the population was reexamined during the six-month virus check-up. We gathered quite a bit of information on them when we issued the first plague ID cards, but this second exam allowed for all existing information to be cross-checked and upgraded. This methodology was quite efficient and speedy, as all of the data on the dead had been purged freeing up a lot of space. During that second examination, we exchanged the National ID cards for the UWC. New jobs and new locations for millions and millions of people are being assigned each day.

"This same UWC card will be further validated every week as each of the citizens places his card in the controller box at their home residence. Credits or demerits for work are issued at that time. We have called them 'dollar credits' to maintain a sense of familiarity. This allows the people to continue to think about goods and services in a common and traditional way. Each job level has its own base 'dollar credit' for that particular job and will afford the individual a certain style of living. For morale purposes, everyone received a raise from previous times and, with our new economy in place, the credit dollar buys a lot more...at about WW II standards, I believe."

With a click, Avery changed the display to a chart. "Each individual's future is based on that person's efforts, and we give quick results. One could, for example start off doing menial work and living in a one-room apartment. That's Level One through One-Hundred. After doing good work for about a year, you could move to a house with a yard and, after a few years, if you're productive and bright, you could end up in a mansion with servants and the best of everything. As a side-note, you could lose everything, even your right to stay alive. To do less is to earn less. Do nothing, and you'll be exterminated. To produce more, means that you will be considered for advancement and receive more. These advancements are awarded each year on the thirty-first of December. This allows the individual to truly start out with good New Year."

Adopting a more professorial tone, Avery continued. "It's a kind of controlled socialism, with capitalist overtones. The UWC card allows them to have free public transportation. As you know, movies, information, music, concerts, sporting events, are all activated by this card. There is a small charge to the individual for each use, and a reduced charge if the individual continues to work well each day. Of course, no entertainment benefits will be allowed if a person fails or falls behind. This same card, when used in the home controller box, enables individual voting on certain public issues, preserving a sense of democracy. Those votes will of course be used in the continued evaluation of the people, as well as provide us some insight as to their thoughts on improving society. The UWC card is the most vital part of a citizen's life. The card contains all information about what they have done, what they are doing and is the cornerstone of their entire life and future. It's been very effective, and is now in use in every country throughout the world."

Billy stood again. Harrison sat down. "Thank you, Regent Harrison."

Evangelical, euphoric, Billy plunged forward with his big speech. "Oh, we really do live in the most fruitful times, gentlemen. Most fruitful, indeed. With your combined efforts executing Plan A, you made me President of the United States. A brilliant success! I presented my Plan B to you and we have now eliminated the obvious ills and misfits of government and the dregs of society and, because of that purge, we are now in the process of constructing a much better world."

Again, the three big screens lit up.

"Now we come to Plan C. The exciting future of man; mankind as a brave new species. As you know, for many years I've referred to you and the others as my Regents. I've never spoken or written of how or what these Regents might be, or exactly how they might operate. Just Regents. I think most of you believed that it was a title—a station or rank to be awarded—and all of that could be very true. The term 'Regents,' however, as used in its traditional sense, is a patriarchal reference that could represent the governance and nurturing we have given the people of the world. In order to have a more perfect future for them, Regents of this kind are definitely necessary."

Billy had the full attention of his men. They knew they were about to hear the final proposition from their brilliant and slightly deranged leader.

"Gentlemen, Dr. Gertz and I have been working on this particular part of our mission for over 18 years. My own ideas have been combined with the great genius of Dr. Gertz and his very capable staff. Finally, our dreams have become a reality. My collaborator, Dr. Charles Gertz, will tell us exactly what our definition of Regents really means, how we spell it, and how it will truly be mankind's reward for living a good and productive life."

Gertz stood and addressed the others. "Thank you, Mr. President. Gentlemen, when Billy and I joined forces many years ago, during those wonderful days at Great Southern Tech, I needed Billy to find venture capital for some of the pretty wild theories I had and to help me develop and market some of these new inventions. Remember, Billy, when I showed you this little experiment?"

The giant wall screens flickered and showed a young Charles performing one of his experiments. The video was of a flower growing from seed to maturity to death as an elapsed time clock on the screen counted 128 minutes.

The scene changed and a slate-frame was seen: "Embryo Growth #41."

Charles continued his narration. "Billy wondered if it could be done with animal tissue. I assured him that it was theoretically possible and went to work. The next experiments you will see show an embryo growing, in a stopped time sequence. You'll see the slow development from embryo to a full-grown chimpanzee. The total elapsed time, gentlemen, was just two months, twelve hours, seven minutes and 13 seconds."

Charles excitedly babbled on. "The obvious next step was to work with human DNA and tissue. Simple cloning had been experimented with for many years. But, in the old days, a laboratory grown fetus, by Federal law, had to be aborted within seven days after conception because it was considered thereafter to be a human being. There have been lots of moral, ethical and legal problems involved in these issues over the years. No one—no one on the record, that is—was ever allowed to grow a human clone to full maturity. But, in that early beginning, we were our own lawmakers. Since my experiments were very private, Billy urged me to go on. I, of course, agreed to try."

Again, the screen showed, in elapsed time, his experiment from the first day through the last.

"And here are the results, gentlemen. From cell to embryo to birth, to maturity to old age to death, and all in less than 13 months. Accelerated growth, a full lifetime in a little over a year."

Charles didn't take a breath. "Then began the real challenge. Could I stop this chronological growth acceleration at the perfect biological time? Stop it, with all its wonderful, youthful vitality, before the aging process began? After hundreds of attempts and failures I succeeded. Yes. I did it! I created a new life and could stop the aging process precisely at the most advantageous time. And then, stop it from aging, forever. Theoretically, this could be life without end!

"During these early experiments in cloning living tissue, we certainly got a healthy new body. But, just as in a normal birth, a very empty brain. You see, every cell contains the DNA pattern for physical reproduction. That kind of cloning is elementary, but another hidden part in the schematic of DNA, a factor I now call RGZ— for 'Regenerative Genetic Zoomorphicides'; these are the genes that contain the accumulated knowledge and emotional experience of that person's life from birth to death as well as his ancestors' tendencies and proclivities. It's a kind of genetic tape recorder.

"I know it sounds impossible, but it's quite real. Using the living DNA in this radical new process, I found that I could accelerate the growth cycle, then stop the aging process during the prime physical age period of the subject, isolate the RGZ factor, and accelerate the growth of the RGZ factor itself so that the subject's lifetime—years of accumulated experience and knowledge—was readily available to the clone."

The men sat stunned, quiet as students, listening in wonder to all that Charles was telling them.

"Am I losing you? I am, aren't I? Well, let me put it in other words. Here it is in the simplest of terms. Let's take an 80-year-old man. He has 80 years of collected life knowledge, plus the accumulated genetic influences of his father, his grandfather, his great grandfather, etc. But he has a diseased and dying body. From the tissue sample, I grow his clone, repair the diseases and other genetic flaws that have caused him to age and die, accelerate the growth of the body, stopping it at say, 25 years of age. He is in prime physical shape, right? Now I isolate the RGZ factor and allow just this part of his DNA to grow at a nonstop rate to the full 80 years. I stop the RGZ growth and: presto-chango, a 25 year old with a perfect body and 80 years of available knowledge and hundreds of years of genetic inspiration. Now, at age 25/80, he returns to his life with use of his accumulated knowledge and continues learning. And the best part is he can live forever—less normal wear and tear—and we can remake him anytime should he wear out or become damaged!"

Billy interrupted. "Understand. One of mankind's greatest laments—'If I only had known when I was young, what I now know today'—becomes obsolete. Amazing. The Chinese assumed for centuries that there was no difference between the mind and the body. The Chinese, of course were right. And, Charles had scientifically proven it."

Charles continued. "Yes, yes. Then Billy asked me if I could clone the DNA of someone who had died long ago. It sounded unreasonable, and quite impossible, but of course, very interesting. This challenge posed problems greater than I could have ever expected, but I love a challenge and went to work."

Charles rested his hand on Billy's shoulder.

"Billy gave me a sample taken from the remains of Albert Einstein. Remember, Billy, I asked you how you got it? I called you Igor, the grave robber, but you reminded me that I, in fact, had become Dr. Frankenstein. After some serious trial and error, I was able to do it. Can you imagine? It really worked! Albert Einstein lived once more. It was more than cloning, you see, because after that experiment, I had perfected a true cellular regeneration. That was when Billy coined the name for the process."

Gertz spelled it on the screen. "Get this gentlemen, it's not R-E-G-E-N-T-S, it is, Regeneration-Genetics-Z which Billy shortened to a sort of acronym, REGENZ."

It was Billy's original idea that the great men and women of the past, should be brought back to life, so they could truly become the Supreme Regents —REGENZ—of the world.

Barnston jumped in. "It's utterly fantastic. I thought *Jurassic Park* was just a fantasy story. You mean to tell me that if you have a speck of tissue you can recreate anyone who has died? Why, this is Biblical resurrection, outdone!"

"Oh, yes, it's all true and I can prove it. Here's an interview with Albert from just yesterday. He is very much alive, you know."

The big screens came to life and showed Charles and Billy sitting with Albert Einstein, having discussions with the brilliant theorist concerning the state of the world today. Each of the members of the circle sat in awed silence and watched this scene with utter amazement.

Avery quietly asked, "Do you have any others, Charles?"

"Yes, Avery, I have Lincoln and Ghandi in growth at this time and I have just received a sample of Thomas Jefferson. Exciting thought, isn't it? But here's the hitch: even though these famous beings are very interesting experiments, they are currently fraught with failure. Keeping them alive is extremely difficult. This was the eighth or ninth Einstein, you know. I have greater results with living DNA. But I'll get it to work. So, let me drop the 'great dead people' stuff and continue with the living REGENZ."

Billy chimed in. "The Einstein experiments proved their point conclusively. The evidence was seen each time we re-grew 'Albert'. It was like we had only interrupted our conversation for a moment and then we continued talking where we left off. It was shortly after the first 'Albert' that I came upon the idea of bringing all of the greatest minds in history back to life. I felt that they could serve mankind once again. They could continue to live on and would progressively grow even more intelligent, creative and productive, year after year, for the greater benefit of mankind. A super brain trust from the past, and for all the ages. True Regents of the People."

Charles took over again. "It's a brilliant concept. I'll continue to pursue it. Of course, Billy, you gave me an opportunity that no scientist in history has ever had. Unlimited capital to work with and the unchanging, sincere devotion of a dear friend and supporter! With that kind of inspiration and financing, gentlemen, I have discovered the secret hiding place of the soul itself! We are the first in history to actually create life, to control life, and resurrect the dead. We have become the gods, themselves!"

Billy patted him on the back. "Yes, yes, ol' boy, I know, I know. He smiled paternally.

Charles continued in a somewhat unrestrained manner. "And then Billy came upon the idea of using this cloning method as the ultimate human control/reward factor. Eternal life. What an incentive! Who wouldn't obey *The Laws* and work hard if they could become immortal? But then, we thought, there's no sense in cloning imperfections. So, I went to work and discovered that there are a great many problems associated with retaining good social attitudes in human DNA. It was very, very hard work, Billy."

Charles clicked a button and the screens all changed to a set of formulas and equations. The numbers and notes were in his own hand and barely readable. "To eliminate the lust and dishonesty and violence so genetically inherent in what we call the human personality, to make it perfect, the DNA must be altered considerably. I found that general evil and abhorrent behavior were located in the mythical 'XXY' factor of the RGZ pattern of the DNA. By altering some of the anerosobine molecules and the nucleotide polymorphisms, the 'XXY' factor—an undesirable quality—then completely disappears. And, *voila*! We have a human with the potential for pure goodness. Now, after the proper DNA alteration, we cloned this mutated genetic material and discovered that we had a totally loyal, happy, productive human without the probability for offensive behavior. A human that will follow directions and never, ever, be upset with the director."

Gertz changed the screen again to show another set of equations combined with a family tree sort of drawing. "But we also discovered that in some people, their ancestry was laden with social or emotional maladjustment quotients and contained many more of the XXY factors than we anticipated. Altering those kinds of people became a very long and labor-intensive process. In some cases, there were so many XXY factors that it was nearly impossible to alter them all. The detection and alteration of the XXY factor is a very long and difficult enterprise to attempt. If we modified everyone in the world...Well, it just became an impractical idea. I concluded that it would be easier to work with the best individuals available—in other words, those with good pedigrees. So, obviously, we still have to monitor those people with flaws, those with bad backgrounds, weed them out, and eliminate them. Killing of the undesirables has happened many times in history and for less important reasons."

The screen changed again and the word "VIRUS" was displayed.

"Billy came up with the answer to the problem. By using his very brilliant plague scenario and all the computerized population information and the DNA genome grid of a perfect 'model human' as criteria, we systematically exterminated the genetically imperfect: the disabled, those that could not think, had no skills, the criminals...the very dregs of humanity. Billy's Plan B accomplished that task and what we have left is a fairly perfect group of humans. Not totally perfect, but now we are going for one-hundred percent! We will create our new REGENZ from the very best of the best."

Billy stood and reluctantly, Charles returned to his seat.

"You have noticed that doctors, dentist, clinics and hospitals—the entire health care system—no longer exist. They are no longer needed. If a citizen with only marginal productive qualities gets sick, injured or killed, there's no repair; simply oxidation. But before the individual is eliminated, since the basis of that person is worth keeping, samples of DNA are evaluated and the genetic structure put in proper order. That genetic evaluation produces a perfect schematic that contains all of the present knowledge, manual skills, and social prowess of that individual. With a lifetime of experience now correctly in order, the individual is then cloned and rapidly grown to his optimal psychical condition, the old, diseased, or injured body is destroyed and the person is reborn into a wonderful new life that could go on forever.

"At this time, the populations of the Northern and Southern Hemispheres have had their six-month plague reexaminations. All have been issued the Universal Work Cards. The National Computer now contains updated information on all of the people and the second phase of eradication is under way. We are now culling the very best from the population. These will be our new REGENZ. Mankind will finally be delivered from suffering, death, and the social ills that kept him from achieving his true potential"

A fresh image appeared on the screen, showing the exteriors of modern buildings with huge signs displaying the letters NWF.

"We are building huge REGENZ centers in all the major cities across the planet. The rest of the world has had the plague inoculations and all of them have been implanted."

"God will speak again to the people of the world. God will announce that He has chosen to give them reason to follow His word. If they are true to Him, He will give them eternal life, physical life everlasting and it will be right here, right now on this earth! We will continue to process them and we will discover a new level of unimpaired, bright humans, thereby creating a fresh new race of immortals."

Billy raised his glass of wine.

"To the brave new future of mankind, gentlemen."

They all stood to approve his proposal. "Hear, hear."

Billy waved his hand and, suddenly, the meeting was over, and the members of the Inner Circle filed out the hidden room.

Collings walked over to Billy, waiting for the last of them to go. "Billy, we need to talk. Tell those clowns to go on without you. This is important."

The President seemed to understand Collings' urgency. "Good night, gentlemen. Please go on without me, Rob and I have a few things to talk about. See you all at breakfast in the morning. Good night."

The elevator doors shut, and they were alone.

"Billy, Sally and Julio have formed an underground resistance."

"What?"

"Fenwick was monitoring their first meeting last night and somehow Julio and Sally and eight other implanted people just vanished off the satellite scanner screen. Blink—they were gone!"

"Julio could be dangerous. He knows too much. And Sally..."

"Look, Billy, she should have gone into the LOES machine long ago..."

"Let's not argue. Rob. A rebellion can spread like wildfire. With Sally's brains and Julio's expertise and the information they both possess... Does Alfred know any more? How the hell did she escape from her apartment? The scanner system should have caught it all. That's what it's there for. You can't hide from..."

"Yes, yes. I know all that. Listen to me. I think you should get

Charles on the phone and ask him about this. He helped design the damned thing. If there's a way to beat it, he ought to know how it could be done."

Billy picked up the phone on his desk and dialed Charles' room. It rang and rang. In time, the house receptionist answered.

Billy barked. "Charles Gertz...Please. I don't care if he said not to be disturbed. What? He's What? Wake him up. This is the President and I want to talk to him now!"

Billy covered the phone and turned to Collings. "Can you imagine that guy? Wherever he is, he's always blocking my calls!

Collings looked at Billy, knowingly.

"Charles? Billy. Call me back on the hidden room number and do it right away."

Within seconds, the phone rang. "Charles? Tell me how a person could beat the scanner system. How could someone avoid being found? ...If they cut their head off? Look you asshole, I'm not kidding. I've got a very serious situation here, and I don't want comedy. I want an explanation! Please, Charles. Think before you answer this time and tell me how a person could hide from the scanners?"

Billy listened and repeated what Charles said to him out loud. "Hmm. Lead foil around the neck and shoulders. We recalled all lead products for use in the LOES machines, didn't we? ...Yeah, that's what I thought, not probable. Okay, what else? ...Inside of a lead-lined container or vehicle or...What are you saying? A jamming device? Is that possible? Lot of electronics. Yeah. Also, not probable, eh? Well look, here's what's happened. We had a dozen or so people under surveillance, had them on the scanner screen, numbers up and everything and suddenly they all vanished...Yes, all of them and at the same time. Yeah, all of them. No, the scanner system has been checked out...It's fine. Think, Charles. How could they do that?... Look for a lead-lined bus. Charles come on!...You're serious now? A lead-lined bus? Okay, old buddy. Go back to sleep or whatever it is you were doing. I'll talk with you in the morning. Good night, Charles."

Collings sounded puzzled then resolute. "Billy, Gertz's explanation is too simple. But if he's right, how do I find this lead-lined bus? No. No, I don't even try. I wait for them to get out of the bus and the scanners will pick them up again and give us the location! Or, we find the glitch in the system, or we override the jammer if there is one and we find them. Okay. Time and patience. I've got the parameters. For now we must be patient. Tomorrow will be a fine day for the hunt. I know what to do. Good night, Mr. President."

Collings left Billy sitting at his desk, thinking over the problem and fooling with the computer terminal. Billy accessed file after file. The red light on his console began to flicker. A window on the screen reported: "Intruder Approaching." Billy made some keystrokes and brought up the CCTV system in the elevator and saw that it was Gertz. Charles was in his bathrobe and slippers and had a strange look on his face.

The door opened and Charles literally charged toward Billy. He was out of breath as he sat down in a chair close to Billy. "We have to talk. I can't sleep, Billy! You called me...'Another problem, Charles'... 'How can the scanner system be beaten, Charles?' Will this ever end, Billy? I have to tell you some things that I know you don't really want to hear."

"What is it, old boy? Speak up. Tell me what's on your mind."

For a moment Charles was silent. He was trying to collect his thoughts "Billy, I'm tired. I've never asked you for a vacation, but I want one, I need one, and I need it, now!"

"Whew. Slow down. You've got it. Could have had it anytime. You never asked. From the report this afternoon, everything is going ahead of schedule. So, calm down. Take a break. Now, what's the real problem?"

"That is the real problem. I am always under pressure. 'Charles, make it work.'—'Don't worry; Charles has the answer.'—'Charles, I need something that will do this or that.'—'Charles, see if you can fix it.' Damn! Damn! Damn! I have more prototype stuff out in the field than can be considered reasonable. Some of this equipment has had only a few tests before you demand that it be put into production. Well, once it's out there, Billy, you forget it. But I live with these new ideas and wait day and night for them to fail. That's too much pressure, Billy; too much. I mean, the scanner system is a good example. You wanted it to be foolproof. Well, my people retrofitted the GPS and we tried our best, but it isn't foolproof.

"Harry Houdini said: 'There's not a lock made by man, that man cannot open.' Nothing is foolproof, Billy. And now the system has failed to do what it was supposed to do. Can it be corrected? Of, course. I've already got notes on things that should have been done. But I'm tired, Billy. My plate is full and you continue to pile on more. I need a rest, just a couple of days, please!"

Billy got up from his seat and approached him. "Charles, a rest is the order. You've got it, and now it's time for you to go to bed. I want you to sleep real good tonight. And tomorrow, my friend, you and I are gonna go alligator huntin' in the bayous. It'll be just like it used to be, and we'll talk about anything but business. Okay?"

Charles got up and hugged Billy. He had tears in his eyes and a quiet smile on his face as he said goodnight. He walked slowly to the elevator and once again Billy was alone.

Billy sat in the quiet of the room. He began to experience a little depression of his own. It had been an odd day. First Collings and Fenwick let Julio and Sally get away and now this little episode with Charles. Billy was tired, too. What Charles had said tonight alerted him that he had probably pushed them all too much. Collings and Gertz and Fenwick had been with him since the beginning, and they had helped him to accomplish everything he had set out to do. It was time to ease off a little and give them all some breathing room before they snapped and ceased being useful altogether. Maybe these meetings with the Inner Circle should be a little further apart, not so frequent.

Meetings. It was always meetings. Billy took a long pull on his scotch and eased back in his chair. Almost immediately, he fell sound asleep.

# 29

## THE FIGHT

At that very moment, Sally Hawthorne and Julio Mondaldo were having a meeting of their own inside a lead-lined, twelve-passenger van. Not all of the lead products had been confiscated by the government. Julio's people had found several rolls of lightweight lead foil and gallons and gallons of old-style lead-based paint in an abandoned industrial supply warehouse in DC. Dr. Gertz was correct in assuming that the satellite scanner system could be beaten. Julio Mondaldo was fast becoming a formidable adversary.

Even before he had rescued Sally, Julio was intent on beating the "eye." He personally did not like the intense monitoring by the new government. The lead foil and paint idea was a good one, and it worked.

They'd covered the inside of the van with several coats of the thick lead paint, making the van invisible to the tracking satellite. Julio fashioned the lead foil into a lead shield covering the neck and shoulders of each of the others, as he'd done for Sally and himself. After wrapped this shield around each of them he covered the foil with high turtleneck sweater dickeys. Ingeniously, they were all able to go in and out of the van undetected by vigilantly observant "eye-in-the-sky." With the lead coverings in place, they were as anonymous as the United States Constitution had promised they should be.

The little rebel had been traveling steadily on the road since leaving their meeting in Washington. Most of the others were sleeping. Only the driver, Julio, and Sally were awake.

Julio crouched down and whispered to Sally. "Sally, your speech last night made me curious. before we left Washington last evening, I linked up with the National Computer. The activity that I saw was... well it didn't make sense. I brought up the general population stats for Baltimore and went back to July 15, two years ago. For a minute, I thought the results were skewed just because of the normal birth and death action at the beginning of the plague. But then I watched in utter amazement as name after name just disappeared. It was too one-sided. Too many deaths and no births. I flipped to New York. Same pattern. I looked at a few more cities. An identical pattern in every city I searched. Sally, you told us last that you had proof that the plague was false and that Billy used it to gain control of the media, the military, the government, and the people. I admit I thought some of it was probably true, but I thought you might be exaggerating a little. Now I know you're right. It has been systematic killing—the cold, premeditated murder of millions of people. We have to find a way to stop Billy and—probably just as important—find out why he is doing this."

Sally sat up a bit straighter. "I didn't want to scare you or the others with too much information too quickly. I know why he's doing it, Julio. He told me everything. He's proud of his deeds. It's the same murderous insanity that Hitler employed, only Billy is using more modern methods. He is methodically eliminating the undesirables of humanity. It's a new kind of genocide. Unfortunately, we're a little late to stop him. This part of his plan is almost over and, as Billy himself said to me, he can't, or won't, bring back the dead. I don't know what his next move is, but I know he's far from finished with the people of the world. This God thing is..."

More fell into place for Julio. "Sally, give me all the details you have on the way you think God spoke to us. I think I know how Billy did it, but tell me what you know."

She was angry. "Well, you set it all up, Julio Mondaldo!"

Julio sat back against the van and looked away.

Sally immediately regretted what she'd said. "I'm sorry. You didn't know what you were doing. All those radio transmitter modifications, all tuned to one 'emergency' frequency, all controlled from the great National Communications Center in New York. Julio, remember the fake plague and the inoculations? Well, as you know, all the people, you and I included, were implanted with a locator ID chip deep in our shoulder muscle. What you don't know is that two tiny receivers are set in the mastoid bones behind each ear. They are perfectly manufactured and are tuned to the same frequency as the emergency radio band. God, or Billy, speaks, and we all hear it at the same time."

"Oh, Jesus. I did do this terrible thing..."

"No, no. You didn't know. No one knew. You're innocent. But now that you're aware, you must help me find a way to undo the wrong that he's done. We have to find out what else this maniac has planned for us and find some way to inform the people of this invasion of their bodies and minds and the total injustice that has been done to them. I have a feeling that our window of opportunity is very short, and it's slowly closing as we speak!"

They sat silently as the van continued on.

The purpose of this van ride wasn't just to escape from Washington or the apparent arrest they all expected. This was a military-style maneuver. Julio planned to make a wide circle around Washington and then meet up with the rest of the resistance group. The others were traveling in a second protected van. They'd agreed to rendezvous at a rest stop at noon, about seventy-five miles west of the capital.

Julio and his rebel units had made plans to go back into the city and strike the first blow for the new resistance. Their target: The National Computer Building.

Finally, the dawn came. At 7:30 a.m., Julio's unit left the rest stop. The van blended into the busy morning traffic and moved along the beltway toward the National Computer Building. Julio knew that the early morning rush hour would give them the best cover for their operation.

Sally took one of the vans and continued west to an agreed meeting spot. There, she waited for Julio and his attack group to return after the raid in Washington.

And so, the fight for freedom began.

Julio and three of the others parked in a public lot near the building. The driver and another man stayed with the van. Julio and another quickly walked into the alley behind the National Computer building and located the water main for the National Computer Building.

One of Julio's men, Sam Gorsky, was a military demolition expert with knowledge of how to use a sensitive new form of munitions known as TN-13. This unique explosive was selected because it was easy to transport and use and could only be detonated by utilizing a special, water-energized catalyst. Because the central computer, as well as the support mainframes, were all water cooled, the scheme was to tap into the water main and attach a cylinder of the thick TN-13 to feed into the pipe. Then, by adding the water-activated catalyst and adjusting the amount that would enter the line, the entire water system would become one gigantic bomb. The high viscosity TN-13 would travel with the catalyst, and when the catalyst reached mass, it would detonate the mixture and a chain reaction would occur throughout the water system. Boom! No computers. No building!

Sam Gorsky was good at his work. It took him a short time to complete the job. At 8:50, twelve minutes after they began, they were finished. As arranged, the driver rolled down the alley. Julio and Sam got in the van and headed back to the freeway.

The traffic going west was light during the morning rush and the ordinary looking van innocently moved along with the rest of the cars and trucks. Julio turned on the radio hoping to pick up a newsbreak that might report their daring deed. Sam lay in the back of the van and looked through a little hole in the rear door as Julio and the driver nervously peered into the side-view mirrors. They had been traveling about twenty minutes when it happened. Way off in the East, a big ball of black smoke appeared. They all cheered and hugged one another. It had worked!

Billy was just drinking his first cup of coffee when he felt a violent tremor and heard the explosion. Seconds later, the private line in the Oval Office rang.

It was Rob Collings. "Billy, your girlfriend just blew up the National Computer Building!"

"Just about to have someone check on that noise. That was it, eh?"

"Yeah. I'm in my car and we're just pulling up...Oh, shit Billy, the whole goddamned building is leveled."

Billy was locked and loaded, speaking in that low, controlled anger-fuelled staccato. "Right. Now listen up, Rob. I want that area cordoned off. Make a quick assessment. Instruct your people to get the bodies out of there. Ship them to the REGENZ center. Call Gertz. Tell him to get on with saving the ones worth saving. Call in the Army engineers to clean up the rubble, right away! Have them set up tall construction fences around the whole area. I want a Seabee operation on this one. Get it started. And then get over here."

Thus far, Billy had no opposition or resistance to anything that he'd ever presented to the public. This act of violence made him nervous. He was sure that Collings was right. Sally and Julio did the bombing. If they got away with this single incident, it would give them confidence to go on and his problems would certainly grow. The brazenness of their act could not be tolerated. Billy decided then and there that Collings should make the killing of Sally and Julio and the destruction of their resistance group his number one priority. They had to be stopped.

But for this, Billy now had total control over the population of the Western Hemisphere, and a very strong command over all of the nations of the world. He had done it without using force. The people had happily followed *The New Laws* and Billy's idea of worshipping one God. Billy was certain that the everyone wanted what he wanted. With absolutely no conflict, the people obeyed his orders and worked harder every day. As a result, the world was truly becoming more and more beautiful.

Billy knew that Sally and Julio could mess things up. So, after a little God-like assessment, he determined that it would be a good time to bring further inspiration, and a maybe a little fear, to the people of the world, and thereby establish in their minds, once and for all, that Billy was greater than a mere, mortal man. Nothing and no one could be allowed to spoil his great success. Now, he would begin to tighten the screws. This final part of his plan would make him a true deity and convince all of humanity that he was God's chosen ruler.

Billy gave the word to Gertz and Osher to accelerate the REGENZ program. All across the world, REGENZ factories were built. Again, the public was unaware. Even the RS Supervisors and RW's, the Workers, didn't know the details or purpose of what they were building. They had been lied to again. They'd been told that these factories were huge hydroponics centers, to be used for growing natural food for the people. Everyone seemed to buy the lie. Work, as usual, continued in earnest.

Billy wanted the final move, his Plan C, put into action immediately.

He again met with his Inner Circle. No one, not even Gertz or Collings, got all the information, for Billy liked control. It was his card game, and the boss always held kickers.

They all filed in and were seated

"Gentlemen, I apologize for another meeting, and Charles, we will do that 'gator hunting that I promised you."

Billy became very serious. "This will be a short, but extremely important. I propose that God should speak to everyone again and without advance warning or ceremony. I want this to be in the 'ancient miracle class,' gentlemen."

Their attention was directed to the video screen.

"On Tuesday next, at exactly 3:30 p.m., Eastern Standard Time, God will speak to the world. God will tell the people the wonderful details of their new immortality. The shock, the bewilderment, the number of driving accidents, industrial mishaps, etc., that are sure to occur will only heighten the dramatic impact of the event itself. Everyone will remember where they were and what they were doing that glorious day when God spoke to them again. Then, later that day, I will broadcast the 'good news' I have personally received from God, and tell the world the criteria for their immortality."

The Inner Circle knew that this was the true final move and they all went to work on the immediate implementation of Billy's Plan C.

And on Tuesday, just as Billy and God had planned, at 3:30 p.m., EST, God again spoke to the people of the Earth:

> *Hear me, O' sons of man. I have observed your attempts to atone for your sins and I am pleased. I will now reveal to your leader—my chosen one—how you will have immortal life for your soul and body. Your leader will explain my new covenant to you. Follow his teachings and obey him. Hearken unto my commandments, O' sons of man. Obey me, and I will give you each life everlasting.*

It was the frosting on the cake. Billy was correct. The effect, worldwide, was stunning. It was perceived as a true revelation. God was speaking directly to man, just as man had always wanted. It was a miracle. No one had to interpret God's word. Everyone clearly understood His message.

Later that day, Billy broadcasted from the Great Hall of the Federal Communications building in New York City. This special place had become a shrine after the first words from God, and was visited every day by thousands of the faithful. As the worldwide broadcast began, the world leaders filed into the Great Hall to hear this message from Billy, and God.

Billy's white hair and tanned skin gave him a heavenly physical appearance. Again, the steps rose from the floor with swell of the music, and dramatic lighting. Billy descended dramatically, regally down the stairs to the podium. He was more than believable as a God-inspired prophet. The people expected the grand and magnificent entrance from this man who had been anointed by God. Billy gave it to them in the style of a true showman.

The lights dimmed and the intense spotlights followed Billy to the dais. A hush came over the audience as he began to speak.

"People of the world, I greet you all with love and affection this day. I have the blessings and the word of God Almighty for you. Our world, our heaven here on earth, is becoming cleaner and safer, more bountiful and beautiful each and every day. You have accomplished this restoration with your hard work and peaceful living. You have repaired hundreds of years of pollution and ugliness in these short years. You have suffered through the worst calamity ever to beset Mankind. And, you have beaten that horrible plague back to Hell, from whence it came."

The spectators cheered enthusiastically.

Billy waited some time for the applause to wane, and then he continued. "God has allowed you to survive so that you can continue to do more of His good work, and so that you can reap the great rewards He has planned for you. Many of the men and women who have lived in history before us have been inspired by our God to do great works. Throughout antiquity, God guided them and directed them toward each of their great contributions and accomplishments. Our great God continues to offer His helping hand to us, even unto this day. God wants us to follow His direction and to hear His words. He wants us to obey Him, for he is the one God, the God of all the universe, and the God of this Earth.

"People, I have been given the good news, and I am here to share it with you. Today, God has spoken to each of us and has told of a new covenant, a new promise for us."

The people listened to Billy's words with great dread. Was God to reward them—or punish them again?

"Do not fear, my people. God approves of your atonement and your attempts to live in peace with each other and to make his world clean and decent once again. God has spoken to me and has told me what He has planned for you."

Billy was baiting them. They waited in silence for his decree.

"Hear me now, people of the world. This is God's covenant with man and a true testimony to His greatness."

Billy paused again, for effect. "God has always promised us eternal life. Our blissful existence for eternity will not be in Heaven, as was promised before. No. Through God's blessing, we are all to be made immortal here on Earth. We will live forever on this beautiful planet in love and plenty. His kingdom has come. Imagine heaven here on Earth, people! God has spoken to me and given me His sacred secrets for immortal life. As he spoke to Moses and Aaron and Jesus of old, He has taught me the design and shown me the methods for the construction of His immortal life temples. These holy places will be built immediately throughout the world for the benefit all of you. There, in these wondrous tabernacles, He will take our tired bodies away, and we will be reborn into the very prime of life. We will live for all time to herald the glory of God. We are all to become His new guardians and keepers of His Earth."

The audience in the massive hall sat stunned and silent as their messiah spoke God's words to them.

Billy continued with the zeal of a true evangelist. "Oh, hear the good news people of the world: God has decided not to destroy us, but to give us life everlasting! This great reward is now easily reached. True immortality. Life everlasting and it all starts today!"

A quiet came into his voice, yet his magnetism was palpable. "But, sadly, there is the possibility that not all of you will receive the honor of His gift. Not all of you will attain this prize of immortality, of everlasting life. You see, in order to receive His gift, you must follow *God's Commandments* and *The New Laws* exactly as they have been written. Those who do not follow these laws for living, as you well know, will die without Heaven. Yet, those who are worthy of His love will inherit God's wonderful beneficence. They shall live on forever, with new youth and perpetual health and continued prosperity in this new Heaven, right here on Earth."

The people were awestruck. They wanted to respond, but the news they had just heard, even though it was joyful, was frightening as well.

Billy concluded. "Go now in the peace and the contentment that the Lord of the Universe and the God this world, has given unto you, what no people in history have ever received—true immortal life; Heaven here on Earth. We must pray to God, now."

The audience collectively closed their eyes and bowed there heads.

Billy, eyes closed, gazed upward. "Great God, we thank you for your blessings and countenance upon us. We all will abide by your laws and will continue to lead good and productive lives. We thank you, O' Lord, and are forever faithful unto you. Amen."

The audience in the Great Hall responded together with Amen.

Billy dismissed them. "Go now, people of the world. Go back to your friends and families, to your good labors with this great news in your hearts!"

Billy had presented them all with a goal that everyone would want to achieve. There was no theological mystery to embrace. The plan was simple: immortality or extinction. Be good and live forever, or disobey *The New Laws* and die a painful death. It all made perfect sense. Finally, mankind had a set of comprehensible and fair rules for living, with everyone on the same plane of understanding.

The joy of this message from God brought hallelujahs and hosannas from every corner of the globe. Billy had assaulted their brains again and the world had bought the act. God had spoken to them once more. Now there would be perfect world order.

This, then, was Billy's absolution and justification for the murder of billions of people; yet he had no remorse. Maybe he was God.

The rebels heard the message, too. They were all genuinely frightened. It was all that Julio and Sally could do to keep their group from going mad. Finally, the two infidels convinced the others that it was not God, but Billy speaking to them via radio transmission. It was obvious to them all that Billy must be stopped. With some general order restored, Julio laid out the next move for this tiny body of resistance. Julio had earned their respect with their first successful attack on the government.

The victory at the main computer center in Washington may have left the building destroyed, but, just as Sally expected, the media didn't report it.

Billy, on the other hand, was concerned that the assault would inspire more acts of violence against the government. He'd ordered Barnston to suppress any coverage of the disaster. The incident was to be treated as a "never-happened."

Immediately after the fire department had put out the blaze, the Army crews with front loaders and dump trucks hauled away the rubble and the bulldozers quickly smoothed out the ground. Within a few days, a multitude of laborers, working day and night, had created a beautiful mini-park replete with fountains and trees. The end result was that it appeared to the people as though the computer building had never existed. Further, it was announced that this new park would soon have an enormous statue of Billy and that the grounds would be dedicated in his name. Hereafter it would be called "Johnstone Commemorative Park." Billy felt the park would foil any real sense of accomplishment by the saboteurs and maybe deter them for a while.

The park was a neat and efficient cover-up, but Sally knew the demolition of the building by them been more than casually noticed by the government. She knew Billy clearly understood that somebody out there didn't like him.

The rebels were not to be deterred. They had bigger plans. Julio reasoned that their next strike should be closer to home. Billy's home —The White House. The same tactical team who had destroyed the computer building began making plans for the destruction of the White House.

Julio tapped into the White House computer system to get the daily activity schedule of the President. They wanted Billy to be inside the White House when the building blew. They wanted him dead.

This time Julio would not go with them. Sam Gorsky would head the team.

A late-night break-in at the DC Water and Power Company netted the necessary water main diagrams. After close examination of the blueprints, the best point at which to introduce the TN-13 was determined.

The water system in the White House used contamination detectors. Julio and Gorsky knew they would only get one chance to inject the catalyst and TN-13. Hopefully, it would force enough "juice" into the system to do the job before the systems automatically shut down.

The time for departure had come for Sam and his team. Sally and Julio wished them good luck and watched them drive away.

Outside of Washington, at a RV campground, Julio and Sally waited Sam's safe return. They were all nervous about this particular outing.

Gorsky's team was instructed to maintain radio silence. Sam didn't like it. It forced them to work alone. Without the aid of communication, each man had to depend on the other completing the work exactly as planned and on time. He didn't like it, but he understood.

An older building, just one block away from the White House was the rendezvous spot. The pilfered blueprints showed that the same water main that would feed the high explosives to the White House was exposed in the basement of this building. This afforded them a safe and easy place to introduce the TN-13 mixture.

The team arrived early in the morning. They put the TN-13 and the catalyst in high-pressure tanks and set the automatic timers on the catalyst so it would be dispensed into the water main at precisely noon. The men worked quickly and efficiently and finished their job within the allotted twenty-five minutes. They covered the tanks of TN-13 with cardboard boxes and junk found in the basement, hiding the tanks and dispensers from the casual eye. Their work done, they quickly left the basement and, one by one, departed the building unnoticed.

Sam was the last out and followed the path to the waiting van. With all of the team accounted for, they moved out just before 8:35 a.m.

The van once again easily mixed with the morning traffic moving west.

After an hour, they pulled into a gas station just two blocks away from the RV camp. Sam called the payphone at the RV grounds.

Julio answered. "Hello...Yes, on my way."

Julio went back to his van, got inside, and closed the door.

The rest of the group was anxious to hear the news of the results. "They're safe. Sam and the others have returned. We'll join them in a few minutes and then travel to the next meeting spot."

No one said a word to Julio. No one speculated as to whether Sam would tell them of success or failure.

The two vans met and separated at a safe distance and began to travel west.

Each had their car radios on just in case there might be a newsbreak. The music played on. No mention of any attack on the White House. They'd anticipated that this incident too, would not be reported.

Because this was an attack on the White House and the President, Julio wanted his group to be as far away from Washington as possible. He knew an assault of this magnitude would probably bring out all branches of the service. The Army, the CIA, the FBI, NSA and the R-SS would come onto the playing field for an all-out manhunt. They traveled as fast as the speed limit would allow.

As a matter for future planning, even though it might be dangerous, Julio really wanted to know the details of how well they had done on the day's raid. If there was no formal news announcement, he had made special plans to find out the extent of the damage via one of the resistance members who remained in Washington. This brave girl would survey the damage, learn all she could, and then be at a phone booth to report when Julio called at 9 p.m.

At 11:30 a.m. they stopped at another rest area. Each van parked at opposite ends of the parking lot. Sam and Julio got out of their vans and went to the restroom. So as not to cause attention they didn't talk or take notice of each other in the restroom. When they finished, both went outside to meet behind the trees and talk privately about the raid. Julio shook hands with Sam and then returned to his own van. He instructed the driver to head out and once again the two vans traveled westward.

After a while, Julio reported to his group. "Everything completed as planned. The explosion should at occur around noon. The traffic in and around the White House will be at a peak then, which will add further confusion. We'll stay tuned to the radio. Maybe we'll hear it on the radio this time."

They traveled down the road for some time with the music playing on the radio. Everyone was quiet. The hourly news, such as it was, reported nothing. Everyone wondered if the plan had failed, or—more likely—the explosion was just not being reported.

Hour after hour they traveled. Late that evening, they stopped to eat and gas up again. After a brief dinner, at 8:55 p.m., Julio gave the signal and both groups got up and went to their vans.

Julio went to a public telephone. He called the phone booth in Washington. The group could see him talking. A smile came upon his face, then a frown. He returned to Sam's van and spoke to him through the window. Julio came back to his own vehicle and told the driver to move out. Julio sat silent for a moment.

"Good news and bad. It was moderately successful. The explosion worked. But it only blew up part of the street and lawn and destroyed the east wing of the White House, not the area we wanted. Billy lives, but he knows he's in trouble."

After a fuel stop, they rolled on down the road and continued their westward movement.

The trip gave all of them time to think. Sally decided that because of the failed assassination, she, herself, should become the instrument of Billy's destruction. She convinced Julio to stop and let her call Billy's private number. She hoped that Billy would answer. At the public phone, Julio dialed several series of numbers, and then handed the phone to Sally. After a few rings, the answer came.

"Hello?"

"Billy. This is Sally Hawthorne. How are you, mein President?"

"Whew. You still gotta lot of balls for a woman—for a man, even!

Sally, Sally, Sally, what a girl. Now listen up, little muffin. Collings has a warrant out for you and Julio. Actually, it's a death warrant. You're to be shot on sight. He knows you two, and your group, were the one's responsible for the White House mess today, as well as the computer building bombing. You were the ones, of course?"

Sally gleefully replied. "Of course, but that was very stupid and a waste of time. In the old days, we would have gotten great coverage and increased support for our cause. Now, well I guess we forgot you controlled the media. Kinda dumb, huh? Hey, do you think the firemen and those cleanup guys you told to shut up might want to join a spiffy new club we're starting?"

Sally stopped the bantering and got serious. "Listen, Billy, I want to talk with you in person, but you've just told me how impossible that would be. I'd still like to try. Is there such a thing as an amnesty in the Fourth Reich, my darling?"

"Only if I give it. No one else can. Would you trust me if I did call a truce, Sally?"

"I wouldn't have a choice. Yes, Billy. You've always been a man of your word. I trust you. You name the time and place. I'll come alone, without Julio. You might consider leaving your attack-dog Collings and his gang at home. I just want to talk and be with you, Billy."

"Can I reach you by phone Sally?"

"Silly you. I'm an outlaw, remember. But I'll call you tomorrow about 2 p.m. Will that give you time to make the arrangements?"

Although Sally had been using a public phone that Julio had routed through a local phone in DC, they both hoped that Billy did not have time to trace the call. Quickly, the rebels piled back into the vans and continued to move on.

Sally had wanted to be in on the action at the computer building, but Julio said one of them must always remain behind to carry on. Now it was her turn. She decided to meet with Billy, the man she once loved and whom she was now determined to destroy.

Sally sat with Julio. "I'm not sure how I can do it, Julio. They'll surely at least use metal detectors or X-ray to make sure I have no means to harm the President. No guns or bombs. Maybe poison. Yeah, that might be an idea. Plenty of places to hide poison. Could even pass a strip search or cavity inspection if I plan it well. Poison, that's it!"

She was silent for a long while.

Then, "How stupid. I can't kill him. He'll just become a worldwide martyr, and Collings would probably ascend the throne and matters would really get worse with that murderous son-of-a-bitch in charge. No, I'll have to figure out something before I get back to Washington tomorrow. Come on, Julio, think! What should I do? Use that good brain of yours! Help me, will you?"

Julio was a patient man, so he let Sally run her course. He did not interfere with her thinking. He waited until she arrived at an impasse.

"Look, Sally, I don't think you should see Billy. I don't think you can trust him, and I don't think Collings would ever let you get near him. We, you and I, do represent a real threat to him. We know too much. He needs to silence us and no matter how he may have felt about you at one time, he will kill you on sight. Trust me. He'll say anything to get you there, but it will be a trap. You..."

"Okay. Okay. Okay! You win! I won't see Billy! Say something helpful. Don't just tell me what you think I can't do!"

Julio was silent.

Sally's anger quickly subsided. "I'm sorry. You're right. It's too dangerous. But, help me, baby. I've just got to do something to stop that bastard!"

Sally thought for a moment and rearranged her previous plan. "Wait, wait. I've got it! I'll call Billy tomorrow afternoon, just to throw him off guard, to mess with him a little. I'll string him along and pretend to be scared. I'll ask him to consider taking me back, that I'm through with you and the resistance, that I've seen the light and I could still be valuable to him again, that I can tell him all about your plans for the resistance, etcetera. Yeah, that'll mix him up. You're right. I shouldn't go back into that mess. But seriously, Julio, can't we figure a way to stop him?"

"Stop him? I don't know if I can figure that one out. Slow him down, drive him crazy, and help to inform the people about this madness, this I can do for you! Yes, I will help you torment him tomorrow."

Sally was getting excited. "Okay, okay. But we need a plan..."

"Please, Sally, listen to me. I do have a real plan in mind, you know. We need to get to one of the computer back-up stations. I can rig an access to the other National Computers, and then we can alert the people via the communication satellites. With some careful planning, we can broadcast all that we know and blow the lid off this whole thing and maybe even cause a people's uprising before it's too late."

"Brilliant! We'll use his own communication systems to tell the people. That's pure genius, Julio. Do you know where the backup stations are located? How far away are they? Is there any way to find out?"

"Way ahead of you, my dear. I know the building layouts and locations of each of them. I planned and directed every one of those installations. We want the one that's most remote and has no personnel. The perfect one for us is about twelve hundred miles west of here. That's where we've been heading since we left DC."

The next day, they stopped on the road again and Sally made her call to Billy at 2 p.m. Eastern Standard Time from a public phone. There was no answer. She hung up the phone and tried the private number at Billy's living quarters in the White House. No answer. If he were at Camp David or the Pentagon his private line would transfer to his cell phone. She tried the number at the WFJ island complex. Sally wondered if the number she had for Billy's private line at the complex was still working. Quickly she punched the number into the phone. It rang and then someone answered.

"Collings here."

"Rob? Sally Hawthorne. Hello, hello, my dear? Is Billy in?"

"Sally!!! He's not here, but thanks for calling. I have a number prefix and your location. You dumb bitch, you're dog meat!"

"My, aren't we getting vicious. Job pressure there must just be terrible, Rob. Careful he doesn't oxidize you along with the rest of the garbage. Well, tell Billy that I'm in DC and that I called his office just like we agreed yesterday, but he wasn't home. He'll never be able to say I didn't try to help. Ta-ta, shithead!"

Sally slammed the phone down and began to laugh hysterically. She turned to Julio.

"Find me, he says. Oh, sure you will, Robby. The LED on his phone says I'm in Washington, but when he calls that number, he'll get a big surprise. Oh, Julio, you're the greatest."

# 30

## *REBELLION KILLED*

"It's Disney World, goddammit. That smart-ass, little bitch!"

Billy laughed out loud. He had been drinking heavily all morning. Somehow this bit of impertinence from Sally amused him, but the drinking caused him to viciously turn on Collings.

"Rob, she's very smart, you know. You didn't think she would call from a legit phone, did you? I'll bet she's not in Orlando or anyplace close to it, either. I think they're both going to give you a merry chase, ol' boy. You ought to be able to win. After all, you've got the friggin' CIA, FBI, NSA, the U.S. Army and Navy, the Air Force, your personal R-SS boys, and the entire goddamned ass-kickin' Marines to help you do it! But even with all that help, Robby, you can't get two little people out of my hair. No, no. Something's wrong with the picture, Robby. You're screwing up bad lately. How could two people and their eight friends slip through your fingers and disappear? How could they bomb my computer building and the White House? Sorry, buddy boy. You're losing your touch."

"I-I-I don't know Billy. I just don't know."

Charles Gertz interrupted Collings.

"Well, I think we should just go out there and get them and bring them in and let me make them into REGENZ. They're both very bright and nice and have many fine qualities that would be helpful to us."

Billy snapped at Gertz. "Oohhh, good idea, Dr. Charlie. But, don't you understand? Little Collings-boy can't find them. Get it? He can't find them, Charles."

Collings was miffed and Charles was instantly hurt. Billy smiled at them and condescendingly whispered. "I appreciate your suggestions, Charles, but I'm sure that our man, Collings, will somehow figure out how to deal with them. Won't you, killer?"

The ability to switch moods and issues was Billy's specialty. "Now the big question for your genius brain, Charles, is can you produce our REGENZ any faster?"

Wanting to please him, Gertz replied, "Yes, Billy, yes I can. You can depend on me. This 'little god' can do anything, you know. Previously, it would have taken us a little over eleven months to complete the average maturity. Now it's done in only 120 days! Quite an improvement, eh, Billy?"

"Fantastic. What about the prototype process?"

"We're way past prototype, Billy. It's up and working. All production designs and systems are valid. Want to take a peek, guys?"

Collings, still pouting, declined. "Billy, Charles, you go on. I've got to get to the bottom of this Sally-Julio thing. I won't rest well until they're both dead."

Charles shook his head. "Sally and Julio to be killed. Such a waste. What a pity," he lamented.

"Yes, it is quite sad," Billy said matter-of-factly. "Well, Rob, you'd better do what's necessary. I don't like to pull rank, but I will hold you personally accountable until they're dead."

Indifferently, Billy turned away from Collings toward Charles and drunkenly acted like a hunchback.

"Carry on, Dr. Frankenstein. Igor will be right behind you!"

After winding through a maze of tunnels and doors, Charles and Billy entered a large open-spanned area. Inside, were rows and rows of clear glass tank-like enclosures set three high inside this huge room. Each of the tanks had a human body floating inside. A steady flow of bubbling fluid was circulating in and out of these tanks. Above each tank a soft, glowing, pinkish-violet light bathed the semi-developed bodies.

"How many of the REGENZ-S?" Billy asked.

"Three hundred here in pink suspension, ready to be transferred to the blue-green radiation grow room, where we have three hundred more ready to mature and over 600 embryos ready to go into suspension. I can match this number of embryos every twenty-one days, Billy."

"So, multiples of 2,000-3,000 for the REGENZ-S. The same for the REGENZ-Ws is certainly not out of the question, is it? Just a matter of square footage."

"Right. We can really handle a few thousand at each venue. Facilities in every major city of North and South America are being completed in existing warehouses. Avery and General Fenwick are locating the buildings and launching the construction as we speak. Professor Osher is at our pilot project at the big New Jersey plant right now. The final details for the installation of all the REGENZ manufacturing equipment will be done this week. New Jersey will be our first 'from the ground up' operating facility."

"Any problems with procedure? Time in, time out, etcetera?"

"Not at all. It really is a marvel, Billy. When the person comes in on the first day, we take a tissue sample. They are given a sedative and put into what I call 'the waiting room,' where they remain on IV, in a state of hibernation for three months while the new person, the clone, is growing. This new person still has all of his memories up to the time of sedation and no outside stimulus will occur to expand the memory during the incubation and growth period. If the clone checks out okay, the old body is oxidized. Of course, the memory of death is never known. The new body thinks it's still the old body and has just taken a nap. The new REGENZ is now, of course, completely immortal. This 'new you' is awakened and goes back into the world happier, healthier and younger, to live forever."

In another part of the complex, Collings was busy at a computer terminal, still upset and fuming about the things Billy had said to him. Collings had taken a lot of abuse over the years, but Billy's megalomania was getting worse. When Billy drank he was totally out of bounds. It seemed to Rob that Billy was developing a Jesus complex, thinking God really had chosen him to save the people. Collings had just about decided to have a showdown with Billy when the computer screen lit up. Finally. He'd found the rebels.

Julio's ID came up on the scanners for a brief period and showed that he was located just east of Denver. It took very little deduction on Rob's part to see that Julio was headed toward a drone computer building located in the northern Rocky Mountains. Sally and the others were presumably with him, and Collings was sure he had them now. Undoubtedly this was the only resistance group. If he didn't stamp them out now, they would surely grow larger and stronger.

Collings paged Billy. Billy's call came back very quickly.

"Billy, I've found them. They're in Colorado, heading for the drone computer center in Wyoming. Sally and Julio have been on the inside of the government operations and that makes them very dangerous. Julio knows what he's doing. If I cut off the head—eliminate those two—the rest of the outlaws will just be rabble. No brains. No plan. No leaders. They will simply and quickly die out or be killed in the prescribed fashion."

Billy was quiet for a moment.

"Kill them, Rob. Kill them all!"

Collings wishes had now been sanctioned by Billy. He decided to allow Sally and Julio to reach their destination. After their arrival, he would send in operatives to monitor the group. He would wait and see if other rebels joined them, then take them all out with one decisive blow. Collings felt that it was very close to being all over.

When this suppression was finished, he could get on with his life and maybe some real enjoyment. He desperately wanted to get out of the killing business. Collings was a tired old warrior, and Billy had promised him a new post once the rebels were taken care of permanently. Collings often wondered what Billy had in mind for him. He began to doubt whether Billy could really be trusted to tell him the truth or keep his word about anything. He was beginning to have serious misgivings about his old friend.

Julio believed that the unoccupied underground "drone" computer center, secretly hidden in the mountains, would allow him to access the National Computer and obtain all the information they needed. He'd found the computer building, all right. But, without knowing, it held nothing inside for them but death.

The computer center was in a very desolate, forested area in the foothills of the Northern Rockies. Collings believed that the rebel outlaws would consider it to be the perfect hideout, a bunker. Collings knew that Julio had designed and managed the installation of this Wyoming computer location. He supposed that Julio was after a link-up to the National Computer and reasoned that the rebel group would all be moving inside to escape the cold winter weather. It was the perfect hideout, warm and full of emergency food supplies. Collings was quite sure that this underground bunker would quickly develop into the temporary headquarters for the resistance, and it was the ideal trap in which to catch them all.

The bunker served primarily as a part of the National Computer redundancy system. Collings had instructed Felix Hanson to have it immediately taken off-line and isolated from the main network. He ordered the "drone center" lines connected to independent computers separated from the main system, and then instructed Hanson to create a phony program that would appear to be data from the National Computer. The erroneous data would go in and out, but it could be observed and manipulated when necessary. There would be nothing but misinformation contained in the fake files, all basically credible, but totally fictitious. The file names would be real, but the data would be false. Felix had four of his best computer designers create the new information system. The data-entry people immediately began to feed the "drone station" terminals the counterfeit computer link. Even before the rebels arrived, the computers were up and could respond to all requests made. Collings carefully and cleverly laid the bait in the snare. The game had begun.

The two rebel vans finally reached their destination. The very tired and hungry group of travelers piled out of their vehicles and headed toward the underground bunker. Julio knew that they could not enter through the main door. That would require entry codes and palm IDs and would certainly alert Washington. He took a few of the men and went about 75 yards away from the entrance to a spot well inside the heavily wooded area. There he located the air vent for the building. The men loosened the grating as Julio called to the others to follow him. It was a nice slide down the airshaft into the huge ventilation chamber. The fans were off and access through the plenum made for an easy entrance. Once inside the building, Julio went to the main security panel and jumped the connections, bypassing all of the alarm sensors and making the big doors operable. They quickly moved the guns, ammunition, explosives and supplies from the van into the bunker. They were safe.

Julio talked quietly with his team. The group now numbered eighteen. Five of them were unadjusted. Sally, Julio and eleven others had the implants.

One man, who had been riding in Sam's van, was a physician. Dr. Victor Jennings—the same Dr. Jennings Sally had met at the inoculation center in DC.

Dr. Jennings had discovered that the mass inoculation was a ruse quite late in the game. Because of his wife's epilepsy, she and the child she was carrying had been eliminated in the LOES units. Shortly after his wife's death, Dr. Jennings deduced that the inoculation centers were not as they seemed. After a little investigation, he found they were nothing more than death camps. After Jennings discovered the truth, and that he too had been implanted, he swore to find a way to stop Billy's purge. One day he feigned a nervous condition and left immediately without permission.

Now he was a wanted outlaw like the rest. Victor Jennings hated Billy even more than Julio and Sally, and he knew the full extent of the insanity they had all decided to rebel against. Over these last few days, while traveling, Victor and Sam had many discussions regarding the implants. Sam proposed that the implants be surgically removed even if there were no proper facilities for the surgery. Victor cautioned them that, under these poor conditions, it could be a very dangerous—even fatal—operation.

Julio put the implant issue to a vote. They agreed as a group that if they were to continue the resistance movement, the surgery to remove the ID implants must be attempted. Sally and Julio had to be first to be freed from the identification chips, for they were the most valuable to the movement and were the only ones, possibly in the entire world, who really knew the inside information concerning Billy's plans and how to stop him.

Julio volunteered to be first. He gathered his people and spoke to them sincerely. "Sally Hawthorne has the detailed plans of our resistance movement and is totally aware of our situation. She knows the decisions that have to be made and has the courage and skill to make them. Should anything happen to me, Sally will be in charge and she will be assisted by Dr. Jennings. Cooperate with them as you have with me. May God bless our efforts and help guide us to freedom. Victor, my friend, let's get on with it!"

This was to be a surgery of times past. No blood or glucose. Iodine and grain alcohol were to be the only antiseptic. No anesthesia. Within this crude, makeshift operating arena, Dr. Victor Jennings only had the few surgical tools that were found in an army medical field pack: two scalpels, a probe, a clamp, a scissors, suture thread and needles, three tubes of antibiotic cream, two bottles of iodine, eight disposable syringes of penicillin and six of morphine, several bottles of aspirin, some swabs, two bottles of grain alcohol, surgical pads, adhesive bandages and surgical tape. Not exactly the equipment necessary for a major surgery. Even with careful dispensing, it wasn't enough to treat eighteen people. Worse, without X-ray equipment, locating the implants would be very difficult.

Victor decided to use clinical hypnosis for this operation to mitigate the pain of surgery and possibly increase Julio's natural antibodies, hopefully precluding postoperative infection. It might even speed up the healing process. During this very radical operation, while part of Julio's mind remained deep in hypnotic sleep, Dr. Jennings would use Julio's subconscious mind to guide him to the exact location of the implants. It was all somewhat theoretical and less than perfect. But Victor Jennings was confident that it could work.

Julio was placed face down on an eight-foot banquet table. His arms and legs were gently tied to the legs of the table with strips of cloth. His head, near the end of the table, was cradled in towels and secured by a wide band of webbed canvas strap. A tent of the lead foil was constructed to cover the operating area. Dr. Jennings removed the turtleneck and the lead foil on Julio's neck and shoulders. Sally assisted

Dr. Jennings by scrubbing Julio's neck and shoulders with soap and hot water and then disinfecting the skin with alcohol and painting the surgical area with iodine.

Several desk lights had been rigged to give more illumination to the operating area. Only Sally and Victor were near the table. The rest of the group sat off in the darkness, waiting, watching, and praying. Dr. Jennings sat down in a chair next to Julio's right side and began to talk quietly to him.

The hypnosis commenced. "Julio, you will rest in a deep sleep during this procedure. You will be awake when I need to you be awake and asleep when I ask you to sleep, and at no time will you will feel pain. You will be my surgical assistant and will be able to talk with me throughout the operation. I will need your help in locating the implants. Your mind and body will become as one. I will begin to probe for these foreign objects and, as I do, you will be able to see the probe and guide me closer to the implants. During the operation, you will never feel pain. After we have completed our work, I will tell you that we have finished and your wound will immediately begin to heal without infection and much quicker than usual. Now, Julio, begin to breathe easy and allow yourself to drift off into a wonderful sleep. You are falling into a slightly deeper sleep, and you are resting easily. You are very comfortable and very relaxed and your sleep is becoming even deeper now. Again, you will feel no pain in your body at any time and no sound will disturb you. You will remain in this deep sleep until I need you. At that time, I will ask for your help. You will respond, talk to me, and you will assist me in finding the implants. When we are finished I will tell you. Now, sleep soundly until I need your help."

Victor awakened Julio and caused him to go back into deeper and deeper sleep. He was making sure that the hypnosis was working as planned. Satisfied, Dr. Jennings made an incision on Julio's right shoulder exactly across the tiny scar the IMPLANTOR had left. The Locator Chip would have to be removed first. Victor deftly separated the muscles in the shoulder. Sally assisted by holding the wound open using homemade retractors bent out of heavy wire.

Victor spoke. "Julio, listen to me now. I want you to remain deep asleep, breathing quite naturally and in this restful condition. You have no pain, you are comfortable and throughout this procedure you and I will be able to talk to each other. All other voices or sounds will not distract you. The sound of my voice will remain dominant. You will only hear me, Julio. I want you to use your inner eyes to see the shoulder area I am probing now and help me find the implant. Can you see the implant or must I go deeper? Answer me, Julio."

All of the spectators were quiet as Julio answered. "No. You are very close to it."

Victor moved his finger slowly through the incision. He stopped. There it was, a little green piece of ceramic about a quarter of an inch in size. It was slightly imbedded in a large ligament. Using the tweezers, Victor worked the locator chip loose and deftly removed it, wrapped it in lead foil and laid it in a pan on the table. One of the resistance group members picked up a hammer, wanting to smash the locator. Sally grabbed his arm and stopped him.

"No. Leave it wrapped in the lead foil. Julio will know how to destroy it."

The MMEA implants at the base of each ear were found to be below the surface of the skin lodged in the mastoid bone and, with some difficulty, they too were removed. The wounds were swabbed clean with the alcohol, stitched closed and painted with iodine.

Dr. Jennings was proving to be an even greater asset to the resistance than had been anticipated. With this one operation, he had pioneered the procedure for removing the implants from all people. Freedom of thought and independence for millions could again become a reality.

Victor had finished. Julio was clean. The implants had been removed.

Victor again talked softly to Julio. "It is done, my friend. Sleep now and use all the great forces God has put in your body to heal these wounds. Let no infection grow in your body. Sleep and heal yourself, Julio."

Jennings turned to the others. "I will not give him antibiotics or morphine at this time. I will save these meager supplies for those who may need them. Julio is quite healthy, and I think he will ward off the infection with no problems. For the postoperative pain, if necessary, we'll use aspirin. We've got plenty of bottles of the stuff. Don't worry. He's going to be all right."

Sally gave Jennings a hug.

"Victor. Just..remarkable.! We all thank you and will forever be grateful to you. If you don't mind, Doctor, I'm going to sit a while with your patient."

Victor nodded his approval and went off for a little well-deserved rest himself.

Sally brought a chair next the table. Julio slept soundly. She looked lovingly at his boy-like face. He looked so peaceful. Sally knew that Julio would be all right now. He was strong enough, and he was very macho. If it did hurt, he wouldn't let on. Julio wanted to show Sally and everyone else that he could survive it, and that they could, too. Macho or not, Julio was actually the stuff real heroes are made of. He was their leader.

Sally had fallen in love with Julio. Secretly, she hoped that Julio loved her, too. This thought, real or not, gave her hope and courage for the future. Now, Sally was sure that she, too, could endure this surgery. The operation had worked and Sally and the rest now had the utmost faith in Dr. Jennings. She longed to be rid of the implants—this curse that had been forced into her body. Sally held Julio's hand as he slept and suddenly she was sleeping, too.

Sally dreamed of Billy. In the dream, they made love and they were very happy. Suddenly, the scene shifted and Billy was on a high throne looking down at her. He was talking with a power in his voice that was so savage and frightening that she began to run from him. When she looked back, Billy was far behind her, still in the chair, but his voice continued to stay at the same high acoustic level as she ran away. The voice grew louder and it followed her no matter how far she ran. The voice was in her brain. She couldn't turn it off and it continued to speak louder and louder.

Sally awakened with a start. The perimeter alarm was blasting. Someone was at the outside entrance door. Sally picked up an UZI and checked to see that her flak jacket was securely in place. Several of the others who had also been sleeping were wide awake now.

They all went to the door and looked at the CCTV security monitor. It was dark outside and the snow was falling heavily. A man stood alone under the TV camera. Sally snapped on the bright quartz lights.

"Identify yourself!" Sally ordered.

"I-A-Way." The man responded

I-A-WA. [I-nsurgence for A-merica and W-orld A-lliance]. The code response was correct.

Sally barked. "How many are you? Are you armed?"

"There are ten of us. We will put our weapons on the ground so you can clearly see them."

From out of the darkness came the rest. Six men and four women. They all disarmed and stacked their guns in a pile near the door.

Again, Sally gave the orders. "Now stand shoulder to shoulder in a single file line with your hands on top of your heads. One bad move and you're all dead. Quickly. Do as you are told."

Sally called to the others inside to cover the door. She pushed a button and the massive blast door unbolted and slowly opened. The people came through. Two members of Sally's group went out and gathered the arms and brought them back in. The door closed again, sealing them all from the fierce, cold wind and snow.

Sally and the others held the machine guns on the new group.

"Okay, repeat who are you and what you want."

"We are here to join you in the fight for freedom."

Julio was awake. He approached the group and smiled at them. "Welcome, my friends. Excuse our slightly uncivil reception. Come and sit with us and have some food and hot coffee. We need to talk with you and find out what skills you have to help the cause."

More tables and chairs were set up to accommodate the new people. The others joined them. This was to be the first combined meeting of the new resistance movement—now a total count of twenty-eight freedom fighters.

As the new group ate and talked with Julio, they listened with interest to the details regarding Dr. Jennings operation on Julio.

Julio rose and spoke to the newcomers. "Do you all know of the implants?"

They all nodded hesitantly.

"If you were inoculated you have the implants. But I have some good news for you. They can be removed. Dr. Jennings has developed the procedure here tonight. I was his first patient, and I can tell you that the operation is virtually painless, quick, and above all, it works."

Soon it was Sally's turn to have the implants removed. The procedure was the same as for Julio. At the end of the operation, Julio pulled his shirt off his shoulder to display the incisions.

"As you see, I have had the operation and now Sally is to be the second to have the removal surgery. You all will have the implants removed from your body, but in your good and difficult quest to find use the satellite has undoubtedly tracked you. Now, I am sorry to say, they will know where we are hiding."

One of the new men interrupted Julio. "There are many of us out there who know about what has been done to us. We talk with the other rebels quite often. One of them spoke with you in Casper, Wyoming. He alerted us and we followed you. They told us of your escape from Washington and how you shielded yourselves with lead.

We have done the same. You are safe. No, no, please, sir. We have not jeopardized your hideout."

"My pardon, please. I respect your ingenuity and bravery. I am impressed. Yet, if we are to operate safely, understand it is imperative that all of you must have the implants removed."

They all muttered in agreement and, as each finished his meal, Dr. Jennings began the implant removals. The surgeries continued on throughout the night and Julio and Sally remained at Dr. Jennings' side for each operation. By morning all but Dr. Jennings had successfully been cleansed of the implants.

Victor turned to Julio. "I believe that I am the last, my friend. You and Sally are veterans of twenty-seven surgeries. I am in your hands now to remove this curse from me."

And so, they did. As directed by Dr. Jennings, they used an injection of the morphine to ease the pain. Sally was acting as the surgeon, with Julio's assistance, and they completed the procedure almost as well as the trained physician they were treating. Victor slept soundly.

Soon Sally and Julio curled up together. They were completely exhausted and quickly fell to sleep.

# 31

## *RULER OF THE WORLD*

Felix Hanson had fooled Julio with his computer tricks. The back and forth data activity from the "drone" computers was operating just as he planned and huge amounts of misinformation were being fed to the rebels in the bunker.

Collings had been right on the money. The "drone" computer center had become attractive as a headquarters for the outlaws. In a matter of days Julio had contacted most of the underground and they were coming to join him inside the drone center, which had become the command center and the base of operations for the rebel movement. Collings allowed Julio's communications to get through to the rebels scattered around the country. He wanted them all in the bunker when he struck the final blow.

After a few weeks of patiently watching the activities, General Fenwick decided that an all-out military assault should be made on the "drone" center. A three-man reconnaissance team had been sent to Wyoming and put in place to watch the rebel activities. Soon they reported that, for more than a week, no one had come in or out of the "drone" center. This last report and the fierce, below-zero weather gave Fenwick full assurance that all of the rebels who were able to get to Wyoming had finally arrived.

The recon estimates reported that over 120 people inside the underground bunker. Fenwick's plan was to seal them all in the solid concrete bunker, which only had one main entrance and an escape tunnel. Cutting off the power supply would be simple. If the outlaws chose to stay inside without electric heat and power, they would soon freeze or suffocate. If they came out they could easily be captured and executed on the spot. Either way, they were dead.

General Fenwick decided that former Captain Collings would lead the military forces against the rebels. A special assault unit equipped with cold-weather gear and rations would be headed by Fenwick and Collings. Both men felt that about fifty men and only light armament would be enough to do the job. A flame-thrower team, two .60 caliber machine guns, an antitank missile team, a bazooka team, a high explosive demolition squad, and a communications team were deployed. The remaining men were armed with automatic weapons and grenades. The remote rugged wilderness terrain surrounding the "drone" center and the winter weather informed the decision not to use trucks or heavy artillery. They would quickly and effectively enter the area by parachute and set up a perimeter holding action. Once the area was secured, the demolition team would go in and do its work.

The blueprint of the "drone" computer bunker showed only one formal entrance and an emergency exit via an underground tunnel on the opposite side of the building. In front of the building, between two huge concrete retaining walls, was an eight-inch, solid steel blast door. The building itself was ninety-eight percent underground and only a mounded rise in the earth could be observed. The ground was thick with indigenous shrubs and trees. Like the rest of the terrain, it was covered with snow, making the bunker very well camouflaged and quite a deceptive target.

As he surveyed the area, Collings recognized that shelling would be useless. He estimated that ten to fifteen feet of earth covered the four-foot-thick reinforced concrete ceiling and walls. It was truly a bomb shelter. The rebels had certainly found a very formidable fortress. The only method that would work was to blast the door and get inside.

Using a metal detector, Fenwick's men discovered the door to the emergency exit tunnel located about one-hundred-and-twenty-five-feet away from the underground building. Here General Fenwick positioned three men and a .60 caliber machine gun. If the rebels tried to use this exit, they would have to emerge one at a time and that would put them in a crossfire and very bad position to defend themselves.

Next, the soldiers located the huge propane tanks that powered the electric generator and water pumps. The tanks were situated about a hundred feet from the bunker and the demolition squad could make short work in destroying all power and water.

As ordered, the communications team made radio contact with the rebels. General Fenwick began a dialog with Julio.

"Well, hello, young man. General Alfred Fenwick here. Strange. The first time I met you, you were a trusted part of this great new administration. Now you're a rebellious traitor who's shacked up with the President's ex-girlfriend. You're attempting to destroy our government and, from what I've seen, you certainly have a flair for this hero sort of thing! Now, let's get to the facts, *Señor* Hero Julio Alvarez Mondaldo. You are now under Federal arrest and you are our prisoner. The entrance to this building and the exit tunnel are now secured by our troops. I order you, in the name of the United States of America, to forget any attempts at resistance. Put your weapons into a pile and surrender. You and your people are ordered to come out now, without violence. You will all be treated fairly. Do you understand me, *Señor* Julio?"

"*Si. Si.* I hear you quite well, General Alfred. This really is your sort of game, isn't it? All the good cards are in your hand. It's just exactly how you like to make war. No, I do not care to capitulate at this time, General. You see, we would expect that your treatment of us would, of course, be akin to blindly walking into a LOES machine. No, we will fight you, *mi amigo*. We will not surrender!"

"Julio, we will cut off the propane. You will have no electric power or water. The battery backups you have will only last six to eight hours and will provide you with no power for heating. You will freeze to death. The temperature out here is ten degrees below zero! If you still don't respond, we will put nerve gas in the escape tunnels. Death is imminent. I know you have women inside, Julio. Do you understand the futility of your position?"

"*Si, General! Si.* Ever since we discovered your reconnaissance team we have been expecting you. It did not take a Patton or MacArthur to figure out what your tactics would be when you arrived. We are prepared to defend ourselves. General, that same lack of power, food, shelter, and bitter cold that you attempt to wield against will first become a curse for you and your men. The cold is not a great threat to us, General. In here it will remain like a cave at fifty-five degrees. Your temperature, however, will be ten degrees below zero or even colder with the wind-chill."

Sally grabbed the microphone from Julio.

"Alfred, this is Sally Hawthorne, one of 'the women' inside. Is Rob Collings with you out there? Never mind. I know he is. He wouldn't miss the chance to kill me for all the gold in the world. Listen to me well, Alfred. I speak for myself and for all of the women in here. We're not coming out. So, have at it, bold General. Have at it!"

Collings motioned to Fenwick.

"Alfred, come over here. I don't think we should use the gas. I think they're prepared for it and have probably sealed off the tunnel. That'll reserve the heat as well as the air. They may have also designed another escape route. They seem mighty confident, Alfred. And Julio's right, you know. We can't maintain very long in this cold without formally setting up a camp. When we do that we'll be off guard and vulnerable. I suggest we try an assault, and we do it now."

The antitank guns and the bazookas were set up about thirty yards from the entrance behind some rocks for cover. This first punch would blow off the outside doors. A second or third volley would knock in the blast doors, allowing large antipersonnel shells to be fired into the bunker. The flame-thrower squad would follow up with a burst of liquid fire to the inside, and a team using rifle-launched fragmentation grenades would send their little pieces of deadly steel deep into the interior of the bunker.

This blitz-style firepower would pave the way for an assault group that would be led by Collings. They would enter the bunker and mop up those who still remained alive. It was a simple plan. Collings was sure it would work.

Fenwick thought that, just for the record, one last attempt should be made to get the outlaws to surrender without bloodshed. This time there was no response to the transmission. General Fenwick told the communications man to announce to the rebels that shelling of the bunker was to commence within three minutes.

A .60 caliber machine gun team covering the exit tunnel opening was alerted to a standby condition. The remaining troops were positioned in a staggered formation all around the bunker in order to take out any of the enemy who might use new, unknown escape routes. Collings' pincers of death were at the ready, and he was beginning to enjoy the "war-play" once again.

When the three minutes were up, the shelling commenced. After salvos from the tank guns and bazookas, the outer doors were blasted in. The guns continued to fire until the blast doors were destroyed. Next, flame-thrower fuel was spewed into the bunker and ignited. A fierce tongue of fire belched from out of the ground.

Quickly, four grenade riflemen lined up in front of the flaming entrance and, on a 1-2-3-4 count, each shot their fragmentation grenades through the opening. They turned left and a second group of four sprang into position with more anti-personnel shells. Then came a final group of four with more grenades. The last of the grenadiers stepped aside as Collings and his squad rushed into the smoke-filled opening.

Outside, Fenwick could hear the burp and chatter of machine guns coming from the interior of the bunker. He held another squad ready to send as a second phase. Suddenly, the ground around the front of the bunker exploded, sending Fenwick's men and weapons flying through the air. A second series of blasts were detonated, killing even more of the men and knocking General Fenwick himself to the ground.

Silence. Everyone stayed exactly in the same spot. Minutes went by and no one moved. Then, without warning, a tremendous blast shook the ground and sent the trees, snow and ground from atop the bunker soaring high into the air. When the debris finally settled, a blazing inferno roared from the entrance door. Smaller explosions continued to come from inside the smoking cavern. Fenwick staggered to his feet, only slightly recovered from the blast. He ordered the remaining forces to stand clear of the area.

They waited as the smoke and fire and unpredictable explosions continued. After a while, General Fenwick called for damage assessment and learned that twenty-four of his men had been killed and nine were severely injured.

The explosions stopped. Still, Fenwick waited. After a short time, he ordered a team into the smoking crater to investigate the potential of further explosions. He tightened the ring of his remaining soldiers around the smoking crater—bringing them very close to the hazy perimeter. Soon, the squad leader emerged and approached General Fenwick.

"As best I can tell, sir, there should be no more explosions."

"Inside. Did you see Captain Collings or any of the others alive?"

"Sir, there is no one left alive inside. All dead. All burned to a crisp. The whole place must have been loaded with high explosives and something like, ah, napalm. It's fried, sir, really fried!"

"Go to that exit tunnel. Put search and recovery teams together while we still have light out here. Get those bodies—theirs and ours— out of that hole and lined up on level ground. I want to be sure there is no one alive who may need our help. Get moving, soldier!"

Only one person was found alive. He was found inside, near the door of the escape tunnel. It was one of the rebels and he had been severely burned and was barely conscious enough to tell what had happened inside before the action began.

He was able to say that, after Fenwick's last communication, Julio had spoken with them and they all agreed to surrender. They had all piled their weapons together and were standing at the door when the assault began. Many were killed instantly. The rest fled to the back of the complex, anywhere away from the fire that was coming through the doors. The man said the interior of the bunker came alive with explosions and fire. The conflagration had burst and spewed into every corner of the building. Then came a huge explosion and the place became a raging inferno.

The man could tell them no more. He was dead.

All afternoon the charred remains were brought out of the open pit. The blackened bodies were laid in neat order on the white snow. The corpses were assembled without identification. They used two arms, two legs, a head and torso as the criteria. The body removal continued until the sun began to set.

In order to resist the freezing weather, Fenwick ordered his remaining troops to locate their tents in a circle. Fires were quickly lit in the front and back of each tent as the encampment of tired soldiers prepared for a bitter cold night. Inside the command tent, General Fenwick was about to speak with the President to give him a report of the day's action. He wished he could keep the death of Collings from

Billy and knew that Billy would take the loss of his dearest friend very hard, yet he was obligated to tell him the truth. The communications man had isolated the high-level security channel and was now ready with the President.

"General. How goes the hunt? Wish I was with you guys right now...any big problems? Probably not. Alfred, is Rob there with you?"

"Mr. President, I have some very tragic news. Captain Robert Collings is dead."

"Ah, uh, Alfred, repeat that again, please?"

"Rob led the assault on the bunker, sir, and after repeated shelling of the interior before he entered, a massive—and I mean massive—explosion occurred after Captain Collings and his group were inside the bunker. Captain Robert Collings, USMC, retired, was killed in action this day, in the line of duty, sir. He is dead!"

There was a long silence.

"You're not to move the bodies from the site, General. We, of course, know your exact location. Charles and I will be there early tomorrow morning. Alfred, find what's left of Rob."

General Fenwick signed off. The he contacted military headquarters and filed his account with the Pentagon.

*SITUATION REPORT:*

*Mission accomplished.*

*U.S. CASUALTIES: 24 dead. 9 injured.*

*4 or more of those injured expected to die.*

*ENEMY CASUALTIES: All dead.*

The general body count at nightfall was impossible to determine. They would resume the search at daybreak. Fenwick settled back and took a long pull on his flask of bourbon. It had happened so fast. It was like the war in 'Nam. Here one moment talking, laughing and then gone the next. Rob Collings dead? A man who, through the years Fenwick had thought of as a son. He never believed that Rob would die in warfare. Now, he was gone. Al Fenwick felt every bit of his 69 years. He was tired and nauseated and growing depressed. He took another healthy slug of bourbon. The radio beeped an incessant signal. The communications man requested permission to answer. It was the Pentagon.

"General Fenwick here...Yes, Mr. President."

"Alfred, I just read your report. Hell of a mess. No way to expect that kind of resistance. Sorry for the losses. I've just instructed the corps of engineers to drop in two 'dozers and adequate men to clean up and bury that area. Please understand, Alfred. This never happened! Is that clear?"

"Affirmative, sir!"

At dawn the next day the silence of the wooded area was broken by the sounds of two huge Sikorsky Sky-Cranes delivering the big Caterpillar 'dozers and a third helicopter that held the group of Army engineers. After the heavy equipment was detached from the mammoth flying derricks, the personnel copter landed and discharged the human cargo. Billy was the first one out, followed by Charles. They were dressed in white Army winter combat uniforms and blended in with the rest of the crew. General Fenwick went out to greet them.

"Mr. President, Dr. Gertz. Very sad day for us all."

"General. Major Fulbright of the Army engineers knows exactly what I want done. Alfred, have you found and identified Rob? It is vitally important that we find him!"

"Billy, we're trying, but they're all burned beyond recognition. Charles, maybe your medical background can assist us."

The three men went to the area that contained the charred bodies. The last of the burnt body parts was being laid in the snow. The bulldozers were fired up and the work of filling in the crater was about to begin. Billy motioned for the big machines to be shut down and await his orders.

Billy and Charles walked slowly among the bodies. Charles occasionally bent down and poked at the remains. Each time, he sadly shook his head.

"Billy, it's impossible. I'll be able to tell you in the lab, but not out here. Not now. You don't want to haul all these bodies back to the Complex. I mean, what purpose will it serve? Just take tissue samples from all the parts of the dead. Within a few days, I can identify them all and we can REGENZ Rob or any others you want. I have living tissue samples on Rob and the other key personnel. Don't worry Billy. Rob will be back alive and with us again."

"You're right, Charles. He's dead now. But he will live again and maybe he will be able to tell us what happened in there."

Charles, assisted by several medical corpsmen, began the ghoulish job of slicing pieces of flesh from each body part that could be found. They were put in small, unlabeled plastic bags. Throughout the day and into the early evening they hunted and collected the pieces of tissue. Fingers, arms and legs were amassed because the idea that one part belonged with another ceased to matter. Even an ear or an eye could hold the truth.

Billy took a break and found General Fenwick.

"Alfred, I want your men to continue carefully, I mean carefully, to assist Charles in obtaining these tissue samples. Then I want your men to place the bodies and parts back in this hole in the ground. Be sure to hold up the final dozing until they've finished the sampling. Charles will give you the green light. In the morning, I want fresh earth put over these people and a memorial service to be performed before the dozing commences."

"Tomorrow, this will become a National cemetery. I've brought a priest with me. He'll consecrate the ground. When the corps of engineers has finished, this area will be revisited in the spring and all will be returned to nature. The official word will be that these military men all died in an accidental explosion in the bunker and there are no remains. There was no resistance movement, no warfare, just a very bad accident. General, you will personally monitor the remaining officers and men that have been involved with this action. If any of them should break the vow of silence, I want them killed immediately. This never happened. Have I made myself clear, General?"

General Fenwick saluted his Commander-In-Chief, and then barked orders to his subordinates.

The day was cold and long. As Billy looked down from the departing helicopter, he remembered the motto, "Everybody goes home!" He hoped that he wasn't leaving his dearest friend behind.

That night, safe in his bed at the White House, Billy retold the official story to Suzzanne. They talked and remembered their old friend. Billy prayed that Charles could resurrect him. Finally, they fell to sleep and Billy dreamed.

It was a gruesome nightmare, all mixed with the gore of the war in 'Nam, the gaping, burned out cavity of the bunker and all the horrible charred bodies lying neatly in the snowy woods. It was a dark and grisly dream.

Then he saw the bodies stacked in the mass grave, one on top of the other. Slowly they began to move. In his dream, Billy shouted at the bodies: "Rob. Rob Collings. Which of you is Rob Collings?"

One of the burned, faceless corpses turned and, with a toothy smile, waved at him and spoke: "Billy, it's me, Rob. I'm here with Julio and Sally and all the millions of others you've killed."

Billy was horrified as the ghastly remains of Julio and Rob picked up Sally's burned and broken cadaver and held her triumphantly above their heads. The three walked out of the rubble and were followed by an endless stream of dead bodies.

In his dream, Billy ran from them. They continued steadily to come after him. It was more and more difficult for him to run. He slowed down. It was like moving through a thick, viscous fluid. His legs wouldn't respond. Billy looked down and saw that he was knee deep in a river of coagulated blood. The dead were gaining on him. They grabbed for him. Lifeless, moving fingers were clawing at his body. He screamed and screamed for help.

Billy awakened, drenched in sweat. The room was dark. Was it just a dream? Or had it been real? He quickly got out of bed, put on his robe and slippers. Stumbling in the darkness of his room, he found a chair and held onto it, afraid he might fall. He was afraid for the first time in a long time.

Was God punishing him for the mass murder of billions of people? Was God punishing him for allowing his dearest friends to be killed? He knew he deserved punishment. He knew he was bad.

He called out loud. "Oh God help me, tell me what to do!"

He stopped talking. Calmly, quietly he left the chair and turned on the lights. Facing the mirror, Billy shouted, "God help me! God help me! Please, God...

Suddenly, he regained his composure.

"I need no help from God, for I am God. And those that are dead deserved to die!"

That next day, Charles had his best people working on the flesh samples. It was easy work, but it took time. Each piece of tissue had to be analyzed to find its DNA. Once the DNA was discovered, it was put into a computerized analyzer and run against the archives in the National Computer. Identification of that individual, thereafter, was simple. So far, Collings had not turned up and neither had Sally or Julio, but there were hundreds and hundreds of samples yet to examine.

Billy's call to the complex was immediately put through to Charles' office.

"Charles, Billy. Anything yet?"

"Not on Rob. Got lots of identifications, lots of duplications because of the mixed parts, but we're making headway. It'll take time, Billy. If he went in there, parts of him had to remain after the blast. Even fire can't eliminate finding some fragment to work with. Be patient, please. And don't worry. Rob will be back with us soon."

Charles hung up the phone and slumped in his chair. He was tired. A knock came to his door. Charles opened the door and a lab assistant came in.

"We've found him, sir. Rob Collings. Good strong tissue taken from a left arm, I think. Please, come look, Dr. Gertz!"

Charles ran, following the man to the section of lab where the tissue examinations were being done. He looked at the computer monitor and then at the DNA analyzer. It was a good match.

Charles called Billy immediately. "Billy, we've found Rob. He was killed. I'll get working on him immediately. But strange as it seems, we can't find a trace of Sally or Julio. It's as though they were not in the blast. What do you think?"

"Not to worry, Charles. They'll turn up. You'll find them."

For the moment, Billy was satisfied. Rob Collings would live again. He could tell him what had happened to Julio Mondaldo and Sally Hawthorne.

Dr. Gertz worked feverishly to bring the REGENZ of Rob Collings to a rapid fruition, but it would take time.

A few months later Rob Collings, the REGENZ, was alive again. Billy wanted to meet with him as soon as Dr. Gertz would allow.

Late one afternoon, Dr. Gertz brought Rob to the oval office. Billy ran across the room and hugged Collings.

"Rob, it is you. Oh, my friend, my good friend, you're back with us again. Tell me how you feel. What's the last thing you remember, Rob?"

"Gunfire. Explosions. Looking at only half my arm. Passing out. Waking up to see that silly ass Gertz grinning at me. Kinda like a bad dream, Billy. Hell if I know. That's all I can remember."

"And what happened to Sally and Julio? Charles has checked all of the tissue samples. Those two were not among the dead."

Collings tried to recall. "Billy, the fire, the noise, I, uh... I don't know. I didn't see them. Maybe they were incinerated to ash, or maybe they escaped. I just don't know."

Charles interrupted. "Billy, I assure you that even from the ash we could identify them. No. Positively, they were not there!"

"Well, don't worry about it. It's a mystery that we may never solve. In reality, I don't care. They're dead so far as I'm concerned. We've heard nothing from them or any rebels, for that matter."

"Gentlemen, they were our only resistance. In whatever way, they have all been eliminated. We win...and they don't!"


But what had really happened to Sally, Julio and Victor Jennings was yet another story.

After the first blast on the outer doors Julio and Sally and Dr. Jennings hid in a storage room near the front of the bunker.

Even with the second blast, the flamethrowers, the grenades and antipersonnel shells blazing, they remained safe in that room.

Returning fire from the rebels against the squad that was led by Rob Collings severed Collings' left arm, and he collapsed to the floor.

The massive warfare inside the bunker caused Julio and his group to flee the storage room. As they crawled across the floor they found the body of Rob Collings.

Dr. Jennings put a crude tourniquet on Collings' arm, and they dragged him toward the ventilation shaft where, again, all hid again from the ensuing firefight.

Julio used the bunker itself as his *coup de grace*. In the original construction, as a security precaution, the interior and perimeter of the bunker had been mined with high explosives. Julio set the timers before Fenwick's assault. The successive massive blasts inside and outside of the bunker were a very effective retaliation.

Before the first massive blast the four of them crawled deeper into the airshaft. They waited until nightfall and under the cover of darkness began their cold trek through the forest.

Julio Montaldo and this little band of survivors continued to walk and struggled through the cold night and into the day.

Late the next afternoon, they came upon a ranch house. The kind people there gave them food and warmth as Dr. Jennings made final repairs to Rob Collings. He was in very bad shape. His face was terribly burned, he had lost a lot of blood and most of his left arm, but Rob Collings was alive.

# 32

## *EVERYTHING'S GONNA BE ALL RIGHT!*

It was a bright and glorious Independence Day and all was well throughout the world. This made Billy happy.

He gazed out upon all that he had done and felt proud.

As it was on that first dawn of time, the earth was again being created and shaped by the hand of God (and Billy). The world and its people had finally grown to look and act as Billy (and God) had wanted them to act. It was perfection.

The people were happy. No one complained or missed the loss of friends and family. No one noticed or cared that freedom and liberty had been redefined. They may have even lost their souls, yet no one seemed to care.

The people were happy. Their new ruler was fair and just. Never before in history had the world experienced such harmony. Never had the people of the world behaved and worked together with this special kind of purpose. Just as God had promised them in His spoken word, Billy was leading humanity into universal peace and prosperity, and it was happening without conflict. The planet and its people had become a beautiful garden of bliss and everyone, everywhere, was joyful and fulfilled.

This particular day, in fact, was to be a great day, and not a time to consider moral issues, for today the Grand Independence Day Celebration was to occur. This special day would commemorate Billy's third year in office.

Much had happened over the last few years, and there was even more to come. Billy had become the hero of the people and on this July 4th. He was to be rewarded by being installed as the first Chancellor of The New World Federation of Nations. Upon taking this office, he would turn over the domestic duties and day-to-day business to Avery Harrison, who would then be known as The Exalted Regent of the United States of North and South America.

Avery Harrison, Henry Gillespie, Irving Penitz, Professor Osher, and General Fenwick had all been REGENZ that spring. These bright "young" men would continue their duties to the NWF and their loyalty to Billy, without the handicap of being old.

Billy would move from Washington, DC to New York City, which was to become the first capital of the New World Federation of Nations. The island of Manhattan had been gifted to the World Federation of Nations by the United States and would become a sovereign nation.

As the Chancellor of the New World Federation, the recently remodeled United Nations building would now become the New World Federation headquarters.

Billy was to live in a newly constructed mansion at the south end of Central Park. This big house stretched from Central Park West eastward to Fifth Avenue. Much of the Park to the north of the mansion had been dedicated for Billy's use, as well. It was the equivalent of Hurricane House and would be the new Chancellor's residence and headquarters.

It was a big day for New York City, the people of the United States, and the entire world. Again, people everywhere tuned in to this coronation ceremony, as it was broadcast live and direct on TV and radio from Liberty Island.

Billy thought the Statue of Liberty would make an inspirational backdrop for this occasion. During the year, full-sized replicas of "Lady Liberty" were sent as gifts to all countries to be erected in their port cities. Now, when anyone sailed into these "foreign" ports, they were always entering the land of the "free and the brave." The words "Liberty, justice and freedom" were now a part of the working vocabulary of the world.

The English language quickly became the dominant language in every country on the face of the earth and to read, write, and speak English was mandatory in all of the World Federation Nations. The older languages of French, Spanish, German, Italian, Arabic, Chinese, etc.,were now, by law, only taught on request and were no longer used in day-to-day conversation.

This festival day was a double-dip treat for the world. Not only was Billy to be installed as the new Chancellor of the World, but the old name of New York City was to be changed to New World City. While some New Yorkers disagreed, they eventually supported the idea. After all, Billy hadn't been wrong yet and the venerable New York spirit was, as usual, fair minded: "If Billy wants it, then it's all right. So, shut-the-fuck-up, already!"

The New World Federation emblem was the giant centerpiece on the mammoth platform and review stand erected on Liberty Island. The newly designed, colorful flags from the nations of the world flanked the sides of the main platform. The NWF emblem dominated all flags utilizing that nation's traditional colors as the background.

Only the very elite were permitted on Liberty Island for the ceremony. Security was tight. The presence of the RSS World Police, in their impressive black and gold trimmed uniforms, just added to the holiday atmosphere. The day was festive and bright, heralded by the media for weeks in advance as the event of the century.

*The New Regents* from nations throughout the world made brief speeches prior to Billy's taking the oath of office. Musicians from each country, dressed in their resplendent NWF uniforms, played musical fanfares before each speaker. Show business entertainment was now employed as part of all official functions. The people liked the happy, up-beat festival style that Billy always gave them.

Television and radio coverage began at 9 a.m. that morning, and at 6:30 p.m., the Exalted Regent, Avery Harriman, spoke to the crowd. After much ceremony, the old City of New York was officially proclaimed the New World City.

The band played the "New World Anthem," and then promptly at 7 p.m., with his wife Suzanne and his best friends Dr. Charles Gertz, David Barnston, Avery Harrison, and Rob Collings at his side, President William F. Johnstone arrived and was sworn in as the first Chancellor of the New World Federation of Nations.

The band played the stirring "Hail to the Chief" and Billy, with genuine gratitude, began his speech: "Citizens of the world. I accept this office of Chancellor of the World Federation of Nations and all the responsibilities it holds. I make one exception to being the Chancellor of the World. I want it clearly understood that this is God's world, not yours, or mine. This Earth, Mankind itself, and all living things in this world are the conception of our God. It is His creation and we love and respect Him. So just do what you know is good and don't worry, 'cause everything's gonna be all right, from now on!"

The crowd cheered.

Billy continued. "And so, my friends, I give to you happiness for the next thousand years!"

The crowd shouted their approval, the music played and the first of many fireworks displays began to light up the evening sky as the people of the world exploded in jubilation.

This man was their living God, and they loved him.

As the band performed Billy led the people in singing the stirring

"New World Anthem." The audience cheered and Billy shouted above their noise. "Oh, yes. Oh yes. Glory be to God, for he has given us much to be thankful for!"

A TV announcer confidently stated. "So, order has finally come to our world. One language. One government. One God. One leader. Chancellor Johnstone has promised us a thousand years of peace."

A young couple near the back of the crowd looked lovingly at each other. The girl said, "Oh, it's true, honey. God's world really is a better place, now that Billy is running it!"

Sally and Julio and a badly scarred one-armed man stood next to the couple. Sally whispered to Julio. "Is that really Collings up there with Billy, or is it a double?

Rob Collings answered her. "Oh, it's me, Sally. A clone of me. I've been regenerated; brought back to life. Christ, Billy is nuts. Now there are two of me. Only this ol' Collings is no longer on his team."

Julio interrupted. "But now, my sweet, Billy must die."

He barked an order into a cell phone: "*Ahora*, Sam. *Ahora!*"

Within seconds, the whistle of incoming mortar shells was heard. With blinding flashes, the missiles hit and exploded on the platform, making a tremendous, jarring roar. The area where Billy, Collings, and the others were standing was directly hit.

All sorts of equipment, bodies and bodily parts were violently thrown everywhere—flying high through the hot, still night air like a slow-motion ballet, rising and then falling lightly again to earth.

For one brief moment, the world stopped. Everyone watched in horror. No one even breathed. Everyone, everywhere, was gripped by the fear that their great leader was dead. They waited and prayed.

Sally and Julio and Collings watched in awe as the platform exploded. Sally almost screamed with delight. In a whisper, she squealed, "We did it, Julio. Billy and those evil bastards are dead!"

No one heard what she was saying, but Julio hushed her.

Little remained of the platform. The people were motionless, waiting. Everything was still. All eyes focused on the pile of smoldering wreckage. The crowd was quiet. Not a breath, not a sound.

Then some of the rubble began to move. A man slowly crawled out from under the wreckage. The man was covered with dust and debris. He searched the ruins of the stage and finally picked up a microphone. The sound system crackled and whined, then they heard that all-familiar voice.

It was Billy. Bloody and staggering, he waved to the audience.

The crowds shouted and cheered. Their great leader was safe.

Wiping his eyes and brushing back his hair, Billy spoke hoarsely to the waiting world.

"Looks like a pretty bad accident up here...Some of them are dead..."

Then, smiling that smile of his, Billy confided in his audience. "But, I'm okay. Not hurt. Still alive. So, don't you worry folks, 'cause you know, everything's gonna be all right...and that's a promise!"

When Liberty is taken away by force, it can be restored by force.When it is relinquished voluntarily, by default, it can never be recovered.

—Dorothy Thompson

# Acknowledgements

From the very beginnings of this book, my daughter Jane's advice and insistence helped to get my original thoughts on paper. We are of the same faith, in that we hope that our glorious country will solve its problems. I owe her great thanks for her love, encouragement and faith.

I also thank my good friend, Brad Small, for pounding me to get this book to become coherent, somewhat literate, suitably punctuated and for putting the concept—and me—on trial until he was satisfied that what I proposed was not only possible, but also plausible.

This story was first published in 2006. This second edition corrects minor typographical, grammatical and formatting errors. No idea or incident was added or omitted; the theme, content and structure are untouched. The story remains as it was.

–SJC

# ABOUT THE AUTHOR

STEVEN J. CONNERS was born in Dayton, Ohio. After nearly four decades in the entertainment industry, Conners "retired" to host a radio show, *The Voice of Reason*, in order to provide a platform for everyone's voice to be heard. His years of traveling the country and speaking with "the average person" inspired his recent fiction efforts, *The Madness of Power* series.

Conners worked in live theatre, creating, directing and producing numerous stage productions that traveled the United States, including *The Great Ghost Show* and *The Magic Land of Mother Goose*, before moving into the management and creation of event-style stunt promotions. In between tours and booking *Dilly the Dragon*, *The Six-Foot Chocolate Easter Bunny*, *The Magic Elf*, *Silkini's Frozen Alive* and *Silkini's Buried Alive*, Conners made a foray into designing and setting up several restaurants and even had a go at running a catering business (Shindigs Unlimited) and his own jazz club (Bozo's).

In addition to *The Madness of Power* series, Conners has written plays, children's books, a biography of showman Jack Baker, and a non-fiction book on the responsibilities of democratic liberty.

He continues to travel and maintains a home base in Reno, Nevada.

# COVER DESIGN ARTIST

JESSE CONNERS is manager of Wasteland Exports, LLC, a firm specializing in design work that "transforms your dreams, nightmares, illusions and delusions from a state of fantasy to reality." Jesse's designs include cast/character makeup, costumes, props, set pieces, web design, digital and print packages for clients throughout the United States.

Jesse makes regular appearances at Comic-Con events throughout the United States. He resides with his wife in Reno, Nevada.

For a look at his work, please visit www.wastelandexports.com.